RED RUNS THE HELMAND

Patrick Mercer joined the army from university. He completed tours of Northern Ireland and commanded his battalion in Bosnia. He left the army as a colonel and became the defence correspondent for the *Today* programme before becoming an MP.

Also by PATRICK MERCER

Dust and Steel
To Do and Die

PATRICK MERCER

Red Runs the Helmand

HarperCollins*Publishers*

HarperCollins*Publishers*
77−85 Fulham Palace Road,
Hammersmith, London W6 8JB

www.harpercollins.co.uk

Published by HarperCollins*Publishers* 2011
1

A catalogue record for this book
is available from the British Library

ISBN: 978-0-00-730276-5

This novel is entirely a work of fiction.
The names, characters and incidents portrayed in it,
while some are based on historical figures, are
the work of the author's imagination.

Map © John Gilkes 2011

Typeset in Sabon by Palimpsest Book Production Limited,
Falkirk, Stirlingshire

Printed and bound in Great Britain by
Clays Ltd, St Ives plc

Mixed Sources
Product group from well-managed
forests and other controlled sources
www.fsc.org Cert no. SW-COC-001806
© 1996 Forest Stewardship Council

FSC

FSC is a non-profit international organisation established
to promote the responsible management of the world's forests.
Products carrying the FSC label are independently certified
to assure consumers that they come from forests that are managed
to meet the social, economic and ecological needs
of present and future generations.

Find out more about HarperCollins and the environment at
www.harpercollins.co.uk/green

To my wife, Cait.

This is the third and final book in the Anthony Morgan trilogy: I will miss him and his friends. I would like to thank my wife, Cait, who has heard every word of this book more times than she cares to remember, my son, Rupert, and the staff of the 66th Regiment's Museum in Salisbury. I canot forget Sue Gray and Edward Barker for their patience and forebearing and, of course, my agent, Natasha Fairweather of AP Watt and my faultless editor, Susan Watt.

Skegby,
February 2011

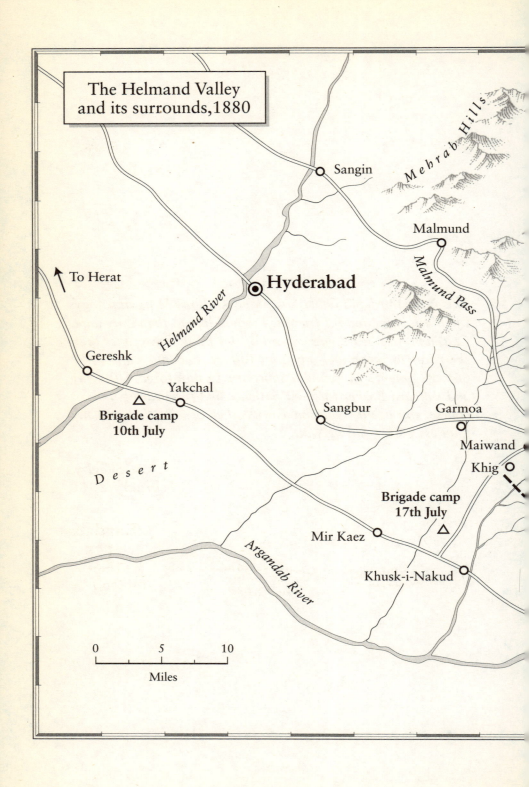

The Helmand Valley
and its surrounds, 1880

Mehrab Hills

Sangin

Malmund

Malmund Pass

To Herat

Helmand River

Hyderabad

Gereshk

Yakchal

Sangbur

Garmoa

Maiwand

Khig

Brigade camp
10th July

D e s e r t

Brigade camp
17th July

Mir Kaez

Argandab River

Khusk-i-Nakud

0   5   10

Miles

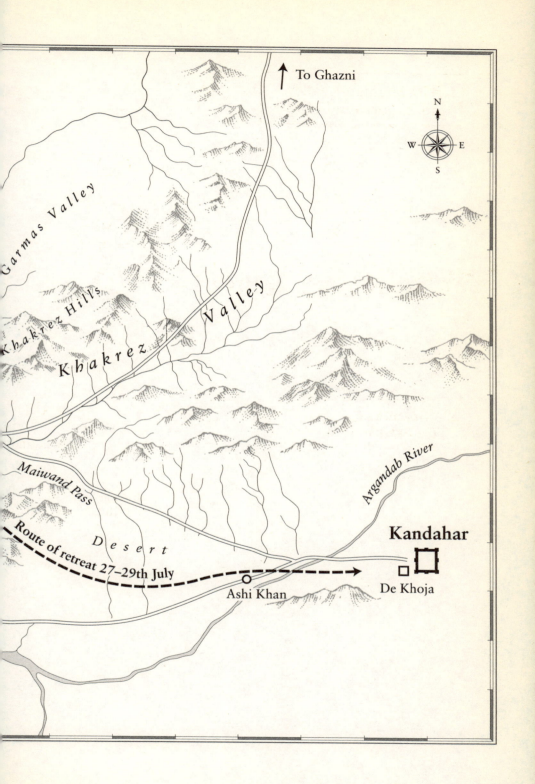

To Ghazni

N
W   E
S

Garmas Valley

Khakrez Hills

Khakrez Valley

Argandab River

Maiwand Pass

Desert

Kandahar

Route of retreat 27–29th July

Ashi Khan

De Khoja

Author's Note

I'm amazed that anyone can soldier in Afghanistan at all. During several recent visits to that country I have found the heat almost unbearable and the ground unforgiving. Today's soldiers have the advantage of wheeled and air transport (well, some of the time) but much of their fighting is done on foot burdened with personal loads of electronic equipment, body armour, helmets and the like that would have horrified their predecessors.

Most remarkably, though, the soldier of 1880, while carrying much less kit, survived on a fraction of the water that his great-great-grandson does. It's noticeable how much logistic effort in the Helmand valley today is absorbed by the carrying forward of potable water – an effort that is directly equivalent to that needed for animal fodder in the 1880s. It has taken me some time to understand the priorities of an army in the field in the nineteenth century and the different privations they suffered.

Another challenge has been to grasp how the relationship between officers and men in the Indian armies actually worked. I've modelled this on the modern Gurkha troops alongside whom I served and the way that their British officers communicated with them. Nowadays, officers in Gurkha regiments have to pass exams in the language of their men. While a similar system was in its infancy at the time of Maiwand, British officers would have been surrounded by native dialects both on and off duty and this, I have no doubt, would have encouraged them to learn the language. But imagine how difficult communications would have been between, say, the 66th and Jacob's Rifles; I've tried to capture some of this friction.

The language of my British characters, for obvious reasons, lacks the casual racism of the later nineteenth century, but I've tried to reflect the humour, candour and pragmatism of the time. In the same way, I believe that relationships then between officers and men in the British Regular Army were very similar to those of today. The film industry is, perhaps, most to blame for the impression that Victorian officers treated their men with a stiff, unbending formality but contemporary diaries and letters would utterly refute that. So, I've taken the heartbeat of the men with whom I served a hundred years later and sprinkled the way in which they spoke and joked with the military patois of imperial times; I hope I've got it right.

Anthony Morgan has now fought in the Crimea, the great Mutiny and the Second Afghan War, fearing much, slaughtering many and seeing more horrors than ten men. I've visited the home of the real Morgan in a delightful corner of County Cork and been treated with great courtesy by his descendants. It was there that Anthony actually retired to raise a family, pursue foxes and all other forms of wildlife and have a walk-on part in the Somerville and Ross books. I suspect that it is now time to let the fictional character enjoy some of the same.

Last, I've taken advice on almost everything in this book. If something is obscure, not covered in the glossary or just plain wrong, then it is entirely my own fault.

Patrick Mercer
Skegby
Nottinghamshire

ONE

Kandahar

'No, Havildar, turn out the bloody guard, won't you? I don't
want these two men standing there like goddamn sacks of
straw. Just turn out the guard!'

I never could get my tongue round Hindi. It was all very
well cussing native troops, but if they really couldn't understand
anything beyond the fact that you were infuriated with them,
what was the point? In my experience, the angrier a sahib got
them, the more inert and immobile they became. It was the
middle of March 1860 and I'd only arrived in Kandahar after
a long journey from India forty-eight hours before. And what
a hole it was. The surrounding country was what I'd expected,
all mountains, vertical passes and twisting, gritty roads; there
was a rough beauty about it after the stifling lowlands of India.
But the old city was not what I'd imagined at all. For a start,
it was so much smaller than I'd thought. True, shacks, mud-
built slums and thatched huts sprawled around outside the wall
of the place, but the town itself wasn't much bigger than Cork,
yet it was packed twice as tight and smelt three times as bad.

Now, this little fracas at the gate came at the end of a long
day when Heath, my brigade major, had proved to be even
more useless than I'd thought. We'd been all round the units
of my brigade, some of which were still dragging themselves

into the town after the long march up from Quetta, although most of them had now arrived. I'd thought the Sappers and Miners' horses slovenly – girths loose and fodder badly stowed. I'd found rust on more than one entrenching tool of the 19th Bombay and now, as I approached the Shikapur, or south, Gate of the city, Jacob's Rifles – who had been the first to arrive and were meant to be finding the city guard – failed to recognise their own brigade commander. And what was that clown, Heath, doing about it? Was he chasing and biting the NCO in charge? No, I had to do it my-bloody-self.

Don't misunderstand me, I was as keen as anyone else to get another campaign medal to stick on my chest, but from the very start of this punch-up, I'd had my doubts about being in Afghanistan. I'd never been convinced of how much the Russians really wanted to get a toehold on the Hindu Kush, but Disraeli had been persuaded by the political officers out here that there was more to it than the Tsar's boys sending missions to Kabul and bending Amir Shere Ali's mind against the British, so we had invaded in November '78. All credit to Dizzy, Generals Roberts, Sam Browne and Stewart were backed to the hilt. Their three columns pushed hard into this miserable country, occupied Kabul after a bit of trouble, drove out Shere Ali and concluded peace with his son, Yakoob Khan, in May '79. They'd bought the wily old lad off for the knock-down price of sixty thousand quid, after he'd promised to behave himself and accepted our Resident, Sir Louis Cavagnari. And there we'd all thought it had ended. If only that had been the case.

While others were grabbing all the glory (like that odious little sod Bob Roberts), I was still in Karachi, thinking that, as a forty-nine-year-old colonel, I'd reached the end of the career road, when news reached us of Cavagnari's murder last September. Before that, there had been some pretty vicious fighting and we had all thought that his being allowed into the capital had marked the end of things – at least for a while. I reckoned we'd done quite a good job right across Afghanistan, but then, as usual, the windbag politicians had failed to open their history books and sent all the wrong signals to the Afghans. Instead of reinforcing success and giving the tribesmen the chance to sample the delights of imperial rule for a few months more, Whitehall listened too closely to the lily-livered press, the Treasury began to do its sums – and the tribesmen soon grasped that we had no plans to stay in their country beyond the next Budget Day. And who paid for that? Poor Cavagnari and his Corps of Guides bodyguard: butchered to a man in the Residency in Kabul. It was all a little too much like the last débâcle back in '42 for my liking.

Then, of course, the papers really took hold. The blood of English boys was being shed for no reason, while innocent women and children were being caught by ill-aimed shells, the Army's finest were being made to look like monkeys by a crowd of hillmen armed with swords and muskets. There were echoes of our last attempt to paint the map of Afghanistan a British red, of MacNaughton and Dr Brydon again. Then, to my amazement, three weeks ago, the Whigs won the general election: Gladstone found himself wringing his hands and 'saving' fallen women all the way into Downing Street. Now, with a card-carrying Liberal in charge, we all suspected we would quit Afghanistan faster than somewhat and certainly before the next tax rise, leaving the job half done and with every expectation of having to repeat the medicine once the amir or his masters in St Petersburg got uppity again.

'What on earth's taking them so long, Heath? We haven't interrupted *salaah*, have we?' I knew enough about Mussulman troops to understand that their ritual cleansing and prayers, when the military situation allowed, were vitally important. 'Well, have we, Heath?' But my brigade major didn't seem to know – he just looked blankly back at me. 'We need to make damn sure that when we're in garrison all the native regiments pray at the same time. Otherwise there'll be bloody chaos. See to it, if you please.'

5

I'd found out as much as I could about the general situation while I was on my way up here to take command of a thrown-together brigade. In it I had some British guns, Her Majesty's 66th Foot and two battalions of Bombay infantry, while the 3rd Scinde Horse was in the cavalry brigade next door. By some strange twist of fate, I had one son in the 66th under my direct command while my other boy was in the Scindis, just a stone's throw away.

Mark you, I was bloody delighted and a bit surprised to find myself promoted to brigadier general – but I was an old enough campaigner to know that a scratch command of any size would need plenty of grip by me and bags of knocking into shape on the *maidan* before I'd dream of allowing it to trade lead with the enemy – particularly lads like the Afghans: they'd given our boys a thorough pasting last year. And what I was seeing of the units that I was to have under my command left me less than impressed. Anyway, it was as clear as gin that if hard knocks needed to be dished out, my divisional commander, General James Primrose, would choose either his cavalry brigadier – Nuttall – or my old friend Harry Brooke, the other infantry brigade commander, to do it, wouldn't he? After all, while they were both junior to me, they'd been up-country much longer.

Talking of being less than impressed, this little mob was stoking up all my worst fears. 'Come on, man, turn out the guard!' I might as well have been talking Gaelic. The havildar just stood there at the salute, all beard and turban, trembling slightly as I roasted him, while his two sentries remained either side of the gate, rifles and bayonets rigidly at the 'present'. Of the whole guard, a sergeant and twelve – who should have been kicking up the dust quick as lightning at the approach of a brigadier general – there was no sign at all. And Heath just continued to sit on his horse beside me, gawping.

'Well, tell him, Heath – I don't keep a dog to bark myself,

you know!' I wondered, sometimes, at these fellows they sent out to officer the native regiments. I'd picked out Heath from one of the battalions under my command, the Bombay Grenadiers – where he'd been adjutant – because he'd had more experience than most and because he was said to be fluent. But of initiative and a sense of urgency, there was bugger-all.

'Sir . . . yes, of course . . .' and the man at last let out a stream of *bat* that finally had the havildar trotting away inside the gate to get the rest of his people. It was quite a thing to guard, though. The walls of Kandahar were packed, dried mud, thirty foot high at the north end, faced with undressed stone to at least half that height and topped with a fire step and loop holes for sentries. The Shikapur Gate was a little lower than the surrounding walls. It was made up of a solid stone arch set with two massive wooden gates, through which traipsed a never-ending procession of camels, oxen and carts, carrying all the wonders of the Orient. Now, the dozen men came tumbling out of the hut inside the walls that passed for a guardroom, squeezing past mokes and hay-laden mules while pulling at belts, straps and pouches, their light grass-country shoes stamping together as the havildar and his naik got them into one straight line looking something like soldiers.

If I'd been in the boots of the subaltern who'd just turned up, though, I'd have steered well clear. I'd dismounted and was about to inspect the jawans when up skittered a pink-faced kid, who looked so young that I doubted the ink was yet dry on his commission. He halted in the grit and threw me a real drill sergeant's salute – as if that might deflect my irritation.

'Sir, orderly officer, Thirtieth Bombay Native Infantry, Jacob's Rifles, sir!' The boy was trembling almost as much as the NCO had done – God, I remembered how bloody terrifying brigadier generals were when I was a subaltern.

'I can see you're the orderly officer. What's your name,

boy?' I knew how easy it was to petrify young officers; I knew how fierce I must have seemed to this griff and he was an easy target for the day's frustrations – I wasn't proud of myself.

'Sir, Ensign Moore, sir.' The boy could hardly speak.

'No, lad, in proper regiments you give a senior officer your first name too – you're not a transport wallah with dirty fingernails . . .' I knew how stupidly pompous I was being '. . . so spit it out.'

'Sir, Arthur Moore. Just joined from England, sir.'

But there was something about the youngster's sheer desire to please that pricked my bubble of frustration. If I'd been him, I would have come nowhere near an angry brigadier general – I'd have found pressing duties elsewhere and let the havildar take the full bite of the great man's anger. But no: young Arthur Moore straight out from England had known where his duty lay and come on like a good 'un.

'You're rare-plucked, ain't you, Arthur Moore?' I found myself smiling at his damp face, all the tension draining from my shoulders, all the pent-up irritation of a day with that scrub Heath gone. 'Let's have a look at these men's weapons, shall we?'

Well, the sentries may have been a bit dozy and not warned the NCOs of my approach, and the havildar's English may have been as bad as my Hindi, but Jacob's rifles were bloody spotless. Pouches were full, water-bottles topped up and the whole lot of them in remarkably good order. It quite set me up.

'Right, young Moore, a slow start but a good finish. Well done.' I tried to continue sounding gruff and impossible to please, but after all the other nonsense of the day, this subaltern and his boys had won me over.

'*Shabash*, Havildar sahib . . .' It was the best I could manage as I settled myself back into the saddle.

'*Shabash*, General sahib.' The havildar's creased, leathery face split into a grin as the guard crashed to attention and Moore shivered a salute. Perhaps, after all, there was some good in the benighted brigade I'd been given.

No sooner had I had my sport with the lads on the gate and arrived at the mess rooms that had been arranged for me than I was summoned to the Citadel to report to my divisional commander in his headquarters, which the great man had set up in the old building. Now, Kandahar had been occupied by General Donald Stewart's Lahore Division during the initial invasion, so when our division had been ordered to tramp up from India to replace Stewart's lot, I'd expected to find the town in good order and all ready to be defended – after all, the Lahore Division had arrived in the place more than a year ago. However, apart from skittering about the Helmand valley, they appeared to have done absolutely nothing to prepare the place for trouble. They'd just loafed about before being ordered to clear the route back to Kabul, leaving us of Primrose's division to put the place in some sort of order.

At the north end of the town, just within the walls, there was a great, louring stone-built keep of strange Oriental design. There may have been some fancy local name for it, but we knew it simply as the Citadel. I'd never seen anything quite like it: its curtain walls were a series of semi-circular towers, all linked to one another, with a higher keep that dominated them in turn. I don't know when it was built, probably more than a century before, but it was solid enough and could have been made pretty formidable. But Stewart's people hadn't thought to mount a single gun on it, while almost two miles of old defensive walls, which stretched in an uneven rectangle south of the fort, had been neither improved nor loop-holed. Meanwhile, the garrison's lines were sited nice and regiment-ally, but with no more thought for trouble than if they'd been in bloody Colchester! Had they learnt nothing after Cavagnari's murder and the bloodbath in Kabul last September?

'Here, General, look at those ugly customers.' Heath, my brigade major, had failed to read my mood, as usual, and was being his normal irritating self. 'Ghazis, you can bet on it.'

Heath, Lynch – the trumpeter who had been attached to me by the Horse Gunners – and I were hacking along from the cantonment to meet our lord and master General Primrose up in the Citadel. There, I was expected to report my brigade present and correct to Himself. I would also be briefed on the situation.

'Ghazis? Why d'you think that, Heath?' I looked across at a handful of young braves who were filing along past a scatter of native stalls on the edge of the bazaar. Lean, tall, well set-up men, their hook noses and tanned skin told me nothing exceptional; they carried swords, shields and *jezail*s slung across their backs, like half of the rest of the men in this town, and looked me straight in the eye, rather than slinking away, like most of the other tribesmen do at the sight of Feringhee officers. 'They look more like normal Pathans to me. I've a notion that Ghazis don't carry firearms.' Those who knew told me that the Ghazis, Islamic zealots from the most extreme sects who had sworn to die while trying to kill any infidel who trod upon their land, did their lethal duty with cold steel only, eschewing muskets and rifles as tools of the devil.

'Possibly, General, but you never quite know how they'll disguise themselves. Look at their arrogant expressions,' Heath continued. When I'd picked him, I'd assumed that, with all his service in India and his fluent *bat,* a degree of common sense and knowledge of the workings of the native mind would come with it. Both appeared to have eluded him – he was even more ignorant of local matters than I was.

'No, sir, they ain't Ghazis.' Trumpeter Lynch had been part of my personal staff for less than twenty-four hours, but he'd already seen through my brigade major. 'If they was Ghazis they'd have buggered off at the sight of us, sir. My mate who was in Kabul last year reckons you'll only see one of them bastards when he's a-coming for you, knife aimed at yer gizzard. No, sir, them's just ordinary Paythans, like the general said.'

Heath might have been wrong on that score, but he was right about their arrogance. They all continued to stare at us. The oldest of the group, a heavily bearded man without, apparently, a tooth in his head, spat on my mounted shadow as it passed them by, expressing his contempt most eloquently.

'A trifle slow off the mark, Morgan?' Major General James Maurice Primrose and I had never liked each other. 'I asked for you to be here at half past the hour. It's five and twenty to by my watch.'

The sergeant of the Citadel guard had been a smart but slow-witted man from the second battalion of the 7th Fusiliers who'd been incapable of directing my staff and me to the divisional commander's offices; none of us had been there before and Heath hadn't thought to check. So, to my fury, I was late and last, giving Primrose just the sort of opening I'd hoped to avoid. We'd first met in Karachi a couple of years ago and, both of us being Queen's officers, we should have got along. But we didn't. He was one of those supercilious types who'd never got over his early service in the stuck-up 43rd Light Infantry and, I was told, envied both my gong from the Crimea and my Mutiny record.

'Still, no matter, we've time in hand. Now, while I need to know about your command, I've taken your arrival as an opportunity to bring all my brigade commanders up to date on developments. Forgive me if you know people already, but let me go round the room.' Primrose was small, standing no more than five foot six, just sixty-one and with a full head of snowy hair. There had been rumours about his health, but he seemed to have survived. Now he pointed round the stuffy,

11

low-ceilinged room with its two, narrow, Oriental-style windows. 'Nuttall commands my cavalry brigade.'

I'd never met Tom Nuttall before but I'd heard his name bruited about during the Mutiny. A little older than I was, he was an infantryman by trade but now found himself in charge of the three regiments of cavalry – including my son Sam's regiment, the 3rd Scinde Horse. He was as straight as a lance, clear-eyed, and had a friendly smile.

'I know that you know Brooke.' I thought there was a distinctly cool tone in Primrose's voice as he waved a hand at Harry. Yes, I knew and liked him for he was a straight-line infantryman like me, a few years younger, but he'd seen more than his share of trouble in the Crimea and China before rising to be adjutant general of the Bombay Army.

'And McGucken tells me you two stretch back a long way.' Again, I thought I caught irritation in the general's voice as Major Alan McGucken reached out a sinewy hand towards me, his honest Scotch face cracked in the warmest of smiles.

'Yes, General, we've come across one another a couple of times in the past. It's good to see you again, Jock.' By God, it was too. Six foot and fifty-four years of Glasgow granite grinned at me, one of the most remarkable men I knew. He was wind-burnt, his whiskers now showing grey, and wore a run of ribbons that started with the Distinguished Conduct Medal on the breast of his plain blue frock coat. I'd first met him when he was a colour sergeant and I was an ensign in the 95th Foot. We'd soldiered through the Crimea and the Mutiny, never more than a few feet apart (we were even wounded within yards of each other), until his true worth had been recognised. After the fall of Gwalior in '58, he'd been commissioned in the field and, with his natural flair for languages and his easy way with the natives, he had soon gravitated back to India. I'd watched his steady rise through merit with delight and pleasure but had been genuinely surprised to hear that he'd been seconded to the Political

12

Department, some eighteen months ago, and then appointed to advise the divisional commander here in Kandahar.

'An' it's good to see you, General. There's a deal o' catching up to do − perhaps a swally or two might be in order?' He was older, for sure, but that rasping accent took me back to good times and bad, triumphs and disappointments we had shared, scares and laughter too many to remember.

But our familiarity clearly irritated General Primrose, who rose on the balls of his feet, peering up at McGucken while shooting me a sideways look. 'Indeed, gentlemen. I'm sure there'll be plenty of opportunity for such niceties once *my* political officer has briefed us all on the possible difficulties we face.' Primrose cut across McGucken's and my obvious delight in each other's company, reasserting his authority and returning the atmosphere to all the conviviality of a Methodist prayer meeting. 'Let's have no more delays. Proceed, please, Major McGucken.'

And with that stricture, McGucken moved across to a map that was pinned to the wall, shooed a couple of somnolent flies off its lacquered surface, cleared his throat and began.

'Before I arrived, back in November last year, while General Stewart was handling his own political affairs, a rumour gathered strength over in Herat.' McGucken pointed to the city, more than three hundred miles to the north and west of Kandahar. 'Ayoob Khan is the governor there and he has designs on Kandahar − he's already declared himself the real wali − and for those of you who don't know, gentlmen, a wali's a regional governor who, so long as he's got the local tribes with him, is extremely powerful. And I can understand why he's interested in Kandahar. It's the most prosperous of the regions and our people in India hadn't made it clear that there was likely to be a permanent British presence here. Anyway, General Stewart took the intelligence seriously enough to report it to the viceroy−'

'But not seriously enough to do anything about preparing

13

Kandahar for any sort of a fight,' Primrose interrupted, bristling away and looking every bit the petulant little scrub I'd always thought him.

'Aye, General, quite so.' McGucken continued: 'But, as you know, things quietened down after the end of the fighting last year and the rumour came to nothing. Some of you gentlemen have already met the Wali of Kandahar, Sher Ali—'

'You haven't had a chance to clap eyes on him yet, Morgan.' I could see how irritated McGucken was becoming by Primrose's constant interjections. 'I'll get you an appointment as soon as possible. He must be in his mid-sixties now, not well liked and without much influence among either the Pathans or the Douranis, but the viceroy decided that he was the man to rule Kandahar as a state that is semi-independent of the Kabul government, so support him we shall. Trouble is, his own troops – who are meant to be keeping the tribes in order hereabouts – are unreliable and we've had a number of minor mutinies already. But don't let me interrupt, McGucken, do go on.'

I knew that look of McGucken's. He'd never suffered fools gladly, not even when he was an NCO, and his expression, a mixture of contempt and impatience, told me all I needed to know about the interfering nature of our divisional commander.

'Sir, thank you.' McGucken's accent disguised his exasperation – unless you knew the man as well as I did. 'The situation is extremely ticklish. You all know about General Stewart's victory at Ahmed Khel on the nineteenth of April. He was halfway to Kabul when he met a right set of rogues and gave all fifteen thousand of them a damn good towelling. But, despite what you might think, that has only made the local tribesmen bolder. Word has come down from the Ghilzais that they nearly beat Stewart's force, and whether that's right or wrong is unimportant for that's what they want to believe, and over the last couple of weeks the locals have become decidedly gallus.'

I smiled as the others knitted their brows at McGucken's vocabulary. His speech had acquired a veneer of gentility to go with his rank and appointment, but his orphan Glasgow background was still obvious if you knew what to look for. And I knew what he meant: the badmashes Heath had pointed out were certainly 'gallus' – far too confident for their own good.

'There's been trouble among the wali's forces while our own troops have been pestered, harassed, attacked, even, by tribesmen here in the city–'

But McGucken wasn't allowed to continue, for Primrose butted in again: 'Yes, that's right. Some of your fellows had a very ugly incident the other day, didn't they, Brooke? Tell Morgan about it.'

'Well, yes, sir.' I could see that Harry Brooke, decent sort of man that he was, didn't want to break into McGucken's briefing, but Primrose was insistent. 'Willis, one of the Gunner subalterns of my brigade, had gone down into the Charsoo – that's the odd domed building at the crossroads in the centre of the town, Morgan, if you ain't seen it already – where the normal gathering of villains was going on around the bazaar stalls. He'd got a couple of soldiers with him and was armed according to my orders, but in the crowd he got separated from his escort – quite deliberately, I'm sure – and a Ghazi came at him with an ordinary shoemaker's awl . . .'

My face must have betrayed my horror at what I knew Brooke was about to say.

'Yes, I know it's hard to believe, but I asked to see the murder weapon after the whole beastly business was over. It was just one of those sharp little iron awls, no more than two and a bit inches long, I'm telling you. The lads who witnessed the attack reckoned that it was an unusually crowded day in the markets, and a lunatic waited till his confederates had distracted them both and then just ran at him and buried it in the poor fellow's neck. The two soldiers saw the assassin running at their officer but had no idea what he was about to do. All they saw was a look of crazy hatred on the man's face and something small glittering in his hand. They'd had all the lectures about what the Ghazis can do and been told about their penchant for cold steel, but the whole thing was such a surprise that Willis didn't stand a chance.

'Anyway, then the mob closed in and the wretched fellow bled to death before anyone could do anything for him. I think even the locals were shocked by the brutality, for intelligence started to come in at once and we arrested the culprit a couple of days later – the cheeky sod was still running his cobbler's business, as cool as you like. We hanged him just yards away from where the murder had occurred – that served as a lesson for the natives – but at least this bit of nastiness has shown exactly what the Ghazis can do. Everyone is on the *qui vive* when they're in and about the town and–'

'Go on, McGucken.' Primrose had cut right across Brooke.

'Sir, as I was saying, we've now received further intelligence that Ayoob Khan is preparing to move out of Herat. He's trying to get his troops – as many as nine thousand we're told – into some sort of fettle, but that's all we really know. It's possible that he's going to bypass Kandahar and move on Kabul, but that seems less likely now that Stewart's force have moved up to Kabul to reinforce General Roberts's troops.' McGucken paused.

'How long would it take a native army of that size to reach us from Herat, and what sort of troops are they?' I asked.

'Well, General, it's hard to know exactly, but I guess it would take Ayoob Khan more than a month, so – if my people are worth their salt – we should get plenty of warning. But they're better organised than you might think, General. He's got regulars, including some of the Kabuli regiments who turned on Louis Cavagnari last year, armed with Enfields and a few Sniders and some guns with, we're told, overseers from the Russian artillery. How many pieces, and of what calibre, we're not yet sure.'

I could see that McGucken had plenty more to tell me but Primrose hadn't yet heard enough of his own voice: 'So, Morgan, gentlemen, there we are.' He was up and down on his toes like some wretched ballet dancer – I knew he would be an awkward man to work under. 'We've got local problems with the troublesome, headstrong folk here in the town and the odd murderous loon in the shape of the Ghazis. The wali's troops are an unknown quantity but will, I suspect, come to heel once the wali takes them properly in hand . . .' McGucken raised his eyebrows '. . . and now the rumour of Ayoob Khan is back with us. I think it's time, gentlemen, to take the soldier-like precautions that General Stewart so signally failed to do. We must not only be ready to take the field at a moment's notice, we must also be ready to defend Kandahar.'

I could see Primrose scanning us all, challenging anyone to disagree with him, as the flies buzzed drowsily and the punkah creaked on its hinges above us. I have to say, it had all come as a bit of a surprise to me. I'd thought our division would be in Afghanistan just to see things quieten down, give a bit of bottom to the new wali and then be off back to India before the next winter. Now it seemed we might have a bit of a fight on our hands and – as Roberts, Browne and now Stewart had found out – these hillmen were not Zulus armed with spears whom we could mow down in their thousands. As well as regular troops and demented Ghazis, it now appeared that Ayoob Khan had guns directed by Russians. McGucken and I had had a bellyful of just such creatures a few years back.

'Well, sir, may I suggest that there are three measures we could start with advantage right away?' Harry Brooke spoke, clear and direct, taking Primrose's challenge head on.

'Please enlighten us, Brooke,' Primrose replied, with a slight edge of sarcasm that caused McGucken to glance at me.

'We must secure fresh and plentiful water supplies within the walls of the town before the weather gets really hot.' Brooke paused to see how this would be received.

'Yes, yes, of course – that's just common sense,' replied Primrose, so quickly that I suspected he'd never even considered such a thing. 'Do go on.'

'Well, sir, if we're to face an enemy in the field, we'll need every sabre and bayonet that we can find so we can't be distracted by foes inside the town such as those you've just described. Should we not expel all Pathans of military age and pull down the shanties and lean-tos that have been built so close to the walls that they restrict any fields of fire? Can we not start to burn or dismantle them now, General?'

The punkah squaled again and I could see that the trouble with Harry Brooke, like all of us Anglo-Irish, was that he was too damn blunt. I'd had much the same thoughts about the clutter of plank and mud-built houses, shops and stalls as I'd ridden up from the cantonments towards the town walls and his comments about the tribesmen made a great deal of sense to me. But, judging by the way Primrose was hopping from foot to foot, Harry's ideas hadn't found much favour.

'No, no, Brooke, that will never do. You must remember, all of you . . .' Primrose treated us to another of his basilisk stares '. . . that we are not an army of occupation. We're guests – pretty muscular guests, I grant you – of the wali under whose hand we lie. We can't go knocking his people's property about and chucking out those we haven't taken a shine to. How on earth will we ever gain his or his subjects' confidence if we behave like that? No, that will never do.'

What, I suspect, the little trimmer really meant was that sensible measures he wouldn't have hesitated to use last year, while Disraeli's crew held sway, simply wouldn't answer now that Gladstone and his bunch of croakers were in charge. Primrose didn't want to be seen by the new Whig regime as one of the same stamp of generals of whom the liberal press had been so critical for their heavy-handedness in Zululand and then for so-called 'atrocities' here in Afghanistan twelve months ago.

I could repeat, word perfect, Gladstone's cant, which I'd read when I'd paused in Quetta three weeks ago, just before the election. It had caused near apoplexy at breakfast in the mess: 'Remember that the sanctity of life in the hill villages of Afghanistan, amid the winter snows, is as inviolable in the eyes of Almighty God as your own,' or some such rot. Disraeli had responded by calling his comments 'rodomontade' (which had us all stretching for the dictionaries) but there was no doubting the public mood that didn't want to hear about British regulars being bested by natives and the murder of their envoys in far-away residences. They were heartily sick of highly coloured press accounts of shield-and-spear-armed Zulu *impis* being cut down by rifles and Gatling guns. If the new God-bothering government caught even a whiff of Primrose's treating the tribesmen with anything other than kid gloves then his career was likely to be as successful as the Pope's wedding night.

'There it is, gentlemen. With a little good fortune, all this talk of Ayoob Khan descending on us like the wrath of God will prove to be just hot air and we can get on with an ordered life here, then make a measured move back to India later in the year.'

I looked round the room to judge people's reaction to this last utterance from Primrose and there wasn't a face – except, perhaps, Heath's – that didn't look horrified at such a prospect. I, for one, had sat in Karachi whittling away over the last couple of campaign seasons while my friends and juniors gathered laurels innumerable, courtesy of the Afghans. And I'd had little expectation of any excitement when I'd been sent for a few weeks ago. But now our hopes had been raised. Perhaps we were to see deeds and glory. Maybe Nuttall,

19

Brooke and I would not be bound for our pensions, Bath chairs and memories quite as soon as we had feared.

But not a bit of that from our divisional commander: he seemed to be longing for his villa in Cheltenham. 'But if we are unlucky and all this trouble comes to pass, then we must be as ready as we can be. So, away to your commands, gentlemen. But not you, Morgan. May I detain you?' All the others were gathering up their swords and sun-helmets, folding maps and despatches in a thoughtful silence, and I'd hoped that the general might have forgotten his summons to me – I wanted to spend some time with McGucken before events overtook us, but Primrose wasn't having that. As I picked up my documents he said, 'We need to discuss the state of your new brigade, don't we, Morgan?'

'What do we do, sir, when we meet a wali? I've never met one before,' asked Heath, to whom I had been about to pose the same question.

'How, in God's name, should I know, Heath? I chose you to be my brigade major because you're savvy with all this native stuff, ain't you?' All I got in reply from the great lummox was a sulky look. 'We'll just go in and salute, regimental-like, and let him do the talking. I hope his English is up to it.'

Primrose had been true to his word: the very next day I found myself bidden to Sher Ali Khan's presence, the Wali of Kandahar. Now Heath and I were waiting in a stuffy little anteroom on the other side of the Citadel from where we'd met Primrose and all the others yesterday. At least the wali had tried to do the place up a little. I didn't know where the furniture had come from – it looked French, with overstuffed satiny fabric and curly, carved legs – but there were some grand carpets on the floor and hanging on the walls. A couple of greasy-looking sentries had performed a poor imitation of presenting arms as we were escorted up to see His Nibs while a funny little chamberlain − or some such flunkey − had buzzed around us, talking such bad English that I saw little value in what was coming next beyond the call of protocol. But I was wrong.

'My dear General!' We'd been ushered into another, similar, room, performed our military rites and removed our helmets as the wali leapt off a low divan, a smile beaming through his beard and his hand outstretched. 'How very good of you to make the time to see me.'

He looked much older than sixty-two. He was short, fat and yellow-toothed; he wore a sheepskin cap that, I guessed, hadn't been removed since the winter; there was a distinct aroma of armpits about him and yet he was utterly, disarmingly, charming. He pumped our fins, sat us down, pressed thimble-sized cups of coffee on the pair of us and made me feel that his whole life had been a tedious interlude while he had waited to meet me.

'No, really, it is very good of you.' His English was accented, slightly sing-song, perhaps, but completely fluent. 'I know what a trying journey you must have had up from India, but we do appreciate it. Now that General Stewart has gone, I'm so glad that you've brought another whole brigade to help General Primrose and me.' The fellow made it sound as if I'd mustered my own personal vassals for this crusade as a favour to him. 'Oh, we shall need them.'

I have to say, the next ten minutes were more useful than anything I'd heard from Primrose or would hear from him in the future. McGucken had, obviously, made a deep and favourable impression on the clever old boy, for he told me (and I don't think it was just gammon) to seek him out if I hadn't met him already. I forbore to mention how well I knew Jock, for I wanted to hear exactly what the wali himself had to tell me, especially about the threat from Ayoob Khan, which Primrose seemed to be playing down.

'Well, yes, dear General, my prayers concentrate upon

21

nothing at the moment but the intentions of that man. Your people don't really understand what he wants and how determined he is to get it.' Sher Ali trotted over the fact that he was a cousin of the amir and that he'd been installed as governor of the entire region in July last year in the clear expectation that he would be kept in post by force of British arms. 'But then your government started to reduce the number of white and Indian soldiers here, and that was when the trouble started with my own men. You see, as far as most of them are concerned, I'm a British . . . a British . . . oh, what's the word I want?'

'Catspaw, sir?' asked Heath, leaving all of us wondering what on earth he meant.

'Eh? No, not an animal . . . puppet — that's the word. Well, they hated that, but they had to put up with it, as long as there were enough British guns and bayonets to subdue them. My troops are not my tribesmen, General. They understand tribal authority more than any rank that is given or imposed — particularly by Feringhees. Oh, I do beg your forgiveness. I don't wish to suggest that your presence is unwelcome!' The old boy nearly poured his coffee down his beard when he thought he might have been unmannerly.

'And this is where Ayoob Khan has the advantage.' He told us again about Kandahar's prosperity, how Ayoob Khan had been eyeing it up as his own for ages and how he'd managed to suborn the local forces with people from the Ghilzai tribes loyal to him but serving under the wali. 'We've been hearing for months now that he and his people are likely to march out of Herat, and if that is the case, we must try to stop him before he gets anywhere near this city. But I worry about taking my troops into the field, General Morgan. As you will know, I'm sure, we have already had difficulties over pay — one of my cavalry regiments threw down their arms only last month when their officers tried to take them out of their lines for training. Now, if he were to come towards us, we should have to try and meet him somewhere here.' The wali pointed to the Helmand river fords near Gereshk on a spanking new map that, I guessed, McGucken had given him.

'Aye, sir, and that's quite a way west over dry country.' The map showed few water-courses and little but seventy or so miles of plains beset by steep heights.

'Indeed so, but he and his elders know it well. And there are more complications.' I heard him sigh when he said this, as if the very thought of what lay ahead sapped his energy and determination. 'He will do his best to raise not just tribesmen along the way, but also the cursed Ghazis in the name of *jihad*. Have you been told about these creatures, General?' I assured him that I had, and that Primrose and Brooke had given me a pretty fair idea of what they could do.

'Ah, but, General, all you have seen of them is odd ones and twos. True, they make trouble in the town, they caused Stewart *huzoor* much pain, and they have started to gnaw at the ankles of General Primrose's new division. But just imagine what such people could do if they were massed against you. That, no one has yet seen. If Ayoob Khan ever ventures out of the west, then be certain, my dear General, that those white-robed madmen will hover around him like wasps . . .'

Two days after my meeting with the wali, I had been up at dawn, ridden out of the town with Heath and Trumpeter Lynch to the lower slopes of the Baba Wali Kotal – the high ground some three miles to the north-west – and made an assessment of where the enemy's best viewpoint would be. Then I'd come back to the mess for a swift breakfast of steak and fruit, before heading to my headquarters. I was just settling down behind my folding desk, preparing to indulge Heath with the things he loved best – detailed accounts, returns and all manner of mind-numbing administration – when news began to filter in of an ugly incident involving the 66th Foot.

The only British infantry that I had, the regiment had so

far impressed me both times that I had seen them. But now there were reports that one of their patrols had killed a child right in the middle of Kandahar, then dispersed with great violence the angry crowd that gathered. Predictably, the first reports were vague and vastly unreliable, so once the dust had settled – literally – and the facts were clear, I had got back into the saddle and come to see the commanding officer, James Galbraith.

It had been an uncomfortable couple of hours' waiting for me, for Primrose had caught wind of it, as had some British journalists who were out and about in Kandahar, and he was pressing me for a full account before the editors in London learnt of it. But I had commanded a battalion – albeit nowhere more demanding than Pembroke Dock – and I knew how irritating pressure from above would be for the commanding officer. Once the matter was fully investigated, Lieutenant Colonel Galbraith had asked me to come into the cramped little hut that served as his office. He rose from behind a trestle table in his rumpled khaki and stood stiffly to attention, expecting the worst.

'Sit down, sit down, please, Galbraith.' Despite my attempts to put him at ease, Galbraith continued to stand. I threw myself into one of the collapsible leather-seated campaign chairs that were so popular at the time.

'A cheroot?' I flicked one of the little brown tubes towards him, but Galbraith shook his head without a word. 'Tell me what happened.'

The 66th had been in India for almost ten years now, stationed at Ahmednagar and Karachi, and I'd been pleased to see how many long-service men they still included. While the new regulations allowed men to enlist for shorter periods – which was reckoned by some to be good for recruiting – I always thought it took some time for a lad from the slums of England to acquire any sort of resistance to the heat and pestilence of India. It can't have been a coincidence that the

Second Battalion of the 8th Foot – almost all young, short-service lads – had been gutted by disease last year outside Kabul.

'Well, General, we had a routine patrol in the central bazaar earlier this morning, an officer, sergeant and six men. They all said that the atmosphere was tense, with a lot of people and beasts bringing goods to market. Suddenly the crowd opened and a child rushed at them with a knife in his hand.' Galbraith had been in command of the 66th for four years now and had a reputation for being as devoted to them as his men were to him. Another English-Paddy from Omagh up north, my father knew his family, but the slim, handsome man, whose heavy moustache and whiskers made him look older than his forty years, had never thought to presume upon this link.

'A child, Galbraith? How old was he?' I found it hard to believe that a fully armed patrol of British soldiers might be attacked by a boy. A strapping youth, perhaps, for many of the Ghazis, while fully grown, were said by those who had had to face them to be too young to have proper beards. But a mere boy behaving like that I found difficult to credit.

'Well, I'm not exactly sure, General, but young enough for there to be an almighty bloody fuss kicked up by the mullahs to whom the press are listening with all their normal even-handedness,' replied Galbraith.

'Are you sure that one of the lads didn't fire his rifle by mistake, hit the boy and now he's trying to cover it up just like the Fifty-Ninth did?' I knew soldiers: they'd lie most imaginatively if they thought it would save their necks. The story was still circulating about a drunken spree by the 59th last Christmas. Two of the men had been drinking and tinkering about with their rifles when one had shot the other. They had made up some cock-and-bull story about a Ghazi entering their barracks and, in an attempt to shoot him down, one man had accidentally wounded his comrade.

'Well, no, sir. The youth was killed with a sword and a number of bayonet thrusts quite deliberately. The men didn't fire for fear of hitting one of the crowd.' Galbraith looked indignant.

'Oh, good. That's exactly what I wanted to hear. So now we don't just have a child being killed, the poor little bugger was hacked to pieces by your ruffians while half of Kandahar looked on. I really don't like the sound of this at all. Who was in charge of this fiasco? I hope you're not going to tell me it was a lad straight out of Sandhurst with some lance sergeant at his side?' When I'd paid my first visit to the 66th a few days ago, I'd been pleased with the appearance of the men but I'd noticed how junior some of the NCOs were. Galbraith had explained that he'd had to leave a large number of sergeants behind in India, either sick or time-expired, and he'd been forced to promote fairly inexperienced corporals to fill the gaps.

'No, sir. Sar'nt Kelly is one of my best substantive sergeants with almost sixteen years' service. He's due to get his colours at the next promotion board. That's why I've put him with one of my new officers.' Galbraith came back at me hot and strong. 'If you'd prefer to hear it straight from those who were there, sir, I've got Kelly and his officer waiting outside.'

'Yes, I bloody well would. Ask them to march in, please, Heath.' My tosspot of a brigade major had been sitting in on the meeting with Galbraith, his expression increasingly disapproving, not a shred of sympathy showing for the men who had been faced with what sounded to me like a thoroughly nasty business.

I saw the pair of them file in, smartly in step. Sergeant Kelly was five foot nine, heavily sunburnt, with a moustache trimmed to regulation length, and the ribbon of the *rooti-gong* above his left breast pocket. His puttees were wrapped just so, his khaki drill pressed as neatly as field conditions would allow, three red chevrons standing out starkly on his right

26

sleeve and his brasswork polished for the occasion. He gave
'Halt,' then 'Up,' *sotto voce* to his subaltern, both men
stamping in time before their hands quivered to the peaks of
their khaki-covered helmets. After a silent count of 'Two,
three,' they snapped them down to their sides. The officer
was taller but slighter than his sergeant. His fair hair curled
just a little too fashionably almost to his collar, his skin was
red with the early summer sun and his moustache still not
fully grown. Holding his sword firmly back against his left
hip, pistol to his right, the single brass stars of an ensign on
either side of his collar, he was my younger son, William.

'Well, Sar'nt Kelly, Mr Morgan, if I'm to put up a good
case on your behalf and keep your names from being spread
over the gutter press, you'd better tell me exactly what
happened this morning.' Galbraith had deliberately not
mentioned that my son was the officer involved – wise man
that he was.

Now Billy cleared his throat and raised his chin before he
spoke, just like his late mother might have done. 'Sir, with
your leave, I'll explain everything . . .'

TWO

The Ghazi

It was hot, and as Ensign Billy Morgan looked up into the cloudless sky he could see a pair of hawks circling effortlessly on the burning air just above the walls of Kandahar. They reminded him of the sleek, lazy-winged buzzards back in Ireland, except that there the sun rarely shone. He wondered how the thermals would feel to the birds – would they sense the heat of the air under their feathers as they scanned the collection of humanity below? And would they have any sense of the tensions that pulsed through the city under them? Then, as he looked at the gang of khaki-clad lads in front of him, he realised just how ridiculous his musings were. The birds cared not a damn for him or his soldiers, or for any man or living beast, he thought. Their eyes and beaks roamed ceaselessly for dead or dying things, for carrion to feed their bellies. Of the feelings and concerns of the men in the dust and grit below them, they knew nothing.

'Is that belt tight enough, Thompson?' Morgan was checking the six soldiers who had been detailed off to patrol the centre of Kandahar. They knew it would be a tense and hostile time, as the villagers pressed into the bazaars for market day.

'Sir,' replied Thompson, flatly – the Army's universal word of affirmation that could mean anything from enthusiastic agreement to outright insubordination. The big Cumberland farmer's lad looked back at Morgan, his face trusting and open.

'Well, make sure it is. I don't want you having to bugger about with it once we're among the crowds. Just check it, please, Sar'nt Kelly.' Morgan hesitated to treat the men like children, but even in his few weeks with the regiment, he'd come to recognise that the ordinary soldiers, dependable, smart and keen most of the time, could be the most negligent of creatures once they put their minds to it.

'Sir.' Sergeant Kelly came back with the same stock response 'Come on, Thompson, I can get this between your belt and that fat gut of yours – look.' Kelly had stuck his clenched fist between the soldier's belt, which had been scrubbed clean of pipe clay on active service, and his lean belly. 'Take it in a couple of notches.' Thompson moved his right foot to the rear of his left, rested his Martini-Henry rifle against his side and undid the dull brass belt buckle, inscribed with '66' in the middle and 'Berkshire Regiment' round the outer part of the clasp.

Thompson was the last man to be inspected. Once his belt was back in place and he'd assumed the position of attention, Kelly stamped in the packed dust just outside the regimental guardroom where the patrol had assembled, slapped the sling of his rifle and repeated the well-worn formula, 'Leave to carry on, sir, please?'

'And is Bobby a vital member of the patrol, Sar'nt Kelly?' The non-commissioned officer's scruffy little terrier-cross, which had followed his master all the way from India, now sat on the ground, sweeping his remnant of a tail back and forth, looking imploringly up at Kelly. Morgan's words provoked laughter from the file of men, and a grin from Sergeant Kelly, relieving the tension. When he had arrived with the 66th, Morgan had been surprised by the deference the soldiers had shown to him. Sandhurst had trained him to expect and, indeed, demand their instant obedience, but he hadn't anticipated how concerned they would be by his inexperienced eye being run over them during an inspection. Now there was the added edge of danger, with the knowledge that previous regiments had suffered casualties among the Afghan mob, and the need for constant vigilance.

'No, sir. Go on, pup, away wi' you.' Kelly's voice was firm but kind as he pointed towards the guardroom while the dog continued to look at him and wag his tail with increased urgency. 'Go on, Bobby, fuck off.'

'One word off you, Sar'nt . . .' Private Battle, the longest-serving soldier in the patrol, murmured, to the delight of the others, Kelly grinning broadly as well. Morgan knew that Battle could be a handful, often nicknamed 'Bottle' because he was fond of his grog – that was why he was still a private.

'That's enough from you, Private Edward bleedin' Battle. Got enough trouble wi' one mongrel that won't obey me without another addin' to me grief. Go on, Bobby, fuck off to the guardroom like a good dog.' The patrol laughed again as the mutt slunk off towards the bell tent that served as the entrance to the 66th's lines.

As the fun died down, Morgan continued, 'Right, Sar'nt Kelly, no one's loaded but ammunition's ready, ain't it?' Kelly simply nodded in reply. Standing orders stated that no firearms should have a round in the breech during a patrol except on the instructions of an officer or an NCO, but that ammunition should be broken out of its paper parcels and ready for instant use in the men's pouches. A number of natives had been wounded during scuffles with the previous regiments and Colonel Galbraith was keen that the 66th should not have the same problems. 'Good. Loosen slings, fix bayonets and stand the men at ease, please.'

Kelly gave a few simple instructions, none of the parade-ground shouting that Morgan had seen with other sergeants, to which the men responded readily, slipping the long steel needles over the muzzles of their rifles before pushing the locking rings home with an oily scrape. Then the leather slings were slackened, weapons slung over shoulders, and they all looked at Morgan for his next word of command.

'Right, lads, gather round and listen to me.' The six men shuffled round Billy Morgan, Sergeant Kelly hanging back, slightly to the rear. Morgan looked at his command. He was the junior subaltern of H Company, charged with leading nearly forty men, mostly good fellows as far as he could see, and few of the sweepings of the gutter that the press would have you believe made up the Army. Morgan was twenty-two, about the same age as most of his men, but they looked older. The product of the new sprawling industrial towns, some from the plough and a few from Ireland, they had been used to a hard life even before they came into the 66th. Now, good food, drill and regular physical training had made them fit and lean, prime fighting material. 'Most of you have been on town patrol before . . .' This was only Morgan's second outing. The first had passed in a blur of new sights, sounds and smells but otherwise had been uneventful. 'We're to make sure that the natives know we're here and alert, and to take note of anything unusual.'

'Like what, sir?' Battle, the old soldier of six years' Indian service, cut in, his brogue as thick as the day he had left Manorhamilton.

'Well, large gatherings of young men, the sight of any modern weapons such as Sniders – to be frank, you're all more experienced than I am and I hope that you've got a better nose for trouble than I have.' Morgan looked around. This touch of humility seemed to have been well received by the men. 'But remember, lads, be on the look-out for the least sign of danger. The Fifty-Ninth found that a mob would know if something was amiss and would thin out at the approach of a patrol.' The only British infantry regiment that had been part of General Stewart's division and had handed over to

31

the 66th had shared all sorts of horror stories with their successors. They'd had a litany of minor casualties and two deaths while patrolling the Kandahar streets. 'So, keep your eyes peeled and if you think we need to put a round up the spout, ask Sar'nt Kelly or me before you do so.'

'But, sir, we're meant to be here to support the wali, ain't we, not to do his troops' work for 'im? The Fore and Afts' – Battle used the nickname of the 59th – 'got right kicked about an' was never allowed to shoot back. If the town's so bleedin' 'ostile, why can't the wali's men deal with it an' save us for the proper jobs?'

There was a rumble of agreement from the other men and Morgan shot a look at Sergeant Kelly, whose level stare merely told him that he, too, expected an officer-type answer to a wholly reasonable question.

'Good point, Battle.' Morgan paused as he measured his reply. 'It isn't like the proper war that was being fought last year. We're here, as you say, to help the wali, but his own troops are unreliable and the town is full of badmashes we need to know about, and then report back to the political officer. Now, if there are no more questions . . .' Morgan was suddenly aware that he and his patrol had been hanging around for far too long.

'Yessir. What do we do if we see a Ghazi, sir?' Thompson, belt now tightened, chirped up.

'Most unlikely, Thompson. They'll melt away at the sight of us,' replied Morgan.

Thompson wasn't to be put off. 'They didn't with the Fifty-Ninth, sir, did they? Why–'

'Yes, well, we're not the Fifty-Ninth, are we? This lot have heard that the Sixty-sixth are here and they won't want to take us on. Now, split into pairs, ten paces between each. Sar'nt Kelly, bring up the rear, please. Follow me.' With that, Morgan's little command stepped out of the tented lines of the 66th, through a gate in the barbed-wire perimeter and away up the gentle incline three-quarters of a mile towards the walls, shanties and sun-lit pall of woodsmoke that was Kandahar.

Morgan walked as casually as he could among his soldiers. The men were moving either side of the pot-holed road in what the Army liked to describe as 'staggered file' – odd numbers on the left and even numbers on the right, no two men in a line with each other. That, he thought, was meant to make a random *jezail* shot less likely to strike more than one man, but he could see how the troops tended to close in on each other for comfort and reassurance.

'No, lads, keep spread out. Don't bunch up, keep your distance,' Morgan said, as lightly as he could, trying not to let his tension show in his voice. He looked at the men that some mistaken fate had placed under his command. They were all polite to him, almost painfully so, trusting him because of the stars he wore on his collar and his accent, more than any proof of competence he had so far shown. Yet he was surprised by how easy he found their company. Sandhurst had told him to expect the worst, that while most of his men would be good, trustworthy sorts, a few would be out to mock him and dun him of every penny he might be foolish enough to carry around. He had identified no one like that. True, Battle was a bit of a handful – he'd come the wiseacre a couple of times over the young officer's Protestantism – but Morgan had managed to slap him down good-naturedly enough.

But, looking at Private Battle, Billy Morgan remembered how his father would tease the Catholics both back home in Cork and in his countless stories about the old Army. Yet, while he pretended to be suspicious of their religion, his obvious fondness for what he called his Paddies shone through. Now the new Army, Morgan thought, had fewer of those Irishmen who'd been driven to take the shilling by the potato blight back in the forties and fifties, but those who had enlisted were good enough and fitted in well with the sturdy English lads that the 66th recruited from around their depot in Reading. No, even in the short space of time he'd spent with H Company, Morgan was beginning to understand the men, to enjoy their ready, irreverent humour (how had they referred to General Roberts in his vast, non-regulation sun-helmet when they saw his picture in the paper? 'That little arse in the fuck-off hat', wasn't it?) and understand their values. How, he wondered, would he have managed if he'd been commissioned into one of the native regiments, like his half-brother, Sam Keenan? Everything would have been so foreign – and even if he'd managed to learn the language well enough to do his job, it would never have been possible, surely, to become really close to an Indian.

But, thought Billy Morgan, that would never have been the case for he was only ever going to serve in a smart regiment – his father would hear of nothing else. As a little boy he'd accepted, without questioning, that he would always get the best of everything while Sam would have what was left over. He could still remember when he was five years old and how bitter the older, bigger Sam had been at having to accept the smaller of the two ponies their father had bought for them. It was the first time Billy had really noticed any difference, but as he matured, he had seen how Mary, his step-mother, had protected the way in which Sam had been brought up in her Catholic Church.

His father had made a joke of it, laughing when Mary elongated the word 'maas' and crossing himself in *faux*-respect whenever something Roman was mentioned. And as Father thought that County Cork was far too much under the sway of the Pope, he would brook no suggestion that Billy should be sent to one of the local schools. Oh, no, they were good enough for Sam, but for Billy there should be nothing but the best: he was to be educated in England, at Sandhurst and then a good line regiment, just like his father.

34

He and his brother had seen little of each other. Only when Billy returned to Glassdrumman in the school holidays would they meet – and clash. Billy knew that Sam resented him and the preferential treatment he received, and on the few occasions that they were together as boys, and then as young men, he wasn't slow to show it. Everything became a contest – no fish could be pulled from a stream or bird shot from a rainy sky without its becoming a test of manhood. At first Billy was always bettered by his bigger brother, who would challenge him to runs over the heather or bogs or turn a fishing trip into a swimming challenge across an icy lough, which he always lost. But as Billy grew, he began to win, so Sam ensured that the contests became more intense.

It was just before Sam had gone off to the Bombay Army, Billy remembered, that things had come to a head. He was home from school and Sam was full of piss and vinegar about his new adventure, full of brag about the Indians he would soon command and the glamour of that country. Then Billy had made some disparaging comment about native troops and the great Mutiny and Sam had retorted with something snide about Maude, Billy's dead Protestant mother. Billy knew he was being daft, for he'd never known his mother – she had died in childbirth, allowing his father to marry again – and he loved his step-mother, Mary, but the sneer was too much and he had flown at his brother just outside the tack-room.

There hadn't been much to it, really. Both boys were scraped and bruised by Billy's first onslaught – he could feel the granite of the stableyard setts even now – before Finn the groom was pulling them apart and promising 'a damn good leatherin' to the pair o' ye if you don't stop it, so'. But, Finn's intercession lay at the root of the trouble even now. Billy knew that if they'd been allowed to fight on, for them both to get the bile out of their systems, there might have been some settlement. Instead Finn had made them shake hands and Sam was away too early the next day for there to be any further rapprochement.

They'd not seen each other since that drizzly afternoon in Cork four years ago, but now Billy found himself at the end of the sun-baked earth, yet within spitting distance of the brother he'd hoped never to see again. The brother, Billy thought, who'd chosen to keep his own father's name – well, God rot Sam Keenan, and the unlucky sods he commands.

Morgan was pulled back from his thoughts by a trickle of tribesmen on their way to market. At first the soldiers passed one or two heavily laden donkeys swaying up the gritty main road towards the town, their loads of newly woven baskets towering above them. Their owners ignored Morgan's and his men's attempts at cheerful greetings, and as the traffic became denser the troops gave up any attempt to humour the population.

'Close up at the rear, please, Sar'nt Kelly.' Morgan had to yell down the street to be heard at the back of the patrol: the closer they got to the Bardurani Gate, the thicker the press of people and animals became.

'Right, sir. Come on, you lot, shift yourselves,' answered Kelly, provoking the last pair of soldiers to break into a shuffling run, their eyes wide at the medley of sights, colours and smells before them. Like his men, Morgan was fascinated by what he saw – camels carrying earthenware pots, herds of bleating goats and sheep, driven by boys with long, whippy sticks, mules and asses with rolled carpets and every manner of cheap, Birmingham-made pots and pans, even a dog pulling a crude cart that squeaked under a load of apricots. And the stink filled his nostrils. Animal piss and human sweat, aromatic smells from little charcoal braziers where urchin cooks touted fried meat and cheese, stale puddles and the universal scent of smoke and shit. The women, Morgan noticed, swivelled great kohl-dark eyes away from his gaze behind the slits of the black *burkhas* that hid them from head to toe. But that

36

was more than he got from any of the men. Tall hillmen, Mohmands, Afridis and Wazirs, each one heavily armed, strode past on sandalled feet while stockmen with broad, flat, Mongol faces and men from the plains – Durrani Ghilzais, Yusufzais – looked straight through him. It was as if he and his troops didn't exist, as if some unspoken agreement between all the men dictated that the Feringhee should be made to feel as invisible as possible.

The noise was vast. Tradesmen proclaiming their wares, the rattle of sheep and goats' bells, the hammering of smiths and, above all else, the Babel of a dozen different tongues and dialects, all competing to be heard above the others. So vast, indeed, that Morgan didn't hear his leading left-hand man's initial shout of alarm; he didn't hear the soldier's cry, 'You little sod!' The first he knew of the attack was when Thompson yelled in pain, which jerked him from his reverie in time to see a blur of white robes and khaki drill, a thrashing bundle of boots and sandals in the nearby gutter, one of his soldiers falling, rifle clattering, helmet rolling, sprawling on what seemed to be a boy as steel flashed and jabbed.

Private Battle reacted faster than his officer. While Morgan groped to draw his sword and understand the sudden bedlam, the older soldier rushed to help his mate, saw the boy pinioned below a shrieking wounded Thompson and a six-inch blade poking time and again into his comrade's side. As Morgan ran he watched Battle's bayonet rise and fall, spitting the brown, writhing form of a boy who, he guessed, could be no more than twelve years old. Now it was the child's turn to cry out as the lethally sharp metal punctured his right arm, then cracked through his shoulder blade before transfixing him to the ground.

'You murdering little fucker!' Battle was standing astride both Thompson and the boy, trying to shake the assassin loose from his jammed bayonet. 'Get off, won't you?'

As Morgan sprinted up to the tangled trio, he looked down

37

into the lad's face. It was twisted in a combination of hate and pain, teeth bared, not yet old enough to be yellowed by tobacco, his dirty white robes and turban stained with his own and Thompson's blood. The more Battle tugged at his weapon, the more the child rose and sagged, firmly skewered on the steel; all three shouted in a rising cacophony.

Without a second's hesitation, Billy Morgan drove his sword firmly into the boy's chest, remembering at the last moment to twist his blade so that it might not stick in the child's ribs. The point passed straight through his target's heart and Morgan saw both dirty little fists grab at the steel before falling away, just as the lad's eyes opened wide in a spasm of shock and his whiskerless jaw sagged open.

Now Battle finished a job that was already done. At last his blade came clear and, with a stream of filthy language, the burly soldier kicked and kicked at the youth's face with iron-shod boots, then stamped down hard until bone crunched and blood oozed from blue-bruised lips and a splintered nose.

'All right, Battle, that's enough − that's enough, d'you hear me?' Sergeant Kelly was suddenly on the scene. 'Help Thompson. The kid's dead enough.' There was something calming, soothing, in Kelly's tone for, despite the gore and horror all around him, he had hardly raised his voice. 'You all right, sir?'

Morgan was suddenly aware that Kelly had taken him by the elbow, that his sword was free of the corpse and that, somehow, a spray of someone's blood was daubed across his trousers. 'Yes, Sar'nt Kelly, I'm fine.' Morgan looked at the attacker's sightless eyes and realised he had killed this boy, but he felt none of the nausea that was supposed to accompany such things and no more regret at having taken such a young life than he would after shooting a snipe. 'How badly hurt is Thompson?'

'I've seen worse, sir.' Kelly was stooping over the casualty, who clutched his left side where several rents in his khaki oozed red, blotching the cloth, his face screwed up in pain. 'He's got some puncture wounds, but none are deep. Come on, son, on yer feet,' Sergeant Kelly helped Thompson – who let out a great hiss of pain – to stand up. 'Get his rifle an' headdress, Hyde.'

But as the wounded man leant against his sergeant for support, Morgan was suddenly aware that the bellowing throng had gone quiet. Where the people had pressed and crowded about their business, Morgan could now see nothing but a circle of hard, silent faces, only the children showing open-mouthed curiosity, everyone else staring with badly concealed hatred. As he looked at the people, though, the crowd parted and a tall, bearded man, armed with a knife, his black turban tied carelessly in a great, ragged ball, pushed his way to the front.

'Who's this bucko, Sar'nt Kelly?' Morgan asked, distracting him from Thompson.

'Buggered if I know, sir,' Kelly noted the deference with which the people seemed to treat the man, 'but these bastards all seem to know him.'

The lofty newcomer paused for a moment and took in the little knot of the 66th, who had now gathered round their stabbed comrade in a loose, defensive ring, their rifles and bayonets pointing at the crowd. Then he strode over to the boy's corpse. Morgan had noticed that the child seemed to have shrunk in death; now he was just a tiny pile of stained and dust-soiled rags, whose beaten face lay in a rusty puddle. The tribesman crouched over the body and swiped away a cloud of flies. The mob was still hushed, but as the man stood and turned towards the troops, Morgan found himself gasping almost as audibly as the crowd. Three or four men, all similarly dressed and armed, had jostled to the front; they looked towards their tall leader, apparently waiting for him to give orders.

'Seems to have brought his gang with him too, Sar'nt Kelly.'

Morgan found himself shuffling backwards towards the others. Now the patrol were practically back to back, facing the surrounding crowd, Thompson moaning softly in their midst.

'Aye, sir, an' 'e don't look too pleased about that nipper we've just turned off. Should we load, sir?' Kelly, so far, had been utterly in control, whether in routine barrack matters or on patrol, available to give sage and discreet advice to his young officer. But now, Morgan realised, as the officer he had to exercise total judgement and leadership. Despite his lack of experience, the men required him to fill the role that his brass stars and station in life suggested. He licked his lips and searched his mind for what Sandhurst might have taught him to do in such circumstances.

The answer was simple: nothing. They'd been told about conventional war, about victories over French and Russians; they'd been shown how to deal with howling masses of 'savage' spear-wielding natives, to read maps, to control artillery, and even how to sap and build bridges. But of operations among supposed friends who were actually foes, of how to deal with fanatical, murderous children in the middle of a crowd of civilians while a critical press corps hovered close by, not a thing had been said.

But Morgan was given no more time to ponder. The big warrior turned to his friends, broke the silence with a gabble of words, then dropped his hand to the bone hilt of his foot-long knife and began to draw it. Morgan didn't even answer his sergeant's question for he knew that if he was going to act he had to do something fast and decisive. Launching himself over the few yards that separated them, the young officer went as hard as he could for the tribesman, knowing he had one chance only to defeat the bigger man. Once that knife was clear of its sheath, his enemy would strike fast and hard − and that would not only be the signal for his henchmen to attack but for the rest of the crowd to swamp him and his men.

The hours of sword training that Morgan had received were ignored. Fencing at school, then cut and guard under the skill-at-arms instructor, even the first fatal thrust he'd just delivered, were instantly forgotten. Instead, visceral instincts took over and he smashed the hilt of his sword as hard as he could into his opponent's face, catching him by surprise and sending him sprawling into the gutter next to the cooling child, a welter of limbs and flying robes. Unwittingly, Morgan had done just the right thing. A neat, deft blow might have dealt with his opponent, but he would have fallen with a dignity that inspired the others. This brawling assault made the tribesman look foolish; he dropped almost comically, which gave the patrol just enough time to seize the initiative.

'Move, Sar'nt Kelly. I'll hold 'em!' But even before Morgan had said this, Kelly was leading the others hard into the throng, making for the gate, pushing and shoving his way through the crowd, bayonets pricking those who were slow to move, while Thompson was half dragged, half carried with them.

The people were mercifully slow to react. Morgan's impression as he dashed and turned, sweeping his sword blade from side to side to keep the Kandaharis at bay, was of a cowering bank of flesh and cloth that pressed itself against the town's walls as he and his men scrambled down the street.

'Let's not wait, Sar'nt Kelly, they're hard behind,' gasped Morgan, as he caught up with his clutch of men, who had paused to get a better hold on the barely conscious Thompson.

'Aye, sir, I can see that . . .' and, as if to reinforce what he knew already, a shower of stones, fruit and whatever else came to hand bounced around Kelly and Morgan as the mob surged up the street in pursuit.

'So, hardly the most glorious start to an officer's career, Mr Morgan?' I knew that all four of those listening, Galbraith, Sergeant Kelly and Heath would be expecting me to show

41

some sort of favouritism to my son. In truth, I'd have been a damn sight less hard on a young officer I didn't know than I was going to have to be on Billy – if I'd been in that horrid situation, I suspect I'd have made a right bloody hash of things and got the whole patrol kicked and stabbed to death. What worried me, though, was how matter-of-fact Billy had been about killing a child.

'No, sir, I know that, but I was fortunate to have a good set of men around me. If they'd got out of control or fired into the crowd, I suspect we wouldn't be here now, sir,' Billy answered confidently, Galbraith nodding his approval almost imperceptibly.

'Quite so, young man. I gather that Private Thompson should recover, but you were lucky that the whole thing didn't turn very nasty indeed. Who d'you suppose the maniac child was?' I asked Billy, but Sergeant Kelly responded.

'Ghazi, sir. Pretty young one, but a Ghazi beyond doubt,' he said, with total conviction.

'What – at twelve years of age? The only possible attraction I can see for being a bloody Ghazi is the dozens of virgins they're promised in eternity if they butcher one of us. Can't see how that would influence a twelve-year-old unless he's a very early starter.' The idea of using children as assassins was preposterous, wasn't it? But, then, the very concept of committing certain suicide in the name of religion was also pretty odd – yet that was what was happening.

'Well, sir, he was dressed all in white.' Billy had taken up the narrative now. 'Apparently he was yelling, "*Din-din*," though I didn't hear that myself. He was quite demented and went for Thompson with a knife rather than a firearm.'

'Perhaps he couldn't get a *jezail* or a pistol.' I still found it hard to believe that anyone could bend a child's mind to do such a thing.

'Ten a penny in the metal-workers' quarter, sir,' Kelly added quietly.

'Yes, I'm sure you're right.' I'd not yet been into the teeming bazaars of Kandahar, the same bazaars in which I was asking boys like Thompson to risk their lives. 'Well, you two, it seems our enemies' beastliness knows no bounds, yet you've come out of this remarkably unscathed. I have no doubt that the mullahs will get to the press vermin and that you'll read all about your own atrocities, but let me handle that side of things.

'Heath, I want a full account of this new tactic that the Ghazis are using sent to all commanding officers – and I'll need to take a copy of it with me when I report to General Primrose, so don't drag your heels.' My brigade major adopted his customary harassed expression as he scratched in his notebook.

'Have either of you anything more to say?'

Both Billy and his sergeant gave me a regulation 'Nosir.'

'Sar'nt Kelly, you should have known better than to let a patrol get into a mess like this and, Mr Morgan, if I hear about any more errors of judgement, then I'll have your balls for bandoleers and you'll be back to India before you know what's hit you.' I knew how lame this sounded and if it had been anyone but Billy standing in front of me, I would probably have given both him and his sergeant a cautious pat on the back – but I couldn't, could I? 'Well, think yourselves lucky. I'll come and visit Private Thompson: now fall out, the pair of you.' I'd tried to sound gruff and to conceal the fact that my son had got himself out of a nasty scrape without a mark on him, but as both officer and sergeant saluted, I caught a look in Billy's eye that concerned me. He knew me – of course he did – and he would certainly know how much I sympathised with him and Kelly, whatever act I put on, but there was no self-doubt in that glance, apparently no residue of regret that the first person he'd had to kill had been just a child.

'One more thing, Galbraith.' I'd stood up, put on my helmet, settled my sword and was preparing to leave my son's commanding officer. 'You'll need to be very careful of such tactics in the future. You'll warn the men to be on the *qui vive*, won't you?'

'Of course I will, sir. In fact Taylor, whose company is just about to take over patrolling duties, is working up a series of instructions to help the men handle just such events in the future.' He looked suitably pained that I should have asked such a question.

'Quite so, quite so. I wouldn't have expected anything less.' I was trying my damnedest not to let my concern for Billy show, but I couldn't quite stop myself. 'I'll smooth things over with General Primrose. And how's young Mr Morgan settling in?'

'He's a most promising officer, sir, and while I know how ticklish things are in town, I think he conducted himself right well today.' Galbraith stared straight back, making no reference to the boy's relationship to me. But I wondered if he knew the question I really wanted to ask.

I wanted to ask him how he would have reacted to having to run his sword through a twelve-year-old's chest. Would he have shown no remorse, like Billy? I knew that − no matter the circumstances − I would have reproached myself. I wanted to ask him if he'd noticed the cold glaze in my son's eyes. But I didn't − I couldn't. I just nodded my understanding, flicked a salute out of courtesy and left the room.

THREE

Khusk-i-Nakud

The 3rd Scinde Horse felt they were old hands, for they had been in Afghanistan more than a year and had a couple of successful skirmishes to their credit; now they were brimful of confidence. As the tribesmen seemed to have subsided into an uneasy truce, there was time for some sport in the hills and valleys around Kandahar: the commanding officer had asked some of the new arrivals from India to join him and his officers for what was insouciantly known as a 'little spearing'.

It was widely accepted that Sam's step-father, Brigadier General Anthony Morgan, regarded himself as a great *shikari*, so an invitation to ride out with a pig-spear, almost as soon as he'd wiped the dust of his travels off himself, had seemed like the most natural thing in the world. Over the past two years, Sam had written and received a few stiff soldier-father-to-soldier-son letters from his step-father, but he hadn't seen him until now. He was wondering how much the prospect of another campaign at this late stage of his career would please him. Then Malcolmson, the colonel, ambitious to the last and delighted that one of his people knew someone of influence, had introduced his officers – the handful of British and twice the number of Indians – to their guests. Keenan was amused to see that his father had changed into mufti while he and the other officers had been required to stay in uniform due, as the colonel stuffily put it, 'to the omnipresent possibility of an enemy presence'.

They'd all been lined up outside the bungalow that served as the British officers' mess, themselves drinking a fruit-punch stirrup cup and the Indian officers unadulterated fruit juice. Malcolmson, no doubt, wanted to give the new general an impression of relaxed *élan*, a study in dash and the spirit of irregular cavalry, but once the man himself and the other guests came cantering up, in an assortment of linen jackets, corduroy breeches and the most battered sun-helmets, the colonel's efforts were made to look a little contrived. Had the officers of the Scinde Horse been similarly *déshabillé* then the ruse might have worked, but the polished boots, the native officers' oh-so-carefully tied *puggarees* and everyone's Sunday-best behaviour gave the game away.

As the general arrived, Sam realised he'd never seen him in circumstances like this before. At home in Ireland it was an open secret that Sam was the bastard son of Anthony and Mary, conceived in the Crimea while Mary was married to a sergeant in the company Sam's father commanded. Everyone also knew that Sergeant James Keenan – a Corkman too – had perished in circumstances of great bravery in India under the mutineers' knives a couple of years later. With the death in childbirth of Maude, Anthony's first wife, the way was clear for the lovers to marry.

Sam, it was true, had stuck to the name Keenan and followed his mother's wishes that he should be brought up a Catholic, but most people knew the truth. Anthony, whenever he was at home, had treated him like the son he was – well, he had treated him in the rather distant, muscular way that, Sam supposed, military fathers were meant to treat their boys, yet there had always been tension between himself and his younger half-brother, Billy. Sam had soon understood that, despite being older, he would always come off second best; not for him the name Morgan and an inheritance, not for him a scarlet coat. No, it was the Indian cavalry for the Catholic Sam Keenan and a life a long way from Dublin drawing rooms. If he thought about it too much it angered him, but just at the moment he couldn't have given a hang, for he was in Afghanistan among people he liked and trusted, being paid to do a job that he would have cheerfully done for free.

Now here was the man who, while he might have made him play second fiddle at home, had given him the chance for this great adventure, a man who certainly had failings but was kind and brave, a man who preferred to ask rather than demand, and that same man had just made his own colonel look like the gauche little thruster he was.

The general had shaken every hand, admired the medals that hung from the native officers' breasts, asked everyone about their home towns (and even looked as though he understood what the rissaldars were talking about) and made friends with them all. Sam wondered how he would greet him, but he needn't have worried.

'So, Colonel, you seem to have turned this gouger into more of a soldier than I ever could!' There had been laughs from Sam's contemporaries at this and a beam of pleasure from the commanding officer. 'May I steal him away from you this evening? I need to learn a bit about fighting the Afghans.'

And so General Morgan won the confidence of the Scinde Horsemen, as Sam had seen him do so many times before with huntsmen, magistrates, police and tradesmen at home. It had never struck him before, but Sam now knew that there might be much to learn about leadership and raw soldiering from his father, whom he knew so slightly. But there were more surprises to come for, towards the end of a disappointing hunt, they flushed a panther from its hiding-place and chased it into a piece of rocky ground that was set about with tall grass, scrub and stunted trees. Long, low, dangerous growls could be heard, echoing from the slabs of rock about them. Then Sam watched his father ride into deep, thick cover after it, quite alone and armed only with a spear. It was in that instant that he saw where his own impulsiveness – his pig-headedness – came from.

Until an hour or so before, the spearmen had had a sparse day of it. There had been distant sightings of pig, excited cries from the native beaters and much galloping hither and yon to no effect whatsoever. But then Sam had been amazed to see a low, sleek, dark form come slinking from a rocky fissure; he had never seen such a beautiful creature before, her black coat groomed and glossy, her ears tipped back and her eyes alight with feral intelligence. The villagers had claimed that the great cat stalked the area, taking withered cows, chickens and goats, and causing mothers to watch their children closely, despite only rare sightings. The native beaters had fired the bush around an outcrop and the creature's supposed lair, hoping to smoke her out. As Sam sat his pony, the short, seven-foot spear in his hand, and watched the grey-blue smoke billow with a bored detachment, he could not have been more surprised when the mythical quarry became reality.

'Hey, goddamn – here, here.' Sam found himself shouting inanities at the backs of the fire-raisers, behind whom the animal ambled, unseen. But as he shouted and dug his spurs into his pony, the panther broke into a gentle trot, dignifying him with a short, disdainful glance before she disappeared into a thicket of grass and scrubby bush.

Sam pushed his mount forward, hallooing as loudly as he could, but the tangle of branches and stalks, combined with the clouds of smoke, gave the advantage to the animal and by the time he'd extracted himself there had been another sighting and more excited cries further up the line of rocks. Galloping as hard as he could to catch the other horsemen, who were now much closer to the cat, he saw two riders hesitating over a body that lay still on the ground.

'A beater, sahib.' Rissaldar Singh, one of the Indian troop commanders in Keenan's squadron, held his horse's reins tightly, flicking his eyes from the inert pile of rags on the ground to the stand of long, coarse grass from which low growls could be heard. 'I saw the cat on him but was too late: *bus*.'

'Aye, and we'll be too late if we fanny around here any longer,' said the other horseman, his voice thick with excitement. 'You two get up towards that gap in the brush just there.' He pointed with his spear to a dark-shadowed, natural hollow in the grass about ten yards from where they all stood. 'I'll poke her up the arse and you two catch her as she bolts. Be sharp about it, though, for you'll get no second chance.' Before either of them could try to stop him, General Anthony Morgan was away into the brush by himself, crashing his horse through the low cover, yelling loudly and shouting, 'Hi, hi, get on,' with his stout little spear held low and ready.

There was to be no argument, that was clear, so Keenan and Singh dug their heels into their mounts, the dead beater forgotten, and in a few seconds were covering the indicated spot. There was just time for Keenan's heart to beat a little less frantically, for the horses to settle, for the general's shouts and thrashing to become less torrid and for them all to think that the panther had slipped away – when out she shot.

Keenan thought of the cats at home as they stalked sparrows around the stables, low on their haunches, all shoulder-blades, flicking tails and rapt concentration. The panther looked just like that as she emerged – but ten times the size and weight, her whiskers bristling and eyes narrowed, trying to weigh up whether to attack the two horsemen or bolt between them. In the fraction of a second that Keenan watched and mused, Singh acted, kicking his horse on, causing the panther to swerve, but still catching her with the point of his barbed pig-spear deep in the rump.

Again, Keenan was reminded of domestic cats, for the panther hissed and screamed in pain just as he had heard two toms do when they were contesting some bit of food thrown on to the kitchen waste. But this cat's enemy was Singh's spear, around which she curled her body, biting at the wooden shaft and clawing so powerfully at the ground that she almost pulled her antagonist from the saddle. Keenan found the writhing, kicking target hard to hit; he jostled his pony alongside Singh's, missed with his first lunge and only managed to prod the panther in the ribs with his second attempt, infuriating the wounded animal even further.

As the horses wheeled and pecked, and the panther scrabbled at the ground to which she was pinned, the dust rose, along with the yells of the two cavalrymen. Then into this chaos panted a third man, a dismounted man, who loped forward with his spear held in front of him.

'Let me in, goddamn you! Clear the way!' rasped General Morgan, as he dodged among the hoofs and flying specks of blood. 'Get your spike into that bloody cat, won't you, son? Skewer it – hold the damn thing down while I finish the job!'

Keenan reached forward from the saddle and jabbed as hard as he could into the fine sable fur, thrusting the point of his spear so deeply that the steel drove through the flesh until it met the dirt beneath. Now, with two shafts holding the agonised beast, Keenan watched as his father closed in.

Although the panther was weak she was still dangerous, and Morgan had to wait for his moment. As the blood flowed from her wounds, so she became more desperate, and as she clawed at the stakes, she finally showed her soft belly and Morgan darted in. Keenan held on to his bucking shaft and watched as his father poked his own spear between a line of teats where the hair was thin and the white hide showed. The general, he saw, was skilful enough just to push a few inches of steel home and then pause until the blood flowed. Once he was sure that the point would find a vital organ, Morgan threw all his weight behind the weapon, thrusting the spear until the metal and wood were deep inside the creature's lungs and heart. Then it was over. One final jab saw the end of the cat's agony. With a twitch that shook the black body from the point of its tail to the tip of its nose, the panther at last lay still.

The horses snorted and shook their heads – almost like a last salute to their humbled foe, thought Keenan.

'Well, damn your eyes, you two, that was a neat bit of work, so it was. The pelt will look grand on your veranda, Rissaldar sahib, well done, *bahadur*! And not a bad show from you, either, my lad.' Keenan saw his father grinning up at both of them as he jerked his spear from the corpse. The general was dusty, spotted with the panther's blood, exhilarated and, clearly, pleased with himself. Yet, Keenan realised, his father, who had taken most of the risk, wanted no credit for himself: how little he knew him.

The day's chase had quite revived my spirits and I rounded things off by sending my clueless brigade major to check that the Horse Gunners had settled into their lines – that was far too grubby a task for a man of his fine habits. Now I could try to enjoy a supper with my elder son and, after today, I suspected that he'd matured into quite a different person from the lad I'd last known. I hadn't seen him for a couple of years – the last time we'd met passed through Bombay and Sam had invited me to a guest night with his new regiment, the 3rd Scinde Horse. I was just a full colonel on the staff then and he was a fresh-minted cornet, straight out of the factory, all new mess kit and sparkling spurs. But what a different sight he'd been when we were after that cat, and now here he was in the dusty courtyard of my living quarters in Kandahar – burnt as dark as any of his sowars, his tulwar swinging by his side, spiked helmet at a rakish angle and a look of such self-confidence in his brown eyes that it took me a second to realise he was my own flesh and blood.

Mind you, Sam had been hard at it for more than a year. His regiment had been right through the first campaign in the Helmand valley, serving under that poor, tired old sod General Biddulph, while my newly formed brigade and I had been rotting down on the lines of communication from the freezing mountain passes up here to Kandahar itself.

'*General* Morgan, sir.' The boy was exaggerating my new exalted rank. 'Mr Samuel Keenan, sir, at your command.' There was a relaxed self-assurance in the way he saluted that I hadn't seen before.

'At my command, Lieutenant bloody Keenan? If you are, that'll be the first time in twenty-four years, you scoundrel! Anyway, son, that was a brisk little business today, wasn't it? You did well . . .' Actually, he'd done bloody well – but I wasn't going to say that. The Indian officer had snagged the panther, but if Sam hadn't struck when he did and hung on like a demon, more would have died than just that poor coolie. 'I want to hear all about your adventures. I had a look at one of the squadrons of your lot on my way to take command of my brigade and a very fair impression they made. Your officers looked a damn good lot today, especially the Indians – they've seen a bit of service, ain't they?'

'We're lucky with our native officers and the rissaldar major is a grand fellow . . .' Sam tailed off.

'I know . . . you've no need to tell me.' His hesitation had told me all I needed to know. 'Malcolmson, your colonel, is a scrub – tell me I'm wrong.'

'Well, Father . . .'

'No, it was all too clear when he had you drawn up drill-yard style, booted and spurred yet trying to loll over fucking cocktails or whatever fancy nonsense they were. I've not seen plunging like that since the Crimea . . .' Sam was looking blank '. . . yes, you know, plungers – don't you use that word

52

any more? Horrible ambitious types – usually tradesmen's sons – who think that licking round their superiors and trying to give themselves airs and graces will somehow give them a foot up the ladder. What does he think he commands – the bloody Life Guards? It's a regiment of native irregulars, ain't it?' I saw a slight shadow pass over my son's face. Without thinking, I'd suggested he might have been consigned to something second rate. 'And bloody good in the field it is too – we depended heavily on your lot back in the Mutiny, you know.' I tried to redeem myself. 'I can see he's an arse socially, Sam, but Malcolmson's done well enough on campaign so far, ain't he? The regiment's got a good name.'

'I think we've done pretty well, Father, but we've only had one serious brush with the enemy and the commanding officer was fine, as far as I could see. Is this your mess?' replied Sam, changing the subject as he ran an approving eye over the single-storey building that stood at the end of the courtyard.

'Yes, it is. Henry Brooke – you know him and his family, Protestant folk from up Tyrone way . . .' Oh, damn it, there it was again: I'd reminded Sam of the differences between us once more when I was trying to find common ground. 'As you know, he's the other infantry brigadier and we've been pals for years. Well, he found the place when he arrived in Kandahar a little after you did. Now he's converted it into a joint mess for both of us and our staff. But you don't have to be over-loyal in front of me, lad. I've seen men like Malcolmson before – a veneer of efficiency that usually hides something much less savoury. Anyway, enough of that. You'll soon know if I'm right or wrong – and I wasn't pumping you up in front of Malcolmson earlier. I really do need to know about this country and the folk we've got to fight. Sam Browne and Roberts have been poked in the eye a couple of times but seem to have come through it, and you tell me that your lot have crossed swords with 'em, so what are they like?'

As Sam started to reply I knew I must concentrate, but my

mind kept wandering away. I thought how little I knew the young warrior who had so impressed me during today's hunt. Why, the last occasion we'd spent any time together had been in Ireland and I'd been daft enough to criticise his skill in the saddle. Yet today he'd been like a satyr while the big cat had spat and scratched around the three of us.

No, I hardly knew him. I seemed to have lavished all my time and attention on his half-brother, William. I had packed Sam off to India as soon as I could into a cheap, but good, native cavalry gang while his brother got the best of schools and a commission in a decent English regiment that nearly broke the bank. Yet, looking at the man, I could see myself a quarter of a century before.

'They're damn good, Father. They'll come at you out of nowhere, exploit every mistake you make, carve you up, and are away like the wind. They nearly gave us a hiding at Khusk-i-Nakud – I thought I'd finished before I'd started when we had to charge fifteen hundred tribesmen who had got into our rear.'

We'd had word of that smart little skirmish when it happened more than a year ago, and I'd been both thrilled and worried when I heard that the 3rd Scinde Horse had been involved. I'd written to Sam immediately, but his reply had been brisk and modestly uninformative and, until now, I'd had no chance to talk to him about his first time in action. 'Tell me about it, Sam. I want to hear every last detail.'

'Take your squadron up to that bit of scrub yonder, Reynolds. I'll hold B and C Squadrons and the 29th Balochi lads down here while you move.' Colonel Malcolmson, commanding officer of the 3rd Scinde Horse, was in charge of the rearguard. 'Then, when you hear my signal, be prepared to fall back behind that handful of buildings over there.'

This looks a damn sight more promising than anything we've seen so far, thought Lieutenant Sam Keenan. I've been here for three months and done nothing but watch other men's battles, picket till I'm blue in the face and freeze my balls off. I wonder if this'll develop into anything more than all the other disappointments? He could hear the colonel's orders to Reynolds, his squadron commander, quite clearly, as could every man in his troop. The sixty or so horsemen of A Squadron waited with the rest of the rearguard in the bottom of the shallow valley, watching the first enemy that they had seen in any numbers since their arrival in Afghanistan. In the low hills above them, dark groups of tribesmen could be seen trotting from cover to cover, firing a random shot or two at the distant British.

Now the men stood by their mounts, lances resting on the ground, easing girths and harness, as they waited with the prospect of action gnawing at their guts. The horses could feel it as well. Just handy little ponies, really, carrying nets full of fodder across their saddles that made them look more like farm beasts than chargers. They whinnied and threw their heads, shook the flies from their eyes and flicked their tails while their riders talked soft Pashto to them, gently pulled their ears and tried to impart a calm they did not feel.

'Squadron . . . mount.' Reynolds's voice carried clearly on the cool, still air as his mostly Pathan troopers swung easily into the saddle, the lance points sparkling in the sun. 'Prepare to advance by troops.' Keenan spurred his horse to the front of his twenty men. 'Right wheel, walk march.' The whole khaki-turbaned column divided into three neat little blocks, immediately throwing up a cloud of choking dust as the hoofs cut the ground.

'Daffadar sahib.' Keenan turned to his troop sergeant, a swarthy, heavily bearded ancient of two previous campaigns and at least thirty summers. 'I guess we'll be dismounting once we get into that bit of cover and moving forward with our carbines. Warn the horse holders, please and let's be sharper than the other troops.'

Daffadar Sayed Miran, one of the only NCOs in the regiment whose English was fluent, nodded and spoke to the men, having to raise his voice above the thump of horseshoes and the metallic jingle of bits, weapons and harness. The ground was dry for February – the snows around the banks of the Helmand had been unusually light that year – but there was still a bite in the wind that made Keenan glad of the sheepskin *poshteen* in which he and all of the men had wrapped themselves. It had been an uneventful few weeks of foraging and inconclusive reconnaissance while Major General Biddulph had scattered his troops up to Gereshk and beyond, trying to find both supplies and the enemy. But the latter had hardly shown themselves – until now.

'Well, the weather's improving and it's clear that the column has done all it usefully can,' had been the verdict of Colonel Malcolmson at the start of the fifty-mile march back to Kandahar. Things had begun quietly enough, with every unit that took its turn on rearguard duty hardly expecting to see the foe. Then, about four days ago, just as the column had entered the gritty valley of the Khakrez, the sniping had started. They were trespassing in Durani country, land that belonged to the people of Ahmed Shah's Pearl Throne, proud and doughty warriors.

At first, Keenan and everyone else would duck as odd bullets whined over the column fired by invisible not-so-sharpshooters. Then, a couple more badmashes had taken up the challenge and a steady drip of casualties had begun. The first violent death that Keenan had seen had been that of a sowar from the 3rd Bombay Light Cavalry, whose pierced body had been carried past his own men on a *dhoolie* two days ago. Even his Pathans had pretended to look away while sneaking little peeps at the inert form whose blanket had come away from its cooling contents. Keenan had seen what had been a husky youth lying on his face, head turned to one side, eyes open with flies feasting at the corners. The wind caught the corpse's moustache, lifting the hair to show stained yellow teeth set in a jaw that had been smashed by a bullet. Blood had spread over the man's khaki collar and soaked, brown, into the grey issue blanket. Keenan had been repelled but fascinated by the sight.

'Left wheel, form line of squadron.' The NCOs repeated Captain Reynolds's orders as Keenan's and the other two troops wheeled from column into line. 'Halt . . . dismount. Prepare to skirmish.' None of the words of command came as a surprise as the five dozen cavalrymen dropped from saddle to ground, secured their lances, passed their reins to every fourth man – the horse holders – and pulled their Sniders from the long leather buckets strapped to the saddle beside their stirrup leathers. But a covey of shots whacked through the leafless branches above Keenan's head, just as his first foot touched the ground, showering him with chips of bark and wood.

'Ah, sahib, it is you the Duranis want – they have heard the great *shikari* has come for them at last!' Of all the native NCOs, only Daffadar Sayed Miran had the confidence and fluency to mock a British officer – however gently. The whole troop had watched Keenan fail to knock down a single duck when they'd been encamped by a lake two weeks ago, although he'd expended much powder and shot. So his reputation as a great hunter – or *shikari* – had been stillborn, and the troops chuckled at the jest.

'That's as maybe, Daffadar sahib, but I want the boys to line that bank yonder, load and make ready.' Keenan was more interested in having his men in place and looking for targets before either of the other two troops than in his sergeant's humour. He was gratified to see how easily the men moved, sheathed sabres pulled back in their left hands, carbines at the trail in their right, each man looking for a good position from which to reply to those who had dared to fire at their sahib.

'Where d'you think that fire came from, Daffadar sahib?'

Keenan had thrown himself down on a dusty bank topped with coarse grass that was deep in the shadow of the trees. He and his men would be difficult to see in cover like this and he pulled his binoculars from the pouch on his belt to scan the ground in front of him.

'I don't know yet, sahib – but our infantry are moving up on something.' Miran pointed slowly so as not to draw the enemy's eye with any sudden movement, indicating twenty or so khaki-clad men from the 29th who were making their way along the muddy banks of a stream about three hundred paces in front of the squadron.

Keenan admired the way that Captain Reynolds had interpreted the colonel's orders for the rearguard. Where he'd chosen to dismount his men allowed him not just a covered position, but a dominating view over the rest of the shallow valley below them. A stand of high trees surrounded a scatter of ruined, weather-beaten buildings at the edge of some unusually verdant fields just to their front, before the valley rose grandly to their south against a powder-blue sky into a series of jagged foothills that dominated the far horizon. If nothing else, the last three months in the field had taught Keenan how to read the ground. Now he could see that while the slope below looked smooth and ideal for mounted work, shadowy folds could easily hide ditches or even wide nullahs that could protect them from any enemy horse, but also make a quick descent to the lower ground very difficult.

'There, sahib, look.' Miran had spoken even before the reports of several rifle shots reached their ears. He'd seen the billows of smoke of the enemy riflemen who had fired at them a few minutes before from the cover to their front, as the next volley sang harmlessly around their heads. 'The infantry wallahs have found them – see.'

'Yes, the Twenty-ninth are on to it, and the Duranis ain't seen them yet.' The winter sun caught the long, thin blades as the turbaned Beloochi infantrymen fixed bayonets, invisible to their enemies in the brush on the bank above them.

'Three fifty, aim at the muzzle smoke.' Captain Reynolds gave the range to the squadron. 'Volley on my order, then fire by troop sequence.'

Keenan knew that sixty rounds all at once from the short Snider carbines should throw the enemy into disarray. Then a steady ripple of rounds would allow the infantry to close in without taking casualties, although, at this range, none of the fire would be precise.

The breech-traps of the Sniders snapped closed. The men fiddled with the iron ramp sights, then cuddled the butts against the shoulder and settled into their firing positions. Keenan watched as the khaki dolls began to clamber out of the ditch before Reynolds gave the order, 'Fire!' and every man bucked to the kick of his weapon. Dust flew; twigs and dry leaves were thrown about as the volley struck home.

'Two Troop, reload, three fifty, await my order,' Keenan yelled, just as if he were at the butts. This was the first time he'd given orders designed to kill other human beings, but he was at such a distance from the damage he was trying to inflict that it all felt remarkably innocent, really no different from an exercise. 'Wait for One Troop, lads.' Keenan didn't want any of his men from 2 Troop to fire prematurely – they would be a laughing-stock if that happened. But as the men to his left fired, so the 29th rushed forward, weapons outstretched. Suddenly his men's sights were full of their own people, charging home amid the thicket.

'Wait, Two Troop!' One or two of his men looked up from the aim towards him, uncertain whether they had understood the English orders. 'Switch right . . . fire!' Much to his relief, every round flew to the flank of the attacking infantry, scything through the brush where further enemy could be sheltering.

'Stop . . . Cease fire. Reload, One and Two Troops. Prepare for new targets.' Reynolds and all of them could hear the

29th's rifles popping in the thicket and see their figures darting about, bayonets rising and falling.

After the crashing noise all about him, Keenan noticed the sudden quiet. Odd shouts and NCOs' brass-lung commands could still be heard on the cool air, but his first taste of action had been disappointingly ordinary.

'Check ammunition, Daffadar sahib,' Keenan ordered needlessly, for the experienced Miran was already overseeing his lance daffadars doing just that. But as the scene of military domesticity took shape around him, men reaching into pouches, oily rags being drawn over breeches and hammers, a strange sing-song shout echoed up from the low ground in front of them.

'Dear God . . .' said Reynolds, as every man in the squadron saw what he had seen. 'Trumpeter, blow "horses forward, prepare to mount".' Less than half a mile to their front, a great swarm of tribesmen, dirty blue and brown turbans and *kurta*s, some armed with rifles, all with swords and miniature round shields, crowded out of a courtyard where they had been lying hidden and rushed towards the platoon of the 29th, who were distracted by the Afghans with whom they were already toe-to-toe.

'How many of those bastards are there, Daffadar sahib?' Keenan asked. He knew that the bugle call was as much about warning the commanding officer, who was at least a mile away, of Reynolds's intentions as it was about getting the squadron ready to attack.

'Bastards, sahib? Do you know these Duranis' mothers?' Keenan marvelled at the daffadar's ability to joke at a time like this. 'About five hundred – Reynolds sahib is going to charge them, is he not?'

His daffadar had obviously read the battle much better than he had, thought Keenan. A charge – the horse soldier's *raison d'être* – in this his first taste of action? Yes, he could see it now. If his squadron was swift and sure-footed, and the commanding

60

officer had the rest of the regiment trimmed and ready to support them, even sixty of them could cut up the tribesmen from a vantage-point like this. Scrambling over the dust and grit, Keenan was pleased to see his syce first at the rear of the little wood, holding his stirrup ready for him to mount even before the rest of the troop's horses began to arrive.

'Troop, form column,' Keenan used the orders straight from the manual that he knew his men understood, as 1 and 3 Troops went through exactly the same evolutions on either side of his men. His command, 'NCOs, dress them off,' saw much snapping and biting from the two daffadars and Miran, but his troopers were almost ready to move before the squadron leader and his trumpeter had come trotting breathlessly through the brush.

Captain Reynolds nodded with approval at his three troops – his orders had been well anticipated. 'Good; troop officers, lead your men to the front of the brush and take post on Rissaldar Singh – he's your right marker. Be sharp now.' Keenan was the only British troop officer, the other two being Indians. Now 1 Troop commander – at thirty-five Singh was the oldest man in the squadron – had been placed to guide the troops as they formed up ready for the attack.

With the minimum of fuss, Keenan's troop followed him forward through the stand of trees before fanning out to the left of 3 Troop, Miran pushing and shoving the horses and their riders into two long, thin lines in the middle of the squadron.

'Right, sahib,' Miran said, which told Keenan that he should trot round to the front of his men and turn about to face them, his back to the enemy. He looked at twenty earnest young faces, every one adorned with a variety of moustache and beard – some full, some scrawny. They could be tricky in barracks, these Pathans of his, but now they looked no more than nervous boys, faces tense in the sun, pink tongues licking at dry lips. Keenan raised his hand to show that his troop was dressed and deployed to his satisfaction, the other two troop officers doing the same at either side of him.

'Squadron, steady!' came Reynolds's word of command that brought the officers wheeling about in front of their troopers, allowing Keenan his first proper glimpse of the enemy. Two furlongs down the slope, a wedge of enemy infantry had charged hard into the rear and flanks of the 29th Bombay and was overwhelming them.

'Drop your fodder, men.' The squadron leader's order caused every man to fiddle with the hay-net that made his saddle appear so swollen. In an instant the ground was littered with awkward balls of crop, while the horses looked instantly more warlike.

'Carry . . . lances,' Reynolds shouted, as the sun caught knife blades that were slicing and hacking at the Indian infantrymen. Sixty or so long, slender bamboo poles, topped with red and white pennons, dipped and bobbed before coming to rest in their owners' gauntleted hands. Keenan looked to either side of him: reins were being tightened, fingers flexing on weapons, every man intent on the target to their front.

'They have not noticed us, yet, Daffadar sahib,' Keenan said, as his sergeant rode up to him, fussing over the men as he came.

'No, sahib, they have not. They're too busy howling about the Prophet to realise they're about to meet him. Look there, sahib: one of the officers is helping those monkeys to meet Allah.' The daffadar pointed with his chin − as Keenan had noticed all natives did − towards a struggling scrum of men right on the edge of the fight. Among the swarthy faces a white one stood out. His helmet gone, a subaltern of the 29th was fighting for his life.

A strange, savage noise: grunting, sighing, the clash of steel on steel was coming from the throng. Then Keenan heard two revolver shots and saw the young officer hurl his pistol at the nearest Durani before dashing himself against five or more assailants, his sword blade outstretched. In an instant it was over. Two robed figures rolled in the dust before steel flashed and fell, knives stabbing, short swords slicing and cutting the young lieutenant's fair skin.

'Prepare to advance.' Reynolds used just his voice rather than the bugle. 'Walk march, forward!' The squadron billowed down the hill, over-keen riders being pulled back into line with an NCO's curse, the horses snorting with anticipation, ears pricked.

'Trot march!' The line gathered pace at the squadron commander's next order, the men having to curb their mounts' eagerness as the slope of the hill added to the speed.

'Prepare to charge!' Keenan had heard these words so many times before on exercise fields and the *maidan*, yet never had they thrilled him like this. 'Charge!' As Reynolds spoke, the front rank's lances formed a hedge of wood tipped with steel, level in front of the soldiers' faces, spurs urging the horses on, a snarl that Keenan had never heard before coming from the men's lips.

Then the ecstasy of relief. Keenan found himself yelling inanely, his mount Kala's ears twitching at her master's unfamiliar noise. The soldiers became centaurs as the trot turned into a canter, Keenan only having to pull gently on the reins to check his mare and prevent her getting too close to the pounding hoofs of Reynolds and his trumpeter, who rode just in front of him.

'Steady, lads, steady,' shouted Keenan, pointlessly, as the enemy loomed hugely just paces in front of them. He could see that the Duranis had been intent upon their prey, crowding over the clutch of Bombay soldiers who had survived their first onslaught, but now they were shocked by the appearance of a charging squadron. Contorted faces, whose owners had tasted easy blood, turned in fright towards the hammering hoofs and flashing spear points.

'Mark your targets, men.' Another needless but self-reassuring order spilled from Keenan's mouth, as Kala jinked hard to avoid one of the enemy who had dropped to the ground. The Afghan had realised, almost too late, that he'd caught the eye of at least three angry Scinde Horsemen. In the first wave Captain Reynolds had cut at him, doing nothing more than ripping his *kurta*. Next, Sowar Ram – the trumpeter – sliced the soft, sheepskin cap off his head, but left the man unharmed. Then it was Keenan's turn. The young officer tried to reach low enough to spit his enemy on the ground, but the Durani had learnt more in the last sixty seconds than in a lifetime of swordplay. First he crouched. Then, as Keenan's blade came close, he sprang like a cat, took the full force of his attacker's steel on the boss of his shield and cut up hard with his long Khyber knife. Keenan was past his target, over-exposed, leaning down from the saddle, and had it not been for the lance daffadar riding close behind him, the knife would have taken him squarely in the back. Instead, an issue lance, with twelve stone of cavalryman behind it, entered the Afghan's left lung, emerged just above his heart and left him dead before he hit the ground.

'*Shukria, bahadur,*' gasped Keenan, as the corpse dropped away. The lance daffadar seemed almost as surprised by the perfection of the blow as the officer was to be in one piece.

The charge slowed and broke, as the horsemen fell upon their enemies, knots of cavalrymen soon surrounded by a sea of Duranis who had quickly recovered from the crashing impact. Keenan found himself in a sandy gully filled with pushing, yelling tribesmen, his own troopers hacking left and right in a desperate attempt to force the enemy swordsmen back.

'More than we thought, sahib,' said Miran, almost matter-of-factly. 'I hope the colonel sahib has got those owls in B Squadron ready to come and help.' The last few words were said with a grunt – the daffadar had abandoned his lance and drawn his sword. Now the blade sickled through a sheepskin *poshteen* and deep into the shoulder of an older, bearded warrior, who quit the fight with a yelp of pain.

'Aye, Daffadar, but they'll need to be quick – look to

Captain Reynolds, won't you?' Keenan saw his squadron leader just a few paces further up the nullah engulfed by a dozen attackers. The trumpeter – who was taught to protect the officer when at close quarters like this – seemed to be down. Keenan thought he'd seen one of the horses roll on to its side as muskets and matchlocks banged all around. Then, at first, Reynolds had slashed all about him, driving the Duranis back, but Keenan saw one bolder than the rest who threw down his shield and musket, drew his knife and scrambled forward. The tribesman had come from the captain's rear, and the long knife poked hard over Reynolds's rolled blanket and darted into the small of his back. The blade disappeared and re-emerged, stained red, and, in an instant, the officer had gone from a fighting man to a semi-cripple: he dropped his sword and yelled in pain, gripping the pommel of his saddle as the rest of the foe closed in and tried to drag him to the ground.

With no further words, the daffadar had dug his spurs into his mount, the pony kicking up the grit as she surged towards the mob. Keenan did the same, Kala barging one man out of her way with her left shoulder before putting her master right among the struggling throng.

Just in front of Keenan, a young Durani had thrown down his sword and seized Reynolds's tunic with both hands, dragging at the wounded officer who was feebly kicking out with the toes of his riding boots while trying to control his rearing horse. Keenan was about to strike a living target for the first time but, despite hours of practice, every bit of training deserted him. His victim was facing away from him, intent upon Reynolds in the noise and confusion that overwhelmed them all – a perfect mark for a deep stab with the point of the sword. Such a strike, Keenan had been taught, would be effective and economical, yet blunt instinct took over as he swept his tulwar over his left shoulder and let go a great scything cut that almost unbalanced him.

The carefully sharpened steel hit the foot soldier in two places at once. The base of the blade struck the man just above the left ear, his woollen cap taking some of the power out of the blow, but not before a great wound was opened on his scalp. At the same time, the forward part of the sword sliced obliquely through the Durani's left hand, neatly cutting off a couple of fingers and carving a wide flap of skin under which the bones showed whitely. The blow had been awkward, clumsy, and his opponent, though hurt and shouting in pain, still clung to Reynolds with fanatical determination.

'Use the point, sahib, finish him properly.' Next to Keenan in the plunging mêlée, the daffadar was jabbing at his own countrymen expertly, while remaining detached enough to guide his British officer.

Pulling the hilt of his sword back over Kala's rump, Keenan lunged hard at his shrieking opponent. The point of the weapon hit the man under his armpit and pushed obliquely through his major organs with surprising ease. One moment the tribesman had been wounded, but alive and dangerous; at the next he fell away, slipping easily off Keenan's blade into the cloud of dust and thrashing hoofs below, a look of horror on his bristly face.

So, that was what it was like to kill, thought Keenan. He glanced at the corpse – it was already shrunken and shapeless in death – but any pang of guilt had no time to develop as the daffadar bawled, '*Shabash, sahib!*' at him and ran yet another of the enemy through the shoulder to send the man corkscrewing back behind them and right on to the lance of a sowar riding with the second rank. Keenan knew the lad, a well-muscled youngster who'd come down from Rawalpindi to enlist last year. He was a wrestler and now every bit of sinew was put into a blow that buried his spear deep in the wounded tribesman's belly, finishing the brutal work that the daffadar had started. Keenan glanced at the cavalryman as he brought his weapon back to the 'recover'. There was no regret, no sympathy, just a vulpine grin behind his beard – a soldier satisfied with a job well done.

The immediate danger was over. Keenan watched as the Durani infantry loped away from his men, dodging among the brush and trees, one or two pausing to fire but most running hard to regroup among the buildings from which they had emerged. Even as Keenan took all this in, however, even as he looked back at the bundles of dusty rags that had been his enemy and the odd khaki figure sprawled beside them, he realised that a badly cut-about, barely conscious Captain Reynolds was being helped down from his saddle by two soldiers.

'What are your orders, sahib?' Rissaldar Singh, the senior of the squadron's two native officers, stood before him, a fleck of blood on his horse's neck but otherwise as unruffled as if he were on parade.

'Orders?' Keenan answered bemusedly, wondering why one of the other troop officers should have come to him for guidance.

'Yes, sahib, orders. You're in charge now that Reynolds sahib is hurt,' Singh continued calmly.

'Yes . . . yes, of course I am.' Despite Keenan's lack and Singh's depth of experience, as the only British officer left in the squadron, command automatically devolved upon him. Now he looked at the enemy. He could see a great crowd of them, probably two hundred strong, he guessed, turning to face his troops from the mud-walled hamlet that lay a furlong away over open, tussocky ground. Even as he watched he could see their confidence returning: they had started to shout defiance and fire wild shots towards the Scinde Horse.

'Let's be at 'em, then. Get your troops shaken out either side of mine beyond this nullah . . .' Keenan pointed to the shallow ditch immediately to their front, but stopped as Singh shook his head.

'No, sahib, we are too few – look.'

Keenan took stock of his new command. Singh was right: not only had the squadron lost its commander and several men, but many of the horses had been cut by swords and knives or grazed by bullets and all were blown. Most of the men had lost or broken their lances and two score simply could not hope to repeat the success of their earlier action, especially now that surprise was lost and the enemy had planted himself among protective walls and enclosures.

'The colonel will want to finish them with the other squadrons — we must hold them with our carbines, sahib,' Singh suggested, with quiet insistence.

'Aye, you're right, sahib. Trumpeter . . .' But there was no one to obey Keenan — he'd forgotten that the signaller had been one of the first to fall. 'Dismount, prepare to skirmish,' he shouted, the command being taken up by the NCOs who tongue-lashed the dazed troopers off their horses and forward with their weapons.

Keenan looked away to his right where the main body of the rearguard had been concentrated before the fight. Again Singh seemed to have been correct: he could see the remaining two squadrons of the Scinde Horse wheeling amid their own cloud of dust, shaking out into line abreast, while the company of the 29th Beloochis were trotting off to a flank to give covering fire, he guessed, with their long Snider rifles. Their own carbine fire, if quick and accurate, would gall the enemy just as the rest of Colonel Malcolmson's horsemen charged home.

'Squadron, load.' The men had flung themselves down behind any cover they could find and now they rammed cartridges into the breech of their weapons and clicked the breech-traps closed. 'Two fifty . . . aim high.' Keenan reckoned the range to be a little less than three hundred yards. The men adjusted their sights. 'Fire!' The snub-nosed rifles crashed out, pleasingly together, immediately obscuring his view of the target with a dense grey cloud.

'Reload.' The gentle breeze cleared some of the smoke, allowing Keenan to see where his men's bullets had whipped and stung the enemy. Where, just seconds before, there had been a dense packet of defiant tribesmen, now wounded men were struggling on the ground and their chanting had been replaced by moans of pain.

'Fire!' Again, the carbines banged out, and the rifles of the 29th joined in from way over on his troop's right. Behind the bank of muzzle smoke, Keenan could see the hundred and twenty lancers of the other two squadrons gathering speed as they trotted, then cantered up the gentle slope towards the village.

'Engage by troops.' Keenan wondered if this was the right thing to do or whether it would have been better to continue to volley fire.

'*Shabash, sahib.*' The daffadar beamed delightedly at his officer as he encouraged his soldiers' frantic marksmanship. 'See them run.'

And, through the smoke, Keenan could see how the Durani formation was beginning to disintegrate. Lashed by bullets, with more and more warriors writhing on the ground, a steady trickle of men was edging away into the cover of the village. Then the remaining two Scinde Horse squadrons charged home. The buildings and walls took some of the momentum away from the assault, but as Keenan watched, and Miran capered with delight beside him, the cavalrymen began their lethal trade.

Lances stabbed and curved steel hacked, poked and slashed; some tribesmen resisted bravely, trying to meet the terrible blades with shields and muskets, but most just melted away through the village, running for all they were worth into the hills beyond.

'Fire at will!' It was the last command that Keenan gave in his first action. As his men blazed at fleeing targets, he took his own carbine, which, until then, he hadn't thought to fire, but now he found a mark. One Durani was moving well from cover to cover, firing a captured Snider at Malcolmson's men as they hunted down the few who still resisted. Keenan watched his man shelter behind a bush, topple a trooper from his saddle with one shot, then rise and scuttle back to his next position. But as the man broke into a trot, Keenan put the metal V of his foresight on the knot of his target's belt, aimed just a fraction more to the left to allow for the time of flight of the round and gently squeezed the trigger. The warrior dropped like a shot rabbit, falling towards Keenan as the lead ploughed through his flesh. There was not even a flicker of life in him: the half-inch lump of lead had ripped it from him.

He's trying to be as modest as he can be, but I know that Sam was in the thick of it – word soon got back to me, especially as he had ended up commanding a squadron when things got tight. Firing his carbine alongside the men . . . I did the same in my first action – well, almost. But I don't see any of the self-doubt that beset me: there's a poise about the lad that I never had and which I've never noticed in him before – must get it from his mother. I expect I've been blinded by setting Billy's course for him, making sure that the Morgan name is held high. Well, much good may that do, for both my boys are out here in Afghanistan now – though I doubt that Billy will get the same chance to earn his spurs that Sam's had. It'll take Billy an age to live down that business in Kandahar with the child.

'Well, anyway, Father, that was months ago. We've seen a little more skirmishing since then, but nothing to compare with Khusk-i-Nakud. D'you think there's likely to be another campaign this season, or will we be going back to India?' asked Sam.

The boy even holds a glass like I do, both hands curled around the base,

'I doubt there'll be any more fighting, Sam. All the spunk's gone out of things now that hand-wringing Gladstone has got in. Mark my words, if we don't show the Afghans who's in charge, the bloody Russians will be in Kabul, like rats up a gutter, and then we'll see just how safe India's borders are. But I expect we'll sweat out the hot weather here and then take a gentlemanly trek back through the passes some time in late summer. I think you may have seen all the action you're likely to get just for the moment, my lad. Just be glad your hide's in one piece.'

'Aye, Father, you're right. A nice silver medal and a notch on my hilt are probably as much as I want. Some of the other officers are full of piss and vinegar – they can't wait for the next round – but a little swordplay with an angry Durani goes a long way in my book.'

I looked at my first son and liked what I saw. It would have been so easy to give his superior officer – and his father – some sort of devil-may-care, God-rot-Johnny-Afghan patter. But, no, he'd tasted blood and once was quite enough for him. I admired his frankness. Mind you, I wonder if I really did expect a quiet summer and a long walk, or was I just trying to calm the lad's expectations? If I'd really thought that things in Afghanistan were all but over that spring, I was sorely disappointed.

FOUR

The March

I'd hung around in garrisons before, but nothing ever like this. In Dublin, Pembroke Dock, Bombay and Karachi, you could establish some sort of routine, some sort of rhythm, to your work and have as good a social life as the people, the shooting and the hunting would allow. Then, when manoeuvres, postings or even campaigns beckoned, you could gear yourself up, *jildi* the men, tighten belts and set about whatever it was that Horse Guards wanted with gusto.

But Kandahar was debilitating. We weren't at war yet we were; we were expecting trouble yet we weren't. The rumours about a troublesome Ayoob Khan in Herat on the Persian border, which had held so much sway when I assumed command of the brigade in April, more than a month ago now, waxed and waned. Meanwhile, fighting was still going on in the north and the town was just as uneasy and bloody unpleasant as it had always been. Patrols continued to be knocked around, scuffles were frequent, and yet we had to pretend that everything was sweetness and light with the wali and his scabrous troops.

At least the dithering gave me time to get to know the units in the brigade and to push them into some sort of shape. By early May I'd visited the two companies of the 66th who were detached to protect the lines of communication at Khelat-i-Ghilzai, eighty-five miles away on the Kabul road, and got a good idea of how the land lay to the north-east. More importantly, I'd come to realise how I would miss them in the event of a serious fight around Kandahar. Their detachment meant that Galbraith only had six companies under his command, and these four hundred and fifty men were the only European troops – other than the Gunners – that I had to my name.

But the 66th were a good lot. Even though Galbraith had never seen active service before, he'd had a fair old time with the regiment and established a pretty firm grip on them. I'd already noticed how many long-service men they had with them and my son's sergeant – Kelly – was typical of their senior NCOs. I was also impressed with Beresford-Pierce, Billy's captain commanding H Company. He and his colour sergeant – James – seemed as close as McGucken and I had ever been in the old days, and it was this company that Galbraith chose to demonstrate to me the 66th's skill at arms.

The British battalion was the only unit to be armed with the Martini-Henry breech-loader; they'd had it for several years now and were thoroughly proficient with a weapon whose rate of fire could be devastating in the right hands. Galbraith and his musketry officer had trained the soldiers to fire eight volleys a minute; a high number of men were good enough shots to have qualified for the extra pay that a certified marksman received. As long as the weapon didn't overheat and fail to eject a spent cartridge case, each rifleman would be crucial if the sort of fighting that Roberts's troops had experienced up north came our way.

The only fly in Galbraith's ointment seemed to be his men's thirst. The Temperance Movement had got a real grip in India with, in my experience, most British units having at least a hundred men or so who had forsworn the bottle. But there were many fewer in the 66th, and I noticed that the regimental prison was always full of lads doubling about in full kit in the heat of the day with an energetic provost corporal in close attendance. Still, there were worse problems, and while there continued to be clashes between the regiment and the toughs in town, there were no repeats of the incident in which Billy had been involved in April.

But when I managed to get some time with my native battalions, I discovered how much work there was to do. The 1st Bombay Grenadiers came with a high reputation for steadiness earned in the Mutiny – but that was a long time ago now – and they had done well in Aden in '65, but I didn't like the way that my brigade major, Heath, talked about them. He'd been their adjutant, after all, and whenever we discussed them he would mention nothing except their steadiness on parade and the various complicated devices they used to ensure that they all took a graduated pace when each company wheeled from column to line. He never mentioned their musketry or their ability to cover miles without a man dropping out and seemed oddly ignorant about which tribe and caste each man came from.

But that was better than the open suspicion that swirled around the other battalion, the 30th Bombay Native Infantry, or Jacob's Rifles. They had made quite a good start in my eyes, being more ready for the field than their counterparts, yet they were a new regiment, having been raised after the Mutiny, and had no battle honours to hang on their colours. On top of this, the vast majority of their recruits were Pathans, the very same folk from whom we had most trouble in Kandahar. As was the way with the Army, someone had decided that the loyalty of Jacob's Rifles was in doubt, so everyone treated them like pariahs, yet Sam's 3rd Scinde Horse – also mainly Pathani – were never criticised for the same thing, not in my hearing, anyway.

Whatever the rights and wrongs of the composition of both battalions, I was more concerned with how they would perform in a fight. Since the Mutiny, it was our habit to keep the Indian units equipped with the last generation of small-arms rather than the most modern. So it was that the Grenadiers and the Jacobs both carried the .577 Snider-Enfield conversion rifles. These were the old muzzle-loaders that I had known in my young day, with a trap affair let into the breech and a metal cartridge and bullet fixed together as one neat round. The result was good enough in well-trained hands, allowing six volleys to be fired per minute with accurate individual fire up to about six hundred paces. But the Snider was prone to jam and fouling and it took a lot of practice before a soldier became really proficient with it. Also, many of our Afghan enemies had the same weapon, which meant that the only advantage we might enjoy would come from stern discipline and plenty of practice.

My strongest card, for sure, were the six guns of E Battery, B Brigade Royal Horse Artillery. The men were smart and sharp, every horse I saw was beautifully groomed and a proper source of pleasure to its driver, while the rifled nine-pounders were lethally well kept.

'Them fuckers'll soon sort out Johnny Afghan, sir.' I let Lynch, my trumpeter, who was on loan from E Battery, regale me with the tools of his trade. 'Aye, we can hit a sixpence up to three an' a half thousand paces with high-explosive or shrapnel rounds, we can, sir.' Lynch was bursting with pride, delighted to be back among his pals with 'his' general under his wing. I allowed him to think that I was a complete tyro in such matters. 'An' the lads can get off four rounds a minute once they've found the range.'

Lynch was right to be proud of his guns and his battery, but our nine-pounders were still muzzle-loading and slow compared with the new breech-loaders that were coming into service. Now I'd seen what well-handled guns could do, especially to native troops, but there was a nasty rumour that Ayoob Khan had rifled guns like we did, and further intelligence to suggest that Russian advisers were to be seen openly in Herat. I preferred to forget how bloody good the Russian gunners had been in the Crimea.

Whatever the strengths and weaknesses of this lot, I managed to get them out of cantonments for two full manoeuvres by mid-May, and saw that they seemed to be settling down. I was still fretting over the compatibility of my two native battalions with my British one when rumours began to filter into the lines of a bloody little affair in which the 29th Baloochis and some of the 66th, who were detached, had been involved near Khelat-i-Ghilzai. I was called to Primrose's headquarters with the other brigade commanders to be told what was in the wind.

'Gentlemen, three days ago, on the second of May, a wing of the Twenty-ninth Bombay and a half-company of the Sixty-sixth under Tanner's command were ambushed on Shahbolan Hill. They'd been out on a punitive expedition along the lines of communication towards Kabul and were returning to Khelat-i-Ghilzai when they got bounced. Now, as it happened, none of our men was killed and we found fourteen enemy bodies.' I hated the way that Primrose strutted about while he told us this. A starched white liner stuck out above the collar of his neat khaki drill while he paced to and fro, hands clasped behind his back, apparently relishing the idea of sudden death. 'But there's far more to this little skirmish than meets the eye. McGucken, would you take over, please?'

'Aye, General, thank you.' The political officer stood up from his camp chair, towering over the scrawny form of our commander. I hadn't seen much of Jock in the intervening weeks for we'd both been busy. I'd knocked into him as he was riding out towards Kabul with an escort of native troopers, himself wearing Afghan dress and looking very much the part with the beard he'd grown, but we'd had no time for the 'swally' we'd been promising each other.

Now he cleared his throat in a way that took me back

76

more years than I cared to remember, swept the room with an uncompromising eye and continued. 'Gentlemen, I canna pretend that intelligence is as reliable as I would like. Simla has been insisting that Ayoob Khan's troops are as good as useless because they continue to have major differences with one another. Sadly, however, this affair up near Khelat-i-Ghilzai is the first real proof I've had that Simla's talking rot.' McGucken's suggestion that our headquarters in India was incompetent – which we all suspected – raised a chuckle. 'No, this was a determined attack by Herati troops. It was well planned but was dealt with by Colonel Tanner's quick thinking and the determination of our men. Some of the bodies are believed to be from one of the Afghan regular units that were involved in the murder of Sir Louis Cavagnari last year.' This prompted an uneasy muttering among the audience. 'It's the first real demonstration of how far afield Ayoob Khan's men are able to operate – and his intention to destabilise the situation here in Kandahar even further.

'You'll all be aware of the guns that we presented to the wali recently.' McGucken looked round the brigade commanders to assess their reaction: there had been all sorts of moaning about the decision to give Sher Ali Khan a battery of brass smooth-bores. Primrose had backed McGucken, whose idea it had been, suggesting that the guns would be seen as a gesture of trust that might lead to greater co-operation from the wali, but I thought back to my brief meeting with Sher Ali last month and his own lack of confidence in his troops. I didn't like the idea of giving away gun-metal that might very well be turned upon its donors. 'Well, that ordnance seems to have served as a key that's unlocked our host's lips. I always suspected that those who might be persuaded to talk to us were being told to keep their traps shut by the rebellious elements in the wali's forces. Well, the wali gave the guns into his son's safe keeping and that young fellow, some of yous gentlemen' – McGucken's speech dropped back into pure

Glasgow only occasionally – 'will have met him already, has suddenly become much more talkative. He tells me that Ayoob Khan plans to move out of Herat in the middle of June, in about five weeks' time. He will try to make us believe that his forces will skirt north of us and go on to Kabul, where he and several thousand troops will then do a spot of gentle lobbying. His real intention, however, will be to fall upon Kandahar.'

'You say several thousand troops, McGucken. What does he actually have?' Nuttall, the cavalry brigade commander, voiced my question.

'Well, sir, we don't know for sure and we won't until he marches – and we don't yet know if his mind's fully made up. Anyway, the wali intends to send a body of his troops up here to the fords over the Helmand river.' McGucken pointed on the map at an area that I could see was a natural convergence of several different roads near Khusk-i-Nakud, seventy-odd miles away, where Sam and the Scinde Horse had drawn first blood more than a year ago. 'He's still getting his own house in order and, as we all know to our cost, Kandahar will only become more volatile with a reduction in the wali's garrison, while the troops themselves are not dependable. I have no doubt, General' – I saw the flash of dislike in McGucken's eyes as he turned to Primrose – 'that he'll ask for some of our regiments to accompany his forces to act as a stiffener.'

'I'm sure he will, McGucken, and as you and I have discussed before, I'm reluctant to diminish what strength I have here in Kandahar for the reasons that you've just outlined. On top of that, I believe in concentration of force' – sometimes Primrose talked like a field manual – 'and I don't want to split what few units I have. But I shall do what Simla tells me to as the picture becomes clearer. In the meantime, I want you all to be prepared to take the field for an indefinite period at twenty-four hours' notice.' He prosed on about musketry,

78

skirmishing practice, preparation of the horses and their fodder, and a host of minor details that Harry Brooke, Nuttall and I had already been working on.

We scratched away in our notebooks to show willing while Primrose tried to tell us our jobs. What he didn't cover, though, were the vital details that we all wanted to know. Eventually he ran out of steam and asked for any questions.

'Yes, General. McGucken's intelligence, understandably, is less than perfect.' Harry Brooke, I knew, had become good friends with McGucken, admiring the Scotsman's plain speaking and direct approach. 'But what do we actually know about the forces that Ayoob Khan might have available to him?'

'He's got about eight thousand regular troops of which some two thousand are cavalry, and as many as six batteries of guns, many of which are rifled pieces, but we lack detail, Brooke.' I could see why Primrose was reluctant to divide his already slender force.

'Aye, General, but that's only really half the story.' This was McGucken at his best. He was by far the most junior in terms of both military and social rank yet the rest of us would hardly have dared to correct Primrose: we were too career-conscious, too much the victims of the Army's strangling habit of unthinking obedience and uncritical respect. But not big Jock McGucken, who wore the DCM and knew that he had naught to fear from men like Primrose for there was nothing they could do for him. His reward was the knowledge that his children wouldn't grow up in the Glasgow slum that had been his home, and the respect that all of us showed him. 'The real question is how many irregulars, tribesmen and mad Ghazis he'll be able to draw to his colours. If he's a halfway decent commander, he could double the number of men he's already got − and we've all seen what ugly buggers the Ghazis and their like can be.'

I was as stunned by McGucken's monologue as the rest of

them. Suddenly there was the prospect of the best part of fifteen thousand men with more guns than we had descending on our three untried and untested brigades in a town that had no serious defences and was riven by malcontents. On top of that, I remembered the wali's words of caution about his own troops' dependability and the dubious attractions of a swarm of Ghazis. Surely he would know better than any of us Feringhees what a ticklish spot we could be in.

'General, I wonder if we shouldn't prepare the town for defence.' Harry Brooke, Nuttall and I had spent hours wondering why Primrose hadn't done what should have been done an age ago by Stewart.

'We've discussed this before, Morgan, but, I grant you, the situation has evolved so tell me what's on your mind.'

I knew from the tone of Primrose's voice that he wouldn't relent. 'Well, sir, should we not bring the troops within the walls of the town and establish a proper defensive routine rather than trying to live in the cantonments as if we were a peacetime garrison? We could then put the troops to work on improving the walls and preparing gun positions both there and in the Citadel. And we ought to start to clear the shanties and mud dwellings that deprive us of any fields of fire.'

'Yes, and that's exactly the point I've tried to make all of you understand.' I'd annoyed Primrose – but Brooke had made a pretty good start on that with his earlier questions. Now the peppery little sod was about to go for all of us. 'Right, everyone except the brigade commanders – you as well, McGucken – please leave us.' The three brigade majors and Primrose's own pair of lickspittles grabbed at their papers and maps and scuttled from the room, only too happy to leave their superiors to face the storm. 'Can't you see that we've got to make this whole situation look as normal as possible and that the least little thing we do' – the man was getting redder and redder in the face as the discussion turned into a rant – 'could upset the whole damned applecart and cause the wali's troops to revolt?'

'All the more reason to have us on top of them, surely. If we're in the town then we can watch them more closely and act more quickly – it makes sense,' McGucken was unable to conceal his irritation any longer, not even adding a perfunctory 'sir', treating Primrose like a particularly dim recruit.

'And I'll thank you not to interrupt, Major McGucken!' The venom in the general's hissed reply shocked me – and it seemed to have the same effect on the others, for there was a sudden silence. Even the flies stopped buzzing, so taken aback were they. 'Do you really think that we could clear the mosques and other religious sites that teem just outside the walls?' None of us replied. 'Well, do you? You all seem to think that we can treat this place as we did Cawnpore or Peking twenty-odd years ago. But can't you get it into your thick heads that this is a new kind of war where I've got newspapers and politicians looking over my shoulder . . .' (I'd have loved to add, 'and dictating our tactics and risking our men's lives', but he was vexed enough already) '. . . and that, no matter what's happening elsewhere in the country, Kandahar is supposed to be the one place in which we're succeeding? If we tear the scab off things here, then the government's strategy to get us back to India without further bloodshed will be ruined.'

It was a shame that the little fellow had lost his rag for he'd just alienated the lot of us.

'So, get back to your troops now, gentlemen, and let's hear no more about ruining Kandahar. If the wali can't deal with Ayoob Khan and we're called upon to do the job, we'll do it in the field as far from this town as we possibly can. That's always supposing our intelligence gives us any warning at all.' Primrose was speaking normally now, but he hadn't grasped how much damage he had done to his standing in our eyes. He hadn't even been able to resist that nasty little dig at

McGucken, which I knew he would come to regret. I was on my feet and saluting almost as quickly as the other three, for none of us could bear the poisonous career-wallah for a second longer.

When Sam Keenan had moved up to Afghanistan with his regiment, he'd known that life wouldn't all be gallant deeds and glory. He had vivid memories of Finn the groom yarning to Billy and himself back in the tack-room at home about India and the Sikh wars in the forties and much of that had revolved around heat and dust, flies and rotting food, good officers and bad. There had been little about blood and flame. Well, he thought, now it was his turn to experience the waiting and frustration of campaign life.

June was the hottest month in these latitudes and the temperature only made the smell of piss-damp straw all the more distinct. It wasn't an aroma that any cavalryman could actually dislike, but in A Squadron's horse lines, which had been established in an old Kandahari stable, it was almost overpowering. There were none of the drains and gutters to which the regiment had become used, and the windows were so narrow that a permanent gloom hung over the place. Now, as he waited for Rissaldar Singh to join him, he peered down the long line of feeding horses, the thin streams of sunlight thick with the dust that the hoofs of the tethered mounts threw up.

Almost eighty horses had been crushed into the stable, sixty or so the private property of each trooper, his pride and joy, and another twenty remounts provided by the government while on campaign. Keenan worried about this so-called *sillidar* system, which was the very definition of irregular cavalry. Each man would bring his own mount as a condition for enlistment – a very considerable investment for these mainly Pathani men who came from poor hilly country – and tend it. Horses became ill or were injured and had to be put down so they needed a cushion of extra animals. But now, as casualties had occurred, the men were being issued with whalers, like any common regular regiment, and Keenan was worried that they would not be cherished as much as a man's own horse had been. The squadron leader had ordered extra veterinary inspections in the certain knowledge that the stabling and relatively little exercise might encourage certain maladies.

Now Keenan, who'd done his basic vet's course at the cavalry school in Nasirabad, looked at his list of common diseases and symptoms as he waited for Singh by the wide doors of the building.

'I'm sorry, sahib, am I late?'

Keenan looked up from his list towards the native officer as he stopped and saluted. 'No, not at all, Rissaldar sahib. I'm early. I've been puzzling over these lists, I hope you know what we're looking for,' replied Keenan, deliberately flattering the man.

In the months that they'd been together in Afghanistan, the two had got to know each other as well as any native and British officer could. They'd ridden together in the Helmand valley last year and fought side by side at Khusk-i-Nakud, but still Keenan was uncomfortable with the relationship. Singh was over thirty, one of the new generation of native officers who had received a viceroy's commission based on merit rather than age and length of service; he had a depth of experience far beyond the young Irishman's. They wore the same badges of rank, were both addressed as 'sahib' and commanded troops of about twenty men. Yet they lived in different messes and Keenan was the senior, for he was a *British* officer, the most junior of whom was superior even to the rissaldar major, the most senior native officer in the regiment. His thoughts unaccountably flicked to his brother. Keenan smiled to himself and doubted that Billy would cope in his plodding, stiff old 66th with the extra layer of officers who were at the heart of the regiment yet weren't really officers at all.

Singh spoke incomprehensibly to one of the four men on morning duty at the stables before turning to Keenan. 'Butt Mohammed believes that one of the remounts may be developing surra, sahib, but we'll soon see.'

Not only could Singh speak English a hundred times better than he could express himself in Pashto or Dari, Keenan marvelled, but he also had a practical knowledge of an ailment of which he himself had no experience whatsoever. But then, he supposed, that was what years in the 3rd Scinde Horse taught a man. As they walked briskly along the straw-strewn floor through the horsy fug, he consulted his *Field Service Pocket Book (India)* in its supposedly waterproof cover. 'Isn't that mainly a camel and donkey disease, sahib?' he asked, freshly knowledgeable.

'It is, sahib, but read on a bit further and you'll see that it can affect horses too,' answered Singh, with a smile.

With the trooper stroking the horse's nose to calm it, both men looked for signs of '. . . repeated attacks of fever during which the animal is dull and off feed, gradually loses condition, gets swelling, spotted membranes, pot belly and finally dies'.

'No, sahib, this is not surra. I have seen it before and it is dreadful. Horses cannot recover, and that is why the men are so worried about it, especially when their animals are around filthy camels and asses.' Singh spoke again to Butt Mohammed before patting the horse gently on its admittedly bulbous belly. 'I think it's no more than a touch of colic.' Keenan thought about that phrase and knew that he would be reduced to charades if he was trying to express such a thing to the men.

That was the only problem to worry any of the men, but the two officers continued their inspection, lifting mares' tails to look for thrush, digging sawdust and muck out of hoofs to check for cracks and mud fever, peering up nostrils for a hint of glanders, and for sores around the saddle area that might indicate farcy.

'What of Ayoob Khan, sahib?' The rissaldar was smoothing down the hairs on a horse's flank having examined an old ringworm site. 'The soldiers say he is bound to march on Kandahar once the weather gets a little cooler.'

'Perhaps, Rissaldar sahib. But I only know what the colonel sahib tells us and he tells you the same. Do any of the soldiers have any contact with Ayoob Khan's people?' Keenan asked.

'Of course, sahib. Many are Pathans from the same tribes who soldier for Ayoob Khan and they have kinsmen here in Kandahar who travel far and wide. Indeed, a caravan arrived from Herat two days ago and brought family news to many of our jawans, and grand stories of the headman's bragging about what he will do to any of "his" people who are taken in the service of the *gora-log*,' answered Singh.

'Does that worry them, sahib?'

'No, Keenan sahib, they don't give a donkey's cock about such things. All that most want is a chance of more fighting and looting – you know our sowars,' replied Singh, making Keenan wonder just how well he did know the men with whom he could hardly converse. 'But, sahib, don't run from this talk – *you* must know, for does your father, the general sahib, not tell you?'

'No, of course not, Rissaldar sahib. He's the chief and I'm nothing but a worm. Why should he tell me anything that he does not tell you?' Keenan realised now that every last sowar must look at him as the receptacle of great knowledge and influence. If only that were true.

'Because he is your father, sahib. He is a general, certainly, and that is why he has gathered both his sons about him to go to war and seek glory. Of course he will tell you and your brother his secrets,' Singh answered evenly.

Keenan snorted with amusement at he idea of Billy and himself being summoned by his father for some sort of ramasammy. He had a picture of Father sitting cross-legged next to the wali, both men pulling at pipes while he and that pup Billy made deep salaams and prepared to advise the elders on what should happen next. But that was what Rissaldar Singh and all the others thought. He must seem horribly naïve in their eyes when he tried to grapple with their tribes, castes and religions.

'And, why, sahib, does your father allow your poor brother to walk to war when he has given you horses and saddles and found you a place in a regiment like the Scinde Horse? Has your brother done something wrong? Has he displeased Morgan sahib yet still bears his name?'

Singh had never asked such questions before, thought Keenan. 'No, Rissaldar sahib, my brother, my half-brother, can do no wrong in the general's eyes and that is why he walks to war and I ride. You see, sahib, I have a horse or two, but that is all I will ever have from the general. I will never bear his name or inherit his house and fields . . . but enough of that! This creature has been rubbed a little by its heel rope, hasn't it?' The native officer had got quite close enough for now.

It's always the way. Something happens or someone says something that causes a bit of heat at the time, but you soon forget it, only grasping its true significance later on. So it was with that conference two months ago – back in May. From that moment on neither the other two brigade commanders nor I had any faith in Primrose. True, he'd sent out the odd patrol, and we'd had some time to manoeuvre in the field – turned a lot of live ammunition into empty cases on the rifle range – and the guns had had some useful practice, but there had been no attempt to improve the town's defences.

Worst of all, the distrust between Primrose and McGucken had become obvious to everyone. I was there four weeks ago in early June when the news reached divisional headquarters that the wali was so worried by intelligence he'd received that he was preparing to march out of Kandahar towards the fords on the Helmand. There the Wali, game old bugger that he was, intended to fight Ayoob Khan well forward, as far away from Kandahar and its skittish tribesmen as he could mange. Not surprisingly, he wanted some British troops to help him. Now, *we'd* all heard that Ayoob Khan had left Herat some weeks ago and was picking up volunteers from the tribes by the hatful as he headed our way, but Primrose seemed genuinely surprised by the sudden rush and fuss among the local troops as they prepared to take the field. It wasn't as though it was difficult to see what was going to happen. A few days before the wali left, McGucken had given me a carefully translated copy of Ayoob's proclamation, which was being distributed by his vanguard.

Then, after a month's dithering by Primrose, we'd marched out of Kandahar in order to catch up with the Wali. Now, as I sat on Rainbow's sweaty saddle, my brigade stretched about me in a fog of dust and grit, I got the proclamation out from my map case to reread it:

Soldiers of the true faith! We march to the conquest of our city of Kandahar, now in the possession of our bitter enemy the Feringhee, whom we will drive back with our steel and win back the capital of the south. The garrison is weak and we are strong; besides, we are fighting for our homes and native land and our foe is not prepared for us with either food or ammunition for a siege. The bazaars are full of British gold and this shall be the prize of the conquerors when we have chased away the invaders from our soil. Let us march on then, day by day, with the determination to conquer or to die.

How could Primrose have ignored this? How could he have continued to tool about playing at peacetime – we'd even had a Queen's Birthday Parade complete with a *feu-de-joie* and other such rot – when the bloody enemy was telling him what they intended? How could he have been surprised, then, when the wali and most of his troops left Kandahar to march to the Helmand river to confront Ayoob Khan? And how could he have been surprised when McGucken piled pressure on him to send British troops to help the wali and his disaffected crew?

As the news of Ayoob Khan's approach grew more and credible, so the other two brigade commanders and I prepared our men – but all that Primrose did was dither. Eventually, after seeking permission from Simla, he made up his mind to do something, and on the last day of June he issued orders for a composite brigade to march to Gereshk, the town that dominated the fords over the Helmand, about seventy miles west of Kandahar, there, in his turgid prose, 'to confirm the fidelity of the wali's troops, overawe the Zemidar tribes and establish confidence'.

So it was that I found myself plodding along in the cool of the night over the dust and the scrubby sand with a sheet of stars above us and only the thump of sandals and boots, and the Ark-like noises of the menagerie of transport animals that accompanied us. I'd got my own guns and sappers, my three infantry battalions and two regiments from the cavalry brigade, with Tom Nuttall himself in charge, though – rather to my surprise – I'd been put in overall command. Two thousand five hundred men and six guns were more than I'd ever dreamed I would command on operations. That both of my sons were with me seemed more than a coincidence.

At first, the thought of such responsibility had made my blood tingle, but the endless hours spent flogging across this wretched desert in the dark had soon blunted my enjoyment. It wasn't helped by the fact that I had soon run out of conversation with Heath, my brigade major. Jesus, he was a dull fellow who knew little about the native troops and their sensibilities, had no discernible interest in horseflesh, beyond the fact that it was a mode of transport, and didn't give a damn for hunting or the chase.

He was a bloody expert, though, on botany – of all things. 'Oh, yes, Lynch. It's remarkable what you can grow in the mild temperatures of Karachi if you water things enough and use just the right amount of fertiliser.' Heath had turned his tedium on poor Trumpeter Lynch, having discovered that I had nothing whatsoever to contribute to such *famtoosh* nonsense. 'Why, I've had all manner of orchids growing, a thing that most folk said could never be done in that part of India.'

'Orchids, sir?' Trumpeter Lynch had, quite plainly, never heard of such wonders. 'Can they be ate?'

Before Heath could reply, we were distracted by a handful of dark figures who came trotting softly up beside us.

'Ah, General, it is yourself, ain't it? We've been looking all over for you.' Jock McGucken's outline was unmistakable, even in the dark. 'I've brought the wali back from his own troops for a wee word with you.'

That was exactly what I'd asked him to organise. I wanted to hear from the person who was likely to have the best idea of what lay ahead, but I hadn't expected him to come to find me.

'My dear General Morgan, I'm so grateful to you.' The wali's seesaw accent was slightly muffled by the cloth he wore across his mouth to keep out the dust. 'McGucken *huzoor* explained to me what a struggle it had been to get your splendid men released from Kandahar. I repeat, I really am most grateful.' Again, the fellow made it sound as if I'd ordered all my serfs to help him, as if I'd called out the *fyrd* solely to oblige him.

'I know you've seen Ayoob Khan's diktat. We should take it seriously and not listen to any rumours that come back from our scouts that he may be peaceable. He wants Kandahar at any price and detects that your new government in London has lost its courage. You must tell your ministers to keep their faces hard, General. Ayoob Khan may send false words of peace and reason, but his message to the people is the true one. He will fight, and you must make your people understand that.'

There was no mistaking the anxiety in the Wali's voice. 'Well, sir, I shall certainly pass on your concerns to Mr Gladstone at the first opportunity.' Luckily, the wali didn't detect the sarcasm in my reply, but Jock McGucken did and immediately cut in.

'The wali was telling me that he's pretty worried about his infantry, but he thinks the cavalry – most of whom are plainsmen from the Kandahar area and from his own tribe – are less likely to turn their coats. Weren't you, sir?'

'I am worried about my own troops, Major McGucken, but I've told the general so before. What concerns me even more, though, is how powerful Ayoob Khan's column is becoming and, even allowing for exaggeration, I believe he has about ten thousand warriors at his command and he's halfway along his journey. If he continues to move at his current rate, he'll have another three weeks or so of marching and sending out his poison letters, which will attract even more men to his cause.'

Once again, I had the distinct impression that the wali had lost all hope of overcoming Ayoob Khan. 'If that's the case, why d'you suppose General Primrose has taken so long to get a force alongside the wali on the Helmand?' I muttered to McGucken, quietly enough for the wali not to hear. 'If we'd set off even a week ago we could have dug positions to hold the Helmand fords and got our guns properly sited.'

'You know why the bloody man has made no decision, General. It's because he's more suited to having tits on his chest, not medals, an' cos he's frit of what the papers might say if he's seen as too aggressive,' McGucken growled. 'It's Ayoob

Khan's guns that worry me most, though, General. Rumour has it they're well served and are carrying plenty of ammunition, and while I've every trust in our Horse Gunners, we've only got six nine-pounders to wipe our arse with.'

'And what news have you of Ayoob Khan's artillery, sir?' I asked the wali, sounding as airy as possible while trying to bury the memory of crashing shells and scything splinters – of which my bad dreams were made.

'Nothing more than you know already, my dear General. He has had some difficulty with the oxen that he is using to drag the guns and one of his best pieces . . . Oh, what is the name of the things?'

'Armstrong guns, sir?' I hoped for bad news.

'Yes, that's right . . . One of his best pieces lost the iron tyre from around one of its wheels, but they soon put that right,' the wali continued flatly. 'He still has many more guns than we do, even when you add my brass pieces that you so kindly gave to us.'

'Aye, sir, and they're grand guns and I've seen your gunners handle them as well as any of my people could,' I lied, trying to cheer the miserable old file up a bit.

'You flatter us, General. Your guns and mine will be the key to keeping Ayoob Khan on the west side of the Helmand,' the wali answered. 'I just hope that the whores that are to use them stay true to their salt.'

'Och, sir, I'm sure they will. Those guns have given your fellows a real sense of pride as soldiers.' Jock McGucken was doing his best to bolster the man.

'I'm sure you're right, McGucken . . .' Then I added for only Jock to hear above the plodding of the horses and the creaking of equipment from the troops all around us, 'Just remind me to check that all our troops have enough spiking nails with them.' I'd just have to hope that Ayoob Khan would be more impressed by us than his propaganda said he was.

＊　＊　＊

91

Billy Morgan couldn't remember any instructions at Sandhurst about guarding baggage – but, then, there wasn't a great deal he had learnt there that had any relevance to what he was asking men to do out here in Afghanistan. The whole of H Company had been detailed off to flog alongside the cavalcade of animals, carts, drivers and gaggles of natives who accompanied the brigade column on the move. At first such moves had certainly been exotic, exciting almost, as camels lurched along blowing great sacs of mucus from their nostrils, cattle sat down when it suited them, asses brayed uproariously and other creatures farted, neighed and whinnied through the night. But now any fascination had long since disappeared. All that he, Kelly and the other NCOs wanted was to keep the men alert and ready for any dark figures bent on mischief who might choose to steal up to the trudging tide. But if he was bored, how did the poor troops feel? They had nothing to do but tramp along with just their thoughts and their aching feet for company.

'Come on, then, Johnny, get that bleedin' thing to stop, can't you?' Private Battle was part of the baggage guard and he'd had quite enough of stumbling across sand and pebbles he couldn't see, tripping on bits of rock and grass surrounded by every sort of beast in God's creation. And their drivers weren't any better: a set of ignorant heathens who'd pretend they couldn't understand his best Hindustani, let alone honest English, and just cheeked him by standing there blinking. It was enough to give a man a thirst, so it was. 'I said, get the bastard thing to stop an' on its knees. I ain't got arms like an ape – I can't reach from down here.'

The camel driver realised how angry the sahib was becoming and he could see that the big soldier wanted the creature to kneel down so that he could get at the wooden rum casks that were slung either side of the animal's back. He looked at the soldier's sleeve and saw no sign of rank, but perhaps he was collecting rum for others. Why, then, as soon as the camel had settled itself did the soldier pull at the left barrel's bung and fill his mess-tin with the precious liquid? That couldn't be right – it was strictly forbidden and more than his slender wages were worth.

'Get your dirty hands off me, you!' The camel driver was pulling at Battle's sleeve, causing him to slop some of the liquid over the lip of his tin cup. 'Fuck off, won't you?' A hefty shove sent the native sprawling on the ground, while Battle's slung rifle slipped from his shoulder to his elbow, causing more of the nectar to spill.

'Oh, you want some more, do you?' said Battle, for the driver was up from the ground, sandalled feet scrabbling in the dust, grabbing and tugging at Battle's arm, gabbling in Hindi, trying to defend his cargo. 'Well, argue with this.' He swung his rifle by its sling with practised ease, wasting no more rum, grabbing the weapon just above the butt, curling his forefinger around the trigger and bringing the muzzle to point straight at the native's face, as the moonlight shone off the lightly oiled barrel. 'Now fuck off and mind yer own business, you little sod.' Battle sank the contents of the mess tin, then filled a spare water-bottle with more illicit rum, his eyes and rifle never leaving the quivering driver. He had chosen a good place for the squabble, as a few scrawny trees gave him some cover from the view of the men and animals that trickled past, the deep shadows concealing most of the altercation.

Most, but not all of it: Rissaldar Singh of the 3rd Scinde Horse had first noticed a shadowy camel fall out of the line of march, then heard a scuffle and an angry English voice. He and his vedette were acting as flank guard for the vulnerable baggage train and too much of their time had been spent already with thrown horseshoes, slipped baggage and broken girths for there to be more delay. A sahib was obviously angry with one of the civilian drivers; he thought he had better investigate.

'Now, what d'you want, you nosy bleeder?' Battle had only just managed to quell the interfering driver when a horseman approached, silhouetted high above him, chirruping in a lingo he couldn't follow. Worse than that, the driver then started shouting the odds to the cavalryman, his voice wheedling, sing-song, bloody annoying. Now, Battle could have coped with all this just so long as neither of these gits stopped him getting his share of the rum. Why should they? What did it mean to either of them? They weren't allowed to touch the stuff anyway.

He could have put up with any amount of jabbering and arm-waving, but then the horse-soldier dashed the mess-tin from his hands – yes, just knocked it on to the deck without so much as a by-your-leave – and started pointing to the badges on his collar.

'And what d'you think those damn things mean to me?' No fucking native was going to talk to Eddie Battle of Sligo like that. The shot sounded huge in the night, the muzzle flash briefly banishing the black and grey of the dark, revealing the khaki of the uniforms, white teeth, shocked eyes and the red blood on the face of the cavalryman as the bullet threw him backwards into a heap on the dusty ground.

But even as Battle stood there reviewing his handiwork, more horsemen arrived, cantering up to the sound of the shot and the angry voices.

Daffadar Sayed Miran and two sowars of the Scinde Horse reined in besides the terrified camel-driver and saw on the ground the dead Rissaldar Singh of their own squadron. Still standing over him was the big Irishman who, even now, worked the lever of his rifle and ejected a single empty round in a puff of smoke from the open breech. Miran grasped the situation at once and, with a few quick words to his men, dismounted and snatched the rifle from Battle's hands as the two troopers pinioned his arms.

'Mother of God, will you get the fuck away, ye bleedin' donkey-walloper?' Half a pint of rum on an empty stomach slowed Eddie Battle's reactions enough for him to put up little fight, but his cursing was as loud as ever, quite loud enough for Lieutenant Sam Keenan to spur his horse over to what he already knew was an ugly little fracas.

'What's going on, Daffadar sahib? Who's that man on the ground?'

Before Miran could attempt to explain to his officer, before Keenan even had time to dismount, Battle was conducting his own defence at the top of a rum-laden voice. 'It's these gougers, sir.' Even in the dark, the soldier immediately recognised a British officer, heard the authority in his voice and hoped for an ally. 'I was just havin' a wee drink, so I was, when one of these dirty natives—'

'You mean one of my "dirty natives", do you, my man? What's your name and number? What unit are you from?' Keenan was bending over the still body of Singh, his brother officer. His voice was hard and flat.

'Sir, nine two seven, Private Edward Battle, H Company, Sixty-Sixth Foot, sir.'

'Is this your work, Battle?' Keenan looked at Singh's bullet-shattered face in the moonlight. The round had obviously been fired from the hip, catching Singh just below and slightly left of his nose, coursing through his moustache before exiting at the top and rear of the Indian officer's skull. Even in the half-light, Keenan could see a great puddle of black blood soaking into the ground, his comrade's eyes staring sightlessly at the stars.

'Sir.'

Keenan would have expected no other reply from Battle. 'Well, my lad, you're in a great deal of trouble. Remove his equipment, Daffadar sahib, and make him a prisoner.' Keenan watched his sergeant bind the befuddled and now unresisting Battle with a leather strap, then broke into hesitant Pashto: 'Sowar Jan Mahommed, away and find the provost – there's a detachment of them marching with Brigade Headquarters over yonder.' Keenan pointed in the general direction of the rear of the moving column where he knew his father was, with his staff.

But just as order began to be restored, boots came thumping through the night, announcing the arrival of a gaggle of foot soldiers. Battle knew who they were even before they arrived. 'Here, sir, over here, Sar'nt, it's me, Battle. These natives have got me tied like a goat – over here!'

Sergeant Kelly had been stumping along with his officer, Ensign Billy Morgan, sharing a pipe and keeping an eye in the dark on their dispersed men. They'd heard the shot and the shouting, had drawn the same conclusion Keenan had and, grabbing a pair of their own men, had run as hard as they could towards the row.

'What's going on, Battle? Who fired that shot?' Billy Morgan knew that something was amiss – it usually was when Eddie 'Bottle' Battle was involved – but neither he nor Kelly had seen the dead rissaldar. All they could make out in the dark was a knot of angry Indian cavalry, a trembling native driver and one of their own men bellowing like a bull, all set against the backdrop of a heavily laden, rather reproachful camel.

'Sir, these bleedin' natives 'as grabbed me, sir!' Battle wasn't going to give up.

'You men, get your hands off that soldier – release him at once, d'you hear?' Whatever the rights and wrongs of the situation, Morgan was not going to have one of his command being manhandled by another unit – especially not a native one. Besides, after the affray in the marketplace in Kandahar back in April, Morgan had become protective of the big Mick, despite the trouble he so often caused. But, like Battle, Morgan hadn't realised that another officer was present – and one who was senior to him.

'Thank you, Mr Morgan. I'm perfectly in control of the situation.'

Even in the night, Billy knew Sam's voice instantly. It wasn't just Sam's voice, though, it was his elder half-brother's voice, redolent of all the stature that two more years gave it, quivering with memories of fights in the nursery and the stables, and alive with a mixture of envy and rivalry. There was a timbre in the voice that suggested the time of reckoning had now arrived: the younger boy, recipient of preferential treatment, who bore the name Morgan and had been brought up to inherit the Cork estate now, in the Afghan desert, stood for nothing.

'Your man, Private Battle, has shot dead one of our officers,' Keenan pointed to Rissaldar Singh's corpse, 'during some drunken assault. I've made him a prisoner and the provost have been called. He'll swing for sure.'

Morgan heard the certainty in his half-brother's voice and knew, if what Keenan said was true, that there would be only one outcome. But he wasn't going to accept things as easily as that. 'Who says Battle shot your man?' he blustered.

'*He* did, actually, didn't you, Battle?'

The soldiers had drawn back in the dark, instantly aware of the crackling dislike between the two officers. Even the Scinde Horsemen, who could hardly understand a word, detected the tension.

'Sir,' came back Battle's muted response.

'Whatever happened, he's one of my soldiers, Sam.' Morgan's use of Keenan's Christian name was the first outward sign of any familiarity between the two subalterns. 'I demand that you hand him over for me to deal with.'

'You'll demand nothing of me, Billy Morgan.' All pretence of formality had gone from the brothers' voices. 'When you have a little more experience you'll realise that matters of this

97

severity cannot be a unit responsibility. The provost must be involved for evidence will have to be taken, statements and all sorts of legalistic stuff. I suspect that that's beyond the skill even of *Her Majesty*'s Sixty-sixth,' Keenan sneered, laying bare the usually unspoken animus that existed between Indian and British regiments.

'The officer's right, sir.' Sergeant Kelly was the only one of the group bold enough to intervene between the two subalterns. So Morgan's case collapsed – the tiff, for once, had gone in his half-brother's favour, and even as he stood there he realised how ridiculous it was that a man's murder should be overshadowed by his own emotions. Mercifully, though, the confrontation was cut short.

'You sent for me, sirs?' The staff sergeant in charge of the brigade's provost section – whose name neither officer knew but both recognised – saluted in the dark. A long-service NCO, with a string of ribbons that suggested earlier experience in a fighting regiment, had arrived quietly with two corporals in attendance. 'The jawan here has done his best to explain . . .' Sowar Jan Mahommed who had been sent to get the policemen spoke only basic military English. 'I gather there's been an accident?'

'A murder, actually, Staff Sar'nt.' Keenan spoke for all of them with the reasoned finality he'd employed before.

'Really, sir? If that's the case, I shall need to take statements from any witnesses,' the provost replied.

'Reckon we ought to leave 'em to it, sir. There'll be all sorts of fannying about now. May I suggest that we get a lance jack to stay with Battle while we go back to the company commander and tell 'im what's 'appened? We didn't see nowt, sir, an' there's fuck-all we can do for Battle until 'e comes up on orders.'

Sergeant Kelly, Morgan realised, was talking his normal sense. 'So what will the procedure be now, Sar'nt?' he asked miserably. He was powerless to help one of his own men – *and* he'd been bested by his brother.

'Why, your man will appear before your commanding officer.' Keenan had been listening to the conversation in the dark and answered Morgan's question. 'He'll be powerless to deal with such a serious case, so he'll remand him for Brigade Commander's orders who, on detached service, has summary powers granted to him. Then Battle will swing – there can be no question of that.'

'Well, we'll see if you're right, won't we?' Morgan could think of nothing more convincing to say, so he satisfied himself by addressing the prisoner: 'Don't worry, Battle. I'll send Corporal Travers to keep an eye on things.'

'"Don't worry, Battle"? The first bit of good advice you've had from your officer, I'd say.' Keenan's voice was quite clear to Morgan, Kelly and the escort as they walked back towards their company. 'There's not a damn thing that anyone can do for you now.'

As if I hadn't enough on my plate. On the night march five days ago, just before we reached the Helmand river, a lad from the 66th was stealing rum and got into some damn-fool argument with a rissaldar from Sam's squadron and shot the poor man dead. To make matters a thousand times worse, the soldier came from H Company and was the same big sot of a Sligo boy who'd been involved with the death of that twelve-year-old Ghazi back in April. So, there I was, exhausted after a night with no sleep, holding my very own assize in the middle of the desert with both of my sons in front of me.

I'd remanded Private Battle in order to take advice when we got back to Kandahar and he'd been marched off in manacles by the provost. I could have dealt with him there and then, swung him high, but I'd seen enough summary executions in my time to be heartily sickened by the whole business. Besides, that was a long time ago, in the madness of the Mutiny, and things have changed since then: you can't behave like Captain Bligh any more without some interfering newspaper wallah reporting it – and imagine Primrose's reaction. Besides, I had no desire to have the blood of one of my own men on my hands when there was still Ayoob Khan to settle. Private Edward Battle would have to wait to meet his maker.

But, selfishly, there was something that worried me much more about the whole sorry affair than the fate of a thirsty boy from the bogs. I hadn't realised until then how much my lads disliked each other. Sam was very cool, very bitter about the loss of his native officer, continually emphasising how much service the rissaldar had seen last year before Private Battle – and by extension the whole of the 66th – his brother and I had even arrived in Afghanistan. Billy had nothing useful to say, having reached the scene of the crime well after the fatal shot was fired. But that didn't stop him being full of emotion, pleading Battle's good character to the rafters. (I knew that was rot but I understood my son's loyalty to his man – misguided though it might be.)

The whole damn hearing had descended into sniping between the two of them and, in the process, I came to see both of my sons in a new light. I'd always been closer to Billy – circumstances at home had made that the case – while Sam had chosen to confide more in his mother than in me before he'd gone off to India.

I'd had an inkling of Sam's strength of character when we'd had dinner together shortly after I arrived in Kandahar and speared a panther. But now here he was, poised and in command, very much the sahib and very angry at his comrade's death. I hoped that he wasn't relishing Private Battle's inevitable fate as a way of damaging his brother. Billy, on the other hand, was still a griff, still the cadet who had swallowed the Sandhurst rule book, not knowing that there comes a point when a subordinate has done something so appalling that to be over-loyal to him makes you look ridiculous.

By God, I had more than enough to think about with twenty-odd thousand Heratis bearing down on us and a set of mutinous rogues who were supposed to be our allies. I really didn't need my junior officers playing Cain and Abel.

FIVE

Gereshk

'What d'you suppose they're up to, General? They're not meant to be milling about like that.' We'd started out nine days ago – it seemed more like a year – and now McGucken and I had ridden up to a low plateau on the Kandahar side of the Helmand to watch the movements of the wali's army over on the other bank, just in front of the scrubby little town of Gereshk.

'I don't know, Jock, but I have a very nasty feeling that everything you've been saying for weeks is just about to come true.' Dawn hadn't long broken on the third day after our arrival at the river. I looked at my watch, dropped it back into my pocket and scanned the mixed horse and infantry with my binoculars. 'It's five and twenty past six. They should be formed up and moving towards the fords by now, but there's no damned sign of that.'

'Aye, General, I fear you're right. As I said last night, my informers told me something was afoot for this morning, that the malcontents would refuse to come back across the river to occupy our old camping ground because they want to keep the river between us and them – and I didn't like the sound of that.'

Then McGucken and I heard a distant popping of shots

that came from somewhere within the wali's tented lines. Even as I watched, the distant horsemen stopped in their tracks and turned to look towards the sound.

'Heath, how far d'you suppose the leading elements of the brigade have got? What time did Jacob's Rifles set off this morning?' My brigade major was performing a little better now we had found the measure of one another, but he had no instinctive feel for what I wanted, seldom having the details I needed at his fingertips.

'Well, General, the two cavalry regiments are already there.' That was a prime example of Heath's lack of understanding. I'd decided to move Nuttall's cavalry to a new camping ground a couple of miles upriver: it was more easily defended than the one we had occupied since our arrival opposite Gereshk. Once McGucken had told me that Ayoob Khan's people were at work among the Kandahar troops and that mutiny seemed inevitable, I'd ordered the wali's men to come back to our side of the river on to ground where we could disarm them. And I knew quite well where the cavalry were because Heath and I had watched them march out last night. Heath was testing my patience. 'Both battalions set off at dawn,' he added.

'I know. That wasn't the question.' It would have been too easy to slap Heath down every time he came up with nonsense like that, but I wasn't going to replace the man in the field. If I decided to, I'd wait till we got back to Kandahar after this bit of bother was over. 'Aren't you in semaphore touch with either Jacob's or the Sixty-Sixth?'

'Yes, General, of course I am. I'll just go and check.' Heath spurred his horse up to the signals detachment on the ground above us. He could have had messengers report to him at regular intervals, but I'd seen the men flapping away with their flags for the last twenty minutes.

At least his departure allowed me to talk freely to McGucken. 'So, Jock, what's to be done? You tell me that the wali's men

103

are going to run off to join Ayoob Khan's people, swelling their numbers further and making life even more difficult for us. Is there any part of his lot who might remain true to their salt?'

'I don't know, General, but I suspect we'll find out in the next wee while.' As McGucken was talking, another scatter of shots echoed up from the mob of men that we could see about a mile and a half away. 'I reckon that the wali's boys were about as much use to us as tits on a bull anyway. Ayoob Khan's regulars and any Ghazis who have fallen in with him will just laugh at 'em. The only thing we need to worry about is those bloody guns we gave to the wali.'

'Well, it was your idea to present them in the first place.'

'Aye, General, I know. I can kick my own arse − I don't need you to do it for me. They served a purpose then and now I'm beginning to regret it. Look yonder, sir − d'you see teams of horses moving out from the camp and heading away beyond the old fort?'

I followed McGucken's pointing arm and focused my glasses on the road that led around the base of the squat stone fortress of Gereshk, which I knew had been the headquarters of the wali's forces. The early-morning sun was winking off a column of bright objects that proved to be the brass barrels of the smooth-bore nine-pounders we had given away.

'I do, Jock. Ayoob Khan's got quite enough guns already. He's not going to have those as well.' I was no Wellington, but I wasn't about to let British guns be taken from under our noses. Besides, such an embarrassment would be all that Primrose needed to damn me for ever.

'You're right, General. How are you going to handle it?' I'd had discussions like this with McGucken a hundred times before, from the Alma to the Ganges, but never on such a scale. I knew, though, that he'd have a plan in mind − it was good to have him around.

'Why, if we move Nuttall's cavalry regiments and the Horse

Gunners now, we may be able to cut the buggers off before Ayoob Khan's scouts even know what's happened. The sabres should be able to cross the Helmand easily enough down there.'

I could see where the river lazily coursed and curved, where the summer sun had dried the muddy flats, and the marks of wheels and hoofs where people and horses had found a shallow ford. 'But even in this heat the ground will still be soft and it may take the guns a little longer. We must move them as soon as possible. Heath!' The brigade major was still buggering about with the signallers and I had to shout for him.

'Good enough, General, but may I suggest that we leave a company or two of infantry to form a rearguard here with the baggage but get the remainder of the two battalions to follow the cavalry just in case they get the guns into action?' said McGucken. He and I had found out in more skirmishes and pitched battles than I could count that cavalry and horse guns can move fast, but it was always wise to have infantry to hand, no matter how unwieldy they might seem at times.

'Quite so, quite so.' My right-hand man had returned to where I needed him. 'Heath, signal General Nuttall that I require both the Scinde Horse and the Third Cavalry. Also, warn the commanding officers of Jacob's, the Sixty-Sixth and the Gunners that they are to move across the Helmand as soon as possible. They're to tell me when they're ready.'

'Yes, General.' Heath looked perplexed by even the simplest instructions. 'May I ask what your intentions are?'

McGucken raised his eyebrows, as exasperated by this question as I was, but Heath got the most measured response I could manage. 'We're going to get those guns back, my lad. The brigade will attack!'

'Don't let them get out of hand, Daffadar – damn all that eagerness!' This wasn't the squadron's first time in action or, indeed their first charge, but it was eighteen months since they had seen the enemy so close and Keenan was amazed by their lack of discipline. 'You owls, get back in line.' Keenan did his best to shout something coherent in Pashto above the din of hoofs, but it didn't seem to work. If Singh had been there, thought Keenan, how much easier would the whole thing have been? The death of the rissaldar had robbed the Squadron not just of a good man, but also one of the few native officers who understood English perfectly – well enough to translate it instantly into phrases that were coherent to the men.

No sooner had they dismounted after morning stand-to than the order had reached the two cavalry regiments to cross the Helmand fords and get after the four six-pound guns and the two howitzers that were being carried away. Keenan and his NCOs had the troop fast back in the saddle and following the lead squadron over difficult ground that was broken by ditches and criss-crossed by canals. The horsemen had coped well with both the country and the ford, but E Battery had been slow to follow. So it was that the 3rd Scinde Horse led the way, unescorted and unsupported, cracking on as fast as they could, skirting the old fort, following the dust cloud that the scurrying guns left in their wake.

'Hark, sahib.' Miran cocked his ear to the bugle call. 'Form line by squadrons.' The dust thrown up by the jingling horsemen was so dense that the officers and NCOs had to rely entirely upon the commanding officer's bugle signals.

'Aye, Daffadar, we must have caught up with those guns. The colonel's obviously going to attack. Tell the men to be ready to face artillery, if you please.' Keenan knew that his Pashto wasn't fluent or fast enough yet to get such messages across to the men, so he had to rely upon Miran. As his troop emerged from the dust cloud, the daffadar was telling the men what to expect.

No sooner had the couple of hundred horsemen swung into

two thin lines, mounts snorting, men pulling the scarves away from their faces, than Keenan could see their foes – men who until just a few hours before they would have counted as friends. 'There, lads. We've caught the traitorous bastards and they've unlimbered to make a fight of it.' The troop caught the urgency in his voice and tensed.

The old-fashioned gun-metal barrels of all six pieces stared blackly, unwinkingly, at them, the gun crew easily visible six hundred paces to the front, more men ready with extra ammunition, the bombardiers crouched, squinting over the sights, firing lanyards tight, ready for the order to fire.

Colonel Malcolmson hadn't hesitated. No sooner had the lines formed than the bugles had urged the regiment into the trot, officers' swords pointing, and as the pace increased, down had come the lances, red and white pennons streaming back against the bamboo poles, bearded faces set and keen – perhaps a little too keen. But all the training, all the discipline that Keenan and the NCOs thought they'd instilled, even the experience of charging an enemy last year, seemed to count for nothing. Whooping and yelling, his troop broke from a canter to a gallop without orders. The once graceful line became a piece of knotted string, his own men fast overtaking him, forcing him to wave them back with his sword, yelling in the dust until he was hoarse.

'Mother of God!' Keenan felt a great sough of wind and was swiped by a vast invisible hand from a gun-shot that was uncomfortably close and caused Kala to swerve. The battery was suddenly screened by billowing white smoke. 'Get back here, damn you!' Stunned as he was, Keenan knew that the lancers must hit their enemies in one solid line. If they charged piecemeal and enemy cavalry or a line of riflemen were waiting for them, all would be lost.

Keenan could see Daffadar Sayed Miran spurring his horse forward with his lance out at a right angle to his mount rather than pointing at the enemy. He was attempting to use the

107

pole to check the troopers who were surging forward, yelling as hard as Keenan, but with no more effect.

'Don't bunch, men!' Keenan had no idea of the native word for 'bunch'. 'Spread out – keep your spacing!' But the ground was against them, a dry, shallow nullah serving to channel the flying manes and thrashing hoofs into a narrow wedge of men and animals – a prime target for artillery at close range.

'Get away, B Squadron, go on, get back to your left,' Keenan bellowed, at a knot of horsemen who'd allowed a great gap to appear in the charging line on his flank. Now they were crowding into his own troop's thundering scrum, barging other horses, clashing knees, squashing the men even closer together.

'This will not work, Keenan sahib,' Miran shouted, from his right, in his stilted English. 'If these scum have any horse waiting beyond the guns, it will be impossible to resist them.'

Miran had echoed his own thoughts precisely, but the next few minutes were to present a much more immediate problem.

The guns fired again. Where the first volley of solid shot had flown just a little too high, the gunners pitched the next shock of iron just as their British instructors had taught them. The rounds hit the ground two hundred paces in front of the muzzles, scarring the earth, skipping low and fast, grazing the dirt and broadcasting blinding, stinging grit, frightening mounts and men. Keenan was tensed for this. He brought his head low between his shoulders, instinctively half closing his eyes – as if that would have the slightest effect against the bounding metal. Even while he shrank from the shot, by a miracle not one round touched a single man or horse. The balls passed invisibly, yet horribly close, but while no one was struck, the screaming iron, the flying earth, the gouting smoke and darting flame spread sudden panic.

'No, no, get on, don't stop.' Where Keenan had tried to check the men just seconds before, now he found himself urging them on. Reins were pulled tight, snaffles biting hard at the horses' mouths, forcing some animals to sit back on their haunches others to rear up, so urgent was the need to stop. 'Don't bunch – for God's sake, get forward!' But Keenan's shouts and those of the NCOs were fruitless.

'Get back, you pig whores!' Miran abused his men in their own language, but his words had no more effect than English had.

Keenan was out in front of the swaying lances and suddenly found himself alone in a fog of dust. As he looked back he could see his men turning away from the enemy, pelting towards the scrubby dip where their advance had formed up, huddled low over their saddle bows, lances awry and faces beset with fear.

'Come, sahib, we cannot charge alone and the jawans are not listening.' Miran was beckoning to Keenan with a gauntleted hand, his own lance now back in its bucket, the leather sling looped around his elbow. 'Turn back now, Keenan sahib – those gunners are slow but even they cannot miss you at this range.'

The young officer looked at the guns, which were now so close. The crews were hurrying rounds forward, sponges and staves pushing at the muzzles, hairy-capped creatures whom he took to be non-commissioned officers yelling frenziedly. As he turned towards the backs of his fast-retreating men, he felt all the courage drain from him. Now his own back crawled with fear, as he expected one of the hurling metal balls to strike him squarely in the spine. His spurs dug deep, as those of his troops had done, Miran beside him, pulling at the loose end of his turban and trying to cover his mouth against the cloud of dust.

'Our guns, Keenan sahib, can you hear?' Miran gave up his attempt to mask his mouth, his face lighting with relief at a distant crash. 'There, sahib, on the ridge yonder.' As they galloped together, Miran pointed away to the flank where Keenan could see gouts of white gunsmoke. 'And see there, those whoresons in the 3rd Light will laugh at us for the rest of their miserable, low-caste lives.'

And Miran was right. No sooner had Keenan understood that the Horse Gunners had arrived and were making their presence felt than he saw the other cavalry regiment lining the lip of the depression where the ill-starred charge had started. His own men were between him and the 3rd Light Cavalry, but he could see the troopers of the supporting regiment standing in their saddles to hoot with derision at the Scinde Horse. Some men of the 3rd rubbed their hands coarsely on their groins, others cupped imaginary breasts; all shouted their disdain.

Then, to Keenan's shocked delight, the scorn of the other regiment worked. His men reined in hard, paused, seemed to shake themselves from the grip of panic, their horses now still, almost as bemused as their riders.

'Come, thou dogs!' Miran cursed his men fluently in their own tongue. 'Don't shame the colonel sahib in front of that bird shit.' The bugles almost drowned the daffadar with their brassy 'rally' followed by 'form line', but the laughter and cat-calling of the 3rd Light Cavalry could still be heard.

'Now, men, dress the line.' Keenan could hardly speak, so hoarse had his earlier shouting made him, but he did his best to yell. 'There are our guns!' He was pointing towards the battery and its ant-like gunners. 'And you, Sowar Thakur Nehala!' The young soldier looked up at the sound of his name. 'Get a grip of that bloody lance – it's not a knitting needle!' It was unlikely that any word of the croaked English was understood yet the trooper grasped the angry sahib's meaning well enough, pulling the long spear upright into a much more martial position.

'Walk march.' Keenan echoed the bugle's call as the regiment turned to advance again over the same ground. But this time there was no hesitation. With the yells of the 3rd Light Cavalry still stinging, Keenan saw his troop settle into its

110

stride, watched the lances come down parallel with the ground as the order blared, while each man checked his comrades left and right to make sure that there was no repeat of the earlier indiscipline.

'Charge!' The bugle sounded again, and every horse surged forward to the touch of the spurs while the officers and NCOs echoed the colonel's order.

Shouting with the others, Keenan sighted down the blade of his own sword. Above the arc of steel he saw the enemy gunners crouched over their pieces, the battery commander just visible to the rear, waiting for the galloping lines of the Scinde Horse to present the best target. Then, even as he watched and tensed for the next hail of spinning metal, he saw one gun crew thrown about like rag dolls amid a vast spray of sand and grit. A sponge stave cartwheeled through the air as the Horse Gunners found the enemy's range.

Then they were on them. Keenan thought back to the tack-room at home in Ireland and of Finn the groom's stories of Aliwal – how he'd lanced the Sikhs and made off with their guns. The stories had thrilled both Billy and himself and the pair of boys had practised endlessly on their ponies for such a day as this. Now that day was here and as Keenan's horse leapt the carriage of one six-pounder, he saw a single gunner sheltering below its axle. Leaning low, he pricked the man with the point of his sword, just two inches of steel in his shoulder that made the gunner yelp and stand, clutching his wound. As he swept past, Keenan glanced over his shoulder to see his target stagger slightly, then pitch violently forward as the point of a lance, then a length of bloodstained pennon emerged from just below his sternum. But there was no time to see whether the sowar in the front rank had speared his man skilfully enough to pull the long pole from the corpse without unseating himself, for the next mutineer stood before him.

The Afghan shifted his weight from foot to foot as Keenan

bore down upon him. The man's long cotton jacket was belted with a bandoleer and he carried one of the old muzzle-loading Enfields that he brought half-heartedly into the aim at the officer and his horse, who were no more than three yards away. Keenan could see indecision in the man's eyes: he hoped that the weapon was not loaded with lead pellets that would give his enemy a much better chance of a hit. But, in the event, it didn't matter, for fear won and Keenan watched the Afghan turn and flee at the last second, presenting an easy target.

Keenan remembered how he'd fouled his first thrust at a live target almost a year and a half ago, so he touched his mare with his left spur just enough to make some more room, brought his right arm back until it stuck out straight behind him, with his wrist cocked forward pointing at the target, never taking his eyes off the point where he wanted the steel to strike. The horse moved left and slowed as he let the bit go slack. Then, at what he judged to be just the right distance, he pistoned his arm forward, leaning all his weight behind the blow, catching the running man between the spine and the right shoulder-blade, sinking six inches of gleaming metal – no more – into the yielding flesh. In a fraction of a second, Keenan saw the dirty cotton smock pucker, the back arch in shock and the man drop almost instantly to the ground, sliding off his now bloody blade.

'Them bastard Scindis made a balls of things, din't they, sir?' Sergeant Kelly lay next to his officer on the sun-dried bank, the pair of them hastily retying their puttees. 'Aye, I thought we was going to lose the guns for a while, sir, din't you?' The Scinde Horse had become H Company's *bête noire* after the affair with Private Battle, while Kelly could only guess at the friction between Morgan and Lieutenant Keenan.

The infantrymen had watched the cavalry's muddle, Billy Morgan hoping to pick out his brother with his binoculars in the mêlée of dust, men and horses. He thought he'd seen a slender, well-mounted figure waving a flashing sword from time to time, but he couldn't be sure. What he did know was that the Scinde Horse – the experienced, battle-hardened, patronising Scinde Horse – had performed badly, much to his delight, and it was only the arrival of the guns of E Battery that had prevented the whole situation turning into an utter mess. That it had been a cock-up would have upset Sam, thought Billy, but that it was in full view of other units, including the 66th, must have really hurt.

As the foot soldiers had been rushed forward, Morgan and his men had had to cross innumerable dikes and ditches that left their boots soaked. This was the first opportunity they had had to wring the moisture out of their socks and to discuss the events of the day so far.

'We'll be needing every last gun and round if our cavalry perform like that again.' Morgan continued to relish his brother's embarrassment, neglecting to mention the eventual recovery of the wali's battery. With his sergeant beside him, Morgan had watched the Horse Gunners' shells bursting over the heads of the wali's traitorous troops, seen the enemy falter and then scurry into the solid cover of a series of buildings that lay in the bottom of a bush-speckled valley. It was obvious to him that the 66th would now be called upon to clear the muddle of huts, shanties and low houses that were set about with mud walls both high and low. He also realised that while Captain Quarry's G Company was due to lead, H Company would soon be called upon to pass through them into the depth of the village.

The rest of the men were still struggling with socks, puttees and boots that were either stiff or slick with mud, and Morgan took the chance to study Kelly who was now ready for action before any of the other men. Not too tall and lithely built, he was wise enough to the ways of the Army to predict almost every move although he'd never been under fire before. As the

113

guns had driven the enemy away from their original position, it had been Kelly who had started to get the men ready to move, checking belts and water-bottles, untying the waxed-paper bundles of Martini-Henry rounds in their pouches, which would soon be needed.

'Oh, and Sar'nt Kelly, we need to make sure that Robbins can keep up better in future. He was finding the pace in and out of those bloody ditches too much for him. What's wrong with the man?' Morgan hardly knew Private Robbins, a slightly tubby twenty-four-year-old from Reading, quiet and unremarkable. But as the rest of the lads in the company had splashed and leapt athletically over the muddy, water-lined irrigation channels, Robbins had puffed and coughed his way forward, his equipment awry and apparently too heavy for him.

''E's just fat and wheezy, sir. Too much boozing is his trouble. Spends every penny on the grog, he does, easily led astray by Battle − the pair on 'em was always in trouble in Karachi. I'll get him out with the gym-wallahs when we get back to Kandahar . . .'

But Robbins's forthcoming torture at the hands of the battalion's master-at-arms could be discussed no further, for with much shouting and the shriek of a whistle, half of G Company rose from the ground where they had been lying a little way in front of Morgan and his men, pulled at their belts, settled their equipment and trotted forward.

As the khaki figures moved off, so puffs of white smoke suddenly erupted from the windows and flat roofs of half a dozen mud and wood-built houses. Dazzlingly white in the morning sun, the beehive-like domes of each dwelling drew the eye, but it was the level platforms round about them that were obviously lined with riflemen. Bullets kicked up the dirt among Quarry's men and whined over Morgan's head, causing him to duck.

''S all right, sir, they ain't aimed at us.' Kelly smiled at his officer, just as unaccustomed to the noise but better able to mask his natural reaction. 'Half of G Company will return fire now while the others try to get round the enemy's flank, but I reckon they'll need us to follow up once they get drawn into the village.'

'I'm sure you're right, Sar'nt Kelly. Get the men to load, please.' Morgan tried to respond as decisively as possible.

'No, sir, not yet,' Kelly replied quietly. 'Let the company commander order that, sir. It's like a ritual for 'im to give that order, sir – sort of marks the start of the action.'

Indeed, no sooner had Kelly spoken than the order 'With ball cartridge, load' was passed down the lines of sheltering men. Each man pulled the lever under the wrist of his Mark II Martini-Henry rifle down and slid one of the .45-calibre rounds into the breech.

'Check the cartridge case, lads.' At Kelly's command, they all glanced down at the delicate wound-copper tube topped with a soft lead slug. 'Make sure it's not dented. We'll be rapid firing in a moment an' we don't want any hard extractions.' The men were well trained and knew how difficult a damaged empty case could be to eject from the breech. The savage steel extractor pawls could rip the base of a cartridge away from its body, leaving the rest of the copper sleeve stuck in the chamber, which made the rifle and fixed bayonet about as useful as a clumsy spear.

'Set yer sights for two hundred and remember to aim low. Once we get into them buildings, targets will be close in and on rooftops above you, so don't snatch yer shots.' Kelly's lecture continued, designed to take the soldiers' minds off their first proper fight. 'And watch the body of troops in front of you – be prepared to pass signals rapidly and clearly.'

Morgan realised that Kelly had fallen into the familiar language of the field manual, using the words as a balm with which to calm the men.

'Right, lads, prepare to move.' Morgan saw Captain Beresford-Peirse, the company commander, and James, his colour sergeant, rise from the ground in front of them, the leading half of the company jumping up around them. 'Wait for the signal.' As the column of khaki figures loped off behind their non-commissioned officers, he licked his lips and listened to the popping of the enemy's muskets and the crashing replies of G Company's rifles.

'The captain's going to take his lot down that line of palms there, sir' – Kelly pointed to a scrubby scatter of trees and bushes that snaked around to the right of the hamlet – 'then use the cover of them walls. I guess we're going right flanking. Yes . . . there's the link-man's signal. Let's be off, sir.' They had both been watching for the lance corporal at the rear of the leading column whose duty it was to pass orders.

'On your feet, men, follow me and watch the roofs and windows.' Morgan sprang up, debating whether to draw his sword or pull his revolver from his belt. Another clatter of shots from the rooftops decided him: he reached under the broad leather flap of his holster and thumbed the hammer back on his Enfield revolver.

'Sir, Captain B-P wants you, sir.'

Morgan had just scrambled forward into the cover of a low wall with his men when a runner arrived from Company Headquarters. So, here it was, the order that he had known must come, the order that would, he had no doubt, put in train a series of events that would test him as he had never been tested before. He pushed his holster back on his belt, set his helmet firmly on his head and gripped his sword as he might have done his cricket bat when setting out to save the match for the first eleven at school.

Following the lad, he was taken past the leading troops in the company, some of whom were returning fire over a decaying wooden fence, to where the captain was directing operations.

'Ah, Morgan,' Beresford-Peirse, a Sandhurst man like himself, had been with the regiment for all of his eight years'

116

service in India. Morgan liked him, admired his horsemanship, his skill with a ball and his humour, and he had expected him to be just as he found him, remarkably collected, despite the gunfire. The captain pointed out the battlefield to him. 'Look yonder – no, you don't need your glasses, just use your eyes.' The two officers were peering through a break in a packed mud wall. 'Quarry has tried to take that orchard affair over there, but he moved before we were in position to give him covering fire and he lost a couple of men.'

Morgan thought he could see a khaki bundle lying in the rough grass about seventy yards in front of his position.

'Now, we'll keep their heads down from here, but I want you to come in from the right, clear those johnnies out of the garden and then return the favour by suppressing those few houses there in the centre of this slum.'

Morgan could see that Beresford-Peirse intended to tackle the hardest part of the position himself, but that he would need to be quick about his part of the plan if ammunition was not to run low.

'Our guns should start to fire on the far edge of the village shortly. Get your bugler to blow a series of Gs when you're ready, then move when my man replies. Any questions?'

'No, sir, that's all quite clear,' Morgan replied, trying to sound as confident as his senior while his belly tightened into a knot of fear mixed with anticipation. Then, out of nowhere, he suddenly had a vision of his brother in the same situation. He felt sure that Sam would have no qualms, no concerns about the responsibility or even about the possibility of hurt or death that lay in front of him and his men. But that thought was enough to push any further doubts from his mind: his brother must not have the satisfaction of knowing that he was scared before this, his first real taste of war.

'Right, off you go, then. Good luck.' Beresford-Peirse reached out and squeezed his hand.

The sprint back to his half of the company, with his escort,

117

Private Thorne, thundering along behind him, attracted a few wild shots from the village that flew high and wide. Morgan tried to keep calm, but by the time he reached Sergeant Kelly and the rest of the men, he was blown, soaked and muddy from the ditches he'd had to cross, and drenched in sweat.

''Ere you are, sir.' Kelly passed him a water-bottle as he threw himself down beside him below the wall. 'I've got the NCOs together for your orders, sir. Are we going first, or is Captain B-P?'

Morgan looked at a half-circle of eager but tense faces, pouches full and rifles at the ready. It took him no time to tell them what he wanted and he concluded, 'We move when Captain B-P's bugler replies with a couple of Gs. Any questions?' He had tried to sound as confident as his company commander had, yet he knew he hadn't: he still couldn't rid himself of the idea that Sam was watching him. But there were no questions from the corporals and they ducked away under the cover of the mud bricks to pass on his instructions to the men.

'Right, Wynne, blow two Gs, please.' As the notes sounded, Morgan noticed Kelly's little terrier sitting in the ditch, studying his master.

'And how's Bobby got here, Sar'nt Kelly?' Morgan asked, more in curiosity than reproof.

'Sorry, sir, 'e just follows, 'e does. Shall I . . .'

'No, Sar'nt Kelly, I'm impressed with his faithfulness. Just don't let him get under people's feet, please.'

Then there was no more debate about the dog's future, for the company commander's bugle returned the signal and Morgan leapt forward, pistol outstretched, legs weak with the fear of failure.

'Come on, lads – stay with me.' Morgan led the column of about forty men crouching under the cover of the low wall while the company commander's party banged away at the enemy, whose clouds of muzzle smoke were now obvious from both the village and the garden that Morgan had to clear. The men stumbled after him, ducking in and out of cover, splashing through ditches full of stagnant water, pouches bouncing and helmets falling over their eyes.

'Keep going, Morgan.' The column filed past Beresford-Peirse's firing line, every man breathing hard and swiping at the flies that crowded round their sweaty faces. 'Get another hundred paces down to my right, shake out and assault only when you hear my covering fire. Give me the normal signal to show you're ready.'

Morgan didn't need to reply. He nodded as he led the trotting line past the rear of the captain's men.

Eventually he reached the crumbling wall that his company commander had indicated and showed the men where to form line left and right of him. 'Last man, Sar'nt Kelly?' The NCO harried the rear of the column, nodding energetically as he scrambled past his subaltern. 'Tell me when the right-hand man is in place, then back here as fast as you can.' Again, Kelly nodded as he pushed Lance Corporal Wyeth − who would be the right marker − along through the bush and low scrub. It took no more than sixty seconds for Kelly to place the last man, but Morgan looked on anxiously, acutely aware that every second wasted meant less covering fire for his assault.

'Right, sir. All ready.' Kelly was pounding back along the path beaten by the troops in the brush.

Morgan glanced at his men to left and right: all of them lay staring at him, chests still heaving with the exertion of the last few moments.

'Fix bayonets,' Morgan gave the order that he'd only ever given on the drill yard or on Kandahar patrols. The long steel needles sang from their scabbards, the locking rings clicked home, and Morgan craned left to wave at Captain Beresford-Peirse who, a hundred paces away, was looking impatiently for the signal.

With a crash and a great billow of white smoke, forty rifles volleyed to their left.

'Up, lads – on your feet, come on!' Morgan jumped up, stumbled over the remains of the brickwork by which he had been covered and forced his way through thorns and twigs into the open. Seventy yards in front of him there was an overgrown wall that puffed and spat as rounds from the other half of the company sang off it.

'Get on, Shiny H!' Kelly bawled the company's nickname. 'Get up with Mister Morgan, lads.' On both sides of the officer and his NCO, men pushed their way into the open, straightening helmets that twigs had knocked awry, a growing line of glittering bayonets thrust towards the invisible enemy.

'Advance – Drummer Wynne, sound the "advance"!' Morgan said to the boy just over his shoulder, then noticed a soldier red in the face and gasping for breath just beyond him. 'Robbins, this really isn't good for your health, you—' But before his sarcasm could take effect, thunder sounded along the wall in front of them and Private Robbins was thrown, like a doll, on to his back, yelping with shock as the ball hit him, tearing an instantly bloody hole in his thigh.

'Is anyone else hurt, Sar'nt Kelly?' Morgan found himself immediately on his belly with the rest of his men, right in the open, sixty yards from their objective.

'Fuck knows, sir. Fire, you cunts! Come on, get some fucking fire back at 'em.' Kelly set an example by half rising and squeezing off the first shot to be returned, a few of the men doing the same, but most just clinging to the earth while bullets whistled and sang around them. 'We can't stay 'ere, sir, we'll be shot to fuck, sir.'

Morgan knew that Kelly was right and that the only thing they could do was to sprint forward and hope to overwhelm the enemy. But his body wouldn't obey.

'Come on, sir, we can't just grovel 'ere.' Kelly's face was

120

contorted with frustration as grit was flung over them by another near miss.

But Morgan hesitated, hoping for Beresford-Peirse's fire to quell the Afghans – anything to make his foes melt away.

Instead, another volley came from the wall, a shriek from Private Ball, then Kelly's yell, 'Fuckin' 'ell, sir, look there – the mad bastards!' as he rose to the kneeling position and fired straight ahead.

Morgan was amazed to see a great scrum of scruffy Afghans bundling out of a gap in the wall, or slithering over the top of it, brandishing an assortment of firearms and swords, some in the dark green *kurta*s of the wali's army, others in dirty robes and turbans all bellowing, '*Din-din!*' or '*Allah-il-Allah,*' as loudly as they could. Some paused and fired, but a knot of at least fifty came straight at Morgan's men in a wild charge.

Then all hesitation left Morgan. With sneaking pleasure he thought of his brother's disgrace that morning, and then of his father's stories about tight corners like this. 'Get up – get up and follow me.' He stood as the bullets whined about while his men stolidly ignored him. 'Come on – before they're on us.' One or two knelt up to fire, but most still clung to the ground. Morgan did the only thing he could, he ran as fast towards the rolling tide of the enemy as his rubbery legs would let him.

'Follow the officer, you fuckers!' Morgan half turned as he ran to see Kelly kicking and dragging at the men. 'Get going – come on, McLaren, Olbey, don't let Mister Morgan have it all to himself.'

As the enemy dashed and yelled towards him, their faces came into sharp relief. All were lean young men and most wore beards, some extravagant, some sparse. Their skins were tanned and leathery and they were shouting, producing a terrifying cacophony. They came closer, and on pumped Morgan's legs. He was driven more by a desire to get his men to follow rather than any particular wish to close with the hedge of swords, knives and other assorted steel that was being brandished.

At five yards' range, Morgan paused, thumbed the hammer back on his pistol and took deliberate aim at a tall Afghan in baggy robes. The man saw what was coming and raised his painted shield, the size of a large plate to protect himself. But as the pistol jerked in Morgan's hand, he saw a bright scab appear in the metal. Then the face of his enemy appeared over the rim, twisted in pain as he slumped to the dust.

'Good 'it, sir.' Kelly was running hard to catch up. 'Fire at the bastards, lads, come on – even you can't miss at this range!'

Morgan glimpsed one or two men firing, a handful of the enemy falling to the ground, and then the sea of Afghans met the khaki, sand and steel.

'Din-din' – the shouts almost deafened Morgan as he punched the muzzle of his revolver into the chest of a man who had betrayed the wali. The soldier had a long Khyber knife in his hand, but he was too slow: the officer ducked below its sweeping arc, well inside his opponent's guard, and pulled the trigger. The detonation cut off his enemy's initial grunt of pain. As the man fell towards him, Morgan looked at a gory, splintered rib that stuck out of the bullet's exit wound and, to his surprise, realised that the man behind, a smaller, emaciated tribesman, was hopping around in agony where the same round had struck him and deeply gouged his cheek.

'There you are, sir!' While Morgan gazed at both of the men he'd shot, another assailant had come at him unseen in the press of bodies. 'Get off, you stinking twat!' Kelly had jabbed his bayonet into the soldier's chest just as he was about to bring a rusty short sword down across Morgan's neck.

'They bloody smell rotten, sir, don't they?' Kelly was almost matter-of-fact as he battered at the next Afghan's face with the iron-shod butt of his Martini-Henry.

'Thank you, Sar'nt Kelly – they do,' Morgan replied breath-lessly – and they did. In Kandahar market he had been overwhelmed by the greasy, unwashed stench of the crowds. Now it filled his nostrils, almost distracting him from counting the number of rounds he had left in his revolver's chamber. 'Three,' he yelled, as his third singed a beard before tearing a bloody hole in a soldier's jaw. 'Four.' His next round missed, despite the density of the pushing, fighting men.

'Get out the way, sir!' Private Millard's rifle boomed pain-fully close to Morgan's ear as the ball tore into the throat of the man he had just missed. 'An' fuckin' stay down, you sod.' Millard poked the falling body with his bayonet for good measure,

'Thank you, Millard . . . five.' Morgan fired another round from his pistol, catching an Afghan in the shoulder. The man dropped his weapon, clutched at his wound, turned and ran. Suddenly a trickle of others were turning away from the fight.

'Get at 'em, lads – they're running!' Morgan, now hoarse with shouting, fired his last round. It slammed a young mutineer hard against the garden wall, while all around him his own men shouted and hooted at the scattering Afghans.

'Cease fire.' Now most of his men had lined the edge of the wall from which the Afghan attack had begun and were firing hard at their sprinting foes. While some shots were telling, most were missing and Morgan, with his own empty pistol, was aware of how low the ammunition in his men's pouches must be.

One more round cracked out at the fleeing enemy.

'Cease fire, Stacey – you fuckin' deaf? Din't you 'ear what the officer said?' Kelly snarled at a young soldier whose shot had been good – Morgan saw another Afghan spin and fall more than a hundred yards away.

'Check ammunition, please, Sar'nt Kelly.' The battlefield was suddenly quiet. The rest of the company had stopped firing as they moved up to join Morgan's men before the next stage of the assault. The Afghan rifles had fallen silent, too – in preparation, Morgan guessed, to resist it.

'Not a bad bit of work, that, sir.' Kelly paused to glance at the enemy dead as he chased and fussed among his own men. There seemed to be no wounded – at least, none that Morgan could see. A few Afghans lay scattered in the longer grass where their charge had been broken, but he counted sixteen lying haphazardly at the base of the wall. The soft .45 lead rounds had done terrible damage, ripping and slashing flesh, poking holes right through bodies whose robes were now wet with blood. Morgan saw two or three whose faces had been smashed with butts and others, quite dead, whose injuries were less obvious. Gore leaked more discreetly from their death wounds, but the soldiers who stood about wiping their bayonets clean with rags torn from the clothes of the dead, accounted for that.

Then he found a man he had killed. It was the heavily bearded one he had shot in the face at point-blank range; he was lying on his back, eyes glassily open, flies buzzing about the thin trickle of blood that came from his nostrils. A neat, red hole had been punched in his cheek, but it was only when Morgan turned him over with his boot that he saw the stark, oozing hole at the top of his skull. He broke open his pistol and loaded six more brass cartridges into the chamber. 'Aye, Sar'nt Kelly, not a bad bit of work at all,' Billy Morgan noted, as he closed the action of his pistol with a satisfying click.

Where some of the distant bodies lay, the young officer could just make out the stump of Bobby's tail wagging hard. The terrier was greedily licking blood from a corpse's cooling face.

'So, Mister Morgan, my lad, how went the day?' Captain Beresford-Peirse was sitting in the shade of a domed brick and mud-built house in the centre of the village while the colour sergeant and the other NCOs reorganised the company around him. He was just as mud-spattered and sweat-stained as Billy Morgan, but still full of energy.

'Fine, thank you, Beresford-Peirse,' Morgan replied, waiting to see if there was some catch in the question. 'Well, fine for everyone except Privates Ball and Robbins. By the time I got back to the place they were struck, the bandsmen had taken them away, but I didn't like what I saw in either case. Both men were hit in the thigh and there was a great deal of blood.'

Beresford-Peirse eyed his subaltern a little quizzically. He was talking about the men slightly too nonchalantly, not expressing the concern he would have expected from someone whose first taste of action this had been. He, Beresford-Peirse, had known both soldiers for two years now and valued them – it worried him that Morgan hadn't immediately sought his leave to go and find out about the lads. He would have refused it, of course, for they were still far too close to the enemy for it to be allowed.

'You'll visit them as soon as you can, won't you, Morgan, and you'll write to their mothers – or are they married?'

Here was the barbed question, but Morgan missed it. 'Oh, I don't know. Yes, I'll get to them as soon as I can.' But this was the wrong answer and he compounded it when he continued, 'Did you see how the Scinde Horse made such fools of themselves this morning? Why, you'd think–'

'No, Morgan, that's not good enough.'

He was suddenly aware that all the normal lightness had disappeared from the captain's voice: now there was nothing but ice. 'I don't give a fig for the Scinde Horse's shortcomings, but I do care about five four five Private Thomas Ball, of Reading, who has a widowed mother and a seventeen-year-old wife back in England, and six zero three Private William Robbins, unmarried, a Newbury man. Why don't you know that, Morgan?'

'I . . . er, I don't know, Beresford-Peirse.' Morgan had come to give his account of what he thought was a pretty little action, still flushed with excitement and with his palm aching from the kick of his pistol.

'Well, you bloody well ought to know. You've been here long enough now to have absorbed such details.' But then his tone softened: 'Look, Morgan, you did well today but don't be so impulsive. If you'd used the ground a little better you might have got away without any casualties at all, and I know that doesn't sound important at the moment − what's two men, after all? − but it is. Every single soldier is vital to us out here, not just because he's another pair of hands but because the men will judge us on the way we look after them. Show them you care − remember that they have young wives or widowed mothers − and that you won't risk them need-lessly. Then they will do anything, literally anything, that you ask. But neglect them or squander their courage and they'll turn sour. They may come to us as guttersnipes, but they're precious, and privates like Ball may one day turn into heroes like your Sergeant Kelly − as long as you don't get 'em shot.'

'Yes, thank you, Beresford-Peirse. I can quite see your point.' Morgan felt utterly deflated. Things had gone so well, he thought. There was a pile of Afghan dead and the village was theirs. Did B-P really need to take on so about Robbins and Ball?

'Oh, and while I'm about it, here's another knock.' Morgan braced himself. 'Don't be so keen to criticise other regiments in front of the men, particularly not native ones. We have enough trouble getting our fellows to treat them with respect, and I can assure you of two things. First, we'll be glad of the Scinde Horse one day and, second, when we make a cock of things − which we surely will − I'd prefer not to have other regiments evening the score. So, please, don't be quite so Sandhurst about such things.'

That last jibe hurt. Billy Morgan had stopped thinking of himself as a callow creature straight out of his apprenticeship

126

after the incident with the child in Kandahar. But then, he supposed, that was exactly what Beresford-Peirse was trying to achieve. He nodded glumly.

'Besides, you've a half-brother, Keenan, in the Scindis, ain't you?' continued Beresford-Peirse. 'I've met him – he's a grand fellow. I'd have thought you'd be quite cast down by his regiment's misfortunes today, not crowing with delight.'

SIX

Eve of Battle

Very few of my brigade had seen any fighting before so I'd allowed everyone a day to collect themselves afterwards. My great temptation had been to get all the commanding officers together at once, to tear a strip off those who needed it, then to buck them up before we cracked on as fast as we could. But suddenly I remembered the first time I had been in battle. I knew that each colonel would want to pause, however briefly, to speak to his men, to help them absorb the shock of death and injury, and to adjust to the fact that much more of the same lay ahead. I let things rest for as long as I dared.

The trouble was that ammunition and provisions were low and here, beside the Helmand, we were too far away from Primrose's forces to get any help if we needed it. On top of that, it was clear that Ayoob Khan and his people would push on fast now that they had been reinforced by the wali's rascals. I wanted to get ahead and intercept him west of Kandahar so there was no more time to spare – I needed to call together my commanding officers to give out orders, timings and all the dozens of little details that would get the brigade moving. But before that I wanted to speak to Jacobs' colonel alone.

'Well, Mainwaring, be so kind as to explain yourself.'

'General, all I can say is that it was the first fight that any of my jawans had been in and — as you know better than I, sir — it takes a bit of time for any soldier to learn what he should and should not do when the enemy's close.' Mainwaring had obviously been dreading this confrontation.

'Close? Do you call that close?' We were about twenty yards away from the handful of mud buildings where I'd set up my headquarters once we'd driven the enemy out of Gereshk. The other colonels were drifting in, so I kept my voice deliberately low to avoid embarrassing the man. 'Why, the Afghans were bloody miles away when your fellows started loosing off at them — I saw it with my own eyes. There was no fire discipline at all, no controlled volleys. Every man seemed to be suiting himself as to when he fired.'

'Yes, General. I know it wasn't good but—'

'"Wasn't good," you say. It was appalling. Your men were just turning expensive shot into hot smoke and firing so wide that I doubt you caused the mutineers to cack themselves, let alone punched any holes in 'em.' I was suddenly conscious of how much I must have sounded like that prig Primrose. I must not humiliate or alienate the man for I would need every pair of hands that we could muster — even inexpert ones — now that the wali's troops had decamped *en masse*.

'As soon as you give me a moment, General, I'll get some more skill-at-arms training in. At least the men know what *not* to do now,' answered Mainwaring. I could see that I was making him squirm, and he kept darting looks at the steadily swelling group of other officers hoping, no doubt, that none would realise he was getting a wigging.

'Aye, well, do that, Mainwaring. You've got a good set of lads there who'll be all the better for having smelt gunsmoke, though I can't promise you any slack time until we've knocked Ayoob Khan on the head.' When I thought about it — despite the good impression Jacob's Rifles had made on me in Kandahar when I'd first arrived, I'd found them pretty indifferent in the field — but he needed encouragement after

129

yesterday's shenanigans. 'That's enough. Let's go and join the others, shall we?'

Mainwaring was clearly relieved that the interview was over, and I could see he was doing his best to look relaxed as we joined the other commanding officers. Although a couple of units had acted like a bunch of schoolgirls, it hadn't been too bad a day. Currie's 3rd Light Cavalry and Anderson's Grenadiers hadn't been required to do much, but had been steady enough, and I couldn't have asked more of the guns and Galbraith's 66th, but Jacob's Rifles – well, they'd need plenty more time and a firm hand.

It was Malcolmson's Scinde Horse that puzzled me, though. By far the most experienced unit in the brigade, they'd made a real mess of their first attempt to get the smooth-bore guns back, only saving the day by a quick rally and a second charge. But Malcolmson, no matter how tricky his troops' behaviour had been yesterday, still had a supercilious old campaigner's air about him that was deeply annoying. If he hadn't been Sam's commander, I'd have brought him down a peg or two.

'Right, gentlemen, relax, please.' Everyone had sprung to attention in the tiny domed building that served as my head-quarters – McGucken had got Heath to set up the maps. It was low and dark inside, full of drowsy flies, but it would serve. 'Well done yesterday. I knew it was just a matter of time before most of the wali's men voted with their feet, but a few have remained loyal. At any rate, we've got the smooth-bores back and had a chance to see what our enemies are made of.' Was that an eye-roll I caught from Malcolmson to his pal Currie? 'But now we've got some hard choices to make. We can't stay here on the Helmand as we have no fodder or flour – the mutineers made off with all that had been pre-dumped in Gereshk. Along with that, Ayoob Khan is reported to be in the range of hills to the west just beyond the town' – Jock McGucken pointed to the map – 'and is now reinforced with the most part of the wali's turncoats.

Explain, please, Major McGucken, what you think Ayoob Khan's intentions are.'

'Aye, General. I fancy that yon Khan will go straight for Kandahar, hoping to bypass us by using one or several of the fords over the Helmand . . . either here at Gereshk, at Hyderabad, or even further north at Sangin' – McGucken pointed out the river shallows on the map – 'then go like shite off a shovel while we bugger about too far away from the city to be any threat to him. But if we can stay ahead of him and get to the area of Khusk-i-Nakud, where we can cover all the main routes to Kandahar, we can get at more supplies and be in a position to block the bugger.' He thrust a finger into the map forty-five miles to the east.

'Are you seriously suggesting that we try to make a stand against superior forces in that fly-blown valley, McGucken?' Malcolmson interjected. 'Why, we met Durani troops there eighteen months ago and they gave us a right good run for our money.'

'No, *Colonel* Malcolmson. *Major* McGucken is suggesting no such thing for he does not command this brigade. *I* do.' I was becoming heartily bored with the commanding officer of the Scinde Horse. 'What exactly are your objections?'

'Well, General, do you not think we'd be better advised to fall back on Kandahar itself? The division is already split and over-extended and, as we found during last year's fighting . . .' Malcolmson paused at that point, just to remind everyone that he'd been out in Afghanistan since God wore napkins and, as a result, was far better qualified to command a brigade than a tyro like me '. . . the enemy will have collected clouds of Ghazis and irregular horse that can move like the wind.'

'He has a point, General.' Now Anderson of the Grenadiers had got his dander up, hunting with the pack.

'Both of you may have a point, but let me read to you a telegram passed to me by General Primrose's headquarters. It comes from GHQ Simla. "You will understand you have full

131

liberty to attack Ayoob Khan if you think you are strong enough to do so. Government consider it of the greatest possible political importance that his force should be dispersed and prevented by all possible means from falling on Kandahar and then passing on to Ghazni." So, gentlemen, I intend to obey orders and seek battle at the most opportune time and place. Please be ready to strike camp at four o'clock and start our march towards Khusk-i-Nakud at six. We'll make twenty-five miles tonight, pause tomorrow and complete the last twenty or so miles the next night. Any questions?'

That, I thought with pleasure, had pissed on Malcolmson's bonfire. All of a sudden the commanding officers were craning at the map, keen to suck in every detail to pass on to their own commands: twenty-five miles across desert at night would not be easy. All dissent melted as the officers concentrated on the task they had been given.

Billy Morgan had found the last four days since the start of the march from the Helmand distinctly irksome. He and the rest of H Company had got used to flogging over the desert by night, and after the incident with Eddie Battle everyone, even the youngest private soldiers, had been keen to do their best to retrieve the name of the regiment. And that, thought Morgan, was all right as far as it went, but now that they were marching *back* towards Kandahar, over the same sand and grit that they had hurried across only a few days ago, all the impetus seemed to have gone. They'd thrashed the enemy at Gereshk, for sure, but now the men were asking why they were moving *away* rather than following hard on the tails of those they had just defeated.

As far as Morgan was concerned, things hadn't been explained properly. Certainly, they had all heard the rumour that Ayoob Khan's host was bearing down on them from Persia in the west, but no one had clapped eyes on it. They had all seen the cavalry patrols come trotting listlessly in from − so it was said – keeping an eye on the foe, but if you talked to the horsemen, the best they could offer was distant sightings of groups of riders. He couldn't help but wonder at his father's decision to pull back from a meeting with the enemy rather than going straight at the rogues bald-headed – but then, he supposed, that was why he was an ensign while his father was a brigadier general. Still, it didn't do to debate such things with the men. He'd obey orders as loyally as he could and keep his own views to himself.

At least they'd now stopped marching. Once the column had come to what passed for a road junction in this part of Afghanistan, they had crowded into an abandoned village from which the whole of the gentle valley they had traversed could be viewed and the routes dominated. They'd fortified the place a little, loop-holed the mud walls, dug some trenches in front of it as best they could in the rocky earth, then set about what the manual would call 'routine in defence'. So, while patrols were mounted, the rest of the soldiers stood to their battle positions for a tedious half-hour at dawn and again at dusk. Otherwise, they were able to get on with repairing kit and worn-out boots, tending the sick, inspecting weapons and completing the myriad small tasks to which an infantryman's hands fall when he has time.

By mid-morning, with the men busy about their chores under awnings to protect them from the sun, Morgan collected Sergeant Kelly and set off to visit the prisoner, Private Battle.

'Anyway, sir, I said to Mister bleedin' Williams, "You're for the guns, you are, me bucko." "Oh, no," says he, "I can't do that sort of thing, Sergeant, the grease and oil will get under my fingernails, and that would never do." Cheeky beggar, thinks 'e owns the place, 'e does.'

'Trouble, is, Sar'nt Kelly, he's a bloody good soldier,' replied Billy Morgan, laughing, genuinely amused at the picture of the well-educated Private Williams taking the rise out of his platoon sergeant yet again. 'You know as well as I do that the other men look to him for a lead, and he did well in the fight the other day. We shall have to put him forward for the next tape that comes up.'

'Well, maybe, sir. I agree 'e's a good soldier an' 'e's spent ages with young George West trying to get 'im to read and write, but you've got to wonder what made a man of his class go for a common soldier, an't you?' replied Kelly.

Indeed, Morgan had often wondered about Williams. After the twenty-year-old had let slip that he'd been educated in Heidelberg, Morgan had found him reading a racy French novel with apparent ease, and he was always pleased to find him on sentry when he was doing the rounds, for it meant that he could wile away half an hour or so in congenial company, with someone of his own class and attitudes. But, when questioned, Williams never gave away very much at all.

'So, he's been detailed off as one of the gun numbers on the smooth-bores, has he? I suppose you'll be spared his company for a while at least,' said Morgan.

'Aye, sir, but it's a rum decision, ain't it, to send infantry blokes off under a set of artillery officers to serve the guns? And it leaves us short-handed.' Kelly was only voicing what everyone else had said when the *ad hoc* battery was formed from men of the 66th.

'Well, I suppose those guns could be vital if we're outnumbered in the way we're told we are. Each piece is worth fifty rifles, so I imagine it makes sense.' It was also a decision that the brigadier general – his own father – would have had to sanction, as the other subalterns had been quick to point out.

'Where's Battle being confined, Sar'nt Kelly?'

'Somewhere over here, sir. I checked with the orderly room and they said that Brigade Provost was in the far corner of the compound. There's a bit of a crowd gathered yonder, sir.' A mixed group of native drivers and soldiers was milling about fifty yards away, a series of shouts and noise issuing from them.

'There's too many troops here, really, ain't there, Sar'nt Kelly? Every bloody unit's tripping over each other. What's all the noise about?' The din had multiplied with a rising pulse, men shouting in time to something that Morgan couldn't see.

'There's a lot of blokes crammed in 'ere, sir, but it makes the place more defendable, don't it? Sounds like punishment parade, sir. Come on, we don't want to miss that.'

Morgan trotted after Kelly over the red dust of the village track towards thirty or forty men pressed together so tightly that it reminded him of a rugby scrum. The crowd was craning forward, intent on whatever was happening within. Sergeant Kelly picked the nearest native, took him firmly by the ear and hauled him clear without ceremony, shouting, 'Officer present, make way.' The man, initially furious at this assault upon his person, skulked off meekly to find another vantage-point when he saw Morgan's badges of rank.

In the middle of the ring that the crowd had made Morgan saw a scrawny Indian driver, of no more than fifteen or sixteen, stretched and tied over an empty wooden water barrel, his bare buttocks pointing towards the sky. A lance corporal from the provost was belabouring the lad with a thin rattan cane. His thick moustache hid much of his face, but he wore an expression of pained determination as each stroke landed.

'What's this all about, Bombardier?' Morgan asked one of the audience, whose badges showed him to be an NCO from E Battery.

'Eh . . . oh, sorry, sir, I din't notice you there.' So intent had the tall, well-muscled Horse Gunner been on the spectacle that he hadn't seen Morgan being pushed to the front of the crowd. Now he braced his arms firmly at his sides, pulled his shoulders back and saluted in the manner approved for when a soldier was bareheaded. 'It's one of us *bhisti-wallahs*. Troop sergeant caught him a-robbing the lads' biscuit ration, 'e did.'

'Couldn't you have dealt with that within the Battery? Why

did you have to hand him over to the provost?' Morgan was genuinely puzzled. The crime was quite a serious one, but he guessed that in the 66th the offender would have been handled within the company – the result would probably have been the same, a vicious caning.

'Dunno, really, sir. We asked the same question, but Bomb' Holman reckoned the officers was frit of the newspapers saying we was mistreating a native – got to treat the 'eathen gits like precious flowers, we 'ave. Anyway, robbing little sod's gettin' a good leathering from the turnkey, ain't 'e, sir?'

'Indeed he is, Bombardier. I hope he thinks the biscuit was worth it.' Judging by the unearthly shrieks the poor man was raising every time the cane bit into his buttocks, the hard-tack must have been very enticing indeed. On top of that, he realised, the high-caste Muslim – for that was what most of the native bearers were – would be appalled at having to expose his backside and genitals to the Feringhee. That indignity, he guessed, would probably be much more keenly felt than the pain.

Repelled by the noise and the baseness of the scene, Morgan signalled Sergeant Kelly to leave.

'No 'urry, sir. I was just beginning to enjoy that, I was,' said Kelly, once they were clear of the throng.

'Glad to hear it, Sar'nt Kelly, but we're meant to be giving the Afghans hard-knocks, not our own people.'

'Sir – but you can't trust these buggers, you can't. Why, it wouldn't surprise me if we woke up one morning and all these greasy sods had fucked off to join the Afghans, it wouldn't. Most of the wali's fellows did – and remember Cawnpore, sir.'

'Sar'nt Kelly,' Morgan replied, with just a hint of exasperation, 'that was more than twenty years ago in another country involving a wholly different set of issues, tribes, castes and all manner of complicated things that are as far from today in Kandahar as a meeting at Fairyhouse races. And, yes, I do

136

remember it. I was there, only as a babe in arms, but there wasn't much else talked about when I was growing up, believe me.'

'Well, you should know better, then, shouldn't you, sir? Anyway, let's find Private Edward bleedin Battle, shall we, sir?'

'That looks like our man over there,' replied Morgan, pointing to a bareheaded soldier in shirtsleeves who was tied by his wrists to the wheel of one of the Army's big grey general-purpose carts.

Battle was watching the punishment of the native with keen interest as the pair approached, but as soon as he noticed them he attempted respectfully to brace up, despite his bonds.

'Thank you, Battle. How are you, man?' asked Morgan.

'Oi'd be better if I weren't lashed like a beast to a post, sir, an' I'm half murdered with thirst, so I am.'

The Irishman seemed remarkably matter-of-fact, cheerful almost, thought Morgan, considering the almost inevitable fate that lay before him. 'Well, I'm afraid I've no porter for you, Battle, but I'm sure no one would mind if I gave you a drop of water.'

But as Morgan reached round for the elliptically shaped wooden canteen, known in Army parlance as 'Italian pattern', Kelly interjected, 'Bloody hell, sir, you'll get us shot as well, if the peelers see you. You should know by now that prisoners under confinement are restricted on the amount of water they're allowed, sir.' He seemed genuinely worried by Morgan's intention to flout regulations so blatantly.

'Yes, Sar'nt Kelly, I do know. But it's bad enough that we treat our own men like animals without trying to kill them with thirst while we're about it. Now, be a stout fellow and just keep a look-out for the provost sar'nt, though I expect he's too busy beating another of our people half to death to worry about us,' Morgan replied resolutely. He pulled the stopper from the bottle and poured a stream of tepid water under Private Battle's hedge-like moustache.

137

'You'll be the fucking death of me, you will, sir,' muttered Kelly, his eyes roving for the provost.

'Now, is there anything else we can do for you, Battle?' asked Morgan, as the soldier wiped his lips on the sleeve of a tethered arm.

'Not really, sir. I was saying to the other prisoners, I was, if you think these screws are bad, you've never been inside one of the Black Bastard's cells back in Sligo on a Friday night wi' a skinful. Now, if precious Mr Gladstone heard about what went on there, he'd stop purging about Africans, Indians and whatever and look to his own.' Battle paused. 'There is one thing, though, sir. If it comes to a fight, can I come back to H? I won't run off after an' I'll stand by you, the sergeant an' the boys an' do me share, you know I will.'

'Well, if I had my way, I'd have you back right sharp—'

But Kelly interrupted his officer: 'There'll be no fight, Battle. We kicked the living daylights out of these rogues at Gereshk, got the guns back and now there's neither sight nor sound of Mr Khan and his army of religious loons.'

Kelly had spoken with a certainty that surprised Morgan. 'Do you really think so, Sar'nt Kelly? The reconnaissance patrols have reported large bodies of troops and flocks of ration animals up in that range of hills yonder.' Morgan pointed through the haze over the flat plain that led first to the town of Sangbur, about eight miles away, then on to the Malmund hills that rose steeply twelve miles beyond. 'And the brigade's been told that we've got to stop them getting past us and falling on Kandahar.'

'Aye, Sar'nt, an' I reckon I heard their drums an' horns last night when the wind came from the west,' added Battle.

'That's as maybe, son, but just because a body of troops makes a fearsome noise don't mean they can fight, does it? Look at them Jock twats with their pipes an' all. They can't knock the skin off a saucer of burgoo, can they?' Morgan and Battle nodded their agreement.

'But if Sar'nt Kelly's wrong, sir, will you put in a good word for me with your da? My da used to beat for him when he came shooting in Sligo before the Roosian war. I'm not asking for no change of judgement, sir, just a chance to die with the old Sixty-Sixth, sir.'

Morgan was persuaded by Battle's simple honesty. 'Well, I shall certainly suggest it to the company commander, Battle, and I appreciate your loyalty. Now we must be off. I'll be back to see you tomorrow.' Morgan gave Battle another long, surreptitious pull at his bottle, as much to pique Kelly as to comfort the prisoner.

'If it does come to a scrap, sir – which it won't – let's just be a bit careful how we handle Battle, sir,' said Kelly to Morgan as they walked briskly away from the provost's part of the village and back towards their own lines. 'I know he a likeable sort of man, sir, and you've got a soft spot for him, but he's a rogue and a murderer.'

'But if we've got Afghani madmen coming over the parapet at us, like they did around Kabul last year, wouldn't a murderer be quite a useful lad to have around?' responded Morgan.

'Sir, he would. But you mark my words, sir. Till this Ayoob Khan fucks off back to where he came from, there'll be more standing to, more false alarms, more marching and more counter-marching than fleas on a dog. If we set Battle free each time a sentry fires at a shadow, you can depend upon it that he'll be away. He probably wouldn't get very far, but he'd be more nuisance than he's worth. 'Sides, we've dirtied our barrels for the last time on this campaign, sir.' Kelly was adamant.

'Well, I hope you're wrong, Sar'nt Kelly, because I for one have no desire to return to rot in Karachi just when I'm getting a taste for this sort of thing,' Morgan replied.

'Getting a taste for it, sir? You'll tell me next that you enjoyed stabbing that kid to death in Kandahar or that that nasty bit of blood-letting the other day was like a walk in the park to you, sir.' Morgan had never heard Kelly talk like this. The grisly affair at Gereshk a week ago had been the first experience of battle and violent death that most of them had seen.

'Well, it's what I'm paid to do, and as long as there are those who come at us, I shall continue to do it. And I didn't notice you hanging back. I owe my life to you, and your bayonet was bent like a corkscrew by the time you'd finished,' Morgan came back.

'Aye, sir, but that don't mean I enjoyed it, does it?'

'Just grab his collar, one of you.' The horse lines of A Squadron 3rd Scinde Horse were pandemonium. A loose terrier, from the unit occupying the buildings on the other side of the narrow street, had flushed a rat from one of the old drains and chased it for all it was worth. The rat scuttled and turned, doubled back and dodged in the dust, but the dog wasn't going to give up, despite the uproar he was causing as he tried to grab his quarry below the legs of the tethered chargers.

'Go on, don't be afraid of it – you women! Get a grip of the cur before it does any damage!'

But it was too late. As Daffadar Sayed Miran bellowed at the troopers, the tethered horses thrashed, whinnied and snorted, metal-shod hoofs flashing as the dog circled and snapped among their legs in pursuit of its prize. Then, in the mayhem, one kick fell meatily against the ribs of another horse, causing the injured animal to bellow through its nosebag, broadcasting bran and barley as it sank to the ground. Still the dog chased the rat.

'You're like a bunch of Hebrew harlots!' Miran was furious, not just with the fools who'd let a dog roam free – crazy white officers playing the great *shikari*, he'd be bound – not just with a precious horse that they could ill afford to lose through injury but with the milksop behaviour of his men.

A dog was dirty, for sure, but it wasn't as if the wretched thing was a pig. 'Why do I have to do everything myself?'

Now the dog had the rat between its teeth. Miran picked it up by the scruff of the neck and dangled it at arm's length, its back legs helplessly akimbo. 'Why, you little fighter, you! You'll not let your enemy go in a hurry, will you?' Despite the chaos that the dog had caused, Miran gazed at it admiringly as the rat hung in its jaws.

'Kill the dirty thing, Daffadar! It's broken my horse's ribs.' An angry trooper swore, as he lay by his injured mount, pulled its nosebag away and stroked its ears as it snorted in pain.

'Nay, my son, this is a *gora-log* dog – see its collar?' The terrier had a cut-down rifle-sling around its neck, with English words burnt into the leather. 'That would never do. The sahibs worship their hunting hounds.'

But the debate went no further for a gang of breathless English troops, off duty in shirt-sleeves and braces, approached from one direction, intent upon finding their errant dog, while the Scinde Horse's Lieutenant Sam Keenan came from the other.

'Oh, Daffadar, that's good of you to catch Bobby for us. Why, I'm most grateful to you. I trust he hasn't caused too much trouble.' Private Posh Williams had been running with game dogs all his life – indeed, his father, the colonel, had his own pack of foxhounds. Sergeant Kelly's Bobby answered him almost as readily as he did his master, and in the sergeant's absence, Williams, Bobby and a small group of trusties got up to all sorts of mischief.

'Sahib, please control your dog better.' Miran couldn't see any badges of rank on the young man who stood before him, but he could just about distinguish between officers' English and that of the soldiers. Now he saluted and passed the dog back to the sahib – rat and all – angry but too tongue-tied to remonstrate any further with the odd young officer whose

141

hair and moustache were worn like a subaltern's, but who had surrounded himself with a bunch of common scruffs.

'Yes, of course I will, Daffadar. Please pass on my apologies to your squadron officers. I'm at your service.' Even before the salute, Williams's accent and general bearing had got him out of another tight corner. 'Well, Bobby, my boy, that's a good day's work.'

Williams was just turning to go back to his own lines with his two companions when a voice that was just as cultured as his own but much more authoritative cut through the air: 'You men, stand still. Stay just where you are.' The latent anger in the words had Williams and his mates bracing immediately to attention, the officer-like tone producing instant obedience in rigorously trained men.

'And who exactly are you, my man?' Sam Keenan addressed himself to the miscreant ringleader.

'Sir, I am 1396 Private Williams, Frederick, H Company, Sixty-Sixth Foot, sir.' Posh sounded as if he were in cells already.

'H Company, indeed. All of you?' Keenan asked suspiciously.

'Sir!' the trio answered together.

'Well, you're under arrest. And you, Daffadar, why were you letting these men get away with all the damage they've caused?' Keenan had instantly taken in the scene of dog, injured horse and general confusion as he'd hurried towards his own lines. He suspected foul play from overbearing white troops towards his own. Too often his men would defer to the Queen's men, even though they outranked them. That the meanest private had a white skin meant, all too often, that his own people would give way to him. There had been that appalling murder a few weeks ago by a drunken lout of H Company, 66th, and now the same lot were at it again.

'But, sir, we were only doing a bit of ratting, sir, just as Brigade orders told us to.' Williams was speaking the truth,

Keenan knew, for he'd read the same instruction to his own men yesterday under the heading 'Vermin Control within Camp Confines'.

'Yes, Williams – you did say Williams, didn't you?' Keenan looked at the three hunters standing rigidly to attention in front of him, with Bobby struggling to be out of his temporary master's arms and back to his trade. Two were mute and sweating, in thrall to the officer's displeasure, but not Williams. He gazed back, level and certain, cocksure almost. 'But that didn't give you *carte blanche*' – Keenan used the phrase deliberately to see whether Williams understood – 'to come irresponsibly into my lines and without permission, damaging precious horses, did it? Now I'm a mount short for the patrol for which this squadron has been detailed and it's all the fault of bloody H Company of Her Majesty's Sixty-Sixth Foot. You just don't seem to have any form of discipline in your regiment, Williams.'

Keenan's tongue-lashing of the three culprits was cut short by the arrival of Ensign Billy Morgan and Sergeant Kelly, fresh from their visit to the provost.

'Well enough disciplined not to break and run from a bit of Afghan shot, like the Scinde Horse did back in Gereshk.' Morgan couldn't resist it. Like Keenan, he'd taken in the scene from afar, recognising his brother and his own soldiers immediately. It was all too much for him. As he had approached, memories of arguments and bickering, of rivalries and old scores to settle from childhood had raced across his mind. He had remembered, too, Captain Beresford-Peirse's cutting words of caution after the fight in the village – 'Try not to be so Sandhurst . . .' Sensing the tension in the scene, he had broken into a trot to get there as fast as he could, trying to restrain himself, but the bilious words had cascaded out.

Meanwhile, Kelly looked at Miran, both men making faces of silent despair to each other, yet neither wishing to intrude in an officers' quarrel.

'You cheeky pup! Why, this regiment was chasing Ghazis when your lot was still in Karachi—' Keenan checked himself. He'd already had one public slanging match with his brother that he'd won conclusively, and now was the time to consolidate the advantage, not waste it. 'I'm not debating the point – you and I have done too much of that sort already. Anyway, I'm glad you can save me the trouble of having to deal with these hoodlums, Mister Morgan. I was just about to go through all the palaver of putting yet more of your men under arrest. Now you can do it for me. Please get them out of my sight and let's just hope that the reconnaissance patrol with which I have been charged is still able to go ahead and gain the information that the brigade commander has asked for.' Keenan let their father's involvement sink in for a moment. 'Carry on, please.' And on that magisterial word of command, he whirled back to the sick horse that still lay entangled among the tethering lines. It left Morgan and Kelly little choice but to obey without further discussion.

'Leave to carry on, sir, please?' Kelly saluted and chanted the rubric even though Keenan's back was turned. 'Squad, squad . . . 'shun. March to the pace I call out. Quick march, lef', ri', lef', ri' . . .' It was a very chastened Posh Williams, with a couple of heroes, whom Kelly marched away in double time before his officer could get them into any further bother with his brother.

Although the Bombay Light Cavalry had been ambushed the night before, Keenan's patrol had eventually been sent forward to the hamlet of Garmao, some ten miles from the temporary camp and just beyond the scatter of buildings and walls known as Maiwand. They were to search for signs of the enemy, question local people and try to gather as much intelligence as possible. But, thought Keenan, almost a hundred mounted men for a task like this was too many: the group was unwieldy and noisy, the men at the back of the column soon losing

144

concentration as they tried to keep up in the cloud of moonlit dust that so many hoofs threw up. Now they were late because Gul Mohammed, one of the sowars, had not cared properly for his horse's shoes.

Miran was only too aware that the sahib was in a foul mood, and had been ever since the incident back in the fort when one of the horses had been hurt. Then there had been the inspection yesterday at which not one set of hoofs had been clipped to his satisfaction, or apparently any set of horse teeth properly filed. Things had improved a little when they jingled out of camp into the cool of the starlit night, but, with the officer's testiness, gloom hung over every man.

'Quietly now, lads.' Keenan flapped impatient hand signals as the patrol fanned out behind him. A third of their number had been left behind in a fold in the ground with the horses and, having worn slippers rather than their issue boots, all sixty-odd of them were moving remarkably quietly. Miran was bringing up the rear, and as the moon beamed down, reflecting off the oiled barrels of the Snider carbines that every man now held at the 'alert' position, his hands tightened on his carbine as he saw the officer sneak behind a low stack of straw and sidle up to the door curtain of a mean little shack from which a weak light shone out.

He watched as Keenan pulled back the curtain and ducked into the hovel shouting, '*Jildi-rao*,' then bundled a man, woman and three children out into the night. Their piercing yells not only woke the hamlet's few other residents but had every dog barking as if Lucifer himself had come to visit.

'Over here, please, Daffadar. Be so good as to translate,' Keenan called. Miran deserted his place at the back and trotted up to join his officer. 'Ask them what all this fodder is doing here and' – there had been a constant bleating of many animals ever since the dogs had issued their warning – 'why they've got so many goats enclosed.'

Miran looked down at the family. The mother was clearly

appalled to be seen by strange men in her night clothes. She nursed a tiny brown wrinkled baby at her bosom, crouching uneasily in the dust with a wrap pulled over her head and shoulders, trying to avoid eye contact with the strangers. An older girl clung to her father, while a boy of about nine hung a little way back in the shadows, his skull cap sitting precariously on his head. But it was the man of the house in whom Miran was interested.

'Keenan sahib, can we not let the woman and children go back inside? Our very gaze is defiling her and offending her husband.' Miran could almost feel the man's growing truculence as he squatted on the ground, his jaw set and beard jutting.

'Why, yes, of course. Is this difficult for them?' asked Keenan.

Miran despaired sometimes of these *gora-log*. The regiment had been in the field for more than a year and Keenan sahib, good and intelligent officer though he was, had neither grasped any of the language nor begun to understand the fierce independence and religious zeal of these hill people. It wasn't as though he was short of material to study either, for almost all of the troopers were Pathan: hadn't the sahib noticed the respect with which most of them treated their wives and female servants?

'Please, sahib, just do as I suggest. This owl is becoming more silent by the moment.' A trooper threw a cloak around the woman and shepherded her and the children back into the byre. Her husband relaxed visibly.

'Ask him why there's all this fodder and—'

'I already have, sahib. I know the questions to which we need answers. Please, just leave it to me.' Miran hunkered down alongside the villager, proffered a quid of tobacco and started a long preamble, of which Keenan understood only one word in ten. There was an exchange between the men, then Miran cleared his throat. 'Well, Keenan sahib, it is as

146

we guessed. The man – he's a good fellow, not originally from around these parts but from Khost so he has no reason to lie to me – says that this area has been full of soldiers for the past two days, driving stock and protecting great crowds of grass-cutters who brought some fodder with them and cut more and piled it here. He says there are still groups of horsemen about, but he's been told to expect a "great swarm of holy warriors" in the next couple of days. They've come far from the west, he tells me, and they're going to pause here for a while before marching on.'

'To where, Daffadar?'

'Towards Kandahar, sahib. This man has seen Ayoob Khan's proclamation and he says that the soldiers were looking forward to taking the city and kicking our arses out of it.'

'But didn't the fight at Gereshk knock the stuffing out of them, Daffadar?' asked Keenan, prompting Miran to return to questioning the villager.

'He says that the scouts made no mention of any other fighting, just warned him not to steal any of the stock or feed. But he says they were laughing at the behaviour of some of the Ghazis who, apparently, spend all day chanting and dancing and whipping themselves up into a lather, the better to deal with all the virgins whom death in battle will deliver to them. The soldiers reckoned they'd be too exhausted even to get hard, let alone put a smile on the girls' faces,' replied Miran.

'Ask him if he knows how many Ghazis, Daffadar.'

'I have, sahib. He knows only that there will be a great swarm of them. You will have to guess what that means, sahib, like Major McGucken will have to. If I may say, sahib, I think we've learnt all we can here. The officers will need to know what we've heard as soon as possible, so unless you want to burn the stores, sahib, may I suggest we go?' Miran had placed a reassuring hand on the villager's shoulder and the man was now almost smiling into Keenan's face.

147

'No, we'll burn nothing. That way the enemy will think it's still safe to come here and at least we'll know his intentions for the next couple of days. So, mount the men, Daffadar, and let's get back to our mud redoubt as soon as we can.' Keenan passed a gold piece to the informant.

'*Tik-hai*, sahib. Come on, you lot, look sharp.' Even though Miran spoke in a whisper, in a language he couldn't understand, Keenan heard the authority in his voice. 'Collect your mounts and let's move, but keep your eyes peeled, all of you.'

The column walked for fifteen minutes, trotted for fifteen minutes, dismounted and led its horses for fifteen minutes, then halted for ten minutes in the two hours it took to get back to the fort.

All had gone well, the night routine of five miles in every hour undisturbed until they were on the last leg. All of them were dismounted, just about to approach the final crest below which lay the brigade's camp, when one of the pair of leading scouts – the only men supposed to remain on horseback – was scampering across the moonlit plain.

'Sahib, one of our own vedettes ahead, sahib.' It was Private Gul Mohammed, whose horse's loose shoe had caused such delay on the way out and who was now riding one of the two remounts that regimental orders insisted should be brought. 'Shall we challenge or wait for you, sahib?'

'How many men d'you see?' Keenan was eager to get back, but he knew how dangerous one's own sentries could be, especially when the foe was thought to be close.

'Five, Keenan sahib, all in the saddle.' Despite his earlier mishap, thought Keenan, Gul Mohammed was one of his better troopers. His spoken English marked him down as a man of potential. 'Five, you say? That's a strange number – and they're all mounted? I'd better come and have a look myself.'

Why five? Keenan wondered. A vedette's normally seven – four scouts, two horse holders and a commander. And why are they in the saddle? They would usually be dismounted unless they've just arrived and a pair of scouts has been sent off with a message.

Keenan left his horse with a holder, took his carbine from its bucket and told Gul Mohammed to do the same. 'Come, thou, we must look.' It was about all he could manage in Pashto, but as the pair of them strode out past the now halted file of soldiers and horses, he caught sight of a group of riders on the skyline about fifty paces in front of him. There was nothing regular about their outlines, no carefully folded *pugga-rees* or any of the distinctive shoulder belts he would have expected to see.

'Where's your pair, Gul Mohammed?' Keenan had crouched in the dark, carbine ready.

'I know not, sahib. We agreed that he was going to stay here while I went back to report, but he did say that it would be quicker if he spoke to the Light Cavalry wallahs.'

'Can you see a riderless horse there?' Keenan was lying almost flat on the ground. 'No, you'll have to get lower, try to see them all in silhouette . . . I mean, against the sky.'

'Sahib, I can see. There's something on the ground that another man's bending over,' said Gul Mohammed, pointing to something or someone on the ground below the horses' legs.

Keenan was in a quandary. One of his scouts seemed to have disappeared into the night, probably the victim of this enemy patrol − for that was what it looked like. Or did it? He'd spent too many nights tripping over himself and other units, everyone scared in equal measure of the enemy and of raising a false alarm. The former might kill you, but that was probably better than the scorn and laughter that 'windiness' would provoke in the brigade.

'Right, Gul Mohammed, we'll advance very slowly. When we get good and close I'll challenge.' Keenan looked at the sowar to make sure the man was following his careful English.

'If they make no reply, I'll fire, then you. That will alert the daffadar, who will bring the rest of the patrol forward, but once you've fired, run back and keep going. Understand?' The trooper nodded, but Keenan was uneasy: he knew he should have alerted the rest of the patrol, but if this lot ahead turned out to be friendly, he would look such a fool in the eyes of his own men.

'Come on, then,' Keenan whispered, and the pair stole forward until they were no more than twenty paces from the horsemen, close enough to hear their whispered conversations and for the horses to detect them, to prick up their ears and whinny quietly. Keenan saw the silhouettes stiffen and then, suddenly, two short firearms were pulled up into the aim, the barrels pointing directly at them.

'Get down, man!' Keenan pushed Gul Mohammed to the ground just as two shots from the dark clutch of figures in front of them shattered the calm of the night. Keenan replied with one shot but missed his man. He scrabbled for another cartridge, just as the horsemen turned towards them whilst Gul Mohammed rose to one knee and snapped off a round that brought a pony crashing to the ground. But the remainder reacted fast, kicking their horses from a confused, gun-frightened stand to a shambling charge, yelling like demons – demons from York, Birmingham and London, Keenan thought.

'Don't shoot! We're friends!' Keenan jumped to his feet and waved his arms as the patrol continued to come. 'We're English, friends, Scinde Horse!' He would have bellowed the password if he could remember it.

'You don't seem very fuckin' friendly, sir.' The lead soldier had dragged his horse to a halt and dropped the muzzle of his carbine, immediately recognising an officer's accent but furious nevertheless. 'If you're such a friend, sir, why've you shot Dabber Baker's horse?' The question was rhetorical: both sides had grasped what had happened – even Daffadar Sayed Miran and the rest of the patrol seemed to have guessed.

Now, in the middle of the night in the middle of Christ knew where, Keenan had to sort this nonsense out, which was completely of his own making.

'What damage have we done and who are you?' Keenan was just glad that he hadn't bumped into an infantry patrol – they would have been bound to be from the 66th, he thought.

'Sir, I'm Sar'nt Mullane from E Battery, sir. We've been sent out on patrol at short notice because so much of the cavalry's out tryin' to find the Afghans tonight, so they are. You've shot Shandy dead, you 'ave, sir. Bloody good shot, hit her right in the 'eart, but Gunner Baker's all right. Good job we took plenty of spare mounts after Gereshk, sir. But if you don't mind me saying, you was a bit 'asty with that shot of yours, wasn't you, sir?'

'Well, I'm very sorry, Sar'nt, but one of my scouts was missing and you do look like Afghan cavalry in those comforters. Why are you wearing them?' Keenan knew it was a poor excuse, but it was better than admitting his lack of judgement – in any case, the woollen caps did look odd.

'Sir, we was just a-talkin' to your lad. *He*'d come up nice an' regular, *he* had – good challenge, so it was. We was just asking him what he'd seen when you arrive and starts treating us to a bit o' musketry, sir. Anyway, least said soonest mended, eh? Oh, an' we always wear cap-comforters at night, sir, don't you? Warm as a tart's thighs they are. But, sir, your man says the enemy's really close, so I reckon we'll have bigger fish to fry than this bit o' nonsense. I'll 'ave to report it, sir, but Shandy's mouth was as 'ard as iron an' – like I says – we've got some spares. So, you'd best get back an' let Paddy . . . sorry, sir, General Morgan know what the *craic* is 'ant you, sir?'

Mercifully, they were dealing with an experienced cool hand, who could see just what was at stake. Christ, thought Keenan, I hope Ayoob Khan comes before this story gets all over the brigade.

He trotted his men down the slope towards the fort, his

cheeks shining brighter with embarrassment than the moon that lit their way.

I'd had a fair night's sleep for the first time in long enough. My blanket roll had been laid out in one of the few clean huts we'd taken over in the village above Khusk-i-Nakud, and I must have been tired for I had spent the last couple of days with McGucken, agonising over whether we'd made the right decision to pull back from the Helmand when we did or whether – as bloody Malcolmson wanted – we should have pushed on to Kandahar. Worse still, it was impossible to make any well-informed decisions without intelligence. While McGucken's scouts and agents continued to give us mixed and confused messages about the strength and rate of advance of Ayoob Khan's people, I'd insisted that our cavalry should go out to find the foe, only for the first such patrol from the 3rd Lights to be ambushed! Well, last night it had been the turn of the Scinde Horse, who'd gone out mob-handed under my son Sam's leadership. All of this should have made for a rest-less night, but exhaustion overtook me.

I'd been up for stand-to, washed and shaved, and was just settling down to some coffee when I was told that the patrol commander was coming in to tell me what he had gleaned.

'So, Mr Keenan, what have you got for us?' I looked at Sam in his grimy tiredness, sitting in front of McGucken and me, and couldn't help but wonder. The lad had been out all night, blundering about the desert between here and Maiwand. He seemed to have gathered some excellent titbits, had had a brush with another patrol and then gone through all the inspection puke so dear to the cavalry before coming up here and reporting to Himself. All that and not a wink of sleep, yet he looked as fresh as a new-scraped carrot – a dusty one, I'll grant you. I wondered if I would have been capable of all that when I was his age.

'Well, sir, when we got to Garmoa . . .'

I let Sam blether on about what he'd found, the stores, the animals, the villager – the whole lot because I'd listened to all the other patrol commanders. In fact, I'd had Sam's written patrol report of what he'd discovered almost before his troop had got the saddles off their horses and it was good stuff. I'd also heard about the nag-murdering episode – it was already common currency – and I'd wanted to see the lad to offer him a bit of solace. I let him talk for about ten minutes before drawing the whole thing to a close. 'Good. You and your troop have done well. But before I ask Major McGucken to summarise, is there anything else I ought to know?' I could see that Sam was expecting the interrogation.

'Sir, on the way back in we bumped a standing patrol of E Battery and shot one of their horses dead.'

The boy had come out with it direct and honest as you like. 'Really, who shot it?'

'One of my men, sir, with whom I had approached the Gunners. But it was my fault, sir. I gave the order and acted without as much caution as I should. I accept the blame totally, sir.'

'So you bloody should.' I watched Sam blanch. 'You're the officer and everything rests with you. Now, you'll get a ribbing for this from the rest of the officers and Malcolmson will tear you into little pieces – he's still smarting after that nonsense at Gereshk. But I can tell you more stories of sentries shooting each other, shooting their own officers during Grand Rounds, shooting civilians, even. It's called the "fog of war", Mr Keenan, and if the cost of one of my best cavalry squadrons learning how *not* to do things is one dead pony that was only fit for dog food, I don't call that a bad deal. Night patrols are difficult and they'll always be blazing away at each other, particularly when the enemy's close.'

I watched how Sam took this. He'd done well on the patrol but was clearly dreading the reputation that Shandy's death would bring with it. He was mature enough, though, to observe how I was dealing with him and to tuck it away for some future occasion when he might have to dish out such a bollocking. His manner was impressive — much more so than his younger half-brother's had been after the child was killed in Kandahar or, more recently, after Private Paddy Whatever's murder of that wretched rissaldar. 'I suspect that we'll all have our hands full of something rather more demanding in the next day or so that will put pony-potting into perspective. Jock, tell us, please, how Mr Keenan's fragments fit into the jigsaw.'

McGucken had been listening to all this, nodding sagely from time to time, remembering, no doubt, all the times out east or in Bengal when he and I had nearly shot our own patrols — and one or two occasions when we did. Now he pointed towards the map and characteristically cleared his throat.

'Aye, sir. The Scinde Horse patrol confirms what we thought. Ayoob Khan will want his next stop to be around Maiwand so that he can re-victual before his last push towards Kandahar. Sources tell us that his leading elements are at Sangbur now.' McGucken pointed at the hamlet about eleven miles from our current fort. 'They stream out behind him for about twelve miles, right the way back to Hyderabad.'

'What's your latest estimate of numbers, Jock?' I knew quite well, but I wanted Sam to understand that it was highly probable that his latest black mark would soon be forgotten.

'Hard to be precise, General, but about three and a half thousand infantry, two thousand cavalry, five thousand-odd Ghazis and, most worryingly, thirty-four guns with plenty of shot,' Jock replied.

'Aye, but we'd be a damn sight more worried had the Scindis not taken that smooth-bore battery back, wouldn't we? So, Mr Keenan, how do you like those odds — five or six to one by my reckoning?' I know I sounded flippant, but I was fascinated by Sam's reaction.

'The odds against their so-called regular units and the Ghazis don't worry me, General.' Sam was staring hard at the map – I'd forgotten that he knew this valley well after his brush with Durani troops last year. 'It's the guns – their superior numbers and how well they'll be laid and handled. I guess you'll be luring them on to the fort here, sir?'

'You're right, Keenan.' Jock McGucken cut across my answer. 'The guns are the key, and while we've got the measure of Herati regulars and know that Ghazis can be dealt with so long as rifle shot and discipline last, the artillery's an unknown quantity. I'll own, though, that the presence of Russian advisers is not encouraging. That's why we've pressed every gun into service that we can.'

'And you're right about the fort here.' I took up the narrative. 'It would be ideal if we could pinch Ayoob Khan up against it, but our informants say that he's expecting us to stay put and will try to blind us here, then bypass and get to Primrose in Kandahar while we're pinned like a butterfly to a board. No, the only answer is to get to Maiwand,' I pointed to the feature on the map, which Sam knew so much better than either McGucken or I did, 'and stop him there.'

'Stop him in that featureless little valley, General?' Sam looked hard at me. 'It'll work so long as the native infantry have sharpened up their musketry.'

'Well, we'll see, won't we?' I paused. 'And the Third Scinde Horse?' I wondered if I would get a blustering reply.

'We'll be fine, sir, provided that luck's with us this time – unlike Gereshk or my own damn nonsense last night.'

God, you had to admire the lad. I saw McGucken smiling slightly at that reply and knew I would never have been capable of such a disarming, thoughtful answer when I was a subaltern.

'Aye, it'll be a gunner's battle I suspect, with – if Major McGucken and I get it right – you and the Light boys only being unleashed when we've shot the heart out of 'em. But just

155

watch those bloody Ghazis, Keenan, they're wild buggers. You know what happened to your brother back in April?' But then I saw a different Keenan.

'Aye, General, I heard. Took his sword to a twelve-year-old, didn't he?' His reply was cold and hard, sneering, quite unlike the young warrior who'd been wearing his spurs just seconds before. I was shocked by his harsh response.

'Well, not quite . . . It was an ugly business.' I could think of nothing more to say, so I changed the subject. 'Anyway, I have orders to give soon, Mr Keenan, and you need every bit of rest you can get for we march to meet Ayoob Khan at five o'clock tomorrow morning. Good luck, lad. Godspeed.' McGucken and I shook Sam's hand.

He looked back at me, even and open, as straight as his grasp was firm. I smiled at him and hoped I wouldn't let him, his brother and all their men down in the test that lay ahead.

SEVEN

Maiwand, Morning

As we topped the rise, I pulled out my watch. It was about ten o'clock on 27 July, and I looked down on a rough saucer of land called Maiwand. Tom Nuttall, my cavalry commander, was with me, a little way in front of the leading troops of the brigade column as we paused to gaze into the valley where I intended first to bottle up Ayoob Khan and then to destroy him piecemeal. The map showed the shabby hamlets of Khig and Mundebad, set about with orchards, walls, ditches, and the shrub-strewn plain bisected at the north-east end by the main road towards Kandahar, up which the enemy would be marching. There was high ground beyond, and as I viewed the whole scene from about two miles away, it seemed that if I could deploy the brigade across the enemy's front and bring the road under artillery and rifle fire, that Ayoob Khan would be hard pressed to get his guns into action before my own people had thoroughly mauled him.

My first view of the place had been promising enough, but as I swept my glasses hither and yon over the nullahs and folds in the ground, I caught sight of dark blobs on the road. The heat made them shimmer and weave, but they seemed to be moving very slowly east and much further forward than

157

I had hoped. 'Well, I'll be jiggered. Look yonder at the road. What do you see there, Tom?' I asked Nuttall.

We'd set off at six that morning in dense fog, but now the sun was up. It had burnt away the mist and left a haze that prevented any sensible view of things much over fifteen hundred yards away.

'It's hard to say,' he replied. 'But I reckon that's infantry and plenty of 'em in just the place we want to be.'

'I think you're right, goddamn it to hell.' We both edged the wheels of our binoculars a little to get the best focus we could. I'd hoped against hope that by starting early in the morning and marching in the cool of the day we'd get here well before the enemy. But we'd been delayed. That great mass of baggage, stores, civilian drivers, awkward oxen and cantankerous camels had taken so long to load. Then when they had moved off they'd been so slow that the rest of the brigade had had to wait for them.

As a result, the infantry were already footsore, the horses and bat-ponies already skittish, the flies on the spree, and no bugger had had time for breakfast. We'd paused once to replenish water-bottles, but as I looked back from the bit of high ground we'd found, the four or five thousand troops, followers and as many beasts of burden looked more like a great blundering beetle than a fighting force.

'My scouts haven't been noticed, yet, General, but some of McGucken's local johnnies have come in and say that the host paused very briefly last night, only long enough to get a meal, then pushed on hard towards Kandahar.'

Nuttall had just confirmed my worst fears: Ayoob Khan, probably without realising it, had literally stolen a march on us and was now hacking across the funnel-shaped piece of ground I hadn't even had time to reconnoitre. 'What we don't want, though, are his guns to move up on to the high ground, yonder.' Nuttall pointed to the low horseshoe of the Malmund hills at the foot of which the road from Sangbur to Kandahar

158

ran, now thick with dark slabs of humanity that wobbled in the heat.

'I doubt Ayoob Khan's canny enough to leapfrog his guns along those heights. Besides, that would be unusually slow and cautious if he ain't seen us yet, but it'll take him no time to get the wretched things up there unless we can bottle them up on the road.' I was as worried about the enemy's artillery as Nuttall was, for it didn't really matter how good our own guns and gunners were so long as the enemy had plenty of metal. That was what we had found at Inkerman – one of the many lethal cess-pits around the world that I preferred to forget.

'Ah, here are McGucken and Heath, that splendid brigade major of yours, General.' Tom Nuttall smiled – as well he might – as the pair approached on their ponies, with Lynch, my trumpeter, trotting just behind them. Even at this distance, it was clear that McGucken was wigging Heath about something. The poor lamb looked awfully tired after his early start – I'd tell Nanny to give him a lightly boiled egg and then put him straight to bed.

'Well, General, it looks as though we might still be able to pull the fat from the fire.' Jock McGucken had been working well forward, listening to cavalry scouts and native informers. Now his neat khaki was sweat-stained, his beard and whiskers full of dust. 'It all depends, though, on us getting across this plain before yon Mr Khan really knows what we're up to. See there, General.' He pointed to Mundabad and Khig. 'Both those villages are pretty well deserted, and there's even the remains of an old fort in Mundabad. Now, it would be grand to hold them, to dig in and wait for Ayoob Khan's boys to smash themselves on us, but that ain't their plan. If we go down there an' just scratch our arses, they'll simply keep a-goin' and flick us the fingers as they do. I might suggest that we leave the baggage there – but we can hardly see the other big feature in this haze. Can I look at the map?'

McGucken leant over my saddle and stared at the chart I had spread on my pommel.

'You see, General,' his finger traced a line where nothing was shown on the paper, 'there's a whore of a wadi that runs south-west to north-east in front of the villages. It's about twenty-five feet deep in places and has a couple of feet of water in the bottom. It's not impassable to horse and guns, but it's difficult. That gives way just north of Khig to another series of dry nullahs that spread out like fingers to the north. The ground that's surrounded on two sides by these ravines is also cut through by irrigation ditches, smaller nullahs, and some walls that enclose the apricot and lime crop. Now, if we can get across that ground and up to the northern stream beds, the infantry can fire at the enemy over the lip closest to the Kandahar road. We can mass the cavalry there and at the same time we can give the guns some cover. But we've got to get there without those wallahs twigging. What d'ye think, sir?'

There was the old McGucken again. We could have been discussing a bloody assault or the merits of a ratting dog: he was no more concerned than I'd seen him a hundred times, although he'd never faced odds like this before.

'Well, as you say, I'd prefer to fight my infantry from solid cover, but they'll just ignore us if we do. No, if we're to maximise the range of the guns and the rifles, we'll have to fight well forward and that means getting across that big nullah and close to 'em as fast as we can. Right. Captain Heath, take a warning order, please.' I might as well have asked the fellow to grow tits, so surprised was he. I ask you, what else was a brigade commander going to do just before battle? 'Take this down, if you will, "The brigade is to advance to attack the enemy south and west of the Sangbur-to-Kandahar road. Infantry are to form a firing line on forward edge of dry nullah: Rifles, left; Grenadiers, centre; 66th − right; 3rd Bom Lt Cav to mark the route. E/B Battery: on completion of support to

160

current reconnaissance tasks, take post to support infantry units at own discretion. Cavalry: on completion of current tasks, detach RHA units and form reserve on my orders. Bombay Sappers and Miners: close protection for E/B Battery and Smooth-bore Battery: conform to their movements. Baggage train: move to village of Mundebad as fast as possible, baggage guard to protect." Right, is that clear?' I watched Heath chew his pencil disconsolately. 'So, you add timings, order of march and any ammunition details that the Horse Gunners need to know. I want the whole lot across that nullah in thirty minutes.' I knew that such a thing should have been more than possible with confident, well-drilled staff, but as Heath positively devoured his quill, I had my doubts.

'Well, McGucken, Nuttall, I think we may have done rather better than we'd hoped. If we can just get a wriggle on across this broken ground and hit them from the flank before he knows we're there, we stand a very good chance of cutting the head off his column, bitching his guns and dealing with him piecemeal in our own time. But it all depends upon the element of surprise.' Both men nodded at me silently. It was a risk, but it was the only realistic course of action open to me if the buggers weren't to slip past and tear off towards Primrose at Kandahar. But, as I said, surprise was everything.

And that we had. The brigade moved well – five minutes faster than the half-hour I'd given them. The great human snake slithered along, band now silent, baggage at last in some semblance of order, over the grit and down into the nullah. It splashed through the water and emerged muddily on the far bank. The sun continued to beat down, mirages distorted ranges and the truth, dust devils spun around the plain while the hawks and buzzards hung lazily above us. As we drew closer to the vast unsuspecting host, my balls tightened and I thrilled to think that we might surprise the very folk who boasted that they could never be surprised. And we

161

might have achieved it, had not some damn fool of a gong-hunting Horse Gunner opened fire at extreme range on his own initiative. Sometimes I wish I could make a rope out of initiative: I'd tie it in a noose and hang Caesar, Clausewitz or whoever the silly fucker was who invented it.

'Action front!' Keenan watched as Lieutenant Hector Maclaine and two nine-pound rifled guns of E Battery slewed in the sand and grit, gun-numbers leapt from the limbers, trails were unhooked and ammunition boxes unclipped as the crews went through their drills as smoothly as if they were in Woolwich.

'Range – one eight-hundred yards. With shell ammunition, load.' Maclaine had a reputation as a firebrand, so when Keenan and his troop had been attached to escort the battery and detailed off to provide close protection for this particular section, he had been prepared for excitement. The crews rammed the rounds home into the muzzles of the steel guns even before the horse teams were properly to the rear, Maclaine busying himself with binoculars and map, assessing the range and the target. Keenan looked around: they were way out in front of the rest of the battery and much closer to the enemy than any other British unit. He suddenly realised he was going to get rather more excitement than he had bargained for.

'I feel a bit exposed this far forward, don't you, Daffadar sahib?' Keenan had just ordered the troop to dismount, to leave their lances with their horses and take their carbines from the deep leather buckets that were buckled to the right and rear of each man's saddle.

'I do, sahib. The rest of the brigade is a very long way off now, and those Afghan horses can move quickly. We must be careful not to be cut off,' said Daffadar Sayed Miran, with, Keenan thought, a real look of concern creasing his face.

'But there we are, Daffadar sahib. We've been ordered to

support these lads, so support them we will.' Keenan was trying to make light of a situation that looked distinctly dangerous to him. Thirty minutes or so ago, he and the other cavalry escorts had been formed up with the battery when the brigade started to move forward. Then young Maclaine had come cantering back from the battery commander, all piss and vinegar, yelling for the guns to 'crack on' and shouting to him that there would be no missed opportunities this time, like there had been at Gereshk. Keenan had had little choice but to set off at a spanking trot down through that great nullah and then up the other side while the guns bounced and jumped over tricky country at breakneck speed. He'd seen another section unlimber and prepare to come into action almost a mile back, but not Maclaine – oh, no: he'd gone rattling on through the heat and dust until the enemy had ceased to be furry-edged mirages and become distinct bodies of foot and horse well within range – and until his men were well within range of the Afghan guns too.

Now the madman was striding about, shouting fuse settings, tinkering with elevation wheels, taking a personal interest in the way that the bombardiers placed their friction tubes and then, without any orders that Keenan knew about, bellowing, 'Number one gun, fire!' A report had followed like the clap of doom, with a geyser of dense white smoke, horses skittering, gunners moving like fat off a hot frying-pan and Maclaine chuckling. 'Watch for the fall of shot, Keenan. That'll brass the buggers up! There it is.'

A black ball of smoke cracked at the right height above the enemy cavalry's heads, but a hundred paces beyond them. 'Drop one fifty, same fuse.' Maclaine paused while the next gun's crew tinkered with an elevation wheel. 'Number two gun, fire!' Another iron round sang from the second barrel, exploding over the same cavalry three or four seconds later, but this time a little too short.

'Drop fifty, both guns go on,' Maclaine continued, to be

163

followed by an instant bang from the reloaded and adjusted first gun, while the second crew strove to catch up.

'Well, Daffadar sahib, I can only think that's what the gunners call "good practices".' Keenan and all of his men were watching the smudged, booming garland of shrapnel smoke that hung in the air above the Afghan horses. Through his binoculars, Keenan could see saddles being emptied and the enemy's cavalry breaking from their ragged ranks trying to find cover – most of them at least. 'But there's no question that they know we're here now. Look hard and you'll see a right good gang of them coming in our direction and spurring on hard.' It was clear to Keenan that the two lonely guns, whose report echoed back from the low hills beyond, were about to become the focus of some most unhealthy attention.

Then two black clouds cracked angrily over their own heads. 'Christ, not bad! The cheeky buggers must have got a brace of guns up on that high ground yonder. They're well sited, ain't they?' Maclaine pointed to a level plateau about seven hundred yards away, now obscured by gunsmoke. Five foot nine of scrawny nervous energy, wispy moustache and side-burns now wet with sweat, he looked, Keenan thought, more like a school cricket captain than an officer practising a lethal trade. The man positively chortled as two Afghan rounds burst short but noisily, the splinters and shrapnel balls angrily kicking up the dust a hundred paces in front of them. It introduced Keenan to a new battlefield noise – an unwelcome one that had his men and him shrinking into whatever cover they could find. 'Right, look out for the next two: they'll bracket us if they're any good at all.'

'He's right, sahib, but those badmashes will be upon us soon, too.' Miran nodded towards the rushing cavalry now no more than six hundred paces away and hefted his carbine expectantly.

'Aye, we'll open fire at about four hundred, Daffadar sahib, just when they get past that line of scrub there.' Keenan pointed to a few spiky thorn bushes past which the cloud of cavalry would have to pass. 'Four hundred, agreed?'

But before the Miran could give his view, the next pair of Afghan shells arrived, bursting about thirty feet above the ground and rather closer to the guns than any of them might have expected.

'That's one fellow gone on pension, sahib,' Miran commented. A young gunner's rammer had been struck by a splinter and spun from his hands, throwing him to the ground, where he now lay shrieking, boots and spurs drumming in the dust.

'Troop, four hundred by bush line, cavalry in open, rapid, await my order.' Keenan was trying to blot out the noise of the injured man. His own soldiers understood this standard military talk and they had now pushed the leather guards off their carbine sights and were tinkering with the numbered steel ramps, pleased to be distracted from the arrival of the next artillery rounds.

'There's about thirty of those sods, Daffadar sahib.' Keenan could now distinguish the green *kurtas* and sheepskin hats of what looked like Herati regulars, their swords held low as they came on at a fast trot.

'Cease fire, prepare to move.' Suddenly Maclaine had broken off the action, his trumpeter's bugle taking up his orders, the gunners moving like machines. 'Keenan, can you hold those bastards while we limber up? We've been ordered back immediately.'

Neither Keenan nor the daffadar had seen the galloper who had arrived from an angry Brigadier General Morgan – he had ordered the action to cease and the guns to be cantered out of danger.

'Of course we can,' replied Keenan, without hesitation, though he had his doubts. 'Get moving and we'll pepper 'em for you.'

'Thank you – seems that old Paddy Morgan thinks we're a wee bit too far forward. If I was commanding the brigade,

I'd bring them up to support us, not the other way round,' said Maclaine, as an Afghan shell soared low overhead without exploding, the fuse having obviously failed.

But Keenan had more important things to consider than Maclaine's ambitions, for as the Herati horsemen came level with the scrub, he ordered the troop to fire. Thirty Snider carbines bucked and spat and a cloud of white smoke was snatched away by the breeze from the face of the firers, but the volley was fired at extreme range. Keenan saw dust and grass kicked up around the cavalrymen, one or two saddles emptied, but the Afghans hardly checked, increasing their pace, he thought, rather than slowing it.

'Reload.' His men had done this automatically. 'Three hundred, wait . . . wait . . .' The blob of cavalry came on, their shouts now quite clear. As they reached the next imaginary line in the sand where the carbines ought to be more effective, he yelled, 'Fire!'

'That's better, Keenan sahib.' Miran was convinced that one of the half-dozen or so casualties who had tumbled to the ground had met his ball. 'That will teach the fools!'

Both officer and NCO might have thought that the match was now uneven, had it not been for the enemy guns turning towards the Scinde Horse rather than to Maclaine's gunners, who were now well away. 'Christ alive, that's too close!' Shrapnel balls skipped and slapped around Keenan's feet, one sowar cursing as a splinter from the shell casing slashed a hole in his haversack. 'Right, move by half troops, Daffadar sahib. You mount and we'll fire. Give it a quarter of a mile or so – by that next line of scrub.' Keenan pointed to a feature that he and the daffadar had already reconnoitred during the move up. 'Then fire us back. Happy? Good. Mount and ride like the wind, *bahadur*!'

Daffadar Sayed Miran needed no further instruction. He scrambled away, followed by half of the troop, just as they had practised it so many times.

166

'That's it, lads, slate 'em.' Keenan knew that his men understood the spirit of what he was saying, if not the words. 'Wait for them to appear from cover and aim for the horses.' Cartridge cases were tinkling about the feet of his men as they picked individual targets among the Heratis who had now realised that a more stealthy approach was wiser. Groups of two or three horsemen were now dashing from cover to cover while the odd enemy carbine shot whined high overhead,

'Start moving back to your horses, lads. The lance daffadar and I will give covering fire.' Keenan knew that Miran would soon be in a position to keep the enemy at bay, but until then he was acutely aware that he was at the sharpest of sharp ends of the whole brigade. The fire from Ayoob Khan's cavalry didn't worry him, but he had been surprised that the artillery had been willing to waste good shells on such an insignificant target. Sadly, the enemy gunners had a rather different view of the importance of Keenan's command and, as the first of his men sprinted back to the horse holders, two rounds burst perfectly above their heads, throwing Sowar Qari Mahibullah to the ground.

'No, sahib, he is *bus*.' A trooper was already cradling Mahibullah's head in his lap as Keenan dashed up. 'Here, sahib, here.' The trooper held up two fingers to show his officer where a pair of shrapnel bullets had struck the young soldier. Keenan looked with revulsion at the neat hole that had rent the shoulder of the lad's khaki, and the mat of blood and hair just below the bottom fold of his turban. The poor fellow must have been bending low when he was struck, he thought. The round had knocked half his jaw away. The mush of gore and bone showed starkly against the dead man's beard.

'Right, give me a hand.' Keenan pushed the other trooper into obedience, standing, catching hold of the corpse's bandoleer and signing for his companion to do the same. 'Come on, drag him!' Through the dust they hauled the heaviest,

167

most awkward weight that Keenan had ever tried to move. The hundred yards back to the horse holders seemed interminable, especially as the rest of the half-troop moved as if they had wings on their ankles, unencumbered by burdens like his.

'Here, help me get him across the saddle.' Keenan's men saw what he wanted. Willing hands pulling Mahibullah on to the saddle face down before his ankles were strapped to his wrists and passed through his horse's girth. The mount was frightened to have her master in this unaccustomed position. She pecked, snorted and pointed her ears, expecting pats and soothing words from the man who had fed and groomed her. Now all she had was his dead lolling face and arms and blood that trickled down her flank.

'God, what's that?' As the half-troop busied themselves around the casualty and prepared to ride after Miran, they all shrank to the ground, flinching involuntarily as a covey of bullets cracked over their heads from their rear. 'Who's shooting at us now?' Even as Keenan bobbed down, he knew the answer to his own question.

'Sahib, it is the daffadar firing over us.' One of the sowars smiled uncomfortably, trying not to show the alarm he had felt as their own lead sang overhead.

'Right, is our friend secure?' Keenan tried not to hurl himself into the saddle but to maintain some decorum for the sake of example, although his spine tingled and crept in anticipation of the next salvo. The men nodded to show that Mahibullah was properly trussed up while they fought with reins, carbines and lances, every bit as anxious as their officer to get away from this horribly open piece of ground. 'Come on, then, follow me,' shouted Keenan, as the little file with its sad burden trotted and cantered over the broken ground.

'Who is that, sahib?' Miran rose from his fire position, carbine in hand, as Keenan joined up with the other half of his troop.

'Sowar Qari Mahibullah, struck by shrapnel, dead before he hit the ground, Daffadar sahib,' replied Keenan.

'Not a married man, sahib – that is good. Thank you for not leaving the body. That was hot fire and you must have wanted to,' answered Miran, looking from the corpse to the Heratis, who were still trying to creep towards them.

'No, Daffadar sahib, even in those circumstances we could not have left anyone. The enemy would defile the body – we both know that – and the men would never forgive me.' Although this was the first of his own men whom he'd seen killed in action, Keenan knew the unwritten rule that all bodies were brought back. To allow the enemy to mutilate the dead would be a grave insult to the men's warrior caste, something they, too, would die to avoid.

'*Shabash*, sahib. Now may we try to catch Maclaine sahib's precious guns?' Miran asked, with an ear cocked for more shell fire.

'Indeed. One final volley from the saddle, I think, then let's be about our business.' After one last ripple of fire at their pursuers, Keenan's troop rode hard and fast after the guns, Mahibullah jolting alongside them, deaf to the occasional shells that hurried them on their way.

I suppose it was a couple of hours since I'd first looked over the battlefield and discovered that Ayoob Khan had foxed us. That had been bad enough, but I'd had to fight to control my frustration in front of McGucken and my brigade staff as the column seemed to move like a dozy slug in response to my orders. I knew I was being unfair, and that I mustn't pass on my worries to my subordinates, for when I looked at the troops through my binoculars I could see that they were making the best speed they could, encumbered as they were by the baggage and the hangers-on. But it was still bloody irritating.

My bladder stopped itching and contracting so much when

169

I saw the Horse Gunners and the cobbled-together smooth-bore battery move forward with an escort of cavalry. At least the guns would be poised and ready while the main body got as close to the enemy as possible before opening fire.

But then disaster: my whole plan looked likely to be ruined. By firing too soon, that Horse Gunner had warned Ayoob Khan that we were not only here, in the haze where he hadn't seen us before, but were here mob-handed. 'That silly bugger's lost us any advantage we might have had, McGucken!' My fury and impotence spilt out. 'And now the sods are getting their artillery on the very bit of high ground I didn't want them to!'

'Aye, General, but it's only native artillery,' McGucken replied, as we rode forward with my headquarters staff around me, rapidly catching the last files of the 1st Bombay Grenadiers who, along with the other two battalions, had now broken into a trot.

'Right. I'd hoped to scrub his artillery before they even got into action, but that ain't going to be the case now. We'll form the infantry up around our guns, try to hit their pieces before they open up and keep his infantry and horse at arm's length with massed rifle fire. We'll have to be careful of their Armstrongs.' I was bloody worried about those – luckily they had only a few. 'But they're thought to be short of ammunition, and if we can bowl a couple of them over, the others will soon lose heart, mark my words. We'll have to keep the cavalry well forward, too. I'll depend on them to use their initiative and break up the Ghazis before they have time to mass.' I hoped that none of my staff had heard the catch of worry in my voice.

The original plan would have worked well. Now this one would have to do, but it relied on the steadiness and discipline of the infantry and the dash of the cavalry. I didn't mention anything about the Russian advisers who were thought to be there, but the dozen or so rounds that had been thrown at the damn fool pair of guns that I'd just reeled back in seemed most unlike any native shooting I had seen before. 'Captain Heath!' The poor man was sweating for all of us as he trotted his horse over to mine. 'Instruct the infantry to form at either side of the Gunners and to be prepared to defend them from cavalry in particular. Tell the batteries to engage enemy artillery as a priority and to fire at will. Get all first-line scales of gun ammunition forward and tell all infantry quartermasters to ensure enough ball is to hand.'

We'd had our only advantage thrown away by some eejit Gunner subaltern, but we were not going to get caught without enough shot and shrapnel, as my former chief, Chelmsford, had been in South Africa last year. Now we had no chance of reaching the cover of the ravine to our front so we'd have to stand and fight and make the best of our cavalry's ability to manoeuvre around the enemy's flanks.

'Well, Jock, we'll just have to trust to our gunners' aim and keep all this bloody infantry and those damn Ghazis at bay with concentrated rifle fire.' Through the haze I could just see disturbingly large bodies of foot soldiers hurrying off the road under the lash of our shrapnel some two thousand yards to our front and disappearing into folds in the ground.

'Sir, you're right, it'll be a slogging match for sure.' Jock McGucken took his binoculars from his eyes for the first time in what seemed like hours and looked straight into my face. 'I just hope yon Bombay battalions have learnt to use their Sniders properly. What I saw of them a couple of weeks back at Gereshk didna impress me.'

'No, but if Ayoob Khan's men attack dosed up on *bhang* and bloody *jihad*, then I suspect they will just have to learn on the job.' I wish that Jock's and my debate could have continued, but as our artillery were still trying to find the enemy's range and our infantry were still moving into the cover provided by a slight nullah, a ripple of shells exploded above our guns. 'And, Jock, if that's the standard of these natives' shooting, then I reckon it could be a long day.'

'Aye, General, but the situation's changed and you've adapted the plan. These lads may not have had as much shot over their heads as we have, General, but . . . ' I looked at McGucken and saw him without grey hair and wrinkles in the rain of the Crimea and the dusty hell of the Mutiny, '. . . as long as we get among them and show them how it's done, though, they'll do rightly.'

'So, Sar'nt Kelly, we ain't going to see any more fighting, then?' The shelling had started at least two hours ago and now Billy Morgan was lying in the cover of a shallow dry nullah while the sun beat down.

'Naw, sir, that's just blank firing you can hear there. I'm surprised at you, not being able to tell the difference between blank and live after all this time in the field. Dunno what they teach you at Sandhurst these days!' replied Kelly, with a rueful smile, as the gun line, two hundred yards to their left, bellowed shells back at the Afghan artillery. 'Them Ghazis will be up in a moment wanting to take tea with you, see'f I'm not right. Here, *bhisti-wallah*, here. Get your bottle filled while we've got the chance, sir.'

'Have all the lads topped up, Sar'nt Kelly?' asked Morgan, as the native water bearer came crouching through the sand with his great *chaggle* almost empty.

'Aye, sir, your turn,' replied Kelly, as Morgan handed his wooden bottle to the Indian bearer and watched the warm, muddy, leather-and-tar-tainted water trickle out.

'So, what do you really think, Sar'nt Kelly?' asked Morgan. He looked around H Company as the men, sweat-stained and covered with fast-drying mud, now sprawled in the safety of the dry stream bed while the battle thundered overhead. Most of the soldiers had removed their sun-helmets and were sponging their foreheads with water-soaked rags before knotting the same bits of cloth around their throats. Belts, pouches and haversacks were eased and loosened, the weight being taken by the sand and grit of the nullah floor. The only things that weren't allowed to touch the ground were the precious Martini-Henrys, each action covered from the dust with a carefully rolled-on sock with the foot cut away.

'I reckon we're in for a right barney, I do. Let's just 'ave a peep at what the company commander's lookin' at, shall we? You lot stay 'ere – and someone 'old Bobby, will you? Come on, sir.' The terrier strained at his collar to be with his master, but Kelly grabbed his rifle and picked his way to the forward edge of the nullah where Captain Beresford-Peirse and Colour Sergeant James lay, scanning the scene before them with their binoculars.

'Hello, you two.' Beresford-Peirse's moustache, normally so spruce, had little drops of sweat hanging off it. 'I was just about to ask you to join us.' Billy Morgan couldn't decide whether or not Beresford-Peirse's careful insouciance annoyed him. What he did know was that the men – to whom the captain was always 'B-P' – liked and admired him, which was normally a pretty good benchmark, he thought.

'Now look at those hills yonder.' Beresford-Peirse pointed to the Khakrez foothills about two thousand yards to their front. 'You'll see the Afghan guns firing from time to time. There – three guns fired at once.' Kelly and Morgan saw plumes of white smoke jet out from a craggy platform before the rounds burst well short and wide of their own gunners. 'The colour sar'nt and I have counted about twenty-four guns in action so far and I believe that the six breech-loaders are right in the middle of their line.' Morgan searched for the fabled Armstrongs, but couldn't identify them.

'Luckily, they're not shooting well, but our own guns ain't hitting anything either so far.' Beresford-Peirse's monologue was interrupted by a section of E Battery returning fire. 'This haze makes the range damn difficult for both sides to estimate.

The colour sar'nt and I were just speculating on where all that bloody infantry we saw might have got to.'

'Was that infantry, Beresford-Peirse? I could see something indistinct in the distance that seemed to be moving, but I couldn't decide if it was the enemy or how many there might be.' Morgan didn't really care any more if he sounded naïve – he just wanted to know what his elders' and betters' assessment was.

'Well, it ain't Scotch mist, Morgan, of that you can be sure,' Beresford-Peirse replied, not unkindly, 'but I think they must have disappeared into the nullah from which we were going to open fire on them, with our own guns supporting us from here. Bloody irritating that the Horse Gunners gave the game away because now all that we, the infantry, can do is protect the guns when the enemy comes at us – and that they will. So, the brigade commander has sent the Grenadiers down to the left.' He pointed to where, five hundred yards away, the three infantry battalions were lying in a curving line that followed the cover provided by the nullah they had chanced upon. 'Jacob's Rifles are in the centre – that's their B Company just to our left.' Morgan saw the Bombay troops going through exactly the same water-guzzling routine as his own men. 'Our own companies are to our right, F, D, C and B on the flank with a couple of smooth-bore guns as the right markers.'

'Including that mouthy Williams – 'e was bouncing along on a gun carriage like 'e was fuckin' born to it, 'e was.' Colour Sergeant James addressed this to Sergeant Kelly, and Morgan suddenly realised how much he missed Posh's banter.

'Commanding officer's just to our rear.' Beresford-Peirse pointed over the lip of the nullah to where Lieutenant Colonel James Galbraith was sitting astride his horribly obvious grey gelding, his staff around him, as oblivious to the artillery duel as they would have been to a shower of rain. A little to his left, Morgan noticed the two young

174

ensigns, Honeywood carrying the great green silk regimental colour and Olivey with the Union Flag Queen's Colour, both billowing in the wind.

'And what do you expect Ayoob Khan will try to do, Beresford-Peirse?' asked Morgan.

'Well, if he's got any sense, he'll attempt to pin us here with some of his force, then crack on to Kandahar, but I don't think that's in an Afghan's nature. His instinct will be to smash us — and that's why he's got all his guns up and in the shop window. He'll want to turn our flank if he can with his horsemen but I suspect he doesn't know just how many cavalry we've got. They'll take care of any Heratis that get ideas above their station. No, I imagine it'll be a grinding match between their guns and ours. Then they'll unleash their regulars and their holy bloody warriors on us. And my money's on Messrs Snider, Martini-Henry and this sweaty bunch of clowns.' Beresford-Peirse looked around his command, most of whom were doing what, Morgan had noticed, came most naturally to them and were resting with their helmets covering their eyes from the sun. 'Colour Sar'nt, Sar'nt Kelly, back to the men, please. Check that everything and everyone's in good fettle, please.'

With a quiet 'Sir', the two NCOs wormed down the bank and trotted off to the troops, leaving the two officers together.

'Well, how are the men going to perform today, d'you think, Morgan?'

Morgan saw a trap in this question from his company commander. 'As you say, Beresford-Peirse, they'll be fine as long as the ammunition lasts and they remember all they've been taught,' he replied, desperately searching his mind for any details he could throw in to show just how intimately he knew his men. The captain's remarks after the fighting around Gereshk had bitten deep but he didn't think he wanted a long discourse on the latest dramas to unfold in Private Dennis's life or Lance Corporal Purcell's prickly heat.

'Hmm, and how about you? This shows every sign of being a right good fight and the lads will need every bit of leadership we can give them, if they're to keep this wretched lot at bay.' Beresford-Peirse stretched his arm out towards the Afghan host. 'So, I shall need you to stand back a bit, to read the battle and not to get too much involved in the business of killing – that's the soldiers' job. Try to take a longer view. Try to anticipate what might happen next and how we might prepare ourselves for it and, above all else, don't let the men detect any hesitancy or indecision.'

Hesitancy or indecision? thought Morgan. He's not suggesting I might hang back, is he? He bridled to himself. He was on the point of retorting with something hot and tart, just as he'd done with his brother the other day, but he bit his words back. 'Yes, Beresford-Peirse. I understand.'

'Good, I knew you would. Damn it all, this is the first major engagement I've seen, but I just feel in my bones that the old Sixty-sixth will be tested to the full today. I don't like the look of either of the native battalions – and before you say it, I haven't let my reservations become public.' He was right – for Morgan had been about to pick him up for criticising native troops. 'No, I reckon we'll be hard pressed in the not-too-distant future and that's why I shall be depending so heavily on you, my only subaltern.'

Morgan recognized that Beresford-Peirse was trying to flatter him – which was better than having his courage brought into doubt, wasn't it? Then it dawned on him what his company commander was doing. In the same way that the officers and NCOs moved among the men cheering, checking and cajoling them at moments such as this, Beresford-Peirse was giving him a fillip. And it had worked: as Morgan scrambled back to join the troops, he felt that he'd been taken into his leader's confidence as an equal for the first time. As he checked that every round was unwrapped and ready to fire and that all oil bottles were full, he looked into the eyes of his men and saw, there, a simple trust – a trust he mustn't betray.

'How, in the name of God, have they got round there, Heath?' It was bad enough to be told that my baggage train was being attacked well in my rear, without the messenger – my brigade major – shaking like a virgin on her wedding night.

'It appears, General, that they came down the big nullah we crossed earlier, but the baggage guard seems to be holding them at the moment.' Heath's notebook was wet with sweat from his fingers.

I could have cursed myself. As we crossed the ravine, I had seen that it stretched north-east before hooking around to the north, its depths disappearing from view at that point. I'd made a note to myself, as if I were still a regimental officer, thinking that it would need to be guarded, but I didn't expressly tell anyone, expecting it to be the most natural thing in the world for the nearest unit to secure any dead ground close by. Jesus! Did I have to do everything myself?

'Hark at that, General.' McGucken was stirrup to stirrup with me, examining the map. 'That's the baggage guard's rifles unless I'm mistaken.'

And Jock was right. If you blotted out the noise of the artillery and listened hard, it was possible to hear the boom of the Sniders and the sharper crack of the Martinis a little way to our rear.

'But it's just a wee bit o' skirmishing. There's nothing very serious there, nothing that the three companies canna deal with at the moment,' said McGucken, as he continued to study the situation to our front.

In truth, I wasn't worried. I'd decided to deplete the infantry battalions of a company apiece to look after the supplies, ammunition and all our kit. If they couldn't keep a few marauding tribesmen at arm's length, then it was a pretty poor look-out. Their artillery was well handled and were giving the cavalry regiments in reserve to the left rear a pasting while they were killing far too many of our horses just behind the gun line. At least, that was what was holding my attention until Jock McGucken saw something very sinister.

'General, look beyond our gunners, about five to six hundred paces. What do you see rising up oot o' the ground?'

I looked through the haze, the smoke, the scrub and the dust, twisted the wheel on my binoculars back and forth until I got the best possible focus and managed to make out dozens of dark, bulky poles jigging about at ground level right across the brigade's front. 'I see what look like flags and standards being brandished and far too many of the damn things for my liking.' I looked at McGucken. We both knew what such things meant.

'Aye, the sods must be in that bloody ravine we were heading for,' McGucken was staring hard through his glasses, 'but they won't be there long, General. They'll come for the batteries.'

'Indeed they will, Major McGucken.' I could just hear trumpets and horns now and couldn't help but be reminded of the Pandies' flags and bugles when they came at us in a great swarm at Kotah. 'Captain Heath, tell the infantry to move out of cover and take post around the guns. Prepare to engage.'

The sun was high in the sky now. H Company had had to endure the sight of nine-pound ammunition being run forward, empty limbers rattling back to replenish their stocks, the crack of guns and the bursting of shells around them without even a sight of the enemy, let alone a shot at them. Now, it seemed, their moment had come.

Billy Morgan had followed Captain Beresford-Peirse's orders, shaking his men out into two ranks before taking his dressing from Jacob's Rifles on the left and their own F Company on their right. Now the front rank knelt and the rear rank stood, loaded, with their sights set at seven hundred, sweating into their khaki. Morgan knew what the first orders would be: the engagement would start with battalion volley fire, each company firing in turn, smoke and flame rippling down the battalion's front as they had practised so many times before. Now, as they shuffled into position, they could all see a long, low, dark smudge of humanity less than half a mile away that joggled in the heat. Just audible between the pounding of the guns was a strange, rhythmic chanting and wild trumpet calls: here was the enemy.

'Sir, why don't that lot fire at us first, sir?' Private Metcalfe, the right marker of the rear rank, asked, as Morgan walked past, trying hard to look calmer than he felt.

'Because, Metcalfe,' he answered, 'they ain't got weapons like the ones we have. There'll be a few Sniders, but most will have the old Enfield muzzle-loaders and muskets like your granddad had.'

'So, we'll give 'em a good leatherin', won't we, sir?'

'We will, Metcalfe, as long as you remember your drills and aim low.' Morgan looked at the two ranks of forty or so lads. Other than the skirmish at Gereshk, this was the first serious fight that any of them had seen and, as Beresford-Peirse had observed, it promised to be hard. The enemy artillery rounds were now banging over their heads as they tried to hit the batteries and their horses, but H Company had eyes only for the slabs of dark- and light-clothed men who were coming at them across the desert.

'D'you think each of them flags marks a platoon or what, sir?' Sergeant Kelly was moving up and down behind the rear rank with his officer. Now they both shaded their eyes and looked as the standards and banners, which were still too far away to have any discernible colour.

'Hope not. There'd be bloody thousands of the buggers if that's the case.' Above the blobs of humanity a forest of flags flew, while strange, brassy notes reached across the desert

179

towards the 66th from Ayoob Khan's musicians. 'No, I guess they're religious rather than regimental.'

'Aye, sir, an' for every bugger 'oo's carryin' a flag, there's one less bundook, ain't there?' But before Morgan could reply to his sergeant, Jacob's Rifles began an untidy fusillade on their left, the roar and smoke of the Sniders drowning any more discussion.

'Sixty-Sixth Regiment, preeee-sent.' Colonel Galbraith's command was repeated by the colour sergeants in every company as more than four hundred rifles were cuddled into the aim. 'Seven hundred, from the left, by companies, volley . . .' Galbraith paused to make sure that each man had heard the orders '. . . fire!'

Beresford-Peirse's and Morgan's swords fell, eighty shoulders bucked, eighty barrels jerked, Bobby yapped and the colonel's horse pecked as a cloud of white smoke billowed in front of H Company. Seconds later F Company fired to Morgan's right, then the others took up rolling volleys right down the line.

'Reload, H,' Beresford-Peirse called out, and Morgan saw the levers of the rifles pulled down and empty brass cases jump out with a wisp of smoke from each breech, but as the cloud cleared in front of them, the enemy still came on, apparently untouched.

'Bit high that, sir, I reckon.' Colour Sergeant James was spotting with his binoculars upwind. 'Try six hundred and aim at their ankles.'

'Six hundred, preee-sent,' Beresford-Peirse was listening for B Company on the far right flank to fire before he fired again and started the regiment's second volley. 'Aim low . . . fire!' and once again the rifles leapt.

'That's better, sir,' Colour Sergeant James yelled triumphantly and, as the smoke cleared, Morgan could see his foes stumbling and flags tumbling as the wall of lead hit home.

'Smooth-bores is firing at 'em now, sir.' Morgan had been

too engrossed in their own volley fire to hear the brass pieces right at the end of the 66th's line coming into action, but Kelly had noticed. 'Looks like they're firing canister, it does, sir.'

'Yes, you're right, Sar'nt Kelly.' Both barrels were depressed level with the ground, and each round kicked up a great sheet of dust about three hundred paces in front of the muzzles where the lowest flying bullets of the 108 in each charge spread out into a lethal fan of iron. 'Bit far for canister, though, ain't it?'

'Dunno, sir. 'Bout six hundred. I thought that was canister's furthest effective range. An' look there, sir, Johnny Af don't seem to like it,' Kelly said, without emotion as the showers of metal bit into the Afghan formations.

The steady rhythm of the regiment's volleys was soon the only noise on the battlefield that Morgan could make out, each ringing crash buffeting his ears, his voice soon hoarse as he spat out the drill-book commands. The pile of empty cartridges grew around the men's feet, the only change in detail between each thumping volley being the adjustments to range as the enemy infantry came steadily on against the sheeting lead.

But then something caught Colour Sergeant James's eye from his smoke-free vantage-point on the extreme left of the company. 'Sir, look there, sir, Afghan horse in that nullah – dozens of the sods!'

Not many heard in the cacophony of the firing, but Morgan looked across to his left where another small ravine ran at right angles to the one that the brigade was lining. About three hundred yards away a multicoloured press of men on ponies were crouching low in the saddle, some with tulwars, some with carbines and muskets, all of them with little round shields either covering their bridle hands or slung across their backs.

'They're going to charge Jacob's Rifles!' James was pulling at the company commander's sleeve, so engrossed had he become in the volley fire. 'They're invisible to 'em in that dip in the ground, sir, and they'll be on the Bombay lads in no time unless we fire into 'em.'

Morgan could see the sense in what James was saying. While the Rifles hadn't seen the stealthy advance of the enemy up the dead ground to their front, neither had the Afghans realised that the flank of their column was exposed to the 66th. The enemy were just as absorbed in their intended target as Beresford-Peirse was in his and Morgan could see that not one turbaned head was turned in their direction.

'H Company,' Beresford-Peirse's voice was even hoarser than Morgan's, 'cease fire.' Morgan repeated the order and watched as the NCOs had to drag the men's attention away from the steadily advancing infantry in front of them to listen to the words of command.

'Open your breeches, lads, let the air cool the metal.' Again, it was difficult to get the men to hear, so deaf were they from the constant detonations close to their ears. Morgan and Kelly had to drop the levers of several of the men's breeches themselves, catching the ejected rounds and pressing them into the soldiers' hands, so mesmerised had they become with the targets in front of them. 'The company will advance . . .' Beresford-Peirse paused to let his intentions sink into concussed senses '. . . by the left, quick march.' Eighty or so men stumbled forward over the sand and tussocks. No more than fifteen paces later Morgan repeated Beresford-Peirse's order to 'left wheel' and the company swung like a gate before being told to halt.

'Fuckin' 'ell, sir, we're going to murder 'em.'

The whole company loaded fresh rounds then knelt or stood ready to pour their fire into the backs of the unsuspecting cavalry no more than two hundred yards away. 'I bloody well hope so, Sar'nt Kelly,' replied Morgan, as every man and one small terrier-cross, seemed to lick their lips in anticipation.

'Cavalry can react awful quick, sir. Wouldn't it be better to get us spikes on first, sir?'

Kelly was right. All it needed was for a body of horsemen to come from another dip in the ground while the company was reloading and they would be effectively unarmed.

'You're right, Sar'nt Kelly. Wave your bayonet at the company commander.' Morgan didn't like to usurp Beresford-Peirse's authority, but as Kelly wagged his long, curved blade high above his head from behind the firing line, the company commander took the hint.

'Fix bayonets!' Every man pulled the slivers of steel from their scabbards with a sibilant hiss and slid the hilts over their muzzles, securing them with the oily locking rings. Fixing bayonets while breeches were open and half of the men were already kneeling to fire was unconventional but, thought Morgan, the troops reacted well, despite the noise and the fear.

'Load.' Rounds were pushed home and breeches closed. 'Two hundred . . .' the men pulled the iron sights down '. . . preee-sent . . .' rifles now tipped with steel came up parallel to the ground '. . . wait . . .' Morgan passed the orders on and watched as the cavalry jostled in the low ground. Beresford-Peirse was clearly waiting for the Afghans to pack themselves as densely as possible before they launched their attack and Morgan's stomach tightened with the horror at the guile of what they were about to do.

The order to fire came, and as the smoke cleared and the ringing in his ears lessened, Morgan could see and hear the carnage that the mass rifle fire had created.

'That should rap their fuckin' knuckles, sir, shoon't it?' Kelly said quietly, as Morgan and he gazed at the chaos. The soldiers had done as they were taught when engaging cavalry and had fired at the mounts. In the scrum of men and animals, about a dozen horses either kicked on their sides or dragged their hind legs across the ground where the bullets had splintered their spines. There were squeals and whinnies of pain and fear, while among the tangle of limbs and harness, wounded and dead men slumped from the saddles.

'Reload.' Morgan looked at the men's faces. So many of these men had learnt to value horseflesh from behind the plough or the dray that there was nothing but revulsion.

'Preee-sent . . .' But even as Beresford-Peirse prepared to repeat the medicine, those horsemen who could – as well as another twenty or so who had been shielded from the fire by the shoulder of the nullah – came shrieking at them, doing their best to pick up speed despite the slope up which they had to attack.

The rifles banged again. Morgan heard lead hit flesh just a few yards to his front as the horses' hoofs drummed on the ground, the smoke hiding everything. But as the breeze cleared the reek, the Afghans were within a spit of them.

'Give 'em the bayonet, lads!' yelled Kelly, and Billy found himself croaking inanities as the ponies and riders trotted by, all force smashed out of the charge by the last numbing volley. The horsemen tried a few half-hearted jabs and slashes as they came past H Company, but all they wanted to do was escape more punishment.

'Get on, you fucker.' Private Metcalfe reached forward as far as he could from the rear rank and poked the last inch of his bayonet into the flank of a passing pony. The animal jerked away with a shriek of pain as the sharp metal opened a gash inches long in its flesh that made it kick its hoofs and swerve away quite out of control. Morgan saw one or two men fire at the fleeing cavalry, who were now being pelted by F Company, before the next order took him by surprise.

'Targets on ground, one hundred, fire at will.' Rifles started to crack individually, hitting single horses and wounded men who squirmed in the sand. Morgan watched as dust kicked

184

up around the casualties, heard the familiar thump of bullets tearing bodies until all was quiet and still among the litter of corpses in front of them.

Despite the ballocks at the start of the action a couple of hours ago, things seemed to be developing as well as could be expected. My guns were getting a bit of a hammering, for sure, but they were giving it back hot and strong. I hadn't seen much of the cavalry, but I was less concerned about them than I was about the infantry action, which now seemed to be general. Fire was erupting all the way down the rough crescent described by the three battalions, but the powder smoke had become so dense that it clung to their kneeling and standing ranks, despite the breeze. Now more Ghazis and Herati regulars were coming at the boys than fleas on a dog's back – but success today, I knew, would rest on these all too few files of khaki topped with turbans and sun-helmets. If the guns were to do their job, the infantry must hold firm.

I was spurring on to the middle of the firing line in order to find out how Jacob's Rifles were faring, when I saw the damnedest thing. A company of the 66th had just pulled off the neatest trick I've ever witnessed on the field of battle. First, they tumbled to ruin a mob of irregular cavalry that had appeared from God-knows-where, then stood against the counter-charge and even saw the buggers off with the bayonet. 'Bravo, lads, bravely done!' McGucken and I were standing in our stirrups – even Heath had stopped chewing his moustache – and as the order was given for the men to break ranks and double back into line, I recognised my son Billy trotting along with his sergeant, both grinning like pooches.

'Ah, H Company, unless I'm mistaken. Mr Morgan, Sar'nt Kelly–' A shell cracked harmlessly overhead nearby, interrupting my eulogy. 'Well done, my boys.' I tried to remember how senior officers had cheered on the troops on other battle-fields as the soldiers poured past me. 'Where's Beresford-Peirse?' Too often I failed the crucial test of a leader by being unable to remember subordinates' names. Sometimes I got it right, though, and what a difference it made – Sergeant Kelly positively glowed with pleasure assuming, quite rightly, that the sins of the Kandahar patrol had been forgotten.

'Over there, General – we put a stop in that lot, did we not?' Billy was the picture of excited pleasure: he might just have scored the winning goal at school rather than sent men and animals to eternity. He'd done well, but I'd also seen the way that the wounded had been despatched and hoped he wasn't enjoying it too much. It was a funny thing, but I couldn't get the reports of the child Billy had killed in Kandahar out of my mind. To me, my son was still just a lad who looked as if he might come bursting round the corner with a couple of trout he'd caught back at Glassdrumman, grinning all over his face. But that was daft.

'You did, son, you did.' As his company commander approached, Billy threw me a salute and sprinted off after his men.

'Bravo, Beresford-Peirse, neatly done.' I leaned on my pommel and tried not to flinch as another couple of shells exploded blackly. 'Word of warning, though, don't let any of those newspaper men see you firing into the wounded – no, no . . .' Beresford-Peirse tried to reply '. . . you and I know how bloody deadly the Afghans can be, especially when they're winged, but just be careful. You and your men have done well.'

Before I could say anything more, McGucken pulled at my sleeve. 'Tom Nuttall wants you, General.' I swung Rainbow around and headed back through the files of H Company, past a pair of E Battery's nine-pounders, before pulling in next to Galbraith and the 66th's colour party, where my cavalry commander was waiting for me. Strange, the horses seemed unfussed by the shriek of gunfire, but the flapping silk of the great flags made them jib like crazy.

'Morgan, there's Afghan horsemen making a devil of a nuisance of themselves over yonder.' Tom Nuttall had the Banbury bit pulled tight on his chestnut to prevent her jumping around worse than she already was. 'They're leaking round the left flank and making it impossible for the Grenadiers' carrying parties to get their ammunition forward and their casualties back. One of the Gunners' limbers has had a brisk little set-to and the *bhistis* are refusing to take the water up because it's too dangerous.'

I looked towards the section of guns six hundred yards away that marked the extreme left of the Bombay Grenadiers' and the brigade's line. While I couldn't see anything of note, except a deuce of a lot of artillery and musketry smoke, I didn't like the sound of this one bit. Not only had the crafty sods got round my right rear, they now appeared to be infiltrating on my left.

'With your permission, I'm going to use one of my squadrons to clear them. Do you want me to leave them on the left flank to support the Grenadiers? I gather that a couple of their British officers have been hit.'

Nuttall was telling me something I really did not want to hear. The Bombay Grenadiers were fine as long as they were well led, but with their officers down . . .

'Yes, by all means clear the ground, but we can't afford any more cavalry casualties.' I knew that both regiments had already been quite badly galled by shellfire. 'Please don't leave them exposed. How long before they move?'

'They'll form up just here, behind the Sixty-Sixth, and be ready to advance at your command in about ten minutes.' With that, Tom Nuttall and his staff saluted and trotted off to give orders. And that left me with a pretty bleak sight. Now all of my brigade was under shell fire and simultaneous attack from both regulars and Ghazis – the whole of the line was cocooned in dense white smoke illuminated with the flashes of the guns and the volley fire from the rifles. Now I noticed, for the first time, little parties of stretcher-bearers carrying the wounded to the field hospital where, my staff informed me, the enemy was already making his presence felt. Indeed, Galbraith had just told me that his surgeon, Preston, had been wounded while treating one of his own lads.

But my view of death, fear and uproar was interrupted by a completely different noise.

'Fookin' 'ell, it's the Runaway 'Orse!' H Company, whose NCOs were trying to get them back into line, were giving full vent to their dislike of the lancers of A Squadron of the 3rd Scinde Horse, whom Nuttall had sent forward. ''S all right, lads, we'll let you know when we need a toothpick,' and other well-worn witticisms were bandied about to the bemusement of the Pathans, but not the British officers and some of the longer-serving NCOs.

And then I saw a curious thing. The three of us, a father and his two sons, were in this little patch of war-torn wilderness, but not even the danger and stench of fear could unite the boys. As the 66th hooted and cat-called, Billy shook with laughter while looking straight at his brother; meanwhile, Sam sat bolt upright on his horse and stared back at his brother without a twitch on his face – he held Billy's eye. God, if Mary were here she'd bang their heads together, so she would.

'Get on then, Shaw.' Another minor triumph: I'd remembered someone else's name just when it was important. 'I want A Squadron to clear these damn marauders out of the rear of the guns and the Bombay Grenadiers. Any questions?'

But Shaw, young though he was, seemed to know his job and in no time, he had the columns of fours wheeling into line and the squadron was away into the smoke and shrapnel, lances all upright and proper, as smart as paint. And that put a bung in the wiseacres of H Company – and no mistake.

* * *

188

'And what else did that owl-shit have to say, Keenan sahib?'
Daffadar Sayed Miran's English was good enough to understand most of H Company's ribaldry. 'Are they not our
brothers? Do we not fight the same enemy? Why, sahib,
most of these jawans' – he looked to either side of him at
the bearded faces of the troop, all of whom were now
tense in their saddles as they trotted forward, lances still
upright, scanning the desert for targets – 'are fighting *for*
Victoria against men of their own blood. Why should they
mock us?'

'Daffadar sahib, I will explain the ignorance of these fools
when we have a little more time.' Keenan was furious, and
humiliated by the actions of his brother's company. He recognised the friction caused by Rissaldar Singh's murder and that
nonsense over the terrier a few days ago and he was also
aware that neither his nor Billy's behaviour was suitable for
an officer. But that comment about the 'Runaway Horse' had
bitten deep. Thank God, he thought, that no one had yet
connected his troop with this morning's débâcle caused by
Maclaine's guns. 'Let's just give some of these badmashes the
opportunity to meet the death they desire.'

Almost as he spoke, the bugle signalled the 'trot march' as
a clutch of turbaned, dark-robed horsemen suddenly fled at
the sight of the squadron. What these men had been about,
Keenan never knew, but they were skulking around, hidden
by some dense thorn bushes. They had obviously been
concealing themselves, hoping that the lancers would not see
them, when something had made them decide to bolt. Now
they burst like a flock of partridge, on handy little ponies that
seemed to respond to a touch of rein or spur far more readily
than one of the whalers upon which many of the Scinde Horse
were mounted. Keenan saw their flying robes, their soft leather
boots and an assortment of carbines, swords and long Khyber
knives, and knew at once that he was chasing tribesmen who
had rallied to Ayoob Khan's colours. What these men lacked

in formal discipline they more than made up for in raw horsemanship and cunning: they were among the finest irregular cavalry that he and his men were ever likely to meet in battle.

Keenan was suddenly breathless with excitement. A trooper was thrown to the ground as his horse pitched into a rat-hole, and another fell to a lucky artillery shell, but nothing checked the lancers as they bore down on their foes. The Afghans galloped in all directions, heels kicking hard at their horses' flanks, hoping to throw the sowars from the chase – but they had left it too late. Keenan watched lance heads flicker and jab as men were speared from the saddle. But the man he had selected for his own attention was mounted better than the others. This man had decided to break away and run alone – he was ten yards from the others when Keenan put his spurs to Kala's flanks and flexed his sword arm ready to strike.

The Afghan rode well, but the march through plains and foothills and poor fodder had left his pony no match for an oats-and-bran-fed Irish hunter. Keenan could almost feel the man's terror as his enemy crouched lower and lower over his horse's flying mane, feet drumming on its ribs, reins whipping at its flesh. But that terror didn't stop Keenan: his sword arm bent at the elbow, he touched Kala with his spurs until she drew almost level with the tribesman, then flicked the shining steel forward, watching with fascination as the blade sank effortlessly into the rider's kidney.

The Afghan arched back without a sound and his horse slowed instantly, allowing Keenan to pull the body from the saddle with the leverage of the sword. Then it was over. The corpse slipped from the blade to the sand, the pony stopped and sniffed its master, while his own mount responded gracefully to the rein. But there was no time for the hunter to dwell over his quarry for the squadron was rallying and re-forming. He turned to join them, and as he saw the blood on his blade he thought of Billy and the scorn on his face.

Runaway Horse, he thought. *I'll give you Runaway bloody Horse, my little brother!*

EIGHT

Maiwand, Afternoon

Along with the inferno of smoke and gunfire came another all-consuming problem: thirst. From where I was sitting on Rainbow, hard up behind the firing line with my headquarters, I could see that each infantry battalion's NCOs and orderlies were keeping the ammunition coming, fresh boxes of cartridges being opened and placed behind every ten men. But water was another matter. I looked at my watch: it was five and twenty past two, we'd been in action for more than two hours now and the sun was unforgiving. The problem was the *bhisti-wallahs*, whose job was not only to keep the men's water-bottles filled, but also to run up and down the line giving each rifleman a mouthful from the great leather *chaggle* and to wash the wounds of the injured.

But the bloody Afghans had enough men between ourselves and the baggage park where the water camels lay to frighten the *bhistis* off their job. What little wretch was going to risk his skinny arse going to fetch water for two *annas* a day? This was going to be as bad as running out of shot; we would have to clear those savages from our rear just as soon as we'd dealt with the buggers who were making life so difficult on the flank of the Bombay Grenadiers.

I'd just watched Sam vanish with his men into the smoke

192

and noise when my own world turned upside-down. The next sensation I had was spitting grit from my mouth and a harsh Scottish voice competing with the thunderclap ringing in my ears.

'You all right there, General?' Hands were pulling me into a sitting position. There was a stink of sweat and that horrid, greasy, carnivorous smell of the butcher's shop. A water-bottle was pushed into my mouth. 'Drink some of this. Can you move your feet?' McGucken tried to find out what was wrong with me.

I heard a scuffing of hoofs and whinnying close by, harsh, urgent words and then a pistol shot.

'I hope you din't pay too much for poor Rainbow, General,' said McGucken, as calmly as if we were at a horse fair. 'The shell hit her spine and there was no saving her − nor Heath, neither.'

I was suddenly conscious that I was looking straight into my brigade major's rather bloody face. He lay on his side just in front of me, and even in my stunned state I had time to study him. His back was arched, his innards spread in a great bluey-red mass of sausagemeat, a puddle of blood rapidly soaking into the ground below him. The poor fellow: he was no more a soldier than I was a botanist. He was more at home in a greenhouse or a drawing room than out here in this God-forsaken butcher's shambles. I'd long suspected that he preferred the safety and relative comfort of Brigade Headquarters to facing the foibles of a regiment on campaign. Through my headache I thought of his parents back in Sheffield (it was Sheffield, wasn't it?), enjoying what the papers told me was an unusually pleasant summer when the telegram would arrive. Even in death he looked confused, his brown eyes staring reproachfully at me, I felt.

'The same round took his guts oot before hitting your charger in the rump, General, and wheeking you arse over tit. Dinna fash about that . . .' McGucken could see me looking

193

down at the blood smeared over my thighs and belly. 'That's no' yours, that's Heath's – he was sitting right alongside you when yous were struck. You all right to stand?'

One of McGucken's many strong points was his complete inability to fuss or exaggerate things. So what if my principal staff officer had been killed in my lap? So what if I'd just been pitched headlong to the unyielding ground? Nothing was broken, was it? At least McGucken didn't deliver his usual line in such circumstances: 'Well, if ye canna tek a joke ye should never have joined!' Instead, he pulled me to my feet, dusted off my helmet and called for one of the spare horses that were kept to hand for just such eventualities.

I shook myself, felt not just my scrapes and cuts, but every day of my forty-nine years and was about to sit down again, pull at my flask, light a pipe and tell some other fool to take over while I had a breather, when I realised that everyone was watching me. And that was why I was getting the gimlet tartan eye from McGucken and that was why I positively leapt into the saddle of the whaler they brought up and busied myself wiping Heath's blood and a battalion of flies off the lenses of my binoculars when all I felt like doing was chucking in the towel.

'Right, so what's happened while I've been on the canvas?' I tried to sound light-hearted – to say it loud enough to convince everyone, even myself, that things were going to be all right.

'Well, the Scindis did well over on the left and the Grenadiers appear to be holding, but I'm a wee bit worried about the Rifles in the centre,' said McGucken – and I could see what he meant. The 66th were volleying like good 'uns on the right while things looked a little quieter on the left, but in the middle of the line our guns were banging away fit to bust, accompanied by screams and crazy yells, trumpets and some sort of snake-charmer music. The smoke obscured everything. Meanwhile, the stretcher-bearers were coming thick and fast from the rear of the Rifles' line. 'Should we not move the pair of smooth-bores from the left into the middle to give 'em a bit more support? That's where the Ghazis appear to be thickest.'

'Aye, sound idea. Get a message to Slade to move that pair of guns as fast as he can – we can't have the buggers getting through in the centre.' Slade was a good man – he'd done wonders in knocking his improvised battery of old guns and infantrymen into shape. I watched as the galloper dashed off with my orders and prayed that the quartermasters had got enough powder, shot and shell forward before the Ghazis started to bugger things up. God's teeth, how my old bones ached.

Billy Morgan smiled ruefully to himself as he thought about all his seniors in the mess back in Kandahar and their predictions of a quiet summer, a restful march to the railhead and then to India. Even Sar'nt Kelly had voiced the same ideas. But that sort of thinking, he supposed, was the legacy of too much time in garrison, the hope of the professional soldier that if they downplayed the prospect of hard knocks, and loudly envied the good fortunes of other regiments who were winning laurels, it might, just might, come true for them too.

Well, now they had it – in full measure. The Ghazis were coming at them like a swarm of locusts and being swiped away by volley after volley of half-inch Martini bullets. Morgan had never realised just how powerful the blunt lead rounds were: no amount of range work firing at board and paper targets could prepare you for the meaty thump of the missile when it struck flesh. Through the smoke of each volley, he watched full-grown men being thrown down like dolls, their crazy, mindless, sprinting, howling bodies grabbed by invisible fists and hurled back into the crowding ranks behind. If the ammunition lasted, the men remembered their training and the battalions on their flanks did their jobs, they might all live to see that gentle march back to India, thought Morgan, as yet another stream of lead and hate split his ears.

They had trained hard, but nothing could have prepared H Company for the strain that continual firing put upon the rifles.

'Well, just wrap some paper around it, Metcalfe!' yelled Sergeant Kelly, above the rolling musketry, the curses of the men and the cries of the enemy. He hadn't a gill of sympathy for the wiry Reading lad. 'Just try not to touch the barrel and use a bit more of this.' He passed some sheets of yellowy waxed paper in which bundles of ten cartridges were wrapped and with which the ground was now littered.

'It still burns me bleedin' 'and, Sar'nt, even through the paper,' Metcalfe whined. He and many of the other men were now finding the barrels of their Martini-Henrys almost impossible to hold.

'Well, I don't give a fuck. Just keep firing unless you want a foot of steel in yer belly,' Kelly growled hoarsely. ''Ow you gettin' on, sir?'

'Oh, guinea a minute, Sar'nt Kelly, thank you,' replied Billy Morgan, as he struggled with one of the other soldiers' rifles. 'These Snider cleaning rods are the answer.' He thumped a steel rod hard down the muzzle and was rewarded by the empty cartridge case tinkling out of the open breech where it had been firmly stuck. 'The heat's made the case expand too much, Wigmore. Try to cool the action whenever you get the chance, but don't waste your time with your Martini rod – it's too short. Shout for me or for one of the NCOs.' Morgan couldn't believe how quickly each man had fired off the seventy rounds he was carrying, or how rapidly the rifles had overheated. Miraculously, though, Colour Sergeant James had appeared with the longer Snider rods when it had become obvious that the Martini pattern was too short to reach the stuck cases.

'I will, sir, so long as Johnny Af leaves off for a minute.

Not much sign of that, though, sir, is there?' Wigmore answered breathlessly, as he pushed another cartridge home, flicked the lever closed, pulled the butt into his shoulder and fired in one fluid movement.

'Good hit, Wigmore,' said Morgan, the boom of the soldier's rifle redoubling the singing in his ears. 'Another one sent to cash in his chips.' The bullet had thrown a Ghazi standard-bearer into the sand. As Morgan looked through the smoke and dust, he saw that the dead and wounded enemy lay so thickly no more than fifty paces in front of the company's muzzles that the next wave of attackers was having to leap over them. Yet on they came, green and black flags being rushed forward and planted in the ground before the carriers fell, ripped by lead.

'What d'you mean you're pulling back to the ammunition lines, Sar'nt?' I could scarcely believe my eyes. The situation on the left centre where the two Bombay battalions met was worrying me, and since my fall from my horse, I knew that I'd lost any feel for what was going on there, so I'd ridden forward with McGucken and what remained of my staff to see for myself. 'Didn't you get the message to move to support the Bombay Grenadiers?'

'I did, sir . . .' I felt sorry for the poor sergeant being pulled up in the middle of a very hot little fight by his brigade commander '. . . but we're out of ready ammunition, sir, an' Cap'n Slade's message arrived just before your'n, sir.' The man had braced to attention in his saddle next to his two guns, which were now limbered up and being towed to the rear with a great plume of dust following them.

'What bloody message, man?' My fury was not helped by my aches and pains. 'I told Captain Slade quite clearly to move you over to the centre here.'

'Aye, sir, I know you did, but we've got no shot left, sir. Battery commander told us to get to the ammunition lines and

197

collect what there is before coming back.' The man answered well enough, but I could see that he was quivering − whether as a result of what I or the Afghans were doing to him was far from clear.

'What − you've got no rounds left?' This seemed incredible to me while E Battery's pieces were still firing as hard as they could.

'No, sir. We was short when we started, and we've fired the bloody lot away into them crazy Ghazis, sir. May I carry on, sir, please?' I saw the wounded man draped across the ammunition limber and realised that one of the traces was short of a horse − all in all, the anonymous sergeant's command was looking a bit dog-eared, yet I could detect no lack of courage. He obviously wanted to find more ammunition and then get back into the fight − though I wouldn't have blamed him if he'd run like a rabbit. Meanwhile, all that my outrage was achieving was more delay.

'Aye, away with you, Sar'nt, and bloody well done.' I hoped that little rejoinder would stiffen his resolve even further. Meanwhile, I'd never seen or heard anything like the din and uproar among the Grenadiers' firing line as the enemy came on yet again.

'We need to find Anderson, General.' McGucken was right. We did need to find the Grenadiers' commanding officer, the man who'd wanted to fall back to Kandahar and had spouted the bloody tactics manual at me as though I was some green-horn. And there he was, sitting on his neat little roan next to his colour party while his Bombay Grenadiers were reeling around like a bunch of drunks. True, the enemy was close and exceedingly vexed; true, the jawans were keeping up a good rate of fire with their Sniders and mowing the Ghazis down by the dozen, but the ranks were uneven and buckled, and too many men were going to the rear, helping to carry the wounded.

'Anderson, what in God's name's going on, man?' I touched

my new horse forward through the smoke and the disorganised turbaned ranks until I was right next to the Grenadiers' colonel. I had to bellow at him, not just to make myself heard but to penetrate the torpor that seemed to have come upon him. At first he just sat there, taking the weight off his horse's back by leaning forward, stiff-armed, on his pommel, looking straight ahead at the tide of enemy dead and wounded that peeped through the gunsmoke. It took me three attempts or more to get his attention and then he almost jumped out of his skin when he recognised me. 'Where are your officers, Anderson?' I demanded, for I could see no Britons among the sweating, struggling, shooting khaki ranks, just the odd jemadar and subadar here and there.

'My officers have gone to get more ball, I'll have you know,' Anderson positively snarled back at me with no 'sir' or 'General', not an ounce of respect. 'We're down to our last few rounds and the bloody bearers are too fucking scared to go and get more. Hughson's dead, Bailey's been struck and the others I've sent off so that we can shoot our way out of this damned mess of yours!'

The man had clearly lost his flint. I'd always thought he had more interest in the parade square than the field, and when he and Malcolmson had lobbied so hard after Gereshk to return to Kandahar, I'd worried some more about him. Clearly I was right to, for his battalion was rapidly falling to pieces around him. What the damned cheeky bastard needed to do—

'Dear God, not again, General!' I just heard McGucken exclaim as Anderson was thrown from his saddle and right across mine by a whistling piece of enemy lead. But at least Anderson wasn't dead. He had a fair-sized hole torn in his shoulder, which was gouting blood, and he was bleating like a child, but at least he was still drawing breath.

'Who's in charge now, err . . .' This time my memory let me down. Anderson was being lifted from his horse by a series of willing Bombay vassals and only his adjutant remained. 'I'm sorry, I've forgotten your name,'

'Hinde, sir, Charles Hinde.' The lad looked no more than twenty-one – though he must have been older than that to be holding the adjutant's appointment – and he was in a suit of the expensively tailored cotton drill that Anderson insisted upon.

'Well, Mr Hinde, tell me what's going on.' But as the youngster started to point out the chaos that was abundantly clear to me, I suddenly became aware that figures were running through the smoke to our left rear, running so hard that they had no breath to shout, running so hard that they had thrown their weapons away and were even stripping off their belts and pouches to lighten their load.

'Jesus, General, the Rifles on the left have broken!' McGucken bellowed what I'd already grasped, just as a shrapnel round seemed to burst directly over young Hinde's and my head. The boy sat there paralysed, gawping round his sepoys, his mouth slightly open, his oh-so-fashionably trimmed moustache just a little unkempt.

'Get your bayonets on, Charlie, my lad, and tell your fellows to form square for whatever has hit the left will be coming our way damn quick.' This scandalised the lad who, along with the rather elderly subedar major whom I had not noticed until then, began shouting incomprehensible orders in Hindi. What I should have expected was Jock McGucken doing what he did best.

One minute the man was mounted beside me. Then, when he'd realised just what a mess we were in, he was out of the saddle like a dart. He'd thrown his reins to my trumpeter and was moving among the troops with the same Glasgow-granite confidence I'd seen from Dublin to Delhi. No shouting, no panic, just quiet words in the troops' own language as he pushed and nudged them into line, helping a shaking hand as it wobbled a bayonet on to a muzzle – I even saw him lowering a sepoy into the kneeling position as gently as if the man were a child. And it worked – where there had been dismay there was now certainty; where the men had been looking over their shoulders and watching their brothers flee to safety, there was now defiance. Though we never managed to form any sort of square before that human wave broke over us, the fact that we weren't smashed to ruins in seconds was entirely due to Jock and the backbone he gave the native officers.

I've never, in all my life, seen anything like the blind bloody courage of those Ghazis. They came in all shapes and sizes, some old, others as young as the youth Billy had killed back in Kandahar, dressed in soiled white robes and not a firearm among them. They didn't co-ordinate things particularly well – there was a bit of firing from the regular Herati infantry – but those zealots came at us in great rushes yelling, '*Din-din*,' and brandishing foot-long bread knives. The Sniders cut 'em down good style, but there wasn't that in-built discipline among the sepoys that there should have been. The rear rank wallah ought to have held his fire until his mucker in the front rank had discharged his piece, reloaded and then vice versa. The jawans were firing anyhow, and running short of lead, while their rifles fouled and jammed with the sheer number of rounds they'd expended.

'Steady, lads, give 'em the steel now!' McGucken was just in front of me among the troops when a handful of *jihad*ists got right up to the Grenadiers' front rank. The Scot had picked up a rifle and bayonet, but not even he could stop one Bombay lad, who had fallen forward lightly wounded in the arm, being grabbed by his equipment straps and pulled into the shrieking crowd.

'Get down – get out the way!' I shouted, loudly enough for the troops below my horse's nose to understand that I needed a clear shot at the foe, and as they barged each other clear, McGucken adding a bit of impetus with the back of his hand, I emptied all six chambers into the bastards.

Now, I've owned revolvers all my life and always distrusted the damn things. That was why, when the quartermaster offered me one of the new Enfield Mark One jobs in the rather odd .476 calibre free of charge, I'd accepted it but with some reservations. I'd fired a few rounds from it in Karachi, found it gave a convincing kick, and had then stuffed it away in my holster where, other than for the odd bit of cleaning, it had been ever since. I had confidently expected never to have to use such a thing again, yet here I was, almost fifty, a general officer, plugging away with the wretched thing as if I were a red-arse subaltern – at least this one didn't jam.

Actually, it was quite effective. At least three rounds told – I saw one unlucky sod stop half an inch of lead just below the eye, which took the back of his head off – but it wasn't enough to save the Grenadier. As my pistol smoke cleared and I scrabbled to break the Enfield and reload, I saw the knife blades flash and fall, stabbing and poking the life out of the sepoy. Eventually, the Ghazis turned and fled, leaving three or four of their number dead or struggling bloodily on the ground, piled on top of the dead soldier whose khaki tunic was rusty with his gore.

'Major McGucken, these boys will have to hold as best they can. Get back in the saddle, man – we need to shore up the right flank now,' I shouted.

But there was one last thing that he felt he had to do before he obeyed me. 'On guard, I'll give ye death wish!' Suddenly, McGucken had lost twenty years and countless promotions. He was back in the Mutiny as a colour sergeant, showing how it should be done. 'Dinna threaten me with that wee bit o' cutlery, boy!' He had stepped from the ranks to deal with a lone Ghazi who had chosen not to retreat with his comrades. The Afghan sidestepped and dodged, rolled up the right sleeve of his robe and stuck out the beard with which Allah would lift him to heaven after his warrior's death. Twice the long knife darted forward and twice it rang against the metal of

McGucken's bayonet as the big Scot stamped forward in the dust, parrying and feinting, mumbling, 'Is that the best ye've got, son?' while the sepoys watched admiringly.

Then he struck. The Ghazi made the mistake of lowering the tip of his knife for a second and it was all that McGucken needed. A perfect blow took the tribesman in the stomach – I saw the tip of the blade tenting the back of the Afghan's tunic as, with a grunt, McGucken pulled the weapon clear and caught his victim a smashing blow with the butt of his rifle across the nose and cheek. The Ghazi fell to the ground.

'Ideas above his station, yon fool,' said McGucken, as his horse, better trained than my screw, stood still and let him find a stirrup iron, despite the hell that was going on around him.

'Think you can hang on, Hinde?' As I gathered up my staff, I looked hard at the adjutant of the Bombay Grenadiers. 'I'll get some of those brass guns to support you once they've got a bit more powder and shell.'

'Yes, General . . . We can hold so long as we can get some more rounds – and water wouldn't come amiss, either.'

I thought the lad looked steadier now. 'Aye, well, my left flank depends upon you and these jawans. You're doing fine, but don't falter now, whatever you do.' With that, my bunch of horsemen pushed between the files of Grenadiers and spurred down to the rear of the companies of the Rifles, who still stood firm, past E Battery and on towards the 66th.

'They'd best hold out, General.' McGucken had drawn his horse alongside mine. The Afghan's blood was still smeared over his hands. 'We've got problems enough to our rear, without anyone else making off, like the Rifles did.'

'You're right, Jock. Let's get those bloody smooth-bores back into action and up among the Grenadiers. I don't suppose we could use a company of the Sixty-Sixth, could we?' I asked, as the sturdy line of Galbraith's men continued to lace

Martini-Henry fire into the Afghans from behind the cover that the nullah lip provided.

Just as McGucken and I came up to Galbraith's party, there was one of those strange lulls that sweep across battlefields from time to time. The enemy's guns were silent – as were ours. The Ghazis and Heratis fell back and I thought we might have a bit of a respite now that the left appeared to be more stable.

'How are the Sixty-Sixth faring, Galbraith?' I asked, as he sat on his grey – as unruffled as if he were at the Aldershot Tattoo.

'We're fine, General,' Galbraith replied calmly. 'We've fired a whore of a lot of shot and you can see the results.' The pause had allowed much of the smoke to be swept away by the wind and there, in the burning sun, lay scores of bodies, some uncomfortably close to the regiment's line, with dozens of flags set in the ground, flapping silently above their dead ensigns. 'I'm worried about the enemy in our rear, but as long as the Bombay battalions don't have any more trembles and we get as much water and shot brought up as we need, we'll be fine. We've only had a handful of casualties so far, nothing like the pasting that the other battalions have had.'

The precise Ulster accent acted almost like a balm. It had not been a good day so far, what with my tumble and then that shocking business with Jacob's Rifles. But this fine old regiment seemed to be brushing the enemy off like flies.

'Here, General, have a pull at this.' Galbraith had obviously seen the blood covering my thighs and my torn breeches – I must have looked a sight – and decided to pass me his flask. 'Ha, well done, lads, get that over to H and F Companies, if you will.' He was clearly pleased to see one of his ammunition-carrying parties taking advantage of the relative quiet. But there was something odd about one of the soldiers who sweated under one of the grey-painted boxes – I knew him but couldn't quite place him.

'Galbraith, ain't that Private . . .' My memory let me down again.

'Private Battle, General. I hoped you wouldn't recognise him, sir, but you have. I decided to release the man from close arrest on my own authority. He wanted to be with his comrades and has done a fine job so far. I know that's irregular, but I hope you won't . . .' Galbraith clearly didn't give a fig for the fact that he'd utterly usurped my authority – and neither did I.

'No. For God's sake, man, we need every pair of hands we can get in this scrap. You did right.' I was just reaching forward to accept a cheroot from Galbraith's adjutant, Rayner, when the situation changed rapidly – very rapidly indeed.

'There's more of those bastards a-coming from the nullah, General, and – unless I'm mistaken – they've got some light guns up with 'em as well.' McGucken had just drawn his first lungful of smoke from his cheroot when the wave of noise drew our attention back to the left flank. First came a wall of screams punctuated by the barking of what sounded like six-pounders very close to the remnants of the Grenadiers, then more trumpets, wailing music and an unmistakable shout of triumph. Even through the smoke, I could see more of the Bombay lads running from the fight.

'Is that the bloody Grenadiers taking to their heels?' Sure enough, figures were beginning to peel away. After all that McGucken and I had done to prop the buggers up – it made you want to weep.

'No, General . . .' Galbraith had his glasses up and, cool as you like, was spotting the colour of turbans or some such hocus-pocus that old India hands prided themselves on. 'It's a mixture of the Rifles, the Sappers and Miners . . . but look there – what in God's name . . .'

And Galbraith was right to be surprised. Through my binoculars, I could see some troops still battling on, despite the tide of others who were doing their best to put as much ground between themselves and the very personification of howling evil as they possibly could. But just this side of what I assumed was the remains of the Grenadiers' square, through the grit, haze and rolling smoke, I saw gun teams pulling most of E Battery's nine-pounders and a brace of howitzers out of action.

'Who the fucking hell has ordered that withdrawal?' I demanded, of no one in particular, realising, as everyone else had, that things must be so desperate over yonder that Slade, the acting battery commander now that his major had been wounded, had limbered up and pulled back rather than be overrun. 'How many can you see, McGucken?' I looked over at him. He was staring hard through his own glasses and counting silently.

'There's at least two that I canna account for, General, an' the ones I can see have got wounded draped all over their limbers.' As that thunderbolt struck home, another block of troops − more of Jacob's Rifles, I guessed − right in the centre of the line, fell to bits, running after the plunging gun teams and even overtaking them in some cases.

I took stock. My first design for battle had been blown to buggery when we had lost the element of surprise and my next plan had rested upon the infantry protecting my guns well enough to allow the lethal nine-pounders to do their work. We had some tribesmen in our rear, for sure, but they were nothing to worry about, and I'd thought McGucken and I had done enough to shore up the Bombay battalions on the left flank. So certain had I felt that I'd even accepted Galbraith's offer of a cheroot. I looked at it: there was barely even a trace of ash on the end of the damn thing. In no time at all most of my line had collapsed, my battery had spread their wings and I'd even lost a couple of guns − and not to the Prussian Guard, mark you, but to a bunch of savages!

Christ, I'd started today confident that my troops had learnt so much from the past few weeks' warfare that a meeting with Ayoob Khan could have only one result. All I knew about fighting native armies rested upon stern discipline, good musketry and the troops holding their nerve. Suddenly I was scared, not for my own skin – that had been scratched and poked very thoroughly already – but for the whole damn outcome of this battle.

'Right. There's only one thing we can do now. Get a message to General Nuttall, tell him to scrape together whatever cavalry he can, and we shall throw these madmen back with the lance.' The time for manoeuvre and clever bloody tricks was over. The one thing that might save us all from becoming a notch on the hilt of a Khyber knife was an all-out charge – and as this was a mess of my own making I'd lead the bloody thing myself.

'Two generals, Keenan sahib. We are very honoured.' Daffadar Sayed Miran rode on Lieutenant Sam Keenan's stirrup at the rear of the two hundred or so sabres that had hastily been pulled together by Brigadier General Nuttall's staff and issued with some very sketchy orders.

'Aye, and we're even more honoured, Daffadar sahib, for we ride behind those warriors of the Third Light Cavalry to whom we owe so much,' sneered Keenan. It had not been a good day for him and his troop. First there had been the nonsense with Maclaine and his guns, then the 'Runaway Horse' taunts, then hanging around in penny packets for no good purpose that he could see, and now, when things looked as black as the shell bursts that had killed two of his men and injured another six, they were being asked to charge as the *reserve* to a bunch of beginners who'd hardly dipped a lance pennon since they had been in Afghanistan, he thought.

'And why should two generals be riding at the head of less than a regiment, sahib? Have Nuttall and Morgan sahib been so impressed with the Ghazis' lust for death that they have turned to face Allah at the last moment?' Miran chuckled at his own dark humour as the single troop of Scinde Horse trotted along through the gunfire.

'Not much chance of that, Daffadar sahib. That said, he's more likely to turn to your man than he is to the Pope.' But Keenan's quip was lost on the daffadar, who was now looking anxiously at the remains of his troop of lancers at whose head they rode.

Keenan took a moment to study the jawans too. They had eaten almost no breakfast and tasted no water for more than an hour now. They had been constantly in the saddle since before daybreak, marched the best part of a dozen miles and then been chasing around the battlefield with little to show for it except a handful of Herat gutter wallahs whom they had managed to spear. And there were fewer of them. Almost a fifth of their comrades had been struck down and now they were being asked to do the job that the bloody infantry should have done, rather than running like rats. As each shrapnel round burst over them, Keenan watched as the men blinked and their heads sank low into their shoulders – the strain, the hunger, the thirst and the fear were beginning to show.

And then he thought of his father, with whom he had exchanged wan grins when he, McGucken and his much-depleted staff had trotted past as the little force was forming up ten minutes or so ago. Keenan had noticed how grim he looked, how tightly he held his reins. He had seen the blood on his father's breeches although he could detect no wounds, and new furrows on his face.

'Sound trot march, Shaker Aamer,' Keenan told his trumpeter, as the bugle notes from the generals' party reached them. The 3rd Light Cavalry ahead of his troop began to pick up pace as the Afghan artillery on the high ground to their left and front tried some ranging shots.

'No, Daffadar sahib, don't let the men bunch together, tell them to maintain the proper spacing,' Keenan yelled, as his own men sought the comfort of closeness while the shells banged above them. Keenan watched two rounds hit squarely in the centre of the Light Cavalry's ranks, hurling one man into the air and bringing down a tangle of horses and riders while the rest pushed closer and closer together as the distance to their target shortened. And this the gunners loved.

'Back, boys, stay back!' Keenan found himself stretching his drawn sabre out as far to the right as he possibly could, reining his horse back firmly, not allowing the thoroughbred to get carried away with the excitement of the charge, the notes of which now sounded high and thrilling from in front of the ranks ahead. His men had become intoxicated with the atavistic noise of the bugle and the pounding hoofs, and were pushing up hard behind him – too hard, forcing him to get too close to the flying horse tails in front. 'No, lads, don't get any nearer – we're the reserve, we must stay a good way back.' He realised, yet again, how little his men understood of his orders.

But it was too late. 'Why do they not push on, sahib?' asked Miran, as he and his officer watched the ranks in front break into individual groups, poking at the Afghans with lance and sabre. 'Why have they stopped?' The Light Cavalry, rather than piling through the Ghazis like a steel-tipped wave – fast, crushing, unstoppable – had allowed themselves to lose all coherence, falling victim to the recruits' temptation to let a charge become a series of individual combats.

'Sound "right incline", Trumpeter.' Signalling with his sword, Keenan swung the troop away from the mêlée. Then he called, 'Sound "left incline",' and brought the troop crashing into the press of bodies obliquely from the right flank.

'*Shabash*, sahib!' The daffadar was delighted with his officer's quick thinking and with the way the troop responded, his lance hitting a Ghazi on the inner edge of his left shoulder-blade, sending the zealot spinning to the ground in a welter of suddenly bloody robes and clumsy sandals.

'Get rid of the lances, Daffadar sahib. Tell the men to draw

209

swords.' Keenan was instantly aware of how densely packed his men had become. The force of his little charge had momentarily thrown the enemy back, but Grenadiers and some stray men from Jacob's Rifles were hemmed so tightly together that the horses had to be checked – too soon for the full effect of his neat manoeuvre to be properly effective, he thought. As the enemy rushed back like an ebbing tide, the lances proved a nuisance yet the men were loath to drop them. 'Swords, lads, use your swords!' Keenan croaked, as he saw one of his troopers pulled from the saddle and slashed by a dozen knives before the man could bring the point of his lance to bear.

But Miran was also in danger. As he threw the broken stump of his lance at one of Ayoob Khan's foot soldiers, while bawling in Pashto for his men to draw their swords, Keenan watched one of the regular cavalrymen who had been loitering on the edge of the lethal scrum, push his pony through the crowd and come at Miran from behind him, tulwar pulled back ready to strike. But while Miran hadn't seen the Afghan, the Afghan hadn't seen Keenan. As the young officer barged his horse forward through the struggling Grenadiers and frenzied Ghazis, he studied his intended victim. In dark green *kurta* and white cotton pantaloons, the bearded man knew his trade well enough to have his reins tight and his elbow tucked in hard in order to protect his vulnerable ribs and chest. But, thought Keenan, he was too intent on his prey. As Keenan brought his own blade far back across his spine and measured the distance between himself and his enemy's lambswool cap, he thought of his father's injunction never to shoot a bird on the ground – it was only fair to let the creature fly first. The thought caused him to hesitate for at least a heartbeat before he stood in his stirrups and scythed his sword squarely down upon his enemy's head.

Keenan expected a jarring blow – he'd only ever practised such a cut against packed straw dummies – so he was surprised to feel the metal slice almost effortlessly through not just cap

210

and hair, but six inches down the man's skull, exposing grey brain and pink meninges until the blade stopped just above his enemy's palate.

'*Shukria*, sahib.' Miran, thought Keenan, looked almost shaken as they watched the dead Herati slump from the saddle and thump to the ground at the feet of the struggling infantry. 'But look, *huzoor*, Morgan sahib needs us.'

Keenan swivelled in his saddle to see a knot of horsemen rearing and plunging among the swords and knives of the enemy and the darting bayonets of their own infantry. He recognised his father's old friend Major McGucken, the political officer, sitting on his gelding, steady as a rock, cutting about him with his sword at every Afghan head he could reach. Lynch, the brigade commander's trumpeter, was more than holding his own, jabbing away like a piston with his heavy gunner's blade, but the brigadier general was in trouble. Keenan could see that a Ghazi, like as not, had crept up on Morgan and hamstrung his horse, for now the animal bucked and whinnied, its nearside rear leg hanging uselessly, bleeding heavily at the hock while its rider tried to cling to his seat.

'Away on, you bloody thing!' Keenan heard his father growl as he brought a spurred heel sharply back into a Ghazi's face, sending the man reeling backwards, but angry hands were pulling at the general's belts and straps as his agonised horse was dragged backwards on to its haunches. Three Afghans were swarming over Morgan's saddle when Keenan and Miran crashed to his rescue.

Miran stabbed one Afghan clear through the loins with his sword while Keenan tried to manoeuvre his horse past a lonely Bombay Grenadier, whose bayonet was impossibly twisted.

'Get out of the way, man!' Keenan yelled at the bemused foot soldier while he tried to get close enough to the general's squealing horse to throw a cut at the Ghazi who was hauling himself up girth and saddlery so that he, in turn, could get close enough to use his knife on Morgan.

211

At last, the infantryman ducked out from between the two horses allowing Keenan to shout, 'Keep low, General!' before he took a swipe at the clambering tribesman. The cut was a good one but, thought Keenan, the Ghazi knew his onions – just as the blade was about to connect with the target's right shoulder, the man whipped his shield, no larger than a dinner plate, from its sling and took the full force of the blow.

'Jesus, boy, you'll have my eye out like that!' blurted Morgan, as Keenan's blade bounced off the shield, almost taking the general's helmet with it. But it was enough to cause the Afghan to check and enough to give Keenan time to recover his sword, pull the hilt way back before driving it unscientifically and too deeply into his enemy's thigh; the blade went straight through the limb and stuck fast in the wooden frame of the brigade commander's saddle. And there the fight hung, like some ghastly frieze – Morgan astride a collapsing horse, a wounded Ghazi skewered to its flank but still holding tight to the general's Sam Browne belt. Meanwhile Keenan was doing his damnedest to pull his sword clear while another Afghan clawed at the off side.

'Leave your bloody sword, son, and shoot the dog before he has me out of the saddle,' bawled Morgan, as he tried to cling to his perch and kick at his next assailant. Keenan could see the sense in his father's command and, despite his every instinct never to drop his sabre, he dragged his wrist from the leather sword knot, fumbled his holster open, pulled out his issued Enfield and fired, the pistol round tearing into his foe's vitals.

Keenan's reaction was fast and fluid. But the bullet failed to lodge in an Afghan bone and travelled straight through the victim deep into the general's charger. The half-inch round ripped into the horse's heart, leaving her dead even before she toppled over on to her near side, with Morgan's left leg trapped firmly below her.

'I'll hold these sons of *shaitan*, sahib. Help your father – quickly now!' Keenan stared hard at Miran as the NCO reined his horse tightly round – the daffadar had never before made any reference to Keenan's and Morgan's kinship.

Keenan slipped from his saddle, looped his reins over his elbow and physically grabbed two sepoys in an effort to make them listen to him in the chaos and din that surrounded them. His father was lying beneath his mount, expressionless, pushing vainly at the saddle pommel in front of him. 'Come on, lift the bloody thing!'

'Here, give me your bandook, *bahadur*.' Keenan was straining for what few native words he had, but he eventually managed to wrest a rifle from one of the men, show the other soldier what he wanted and then grab the general by the armpits while the two Grenadiers used their weapons as levers. With much grunting and sweat, the dead horse was finally raised enough for Morgan to wriggle out while Miran and McGucken protected him. He rose to his feet, swiping the dust and sand off his bloodied khaki drill.

'This is turning into a bit of a day for you, General, is it not?' McGucken grinned down at father and son, his sword blade red as the sun reflected off it. 'Still, nice for ye to bump into your laddie like this.'

Keenan offered his water-bottle, then passed him the reins of his own charger. 'Here, General, take Kala. She's from Meath, as Irish as we are.' Morgan pushed a dusty boot into the stirrup and vaulted into the saddle with, Keenan thought, surprising vim for a man who had obviously been through so much.

'Thank you, lad.' Morgan patted the thoroughbred with obvious pleasure. 'But what of you?'

'He'll ride with me, General sahib,' Miran said, offering a gauntleted hand to his troop officer, 'until we can catch a stray mount.'

'Aye, so he can, Daffadar sahib, thank you.' Morgan looked

relieved as Keenan was pulled up behind his sergeant's saddle. 'Find yourself another sword while you're about it, Mr Keenan. That last one cost me a king's ransom and I'll not buy you another. And the next time you decide to rescue some unlucky sod, try not to slice their head off and don't shoot their bloody horse. Oh, and one more thing, Sam,' the general added, with a tired smile, 'don't you dare mention this to your mother!'

Billy Morgan was aware of many hoofs in the dust behind him. Some of the men had even been distracted enough from their own crisis to yell derision as the cavalry hammered by – but not for long. He knew that things were snug enough for the 66th in the centre of the brigade line of battle, so long as their flanks were secure and they had enough ammunition. Despite his numbed ears, he was getting used to the pulse of a major battle and the presence of sudden death and wounds. He'd grown accustomed to the rolling rifle fire, the shriek of shells and the cacophony of their bursts, but most of all he had learnt to listen to the cries of his foes. Their yelling and drumming would build up as they massed unseen under cover of the nullah. This would rapidly increase until, with uncontrolled shouts, they came pouring forward to be met by crashes of lead, the voices of British and Indian NCOs quite audible through the din.

But then the tempo changed. Away to the left the cries built up, but the firing never came to a crescendo. Rather than the crash of musketry subduing the war cries, the shouting just went on and on, coming closer and accompanied by wild-eyed men of the Bombay Grenadiers, some bleeding, some not, but all running like hares.

'Morgan, face the rear rank of the left half-company about.' Captain Beresford-Peirse reacted faster than anyone else as the native regiments to the left of the 66th were overwhelmed and ran. Ensign Billy Morgan soon realised the danger, though, and with Sergeant Kelly's help, they pulled and shoved the dazed and deafened troops into some form of order.

'Come on, lads, back to back now, leave a bit of space for more ammunition to be handed out.' The young officer was doing his best to calm the men who were now faced by hordes of Ghazis to their front and a stream of mixed sepoys, being chased by Ayoob Khan's regulars, to their rear. A few men from Jacob's Rifles and the Bombay Grenadiers ran to join H Company's ranks, but only a few.

'That's us with firepower halved, sir, just when we need it most.'

'I know, Sar'nt Kelly – don't I bloody know!' Morgan replied. 'Well done, Battle, keep that ammunition coming.' Private Battle and Private Honor were trotting between the two ranks, handing out extra rounds from the grey wooden box that they carried by its rope handles. 'You ain't got any Snider shot for our guests, have you?' Almost every Rifleman and Grenadier was indicating that his pouches were empty.

'Why would we, yer honour? Four-five Martini rounds only, so it is,' answered Battle, airily.

'And they're good ones, sir, Brummagem made. Look here.' Battle pointed to the diamond-shaped cut-out window near the base of one of the cartridge cases. It showed that each cartridge was made out of two layers of thin brass sheet – 'None of that shoddy Dum-Dum stuff.' That, at least, was a relief, thought Morgan. The last thing he needed now was locally produced ammunition – it had proved terribly fragile in the intense fighting of last year.

'Fucking nuisance them old Sniders, sir . . . You're firing low, Churcher, notch yer sights up a bit, son.' Sergeant Kelly had made the point before the battle that rifles of different calibres and types among the infantry battalions were likely to be a problem – and, Morgan realised, he was proving to have been disastrously right.

The enemy was pushing hard from the front now. A cloud

215

of Ghazis mixed with tribesmen came running at H Company with powder smoke erupting from their advancing line while bullets from *jezails*, muskets and a few Enfield rifles sang around them. Morgan saw Private Ayling dashed to the ground by a piece of lead before his attention was drawn to one of the enemy.

'Look there, Sar'nt Kelly.' Morgan pointed to a flag-bearer who was racing towards them, brandishing a great black cloth attached to a crude pole. A dense crowd of Ghazis followed, all howling at the tops of their voices and waving their weapons. 'Is that a woman?'

'Aye, sir, looks like a bint from 'ere. And there's a fair bit of cutlery following 'er an' all,' answered Kelly. 'Go on then, Churcher. If she wants some, shoot the bitch in the itcher,' he continued calmly, as Private Churcher, a Londoner and, at twenty-six, one of the oldest men in the company, fired and sent the girl and her banner flopping into the dirt.

'What the hell's she doing here?' asked Morgan, bemused by the sight.

'Buggered if I know, sir – probably the advance guard for all them virgins we keep 'earing about,' replied Kelly, as he took careful aim with his own rifle and dropped an Afghan who was just ramming home another charge. 'Hark to the bugle, Mr Morgan, sir.'

And it was the warning notes of 'prepare to move' that, Morgan thought later, marked the turning point in the battle both for him and for H Company. Like Sergeant Kelly, the rest of the non-commissioned officers began to yell the cautionary order and the men left off firing to hear what their leaders wanted. At the same time, Captain Beresford-Peirse – right in the centre of the company and visible to most of the men – was felled by a bullet. In fact, Morgan gathered later, the round passed straight through his helmet without touching him, though the impact knocked him down. But it was enough to distract and shock the men at a crucial time of the enemy's assault. In the few seconds that fire slackened, Morgan saw a howling wedge of Ghazis break right through the centre of the company only a few paces to his right.

'Fire into them, lads,' he tried to croak, as he snapped off two rounds from his pistol. The first missed but the second hit a tall native in the groin, causing him to hop about with both hands clapped over his genitals and Sergeant Kelly to remark, 'Good job Churcher shot that tart, sir. That youth wouldn't be able to put a smile on 'er face now, would 'e, sir?'

'Form square, lads, on me, form square.' Morgan did his best to make himself heard before a dozen or so men of H Company, a stray Gunner and a handful of Bombay lads formed a tight circle around him and Kelly, firing at the enemy or taking the occasional lunge with their bayonets at any who came too close.

'Right, come on, sir, let's get moving,' Sergeant Kelly shouted. Unlike Morgan, he had noticed that the rest of the company to their right had melted into the smoke, although no further bugles or words of command had been heard. 'No point staying 'ere on us own. Shoot and move, lads. Keep the bastards at arm's length.'

And so the little bunch moved off, shuffling like a dangerous hedgehog, pausing only to ransack the pouches of any dead they encountered and hastily bandaging Lance Corporal Eugene Mahoney when a bullet nicked his elbow.

'Don't shoot – don't shoot, for Christ's sake!' Morgan had to caution a smaller group of Jacob's Rifles whom they came upon, clustered round one of their own dead, as they eventually reached the lip of the deep nullah they had crossed less than two hours before.

'Hey, sir, there's Cap'n B-P down there, sir.' Kelly was looking at an almost vertical part of the deep ravine the loose soil of which had been furrowed by, Morgan guessed, men in a fearful hurry. 'And the colour sar'nt's with 'im – looks like 'e's stopped one, it does.'

Billy Morgan gazed at the knot of figures below him. He was surprised how pleased he felt to have found his company commander and so to be relieved of some of the weight of responsibility for his handful of men, but there were only a few of H Company men there and they were bending over Colour Sergeant James who was clearly in agony.

'Ah, Morgan, I was wondering where you might have got to.' Beresford-Peirse was mud-stained and had a bullet-hole through the crown of his sun-helmet, but was otherwise as calm as could be. 'How many boys have you got with you and how much ammunition and water?' he continued, apparently undisturbed by the whimpering of his senior NCO who, Morgan could now see, was clutching at his stomach.

Morgan did his best to answer. 'Sir, I've got nine unwounded. Corporal Mahoney is badly hit and out of it, Private Lord's burnt his hand on his own barrel but is still fit for duty, three Bombay lads who've been pretty stout and an odd Gunner. We've less than ten rounds a man and the water's finished but we're all right to fight on. What's happened to Colour Sar'nt James?'

'Never you mind about the colour sar'nt,' Beresford-Peirse answered, a little too quickly. 'Get your men across this nullah, hook left into the village and find the colonel, who's rallying there. Tell him I'll be with him directly. There should be more four-five ammunition there – try to find some Martinis for the Indian boys and take water-bottles off any casualties you come across.'

Morgan had no idea how Beresford-Peirse knew where Colonel Galbraith was, but there was something enormously reassuring about the idea of the regiment gathering around him.

'Be ready to let me have Sar'nt Kelly to act as colour sar'nt if I call for him please, Morgan. Reckon you can manage without him?' Beresford-Peirse had lowered his voice so that the fatally wounded James should not hear him.

'Well, I'd rather keep him, but if you need him then I'll certainly shift with one of my corporals in his place.' Morgan thought that the captain was being rather optimistic – H Company seemed to have shrunk so dramatically that the colour sergeant's job would be superfluous.

'I was right about those Bombay lads, wasn't I, Morgan? I don't know what it was, but there just didn't seem to be any substance to them. They looked good enough on parade and at musketry, but on the march they were awfully flat and quiet – bad sign in native troops, I've always thought.'

Beresford-Peirse seemed to want to detach himself from the horrors that surrounded them both, thought Morgan. 'Yes, you were . . .' Billy Morgan almost added something about the inadequacies of the Scinde Horse, but thought better of it. 'You were also right about our lot being tested to the full.'

'Yes, the old corps will have earned whatever battle honour they choose to give us for this scrap. I just hope we've got some colours left to stick it on. We've lost too many men today, Morgan, and it's far from over. Your fellows have done well enough, though,' Beresford-Peirse added.

'They've been magnificent, especially Private Battle – I'd always thought he was more nuisance than he was worth,'

'It's often the way, Morgan. I've seen it before – men who are a pest in barracks and on routine duties are bloody excellent in a tight corner. I thought he would turn out well after that affair in Kandahar, but then he rather let the side down when he killed that poor rissaldar, didn't he?' Beresford-Peirse replied, peering out from under the peak of his helmet.

'Yes, it wasn't the most sensible of things, was it?' Morgan was aware that he was unintentionally copying his company commander's taste for understatement. 'No, the boys have been a marvel today.'

'And, Morgan,' Beresford-Peirse looked at him and smiled briefly, 'you've done bloody well, too. Now, off you go. Leave me to sort out James.' He turned back to the group of men surrounding the stricken colour sergeant, just as Kelly came over to join Morgan.

'What happened to the colour sar'nt, Sar'nt Kelly?' Morgan was pleased that B-P hadn't needed Kelly. Now he and his little group were hurrying up a lower part of the far bank of the nullah, taking advantage of the cover from fire that the ground offered. 'Was he badly hit?'

'Sir, he's poorly. We won't be seeing 'im again this side o' the pearly gates.' Kelly avoided Morgan's direct question.

'I'm extremely sorry to hear that, Sar'nt Kelly. Are you sure he won't live?' Morgan was appalled by the prospect of Colour Sergeant James's imminent death. James had always been at the heart of H Company; he had been the first man to make Morgan feel welcome when he'd joined in Karachi and was always ready to give paternal but respectful advice to a young officer, never familiar but always cheerfully blunt. Now, thought Morgan, he lay dying in a nameless ditch. 'What hit him?'

'Sir, he's *bus*. Keep it to yerself, sir – promise you won't breathe a word?' insisted Kelly, as they scrambled up the crumbling bank. 'He got pushed over the edge by some bunch of *bhistis* 'oo 'e was trying to get water off when all they wanted to do was to run. 'E went over so 'ard he fell on his own sword scabbard an' it stabbed him through and through, it did. I saw it sticking out the poor old bloke. But not a word now, sir. 'Magine if that got out! The Sixty-Sixth would never live it down.'

Morgan could see Kelly's point and might have said something but Kelly jerked him back to more immediate difficulties. 'There's the village, sir.'

They came over the lip of the ravine and Morgan could see a low clutch of mud and wood buildings that shimmered white in the sun. Most had flat roofs, but some had the domed tops characteristic of this part of Afghanistan. Featureless walls – concealing gardens and vegetable plots, he guessed – connected them, creating alleys and lanes.

'Where did Cap'n B-P say the colonel was?' asked Kelly.

'Well, he didn't exactly. He just said he was somewhere in the village, but judging by the noise . . .' Morgan could now hear firing and wild shouts coming from the far side of the buildings '. . . he's over yonder. Get the men into file and let's join up with him as fast as possible.'

The party scurried through the buildings – stopping only to let Private Battle squat in the apex of two garden walls having declared himself 'so full of shite, me eyes have turned brown, so they have' – heading towards the sound of the fighting.

'They're at it hammer and tongs by the sound of things, sir. Bloody hell, Battle, bet you don't know whether to leave that damn thing for the flies or tek it in yer arms and baptise it . . .' Kelly's age-old jest got a brief laugh. 'Come on, you lot, don't tek all bloody day.' As they got closer to the combat, Kelly had found a muddy irrigation ditch and there the party paused to fill water-bottles.

'Aye, we'd better be a bit canny here—' Morgan's sentence was cut short by a new din. 'Christ, that's artillery firing and bloody close, too. They've got to be ours, ain't they, Sar'nt Kelly?'

'Not sure, sir. Sounds awfully like them poxy little galloper guns that Johnny Af was usin' earlier.' Kelly looked directly at Morgan. 'Leave it, Bobby!' The scruffy terrier had been following the party throughout the retreat and was now licking blood off the face of one of the few dead Afghans they had so far seen in the village. 'There's only one way to find out. Should we shift ourselves, sir?'

And with that the dozen men moved cautiously off again, Morgan, sword at the ready, leading the way. They crept down alley after alley getting closer and closer to the fighting until Morgan realised – from the musketry that crackled invisibly close to them – that they were approaching an outpost of some sort.

'Someone's just around the next corner, Sar'nt Kelly.' Morgan had signalled for the column to crouch down in the filth of the alley and wait for him to issue orders. 'I'll just go and have a look-see.'

'Sir, but take Battle with you as an escort,' replied Kelly, whispering cautiously despite the noise that raged just a few alleys away from them.

Morgan nodded and moved off towards the firing, with Battle close behind. As they came to the junction, the young officer sank to the ground, took off his helmet and was just preparing to peep round the corner at ground level (as the *Field Service Manual* said it should be done) when Battle cautioned, 'Watch yerself there, your honour. It'll take a devil of a lot of scrubbing to get that out of your kit.' He nodded at a slurry of chicken dung that Morgan had somehow managed not to see.

But no sooner had he eased his head around the base of the wall than Morgan was back and whispering urgently, 'Bloody hell, Battle! There's twenty or so of Ayoob Khan's men there, not our lot. They've got round the back of the Sixty-Sixth and are lacing into 'em.' He paused. 'Tell Sar'nt Kelly to get everyone up here now – we'll surprise them with the bayonet.'

'Twenty, sir? But there's only about ten of us an' Corporal Mahoney's hurt bad.' Morgan glared at him in reply. 'All right, your honour, I was just sayin'. Makes no odds to me, I'm a dead man anyway,' Battle muttered, as he scurried back the few yards down the alley to get the rest of the party.

Within minutes the handful of fit men came crouching and filing up to Morgan, every one of them with his bayonet fixed except the nameless Gunner, who had armed himself with a short spear he had picked up. It was, Morgan thought, probably every bit as good as anything that the Board of Ordnance could provide.

'Right, lads, on my word, follow me. Form line as sharp

as you like and then at 'em without a sound. No firing, no cheering, try not to let your boots scrape on any stones...' Morgan looked at the three sepoys, whose flat leather *chaplis* – normally so unsuitable for this sort of country – were much better for close-in work than his own men's heavily nailed footwear. 'Any questions?'

'Sir, 'ow many Afs are there?' Private Churcher asked nervously.

'About twenty, so let's surprise them, shall we?' Without waiting for anything more, Morgan was up and off, bent double, sword in one hand, pistol in the other.

The first man to land a blow, Morgan noticed, was Private Battle. With a snarl on his lips, the Irishman thrust his bayonet into the side of an Afghan who, like the others, was firing over a crumbling mud wall. In the noise and excitement, none of the Afghans had heard Morgan's little charge until Battle's victim cried out in shock and pain – but by then it was too late. Some of the natives fought back well, dropping their rifles and muskets and reaching for their knives. Churcher took a cut on the forearm that made him yelp, but he recovered well, ducking under the man's next slash before ramming his bayonet into the pit of his attacker's stomach. Morgan killed one man with his sword but, in a frenzy of steel and iron-shod wooden butts, the Herati infantry were quickly stabbed and thrashed to the ground.

'Didn't stand a fucking chance that lot, did they, your honour?' Private Battle, chest still heaving with the strain and adrenalin of the assault, stood over his second target, looking with undue satisfaction at the blue-bruised flesh and splintered bone that repeated blows from his rifle butt had inflicted on the man's face. 'Classy wee poke you gave that big fucker, sir.' Battle pointed with his chin towards a towering man whom Morgan had run through almost as soon as the attack had begun.

'Yes, but I jarred my hand and broke the point of my bloody sword doing it,' Morgan replied, not really knowing why he was telling Battle that he'd stabbed his opponent unskilfully hard, pushing the sharp steel right through his body in his lust to kill until the blade ground into the wall over which the Afghan was firing, snapping off the top half-inch. 'Everyone all right?' He looked around his troops, all of whom were now crouched behind the wall for cover and surveying their brutal handiwork.

'Aye, sir, everyone's fine. What now?' Sergeant Kelly asked, as he pulled a palmful of Snider rounds from a pouch of one of the cooling dead and passed them to a Rifleman.

'Stay here while I go and tell the lads that we're coming in.' When they had attacked, Morgan had glimpsed a couple of hundred khaki-clad troops about seventy paces in front of them on the other side of the garden that the walls enclosed. They seemed to be thickest around the colours, but even a brief peep showed that they were under heavy attack from their front with no real idea that other enemies had got into their rear. Despite this, Morgan was under no illusion about how jumpy and trigger-happy his comrades would be; approaching from their rear would be risky and he had no intention of exposing his men to needless danger.

'No, sir, wait!' But Morgan ignored Kelly, vaulted over the wall and was away as fast as his feet would carry him. With bursting lungs and leaden legs, the young officer sprinted across the furrowed earth of the garden, brushed aside a few canes and a low wooden fence, shouting as hard as his sucking lungs would allow him.

'Officer coming in! Officer coming in!' Even that didn't prevent one frightened young soldier from spinning around and putting a Martini-Henry round uncomfortably close to Morgan's head.

'Stop shooting! It's me, Mister Morgan, H Company – stop shooting, you bloody idiot.' The young officer realised how lucky he would be to come through this terrible day alive – even if the Afghans spared him.

'Ah, Morgan.' Lieutenant Maurice Rayner, the adjutant, had seen him. With no word of enquiry about him or his command, he added, 'Get over to the commanding officer, won't you, and take hold of the Queen's Colour? Olivey's wounded and needs to be relieved.' Morgan blinked. 'And straighten your helmet – don't set the men a bad example.'

With some muttered words of explanation about Sergeant Kelly and the others who were still waiting for him to guide them into the garden from behind the wall, to which the adjutant promised to attend, Morgan scuttled off, obeying his superior as if they were still on the barrack yard. Only as he sidestepped to avoid the wounded and their attendants, recoiled from the noise of the enemy guns and pushed through yet another desperate firing line did he realise how absurd Rayner's words were. How could his tilted helmet possibly set a bad example to this set of ragamuffins? Hardly a man that he could see still had all his kit and clothing; all were filthy and many wore bloodstained bandages. Most had wrapped cloth or ammunition paper around their rifle stocks and many had draped their heads and shoulders in native *puggarees* that they had picked up to protect them from the sun. They were as far from the colonel's pride that had graced the square in Karachi as could be – yet he adjusted his helmet.

'Good man, Morgan. How are you, my boy?' Lieutenant Colonel James Galbraith stood with the green silk regimental colour in one hand and his sword in the other. His grey charger lay dead a few yards away while his helmet – far from being worn at a curious angle – had disappeared completely. 'You been struck? No, well take the Queen's from Olivey like a good fellow.' Morgan said nothing about the group he was supposed to be leading. 'And show front.'

And show front. Hadn't his father told him some story about being told to 'show front' with his regiment's colours at the Alma? And hadn't he said that they were the worst few moments of his life because every Russian gun and sharpshooter used

225

him to hone their marksmanship? Morgan wondered where the general was now and how this day compared with other days on other battlefields. He even questioned, with sudden, unexpected affection whether or not his doughty, always cheerful father was still alive.

But the general's memories soon proved to be uncomfortably accurate. A funnel of iron canister shot cut a gap through the troops in front of him, nicked the colour pike just above his hand and swiped the other standard with Colonel Galbraith to the ground.

'No, lad, leave me be.' Morgan thrust his sword under his left armpit and, while struggling to control the vast Union flag, bent to help his colonel. 'I said show front – keep one damn colour flying, won't you? These folk cannot think they've done for us.' Morgan was shocked to see blood pulsing from the colonel's thigh, yet still Galbraith struggled to one knee, scrabbling to lift the regimental colour from the dirt.

''Ere, sir, let me help you.' As Morgan watched, a cameo took shape in front of his eyes that, he suspected, might have come from the front cover of one of the more lurid boys' magazines. Sergeant Major Cuppage – the regiment's most senior non-commissioned officer and Galbraith's right-hand man – took the colour from the colonel while trying to help him up. Morgan had been told that the two men had joined the 66th almost on the same day and had been together since one was an ensign and the other a private soldier. Now they both shielded the precious symbol of the regiment in some squalid vegetable patch while guns thundered, tribesmen screamed and the pair of them stared death in the teeth as stoically as they might a lost football match in Colchester. 'Well done, Mr Morgan, sir. You 'ang on to the Queen's Colour while I get the colonel gingered up,' said the sergeant major. Morgan marvelled not just at the calmness of his words but also at the fact that his helmet was as squarely on his head as the *Manual of Drill and Ceremonial* required it to be.

But Morgan never really knew whether the colonel was gingered or not, for even before his ears had stopped ringing with the noise of the enemy's guns, a swarm of shrieking swordsmen had barrelled through the gap in the firing line. A maddened throng of regular infantry and Ghazis slashed, shot and stabbed at the fragile khaki line, pulling exhausted men to the ground before a dozen knives flickered around the victims, some poking deep, bloody holes in the struggling bodies, some even cutting the belts away in order to take the ammunition that each man carried.

'Here, Sar'nt Kelly, on me, protect yer officer.' Sergeant Major Cuppage grabbed the breathless Kelly, Battle and Churcher, the stray Gunner and a handful of others from Morgan's party who had come sprinting across the walled enclosure just in time to throw a protective hedge of bayonets around the subaltern and his colour, just before a wave of Ghazis burst upon them.

'Good 'it, sir!' Sergeant Kelly panted as Morgan slashed a white-robed man straight across the face, sending him reeling back into the others who were pressing closely behind. 'Get yer hands off that, you fucker,' Kelly growled, as he shot another of the enemy through the throat, just as the Afghan had grabbed hold of the regimental colour that Colonel Galbraith was still trying to raise aloft.

But that was the last Morgan ever saw of his commanding officer for the next few moments raced past in a horror of blood and flashing steel. The press of bodies was closer than any rugby scrum he had ever experienced, his overwhelming sensation being the stink of unwashed, frightened flesh, of sinewy hands clawing at the pole of his colour, of his utter vulnerability with only one arm free to defend himself, the other holding a useless flag that common sense told him to ditch. Honour would not allow it.

'Ye great, stinking savage, ye!' Private Battle and he were both holding the colour pike with desperate strength, all weapons abandoned, while three Ghazis clutched the cloth and the other end of the staff, all locked in a deadly tug-of-war while around him iron, steel and lead clashed and banged. 'You'll not have it, you won't!' Battle continued, through gritted teeth, as his boots scrabbled and rasped in the dirt.

'Mister Morgan, sir, and you, Battle, when I say, let go of the bloody thing.' Sergeant Kelly jabbed and feinted at their enemies with the long, curvy blade of the sword bayonet with which the sergeants were equipped,

'I'll do no such thing, Sar'nt Kelly,' replied Morgan, as he tried to keep as firm a grip as the sweat on his palms would let him. 'I'll not let this go now!'

'Will you just do as I tell you for once, sir?' shouted Kelly, in such outraged tones that Morgan realised he would brook no more argument. 'Let it go, the both of you. Let it go, do you hear?' Battle and he did so.

The result was almost comic. Morgan was delighted as his three opponents sprawled in the grit, robes flying and sandals akimbo while Battle chortled, but there the comedy ended: hardly had the enemy trio collapsed than Kelly, Churcher and a nameless sepoy were upon them, bayonets rising and falling, hard metal jabbing and jabbing again into soft flesh until all three ceased to squirm.

'Come on, Mr Morgan, sir, get hold of the bloody colour and get a move on yourself.' Kelly pushed and bundled Morgan away from the bloodbath as the young officer struggled to pull the gaudy silk from below the body of one of the dead Afghans.

'But we can't leave the colonel and . . .' Morgan knew that the fear and the blood had engulfed him, that he was mesmerised by saving the great, red, white and blue flag with which he had been entrusted and that orders and bugle calls were echoing about to which the horror had made him deaf.

'Leave him, sir, he's down an' so's the sergeant major. Come on, sir, our only chance is to stay with the others!' Sergeant Kelly had seen the circle of men fall back to a piece of ground where they might make another bloody stand.

Morgan felt almost detached from the race through the straggle of alleys and open bits of ground that linked the first part of the village with a handful of buildings at its south end. He knew that bullets snapped about him from the roofs and walls of the mud houses. He heard the shouts of Kelly and the little group that surrounded him; he saw the Gunner, who had joined them from nowhere and who had fought so well, sprawl headlong on the ground and lie still, and he heard the incessant, excited yapping of Bobby, who measured their mad scramble pace for pace. Yet he didn't feel part of it.

When Sergeant Kelly announced, 'Here they are, sir, here's the lads!' Morgan saw Captain Beresford-Peirse wearing his ridiculously holed helmet and the adjutant, Rayner, miraculously sitting his horse. Then he began to feel part of that blood-drenched day again.

'Morgan, thank God, you've still got the Queen's. What of the regimental colour?' Collected but clearly deeply worried, Lieutenant Rayner was trying to rally the hundred or so men who remained.

'I don't know.'

Sergeant Kelly cut across him impatiently: 'Sir, the regimental is lost. I saw the colonel fall across it shot dead – he broke its pike with his weight, he did. We 'ad to get goin', sir, or we'd have lost both, sir – fucking Ghazis was all over us.' Kelly paused, then added, 'An' the sar'nt major's dead, sir.'

'What?' Rayner exclaimed. 'No, he's not – look, he's yonder.' All of Morgan's party gaped as Sergeant Major Cuppage came staggering across the walled enclosure with an open ammunition box held awkwardly across his midriff.

'Well done, sir, Sar'nt Kelly. Give that 'ere.' Sergeant Major Cuppage threw the ammunition box down and took the colour from Morgan. 'Take some shot and get yourselves to Cap'n Beresford-Peirse – he's over there.' The senior soldier of the 66th jerked his thumb over his shoulder towards a gate in the rear wall.

'But I saw you lying dead with the colonel not ten minutes back, Sar'nt Major, we both did,' said Morgan. He and Kelly were goggling at the apparition.

'You're right about the colonel, sir – God rest the man. And so I'm just a fucking ghost, am I, sir?' Cuppage, Morgan noted, despite all the danger and personal grief he was enduring, was still the rock-like figure he had always admired. 'Now be a good young gentleman, sir, and get over to your company commander – he needs a hand. These Ghazis won't shoot themselves, you know.'

Morgan saw the sergeant major, colour in one hand, loose ammunition in the other, pressing rounds into the hands of the mixed bag of troops who were firing and stabbing at the wave of warriors who continued to throw themselves at the British and the Indians. As he ran across to Beresford-Peirse, he just caught sight of Rayner being bowled from the saddle by a gunshot – yet his helmet, Morgan saw, was still worn at the correct angle.

'And where have you lot been?' Beresford-Peirse was hastily reloading his pistol while around him twenty or so men – mainly of the 66th – were scrabbling in an ammunition box and stuffing a few rounds apiece into their pouches. 'I thought we'd lost you at the nullah.'

'And we thought you were a goner, too, Beresford-Peirse,' replied Morgan, amazed at the way the dead seemed to be coming to life.

'No, my lad. You'll just have to wait a little longer before you get your grasping hooks on H. Now, the colonel's dead and the regiment's down to a little over a hundred still in action,' said Beresford-Peirse, very calm, very measured. 'Colonel Mainwaring of the Rifles has taken command and wants us,' he waved his sword blade around his tired, tattered troops, 'to gather together whoever we can and be prepared to give covering fire to his lot. As far as I can see, the rest of the brigade is heading back towards the baggage park, and as soon as we can break clear from these mad buggers—' he was interrupted by another shattering blast of artillery fire that caused fresh screams from the party they had just left '—they'll cover us back so that we can regroup.'

Morgan thought how rational, how ordered Beresford-Peirse made everything sound, but as he looked at the struggling, thrashing, slashing bodies around the colour, at the frenzied bravery of the Ghazis, at the smoke and the numbing gun blasts, he realised he hadn't the least idea of what was going on. He knew that the colonel and too many others were down, that people he thought dead kept being resurrected, that a sacred colour had been lost and that the vibrant living creature that was the 66th was quickly bleeding to death. And he also realised that unless he shook himself out of his reverie and metaphorically adjusted his helmet, he and his men would soon just be names on some God-forsaken obelisk back at the depot in Reading.

'Right, Battle, Churcher, all of you, check your pouches get some water down you and listen in for the company commander's orders.' Morgan felt better to be back in charge, to be divested of the frustration and responsibility of the colour, and part of a larger group that didn't seem quite as forlorn as his own handful of men had done. Once the few rounds they had were redistributed, Beresford-Peirse, he and Sergeant Kelly were just beginning to get the men into a firing line when the insistent notes of a bugle, very close among the buildings to their rear, began to play the 'retire' over and over again.

'Sir, your honour, look there – it's your da and the big Jock.' Private Battle, who had been posted in the gateway and told to shepherd in any stragglers, was astounded to see the brigade commander and Jock McGucken come clattering up the alleyway on their horses, a bugler from Jacob's Rifles trotting obediently along on foot behind them. 'Halt! Who comes there?' challenged Battle, as he pushed his rifle and bayonet forward, suddenly and needlessly regimental, thought Morgan.

'Who the fuck d'ye think it is, ye daft Paddy?' retorted McGucken, as both he and the general kept their horses moving with soft touches of the spur in order to throw the aim of any sharpshooters.

'Are there any officers present?' demanded the general, while casting a quizzical look at the too-familiar figure of Private Battle.

'There are, sir. Is it your wee boy you'd be wanting?' Before General Morgan could reprove Battle for his familiarity, the big Irishman was yelling, 'Your honour, it's your da come to see how you're getting on.'

'Ah, Mister Morgan.' Brigadier General Anthony Morgan knew the Irish too well; he ignored Battle, his face splitting into a grin at the sight of his son. 'Still in one piece? Do I recognise Beresford-Peirse over there? Where's the commanding officer?' The questions came almost as thickly as the bullets that cracked around them all.

'Sir, I'm fine but the colonel's dead.' Billy Morgan tried to sound as flat and unmoved as his superiors had done. 'And, yes, that is Beresford-Peirse.'

'Is this all that's left of H Company?' General Morgan interrupted his son, looking around at the score or so of men who lined the inside of the wall,

'No, sir, that lot around the colour,' Billy Morgan pointed to the mêlée fifty yards away, 'and ourselves, we're all that remains of the whole battalion . . . the whole Sixty-sixth, sir.'

The general paused and looked at McGucken. 'Damn me. Tell whoever's in charge to obey the bloody bugle. You're to move back now to protect the brigade's flank.'

'Very good, General. We've been told to give the other

232

party covering fire.' Billy Morgan pointed to the scrum around the colour. 'Once we've done—'

'No, lad,' the general said, with an edge of steel in his voice, 'they must shift for themselves. I need you now if we're to stand any chance of keeping Ayoob Khan at bay on this flank.'

'But, General—'

'Do as you're told, Mr Morgan,' the general growled. In all his years, in all his childish tantrums and the spankings that had inevitably followed, Billy Morgan had never seen his father as icily cold as this. 'Tell Cap'n Beresford-Peirse that I'll have you people out of the village and shielding my flank within ten minutes or I'll want to know the reason why.' With no more discussion the brigade commander's party turned and was away.

Beresford-Peirse, of course, could see exactly what the general wanted, and even before the men had time to settle their equipment, his party was doubling away through the village, away from the pile of bodies and flashing steel, away from the great, raw, primitive noises of death.

'Here, Bobby! Here, ye daft mongrel.' Sergeant Kelly, the last man of H Company to leave, was whistling and shouting hard for his dog.

'Come on, Sar'nt Kelly, don't hang back.' Now it was Morgan's turn to drag at Kelly's arm, but the sergeant kept calling, despite the clash of battle. Morgan looked back at the others. Above the thrashing, hacking bodies floated the Union flag — Morgan thought he recognised the sergeant major still holding it. And there, amid the skidding boots and sliding sandals, quivered a small, scruffy terrier, barking hatred at the merciless men who were cutting down his comrades like wheat before the scythe.

NINE

Retreat

A battle's a strange thing. One minute you're in the jaws of hell with madmen trying to claw you from your saddle, shells bursting over your head like the clap of doom and folk spilling their lifeblood everywhere, and at the next everything is calm. Well, that was exactly what happened now. Suddenly the storm abated, the guns fell quiet and the screaming stopped – it was just one of those unaccountable lulls when it seems that everyone, as if by some unspoken agreement, pauses to light a pipe. And I found myself thinking about my lads and that ridiculous homely comment from that great daft Paddy, Private Battle.

'Wee boy' indeed! There wasn't much about Billy that reminded me of a wee boy any more. Hard-bitten young killer, more like – and a damned argumentative one to boot. Still, he was in one piece and seemed to have had a bit more luck than I was having. In fact, both lads were untouched – at least, I hoped Sam was still in the land of the living and had found another horse – and that was more than could be said for a good slice of my brigade. Shame they seemed to loathe each other so much – all my own fault: I should never have let Mary bring up Sam as a Papist. It was always bound to cause trouble. And . . .

'Watch yerself, General. Best have your pistol ready in these alleyways. Lynch, put that bloody sword away and get your carbine out.' Major Jock McGucken could still be the colour sergeant when he wanted to and, frankly, things were such a mess that I probably needed him to look after the deadly little details that, if neglected, could easily get us all killed. Mark you, I felt a bit sorry for Trumpeter Lynch when he found that his bugle had been cut away without his knowing during one scrimmage or another. Jock McGucken had torn a strip off the lad and we'd had to grab one of the Rifles' buglers to do his job for him.

'We'll try to form a rearguard, McGucken.' I forced myself to think about what I could do to minimise the bloody disaster that the day was turning into. 'How many guns did you see when we passed the gun-line? I was so taken up with our bold Grenadiers that I hardly had time to count.' In point of fact, when I'd purloined Kala from Sam, and the remnants of Brigade Headquarters had eventually cut ourselves out of the mêlée among the native battalions, I was bloody amazed to see Slade and his battery unlimbered about one thousand yards behind his original position and giving the Afghans what-for with shell and canister. I'd quite expected never to see them again, what with that wretched boy firing his guns too early at the start of the action and setting off a chain of events that had led to the débâcle I could see around me now.

'Six guns, General, but several of their horses was missing. We can tell Malcolmson to get some of the Scinde Horse to escort them and there's Beresford-Peirse's lads and another few of the Sixty-Sixth guarding the baggage that we can pull together.'

'Aye, that'll have to do. Scribble a quick note, if you please. Put Cap'n Slade in charge and tell him to keep a gunshot behind the back end of the main body and to work on his own initiative − you know the form.' But while McGucken worked at his notebook with a stubby pencil, having given

Trumpeter Lynch the unwelcome task of carrying my despatch, I suddenly became aware of a horrid loud moaning from behind one of the low mud walls that hemmed us into the alleyway. I pulled my Enfield from its holster and walked the big chestnut forward to investigate.

Tucked just inside a gap in the walls a few yards further forward, a British officer was lying half on his side and half on his back with the riding boot of his left leg sticking out at the oddest angle. His crying was strange and piercing; around him were a couple of sepoys from the Rifles, both looking worried about their wounded *burra-sahib* and incapable of doing anything, except feebly pour water down his throat. When I listened properly to the noise, though, I realised it was a stream of fluent Hindi, delivered with the shrillness that, I had noticed, native troops adopted when hurt.

'Iredell, ain't it?' By some miracle I had remembered the name of the Rifles' senior major. I dismounted to get a better look at the casualty. Both soldiers almost fell over themselves to get out of my way and so pass on the responsibility for their wounded officer.

'General . . . sorry, I can't stand up.' It was a curious thing, but as soon as Iredell realised that another European was present his behaviour changed at once. Stoicism came flooding back. 'I seem to have been hit.'

'Aye, so you have. Your leg's broke.' A bullet or perhaps a ricocheting stone had dented the leather of the major's boot just below the knee, but not penetrated, snapping the bone and crippling the man. I was just bending down to look more closely when I heard hoofs on the cobbles of the alleyway to my rear and Jock McGucken's voice.

'General, I've got the wordi major of the Scinde Horse here. Thought you might like to hear what he's got to say.'

The senior native officer of Sam's regiment sat stiffly to attention and, despite the hum of bullets and the crashing of musketry no more than a couple of hundred yards away, he saluted as regimentally as he might at evening stables' parade. His face was so lined and his beard so grey that he could have been a hundred; he wore the Mutiny and Abyssinia medals but sat as bolt upright as a man thirty years younger. And in brief, clear English, obviously learnt straight from the dictionary, he explained that the regiment had lost many men and even more wounded but that Malcolmson sahib was with Nuttall sahib somewhere on the far side of the baggage park. My first instinct was to ask about Sam and then to enquire of the poor man why the blue blazes my cavalry commander was that far back – but the wordi major, all turban and Mahratta-style *puggaree*, wouldn't have been able to answer.

'Right, you two, get Iredell sahib up here on my charger.' The two Riflemen just gaped at me. 'Wordi Major, *huzoor*, tell these owls what to do please – and get him out of here *ek dum*.'

'General, you're no' giving that beautiful horse away, are you? It's worth a fortune – an' what will you ride, may I ask?' McGucken was appalled, not so much by my sacrificing my own ability to get around the battlefield, but more by the hard pounds, shillings and pence that Kala represented. Bloody tight-fisted Jock. Though, I had to admit, not just the horse-flesh but the hussar saddle and the splendid tack that the horse had was hardly complemented by Iredell's skinny arse and floppy leg as he was slung, belly down, across the animal's back. I hope the man realised what a good deal he was getting.

'I'll get up here behind the wordi major, McGucken. This is my bloody mess so at least let me see it through as I choose.' I don't think that the bemedalled old Scinde Horseman thought that two on a horse befitted either his or my dignity. 'Take me to wherever you saw the Horse Gunners last please, *bahadur*,' and with that we trotted away, myself clinging to the rump of a mount no bigger than a polo pony and adding a squashed knacker-bag to my other aches and pains.

*   *   *

237

It had been a long day. As Keenan and his men waited for the rest of the rearguard to form up, he had a sudden, ridiculous, vision of the scruffy mud hovels among which they stood turning into a British officers' mess. There was no shell fire, no smell of burning wood and singeing flesh, no harsh shouts as NCOs called men together and checked equipment, and at about this time of the afternoon, tea would be served. Darjeeling, he fancied, poured from the familiar silver pot with a tiny crescent of lemon. But he was jerked back to reality – filthy, noisy, frightening reality – by his troop sergeant and one of his men leading an obviously captured horse.

'Well, Daffadar sahib, I'm grateful to you.' Sam Keenan hardly needed to hoist himself into the saddle of the Afghan pony, so tiny was it. 'Does its owner not need it any more?'

'Sahib, he is with his friend *shaitan* sampling the rewards of a true Ghazi. I hope he enjoys them more than the ball from Mohammed Azem's carbine.' Daffadar Miran smiled one of his wolfish grins, exposing his betel-stained teeth. 'A good man, aren't you, Mohammed Azem?' Miran and Azem had killed one of the few Ghazi cavalrymen and taken his horse so that their officer might be more useful both to himself and to the troop. Now Azem – in typical Pathan style – was being shown off to Keenan, brought forward for official recognition.

'*Shukria*, Mohammed Azem.' Keenan knew the swarthy twenty-year-old to be a good horseman – he remembered him winning the tent-pegging competition at the camp at Thul Chotiali last autumn – but he had never had any other cause either to congratulate or castigate him. 'What state are you and your horse in, lad?'

Miran hastily translated before the boy did his best to reply to his officer in English: 'Sahib, horse good.' Azem patted the beast affectionately; it belonged to him rather than the government and represented a considerable investment

238

for his family. 'But dry.' The sowar gestured with his leather glove and pushed his tongue out at Keenan.

'Jesus, Daffadar sahib, Azem's tongue looks like a sausage roll.' Keenan realised what a ridiculous thing that was to say to Miran who, even if he knew what a sausage roll looked like, was extremely unlikely ever to have examined such a defiling thing in any detail. 'I'm bloody thirsty myself, but I'm not yet in that state. The men have been guzzling their water again, ain't they?'

'Sahib, I cannot say. I have been busy with keeping you alive, Keenan *bahadur*,' Miran shot back at him. Keenan realised that his daffadar would not take the blame for what should have been a matter of individual discipline.

'Aye, quite so.' Keenan felt for his own water-bottle – it still contained a splash of liquid. 'But their water-bags are all empty, Daffadar sahib, I can see them from here. Will you see if you can find something to drink while we wait for the guns and the infantry?' Uniquely, the Scinde Horse all carried a large leather water bladder on their saddles so that their mounts should never go thirsty, but all of the twenty or so horsemen that Keenan had managed to salvage from A Squadron seemed to have run dry. Now the men stood exhausted, some offering a few oats to their mounts, some listlessly cleaning their tulwars and carbines. But even as Keenan watched, one of the troopers buckled at the knees, half falling before recovering himself. Exhausted by the hours of riding and skirmishing under the blazing sun, by the lack of drink and food and by the stress of danger and fear, he had fallen asleep as he stood.

'Sahib, you stay in cover behind these houses. I've posted sentries, so you won't be surprised by Ayoob's Khan's clowns. Please blow two Gs if you need us back quickly.' He addressed a few unintelligible words to Mohammed Azem, then the two men were away on their vital search. As he watched them go, Keenan realised just how lucky he was to have a troop sergeant

239

like Miran. He knew that the rearguard he had been told to join would be a difficult and dangerous task — he would need Miran's rock-like presence.

'Sahib — sahib, *tatt* gun here.' One of the dismounted sentries who was watching the front of the buildings behind which his men sheltered was trying to get his attention. 'Wordi major and gun, sahib.'

Keenan led his Afghan pony forward, suddenly aware of how weary he was and how deeply unappealing the prospect of exposing himself to bullet and shell once more. He saw, trotting down the dusty slope into the little saucer where the buildings lay, Ishaq Abu Afgoye, the wordi major of his regiment. Every man in the 3rd Scinde Horse could recognise his posture and the set of his turban at a thousand paces but Keenan could not make out what the odd shape was behind the wordi's saddle. As they came closer, he realised that another man — a rather bedraggled one — was leaving the field in exactly the same way that he had behind Miran.

Another pair of horsemen followed the wordi major, and as this trio dipped below the near horizon and into ground that was safer from the enemy's artillery, Keenan saw the first of their own guns rattling along behind the mounted figures. They were a couple of hundred yards away and the details were difficult to make out in the dust and the glare of the sun, but he could see that each limber and even the axles of the nine-pounders that led the cavalcade were festooned with men, some obviously alert and ready for action, others draped lifelessly over saddles and carriages.

'*Ram-ram*, Wordi Major sahib.' Keenan walked forward to greet a man who had seen many battles. He wondered if he had yet seen any as bloody or as disastrous as this. His expressionless mahogany face gave nothing away. Neither did the faultless salute. 'Have you seen the infantry who are meant to be with us?'

240

Before the wordi major could reply, the crumpled figure behind him slid from the saddle, pulled his jacket and belts down, wiped the dust from his whiskers and smiled slightly.

'I was just about to ask you the same question, Mr Keenan,' said Brigadier General Anthony Morgan, even more grimy and war-stained than when Keenan had seen him last. 'Do I take it that you form the cavalry of my rearguard?'

'Sir, you do. I've got about twenty sabres with me,' answered Keenan, 'and we're just trying to water the horses. I've sent the wounded to the rear and we've lost a couple of animals, lame, but—'

'Aye, good stuff, lad. I can see all that I need to know. Ah, Slade, are all your guns complete now?' The general turned towards the artillery commander, who came trotting up. The officer was every bit as filthy as his superior, Keenan noticed, yet apparently unhurt.

'Yes, General. We've lost two of the nine-pounders.'

The general interrupted, 'I hope the bloody things were spiked?'

'I don't know, sir. I was with my smooth-bores at the time,' Slade replied, with evident discomfort.

'Don't give me excuses, lad. You should bloody know. Whose guns were they and does he know if the next time we're going to see the damn things is when we're gazing down their fucking muzzles?'

Keenan had never seen his father like this before. He'd seen him frustrated by his mother's vagaries, he'd seen him in a theatrical rage when an incompetent huntsman had let a fox get to earth back in Cork and he'd seen him in at the death of a panther, but he had never seen him in a flat, exhausted, end-of-his-tether fury like this.

'They were Hector Maclaine's guns, sir,' replied Slade.

Keenan sat up when he heard that: the very guns he had escorted at the start of the action, the very guns that he might have predicted would be risked and lost.

'Maclaine!' growled the general. 'Is the young gentleman still drawing breath and, if so, where is he?'

'Just there, General . . . Mr Maclaine, a word with you if you can spare a moment,' Slade shouted, with exaggerated courtesy, as the battery, with its battle-torn gunners and their mounts, came snorting through the choking dust. The young Gunner subaltern walked his horse over to his battery commander. 'I think the brigadier general may like to speak to you, Maclaine.'

Keenan watched as his father attempted to roast Maclaine. But the youngster, still in the saddle, towered over him.

'Get down here and look me in the eye, damn you,' spat Morgan. 'It was your guns that started firing without orders, was it not?' Maclaine tried to speak but Morgan carried on: 'You gave away any element of surprise, you bloody griff!'

Keenan watched his father's six-foot frame almost burst with anger.

'I'll wager you didn't even spike the pieces you handed over to the Ghazis, did you?' The general was shifting from foot to foot, so furious was he, his fists bunched, his face red under the tan. Keenan expected him to round off the onslaught by blaming Maclaine for the whole fatal imbroglio, with a threat of court martial or, perhaps, both. But the storm left Morgan as soon as it had blown up; his body relaxed, his fists unclenched. 'Well, be off with you and learn a lesson.' The tirade had ended with a simple caution and the kindly, thoughtful man Keenan knew had returned. But he could see how tense Maclaine was as he saluted and turned his horse away; it was clear that he bitterly resented being upbraided by the general.

'And you can take that vexed expression off your face, Mr Keenan.' The general now turned to look at his elder son. 'Your precious Kala is alive and kicking somewhere in the rear by now, I expect. I'll not give you the chance to shoot a horse from under me again − and I don't want that damned native screw you're riding now. Have you seen yourself?' Keenan wondered if his father had taken a moment to look at his own extraordinary state of gore-caked scruffiness. 'You look like the scratchings from Skibbereen fair, so you do.' With a slight smile, the general turned away before raising his voice as a flock of Afghan shells winged overhead: 'Will no one get me a perishing horse? The place is running with the creatures!'

'Here you are, General,' said McGucken. He had come into the bowl leading a stray whaler by the reins. He had hung back for a time while Morgan got his fury out of his system before coming forward, calm, properly dressed and reassuring. 'Enjoy that wee paddywhack, did you?' he asked, rather as a tolerant father might enquire of a petted child. 'Here's a good, strong horse for you and there's a half-company of the Sixty-Sixth just about to join us, so things ain't so bad, are they?'

Billy Morgan trotted alongside his sergeant towards the little group of buildings that had been chosen as the forming-up point for the makeshift rearguard. While he was desperately tired and thirsty he wasn't going to let the men see it.

'Here we are, sir.' The little column topped a low rise, allowing the remains of H Company to see the entirety of the village and the scratch force that was milling about behind the cover that the houses provided. 'Most of the guns is 'ere and Himself with Major McGucken. But, oh, for God's sake – you're going to love this, sir. Look there – the bloody cavalry's only the Runaway Horse, sir, and your big brother. You wouldn't warrant it, sir, would you? The whole friggin' brigade to choose from an' we 'ave to end up with those donkey wallopers again,' Sergeant Kelly said disbelievingly. Morgan knew how exhausted Kelly must have been, but it didn't show. 'Bloody good job Bobby's gone west. He'd have bit one of their precious bleedin' nags again, he would.'

243

'I really don't want to hear that, Sar'nt Kelly.' Billy Morgan and Sergeant Kelly were doing their best to make the forty or so men they had scraped together from the remains of the 66th Regiment maintain a shuffling run. After their orders from the brigade commander to hold a flank, they had received another message that caused Captain Beresford-Peirse to set off at the double the six hundred yards from the village of Khig to Mundebad to act as part of the rearguard. 'We've got only a handful of rounds per man, half a bottle of water and most of the boys are more dead than alive with sheer exhaustion. We don't need that bunch of mounted clowns to nurse as well.'

'I know, sir. I'm not sure that Titcombe will be of much more use to us.' Kelly looked at the young soldier from Windsor who, badly sunstruck, was being half carried and half pulled by two others. 'And Corporal Mahoney can't use a weapon no more.'

'No. It's going to be tricky unless the guns have enough shot to help us out.' Billy Morgan had acquired a Martini-Henry for himself and was also carrying Private Titcombe's in the vain hope that the man could be brought round to fitness once they had found some water for him.

'Cap'n B-P wants you, sir.' Sergeant Kelly had seen the company commander turn to face them, wave and touch his shoulder as the column concertinaed to a halt in the bottom of the dusty bowl. 'Look, sir, he's signalling for you.'

As Morgan loped up to his captain, he saw a group of horsemen sheltering from any stray shrapnel balls behind the walls of a low house.

'Come on, Morgan. We've been summoned by the brigade commander, no less. It's not every day that crows like us get to be spoken to by a general.'

Beresford-Peirse, thought Billy Morgan, was trying to play the cool hand just a little too hard; his next comment confirmed it.

'That said, you've probably heard too much of this particular one in your time. Halt and salute smartly, now.'

That was B-P, thought Billy Morgan. That was the bloody 66th! Not many officers who'd had their hair parted by a bullet, stood back to back and hacked at Ghazis, who'd watched their company wasted by shot and steel, all without food, water or rest for many hours, would worry about such niceties. But Beresford-Peirse did and that, Morgan realised, was why H Company was still in the field and still earning the Queen's shilling. A feeling warmer even than the beating sun crept over him.

'Captain Slade, I want you to command my rearguard as I warned you in my message.' General Morgan had dismounted in order to speak to all the officers in the improvised force. The Gunner officer nodded his understanding. 'Mr Keenan, be prepared to keep the Afghans at arm's length. I will not accept the loss of any more guns. And I need you to keep riders in touch with my headquarters at all times – is that clear?' Sam Keenan nodded as well. 'Captain Beresford-Peirse,' the general's eye swept over Billy Morgan, his second son who was standing by his captain, 'the 66th will have to make every round count and, just like the Scinde Horse, I want you to protect the artillery. I must see every barrel back in Kandahar as soon as possible.

'Listen to me. You've all fought damn well today and brought credit on yourselves and your regiments, but now's the time to carve a place in history. We will only halt once we're back in Kandahar and that's more than thirty miles away. If you fail to keep the enemy at bay, our column will be overwhelmed. We must not let Ayoob Khan turn this withdrawal into a rout. Gentlemen, I'm expecting much from you and your tired troops, but I've never before seen soldiers like you. Now go to it.'

And with that the general mounted and trotted away, leaving Billy Morgan – and all the other officers, he suspected – standing a little taller, thirst and fatigue forgotten, determined to do their utmost for the man. Morgan looked across at his brother Sam. The cavalryman was every bit as filthy as he was, yet he could tell that their father's speech had found its mark with him just as much as it had with himself. He watched Sam fold his notebook shut and tuck it into his sabretache. He expected him to glance up, to catch his eye and make at least some sign of recognition. But no. As Captain Slade ordered, 'Captain Beresford-Peirse, Mr Keenan, close in now, I can't shout above all this damned noise . . . the rest of you, back to your men, please,' there was nothing. But what else could he expect? He'd hardly gone out of his way to make a friend of his brother, had he?

Keenan eased himself in the odd, narrow saddle he had inherited. He stroked the little pony's mane for it had carried him well since the death of its first master and had drunk deeply from a canvas bucket that one of the sowars had found for it when they stopped to water less than an hour ago. Now the rearguard rested on a flat stone plateau that overlooked the track along which most of the brigade had already fled. They had been constantly sniping and galloping, ambushing and counter-attacking for five miles or so along the road to Kandahar. Now, in the moonlight, Keenan could see an abandoned stores wagon, one dead horse still in its traces and two shapeless lumps that he took to be lifeless or, perhaps, sleeping men. If they were asleep, he couldn't blame them, for almost all the rearguard was doing the same. He thought back over the past three or four hours and could scarcely remember a moment – until now – when they hadn't been chased and harassed by the enemy.

'Well, Daffadar sahib, how's our ammunition?' As the horses and men rested, Keenan and Daffadar Miran had taken the opportunity to pull on their sheepskin *poshteens*.

'Sahib . . .' Miran shivered slightly for the thick coat had yet to provide any warmth in the sudden chill of the darkness '. . . everyone has redistributed all that they have. I took

Koreshi Mohammed Yusuf's ammunition when he fell and now we all have eight rounds. Not much, eh, Keenan sahib, but we still have our swords.'

'We do, and I suspect that we've not seen the last of the Afghan horse tonight. They'll be as tired as we are and they'll need to pray, rest and eat, but once that's done . . .' Keenan was talking to himself as much as to his troop sergeant.

'They will, sahib, but the greatest blessing is that those dogs' cocks will be busy looting the baggage that the brigade has had to abandon. There's drink there, sahib, and it's a wonder how the words of the Koran become so meaningless, even to a Ghazi, when the Feringhees' grog is there to be had.'

Even Miran, Keenan saw, was beginning to sag. His voice was flat and listless and he kept rolling his head back and turning his beard to the stars in a sign of tiredness that Keenan had never seen from a European. 'Get some sleep, Daffadar sahib, even for ten minutes. I will stand watch. Everyone else is asleep and there's no sign of the enemy just at the moment. Go on, *huzoor*, do as I say before I fall out of my saddle and find a dead Ghazi for a pillow.'

'Sahib, for once your orders are easy to obey.' Miran's teeth flashed in the dark. 'Give me those ten minutes then I will repay you.' Without further discussion, the daffadar patted his horse's neck, slipped his feet from the stirrups and was sound asleep on the ground with his reins looped over his arms.

Slade's guns had kept away any serious attacks by the Afghans, but he and his sowars had constantly been dismounting and firing their carbines, remounting and moving while the rifles of the 66th covered them, and flying around the flanks keeping marauding Herati cavalry at bay. As if this weren't enough, he had had to keep one eye cocked over his shoulder, watching the tail of the increasingly weary brigade.

'Don't you challenge a stranger, lad?' Keenan had walked

his Afghan pony over to the gun-line where he could see the dark shape of a sentry prowling about in the way that sentries did when they feared that sleep was stalking them. The man had turned to face him, had initially brought his rifle to the shoulder but had then relaxed, saying not a word. Keenan wondered why the black form was carrying the long infantry rifle until he realised that the closest gun was one of the brass smooth-bores and, therefore, manned by a scratch crew of the 66th.

'Not if I recognise him, sir,' the sentry replied, in an educated voice that took Keenan quite by surprise. 'You're Lieutenant Keenan, sir, Third Scinde Horse.' The man tapped the sling of his rifle in salute.

'Indeed I am, and who are you?' Keenan wondered if he was talking to another officer in the dark. But, if so, why would he be standing sentry and carrying a rifle?

'Sir, I am Private Frederick Williams, Sixty-Sixth Foot, now with Captain Slade's battery, sir.' There was courtesy but no deference in Williams's voice, thought Keenan, and there was something familiar about the man. 'Our dog Bobby caused your horses to get awfully uppity, sir, when he was chasing a rat.'

Keenan could tell that the man was tired, but there was a note in his voice that might just have been slightly mocking; it put him on the defensive. 'Yes, it was a bloody nuisance. Each of my sowars owns his horse—' Keenan was starting to answer when Poshie Williams interrupted him.

'I know that you're *sillidar* cavalry, sir, and I can appreciate how attached the men are to their own animals.'

'No, lad, you can't know because, as an English infantryman, you've never been asked to bring your most prized and expensive possession into the Service. The injury that your terrier caused cost one of my men dear and imperilled my patrol.' Keenan was suddenly aware that he was talking to the man too much like an equal: he had no need to justify himself to an ordinary soldier.

248

Williams understood the silent reproach as well and fell back on the stock 'Sir,' rather than continue an argument that he could never win.

'Anyway, that's in the past now. What do you make of things, Williams?' asked Keenan, more to keep himself awake than because he was especially interested in the reply.

'It was a pig's bastard.' Keenan noticed how Williams dignified the typical soldier's curse with a long *a* in the last word. 'Sir, we'd fired all our ammunition before the Ghazis had even got into their stride, and when we were told to go back to replenish our limbers, sir, Johnny Af was hanging off our nags, jumping all over the pieces and cutting and slashing at anything and anyone who came within reach. I fired nearly fifty rounds myself and bent my bayonet. We lost eighteen men before we managed to break clear, sir, and do you know—'

'Ssh . . . hush a minute, Williams.' Keenan cut across the soldier's tale. 'Look at my mount.'

'I was, sir – hope you're not planning to show up on him in Phoenix Park . . .'

Keenan signalled to Williams to hold his tongue for the horse was throwing his head with an animation that Keenan hadn't seen all day. His ears were flicking to and fro and he was swishing his long tail.

'My stallion's got the scent of a mare in season,' whispered Keenan, just tightening his reins a fraction.

'Sir, you're right there. But our horses are still limbered up and they're downwind anyway. Has your boy noticed any of our mares before?' answered Williams, betraying a good understanding of horseflesh that was unusual in a private of the line, thought Keenan.

'No, I don't think so . . . Listen there, upwind, away to the left.' Keenan pointed in the dark. 'Can you hear hoofs?'

'I'm still deaf as the mainmast after today, sir.' Williams had turned to face the sound, cupped both hands behind his ears and opened his mouth to magnify any noise.

'Yes, there are horses a little beyond that ridge. Stand your gunners to and get a piece swung round, sharp as you like.' As Williams scuttled off to wake the gun crews, Keenan kicked his priapic pony into a trot for he had to rouse the men of the 66th.

'Stand to, lad, and get the company to stand to as quietly as you can now.' Luckily, thought Keenan, the sentry was sensible – and probably frightened enough to be on his toes. He asked no questions, but simply shook the man closest to him, then ran along the sleeping ranks pulling and kicking everyone awake.

'Where's the company commander?' But even as he asked, Keenan saw that the infantrymen were resting as they would fight, with the NCOs two paces behind them and the pair of officers another pace to their rear in the centre of the line.

Keenan dismounted and grabbed the sleeping shoulders of both bundles. Captain Beresford-Peirse sat up immediately, blinking, coughing, but instantly alert. The other figure was less lively. Billy Morgan was sleeping the exhausted sleep of a lad barely out of his teens. He came to slowly, his hair stiff with dust, yawning and stretching his arms as his elder brother had seen him do a thousand times in the nursery when they were boys.

'Quickly now, Beresford-Peirse.' Keenan ignored his brother. 'I believe we're about to be rushed by Afghan horse from up on the left flank. The guns are coming into action, but we'll need a volley from your men if we're to see them off.'

'Where are they and how many are there?' Bereseford-Peirse was instantly on his feet, easing his pistol in its holster and clapping his helmet on to his head.

'I don't know how many, but I guess they're about a hundred paces away up yonder behind that bit of rock. I'll get my men in the saddle and try to work around their flank.' Keenan threw himself back on to his horse as the infantrymen came back to life remarkably quickly. But as he left the two officers, he heard his brother mumble, 'What's he bloody flapping about now?'

Then, before Billy Morgan had time to snipe at his brother any more, the half-hundred or so men of the 66th who formed the rearguard had to act even more urgently, for two shots lit up the night followed by another two.

'Those are our sentries firing, Morgan. Get the men on their feet and formed up, for Christ's sake!' Morgan had never heard such abruptness from Captain Beresford-Peirse before. Even in the worst of the action earlier that day, the man had been studiedly calm, almost theatrically so, but not now. 'Come on, that's cavalry — and dozens of the sods by the sound of it.'

Morgan was suddenly aware of the noise of hoofs and saddlery in the night but, unusually, no shouts of '*Din-din*' which had become horribly familiar over the past few hours. 'Sar'nt Kelly, get the men—' but Morgan need not have bothered for his sergeant was already turning exhausted soldiers towards the dark, pounding hoofs. Morgan just had time to admire the fact that Kelly was already fully dressed and ready for anything when the first horseman stormed into the confused infantry. Swords flashed in the moonlight, one or two bayonets flickered in response, but the relative quiet of the whole scene was soon broken by English shouts and screams and the eldritch battle-cries of the Afghan cavalry.

'Get down, you fucker!' Sergeant Kelly fired his rifle into the belly of a horse, which toppled hard on to its nose in the scrum of bodies, pitching its rider in a tangle of reins and robes to the ground at Kelly's feet and below his hungry bayonet.

'Get into a circle, lads — quick, back to back, keep them away.' Morgan could only think of what Beresford-Peirse had done earlier in the day. He poked at a galloping horse's flank with his borrowed bayonet, felt the blade bite flesh and heard

251

the horse squeal as his men were barged and buffeted against him by the physical shock of the charge.

'Steady, lads, keep your blades up, don't waste any shot now.' Captain Beresford-Peirse obviously agreed with Morgan's instinct for he now took control of the little group as they stabbed and thrust at the horsemen who swirled about them. 'Right, men, make sure you're loaded but only fire on my orders.' He was completely aware of the shortage of ammunition, thought Morgan. 'Now move down towards the guns while we've got a breather.' The Ghazis had pulled back beyond the reach of the 66th's bayonets. 'Slade . . . Slade, we're on our way, give these buggers some canister, can't you?'

Confused shouts came back through the dark from seventy paces away. Slade's battery was in just the same state of exhausted chaos as the 66th.

'What's that they're saying? I'm too damn deaf to hear a thing,' said Beresford-Peirse.

'They say to make a run for it,' replied Morgan, just a few feet away from his captain in the circle of bodies. 'We're masking their fire.' At least, that was what Morgan thought he'd heard a voice remarkably like Slade's say, as the porcupine of bayonets shuffled slowly towards the gun-line.

'Aye, they're right. They can't get a clear shot at Johnny Af while we're between the two of them. Right, lads, when I say so, break formation and run like buggery towards the battery. Form up round the nearest pair of guns once we're there. If we're quick about things, we'll wrongfoot the Ghazis. Everyone clear?' Morgan looked at the pale, haggard faces that nodded below helmets, bandages or improvised turbans, acknowledging the company commander's words. 'Right, go – go like the devil's after you!' The men did just that.

Morgan was reminded of one of the lung-bursting contests that his wretched brother would organise when they were boys. How many times had they been out on a picnic with Mother when Sam had turned a pleasant day into an impromptu test of manhood, a race to a rock or lone tree and back suddenly becoming a matter of overwhelming importance? This time, though, the marker was the barrel of a howitzer and the competitors' lives mattered more than his mother's delight.

'Get out of the way – get fuckin' clear.' As Morgan and Kelly vied with the men around them to be first to the guns, a great, coarse voice bawled through the dark. 'Get out my field o' fire, you idiots!' Just visible in the light of the crescent moon was the steel of a nine-pounder, a gang of men gathered about it and the dark outline of another shouting, swearing and waving at them,

'Get down, your honour.' Out of nowhere Morgan was grabbed by strong hands and almost pulled off balance before he realised that the enemy was close behind and the gunners were itching to fire. 'Jesus, Mary and Joseph!' Down on his belly, he heard Private Battle exclaim from the ground next to him as a great belch of flame leapt over them and a sheet of iron canister rounds swept into the foe.

'Mother of God, that was close. Come on, sir.' Battle was as quickly up on his feet as he had fallen to the ground, pulling Morgan after him towards a mob of silhouettes who flailed rammers in the dark and pushed at the wheels of a gun with silent slickness.

'On me, lads. Form round the guns.' Beresford-Peirse's voice hung hard on the roar of the shot as order was created out of the confusion of his sprinting men. With their lungs soughing for breath, Morgan, Kelly and the other non-commissioned officers placed the weary remains of H Company into a defensive ring around the artillery pieces on the left part of the line while more of Slade's men pushed and hauled at the trails of the other guns in an attempt to get them to bear on the rest of the Afghan cavalry.

'Can you see any more of this lot, Sar'nt Kelly?' Morgan asked, as he peered into the darkness trying to use what little light there was.

'No, sir.' Kelly, like Morgan, was trying to control his breathing. 'But I think I can hear summat back there where we came from.'

Then the horror came again. The Afghans had seen the way that Slade and his men had wheeled their guns around and came out of the dark from an angle that put the infantry between them and the louring muzzles of the artillery.

'The fly fuckers!' muttered Sergeant Kelly. 'They've scotched the guns, clever sods.'

'Front rank, kneel,' Beresford-Peirse shouted, with more optimism than accuracy for the defensive circle of infantrymen was just that, a loose ring of men with no strict formation, just a deep, common desire to cling together in order to survive the next onslaught. 'Preee-sent,' the captain's command brought the rifles' muzzles and their shafts of steel into a menacing line as the troops at the rear of the circle turned about to fire over their comrades' shoulders. 'Wait, lads – go for the horses . . . Wait.' Morgan was staring down the barrel of his rifle, finger curled tightly around the trigger, first pressure taken, gasping to ease the crescent of steel another fraction of an inch and feel the butt kick back hard against his flesh. 'Wait . . .' Beresford-Peirse was letting the Afghans get dangerously close, for Morgan could now hear the drumming of the hoofs, even above the shouts of the frustrated gunners behind the 66th who were grabbing for their carbines.

'Where's the Runaway fucking 'Orse when we need 'em, sir?' Sergeant Kelly voiced Morgan's own thoughts as both of them squinted down the sights of their rifles.

'Wait . . .' The horses were now plainly visible, the white clothes of their riders reflecting the starlight; Morgan even fancied that he could see the teeth of one of the snarling riders as the cavalry came within yards of the waiting muzzles.

'Fire!' Morgan felt the stock of his Martini-Henry jump in his hand as a great cloud of white powdersmoke shot out in front of him, obscuring his view of his target. Through the reek and the darkness, horses' squeals and men's shouts merged into the automatic metallic clicks and deft gestures of well-trained troops.

'Get to fuck!' the men jeered, and raised a tired cheer as the Afghans who had not been hit by the volley sheared past the 66th, their horses, despite kicks and thrashes from the riders' reins, refusing to impale themselves on the steel of the ragged square. One or two more rifle shots followed them, to be greeted by roars of 'Cease fire, don't waste your ammunition,' from both officers, Kelly and the clutch of NCOs.

'Can you see anything, Beresford-Peirse?' asked Morgan, aware that the enemy had fallen back out of range, although their tack and weapons could still be heard in the shadows cast by the nearby outcrop of rock.

'Nothing, but they're there and they'll be back – of that you can be certain. Everyone, make sure that you're loaded and no jammed cartridges. Anyone hurt?'

Just as the company commander started the checks, which, after that day, were becoming depressingly routine, there was a bang from the gun-line behind them, followed by another that made all of them duck.

'What the bloody hell are they firing at, Sar'nt Kelly?' asked Morgan, bemused by what the guns had seen – unless there were yet more foe whom their exhausted senses had failed to detect.

Sergeant Kelly paused a moment before answering. 'There, sir, look upwards,' He tilted his head towards the sky. 'Star shell – look at the trail.'

And, sure enough, as Morgan looked up he saw two scarlet trails of sparks speeding upwards like angry comets. 'That must be the new illuminant they've been talking about . . . Bloody hell, it's like daybreak!' The dark was swept back by the magnesium balls, twenty-one from each round, that sent the shadows racing and showed a score of Afghan horsemen moving forward from their rocky shelter, ready for the next assault. Morgan watched for the enemy's reaction – it was the same as his. The Ghazis froze in their tracks, awestruck.

But not Sam Keenan and his men. As the harsh white light drenched the desert and its scrubby bushes, the Scinde Horse spurred forward, straight into a gallop from a cautious walk. Morgan saw how the sowars' battle cries forced the Afghans to wrench their heads around and how the combination of light and fear threw the Ghazis off course.

'They're bloody running, so they are, your honour!' Private Battle had jumped to his feet from the kneeling position. 'Permission to fire?' Before anyone could grant his wish or forbid it, Battle fired, hitting an Afghan neatly in the back at seventy yards, throwing him from the saddle, while a handful of others joined in until Beresford-Peirse, Morgan and the NCOs screamed, 'Stop firing – stop! You'll hit our people!'

'Aye, let the bloody *tatt-wallahs* do some fighting for once.' Similar shouts of derision came from the other soldiers while Morgan watched, his sweat-slick fists clenched tight round the furniture of his rifle, thrilled by the sight of shouting, howling Scindis piling into the frightened enemy with vengeful joy. The light of the star shells bounced and slid off the blades of the Indian cavalry as they hacked and jabbed at the Ghazis. The impact of the miniature charge was too much for Ayoob Khan's troops, who were overwhelmed by the sheer aggression of Keenan's men. As the Afghan horse broke and fled into the night, Morgan found himself cheering alongside Kelly and the others. In the best tradition of the *Illustrated London News*, the 66th twirled their helmets round their heads and some, unable to resist the popular image, went so far as to raise them on the points of their bayonets.

Even Private Battle was as generous as he could be towards his old adversaries. 'Why, your honour, that's a grand sight. But them boys would be twice as fierce wid a drop of the devil's piss inside of them, so they would!'

* * *

256

This night, thought Morgan, would never end. His brother's charge had bought them a little respite, but no sooner had they fended off one set of Afghans than another sprang up from nowhere. Since the cavalry charge an hour and a half ago, there had been no more serious attacks, but *jezails* and Sniders continued to spit from the dark, happily hitting no one but preventing any rest and keeping everyone on a knife edge of tension. As he and his men waited in the lee of a some low boulders beside the road for Beresford-Peirse to come and give his next set of orders, Morgan looked up into the sky in an effort to stop himself falling fast asleep. He fought back his exhaustion, trying to compare this carpet of stars with the few that sometimes managed to peep through the rainclouds back in Cork. But such homely thoughts shrivelled as the scrape of boots and a low cough announced the arrival of his commander.

'So, Morgan, I'll escort the guns back to the next delaying position. You keep the eighteen men that Sar'nt Kelly has detailed here with the cavalry and make sure that any more of these rogues keep their distance. As soon as you hear our call and then the "retire", get back as soon as you can, but don't let the cavalry outstrip you.' Beresford-Peirse, thought Morgan, was just a little less polite now, just a little less studiedly courteous – he rather preferred it. 'Oh, and another thing, Morgan, collar any stragglers that you can and search every pouch you find – we're down to ten rounds a man now.'

Morgan knew how a rearguard should have worked – he'd practised it enough at Sandhurst and the tactics course at Hythe – but the reality was rather different. Now he and a dozen threadbare men were left with a gang of cavalry who couldn't understand a word he said, commanded by someone who wouldn't lift a finger to help him even if all their lives depended on it. Worse than that, he and his wretched brother were now responsible for seeing that the remnant of their father's command got away without further disasters.

'Sir, what do you want me to do about Sutton and Cooper?' Sergeant Kelly had done as he was told and numbered off half of the tiny force to stay behind under Morgan's command. But two of the men had collapsed during the skirmishes with the Ghazis while the guns – the only available transport that might have been used to get them to the rear – had gone before Kelly had had time to deal with the two sick men.

'Do you know what's wrong with them, Sar'nt Kelly?' Morgan had seen both men unconscious on the ground, apparently unwounded but not responding to anything that he and the others had tried.

'Sir, it's sunstroke – combination of thirst an' exhaustion, I reckon. They was both wobblin' a bit earlier on and Sutton said 'is head was so bad he couldn't hardly see. Come across this before, I have, sir. They'll be fine if we can get them some rest an' plenty of water.' Sergeant Kelly was kneeling next to Cooper, cradling his bare head in his lap and pouring drops of precious liquid from his own water-bottle carefully down his throat.

'Aye, and both are in short supply,' replied Morgan, as he saw that the rest of his men had fallen instantly asleep on the ground while still holding their weapons. 'How are we going to get them back? None of us has the strength to carry them and every fit man must be available to use his rifle. What's to be done?'

'The Scindis will have to carry 'em, sir. If they can't put 'em on their nags, they can rig one of them dhoolie things they drag behind their hosses – you've seen 'em,' replied Kelly.

'Yes, I have.' Morgan could picture the jury-rigged stretchers he had seen Afghans using: two poles and a blanket were attached to the horse while the other ends of the wood skidded along the ground. 'I'll go and speak to Mister Keenan. We need to get this sorted out as soon as possible. Captain Beresford-Peirse will be blowing for us before we know it.'

'Good luck, sir,' replied Kelly, sardonically, as Morgan

walked over to the Scinde Horsemen who were resting a little way off the track.

Their horses slept standing or lying down, saddles and tack still on while, apart from a pair of pacing sentries, the sowars lay fully dressed on the ground, carbines and sabres beside them, all in that state of the instant comatose sleep that only comes with utter exhaustion.

'*Ram-ram, bahadur,*' Morgan began. His presence was acknowledged by the grimy sentry with a flick of a salute. A bearded chin pointed to a motionless body on the ground when he asked, 'Keenan sahib?' He walked over to a khaki bundle and saw a spiked helmet lying beside it in the starlight. He crouched down and looked at his brother. The older man had a luxuriant moustache, though the rest of his hair was cropped short. The deep tan that Billy had seen on most of the other sahibs who had spent time in India hadn't yet fully taken hold of his brother's complexion, but he saw that Sam's mother's dark colouring meant that her son would soon be burnt as brown as any of his men. The thing that struck Billy, though, was the dust that ingrained Sam's clothing and equipment. Even in the dark, he could see that the cavalryman had been just too tired to beat the dirt from his clothes before he sank to the ground. He reached to shake him awake, even as the dark shape of Daffadar Sayed Miran stalked up, as silent as a cat, to protect his officer's vital rest.

'You need the *burra-sahib*, sahib? He is tired. Will I not do?' Miran recognised Morgan at once and saluted, suspecting, somehow, that the purpose of the visit was far from being a family reunion.

'No, Daffadar sahib,' Morgan began, then checked himself. He had noticed how poor his own people were with the native soldiers, always insisting that a British officer should be brought to speak to them, even for the most trivial of things. But, then, had he not seen Indian troops perform bravely and every bit as well as his own men today? It stood to reason

259

that an Indian NCO would be just as used to responsibility as one of his corporals or sergeants. Furthermore, the daffadar would probably know more about heatstroke than any of them did and he had no wish to ask anything of his brother. 'Yes, of course, Daffadar sahib. I have two men who are struck down by the sun. We cannot carry them. Can you?'

Just as Miran was considering the request, Keenan sat upright on the ground, rubbed an already gloved hand through his gritty hair and demanded, 'What's wrong? Has Slade blown for us?'

'No, sahib . . .' The daffadar explained the situation to Keenan who, Billy Morgan could tell, was becoming increasingly impatient with yet another worry being added when all he wanted was a little rest while the Afghans allowed it.

'Oh, it's you, Morgan.' He was fully awake now. He rose to his feet, rolled his neck and shoulders, as if to ease some deep ache, clapped his helmet on his head and demanded, without any warmth of recognition in his voice, 'Show me what the problem is.'

Had Morgan not been so tired, he might have expected the next encounter. Chance, of course, had dictated that the very man to be tending the two sick soldiers when Keenan arrived on the scene was Private Eddie 'Bottle' Battle. He looked up at Keenan, recognising him immediately, then dropped his chin, hoping to avoid the officer's attention.

'What's wrong with these two, then?' Keenan asked Battle, without a trace of sympathy. 'How long have they been unconscious?' He knelt down to feel the forehead of Private Sutton. 'This man's as hot as hell – how long has he been like this?'

Battle did not reply.

'Well, don't you know, man? Cat got your tongue?' Keenan, already irritated by the way that things were developing, looked hard at the silent soldier who crouched next to him before almost spluttering, 'Devil take it! You – you're that drunk who shot my rissaldar. What in the name of God are you doing here? Are you on the run, you blackguard?'

'No, Keenan, Private Battle was expressly released by *Colonel* Galbraith.' Billy Morgan stressed his commanding officer's rank. 'Battle's fought well throughout the day and—'

'Well, Galbraith's a bloody idiot to set free a lout like this,' Keenan snapped back.

'An idiot, is he?' Morgan riposted, hot and sharp. 'Well, he's a dead brave idiot, who fell with the colours of the Sixty-Sixth in his hand. And where is the commanding officer of the Third Scinde Horse, Malcolmson *bahadar*?' sneered Billy Morgan. 'A bloody long way from here, I'll wager – as usual.'

'Now stop it, the pair of ye.' Private Battle intervened between the two brothers with no more ceremony than if he were stopping a fight in the wet canteen. 'Ye're meant to be off'cers, setting an example to creatures like me, not squabbling like nippers. Stop it, won't you?' And such forthright talk, from the sort of man both subalterns recognised from their childhood, defused the situation. The pair reined back and the tension eased.

Then Sam Keenan reignited it: 'I've no spare animals to carry these two – every sabre and horse will be needed to cover the rest of the rearguard. Besides, they're not sunstruck. They're dead drunk and no use to either man or beast.'

'What?' Billy Morgan erupted as quickly as he had subsided. 'They're not dead drunk, they're dead beat. They've been hard at it with the Afghans all day and I'll not have you—'

'They're no more drunk than I am, your honour,' cut in Private Battle, with a less than helpful intervention. 'Why, Josh Cooper's a temperance wallah and Jim Sutton's just a lad, so he is.'

'And they both stink of drink,' retorted Keenan, angrily. 'Are you never going to learn about the men, Morgan? Will you always be so naïvely loyal, even to murderers and sots like these?' He pointed at the two men on the ground and Battle.

261

'I'll take that from no one,' Battle stood up, his fists bunched, 'officer or not!'

'That'll do, Battle. Get your kit and rejoin the rest of the men.' Sergeant Kelly loomed out of the darkness. 'Come on, lad, *jildi* now.' The quiet authority in his voice made even Battle obey instantly.

'So, you can't help these men, sir?' asked Kelly, evenly, while Morgan stood by, speechless. 'We can't carry them for the same reasons you can't, sir – and we can't just leave them, can we?'

'I'm afraid you'll have to, Sar'nt Kelly. They're not fit for duty and they'll endanger other men. Take their ammunition and smash their weapons and— There's the bugle call.' The notes blared across the windless dark, indicating that the other half of the rearguard was now ready to protect Morgan's and Keenan's men as they moved back. 'Let's have no more nonsense. Get a move on now.'

But as Keenan rose to rejoin his troopers, Billy Morgan blurted, 'But you can't just abandon two good men to these savages, Keenan!'

'Can't I? What else do you suggest we do? You've got no ideas, have you? When will you get it into your dumb head that war's a nasty business – people get hurt, just like Rissaldar Singh did when your man Battle elected to make a beast of himself and then shoot him dead. Now do as you're damn well told and be quick about it.' Keenan was off, brooking no more argument.

'There's nowt else for it, sir.' Sergeant Kelly took a handful of rounds from each supine man's pouches and reached down for one of the rifles.

'We've got to leave them with some protection, Sar'nt Kelly – we can't just cast them off.' Morgan was appalled.

'We need every round, sir, and I'll never forgive meself if we give Johnny Af better bundooks than they've already got. I know it's hard, sir, but these two lads won't see another

262

dawn, not even if we do carry 'em. They need treatment and they need it urgently – and we just can't do that. They'll know bugger-all about things when the Ghazis get here, sir. So, unless you want to put them out o' their misery 'ere and now, I suggest we don't draw any more of the troops' attention to it. We need to get back to Cap'n B-P as quick as we can.'

Billy Morgan looked down at his two men. He understood everything that both his brother and his sergeant had said, but he still recoiled. For a moment his hand went to his pistol holster, but he got no further than fiddling with the fastening stud.

'No, Sar'nt Kelly, I can't do that either.' Morgan's hand fell to his side. 'But neither of these men has drink taken and I cannot forgive Mr Keenan for this.'

'Aye, sir, well, that's between you and 'im, it is. Let's get a move on now, sir, before the bloody Ghazis pokes us up the arse,' replied Kelly, pulling his officer gently away from Privates Cooper and Sutton.

How he'd endured another day of this torture Billy Morgan couldn't tell. After leaving Cooper and Sutton, they had moved and stopped, moved and stopped all the way through the night, harassed by sharpshooters and pestered by mounted scouts. They had managed to get by without any serious casualties, but they'd had not a scrap of rest either. That had had to wait until the heat of late morning when orders had come to find water and get some sleep. They had sunk down by the side of the Kandahar road and immediately obeyed.

Scarcely had Morgan's eyelids closed than it had been up and off, impelled by rumours of more Herati cavalry as the two parts of the rearguard leapfrogged past each other, if a bone-tired shuffle could be described in such energetic terms. Finally, night had come again and heat was replaced by cold. They had made about fifteen miles since the retreat had started – or so the map told them – and now they had halted, just as Beresford-Peirse had ordered, beside an apparently deserted village that stretched away into the darkness. Morgan was just turning his thoughts to checking ammunition, to the state of the men's feet, a blessed brew of tea for everyone and then, perhaps, some rest when a crackle of gunfire made him scramble for cover.

'Can anyone see the enemy?' He cried the textbook query just as he realised the absurdity of what he had said: it was dark so no one among his handful of men could see the enemy. 'Any muzzle flashes seen?' he corrected himself, only to be met with a series of muted denials from his tired, listless men.

'Sounded like muskets or *jezails*, sir. Probably villagers joining in for the badness of it.' Sergeant Kelly had come doubling up to his officer when the hail of shots had come sheeting over as they lay on the side of the sandy track down which the exhausted, sun-dried tail of the brigade was shuffling. 'These bints an' *bhisti-wallahs* don't half take on, sir, don't they just?'

Though the firing had been wild, the shots were enough to terrify the miserable crowd of camp-followers and servants who, after more than twenty-four hours of harrowing retreat, lagged far behind the remaining troops.

'Yes, they make a right bloody din at the slightest thing – but you saw what the Herati cavalry did to those camel wallahs this afternoon, didn't you, Sar'nt Kelly?' Morgan had been as shocked as the rest of his men when they had rounded a corner in the track to find a dozen enemy horsemen who had outflanked the rearguard. The fire of the 66th had driven them off, but not before they had ritually carved up five native drivers.

'Aye, sir. Not seen that before, I ain't,' Kelly answered matter-of-factly. 'We've all known what those butcher's knives can do, but sawing off the poor blokes' cocks an' sticking them in their gobs is out of order, ain't it, sir?'

'Yes – utterly. But you can see why the bearers get excited – especially when they must have thought that things were getting quieter,' replied Morgan, as he searched the edge of the village just a little way off the track with his red-rimmed, dust-rimed eyes. Two more shots boomed from about a hundred and fifty yards away, the flashes this time quite clear. Three Martini-Henrys cracked in reply – and then silence from the village but more uproar from the flotsam on the road.

'All right, lads, that'll do. Save your rounds.' Morgan hoped that his men's fire might have found a mark, for while they had managed to filch some more ammunition from a dead mule they had found just before daylight faded, the party was still desperately short.

Ignoring the panicking litter of camp-followers, Kelly asked, 'Do you reckon we've got time to get some char on, sir? Cap'n B-P was letting his party get some doss while Cap'n Slade was buggering about with that gun they'd got stuck.' If Kelly was sufficiently unworried by the musket fire, thought Morgan, then he supposed that he might be as well.

'If we've got enough water between us, then please do so, Sar'nt Kelly. Ayoob's boys seem to have got bored with chasing us for the time being – thank the Lord – and those Gunners' screws looked completely done up to me. They won't pull that howitzer out of the nullah in a hurry.' As Morgan's detachment had passed the artillery and Beresford-Peirse's party, the crews had been heaving and straining to get one of the brass guns out of a deep ditch where it had tumbled, but the draught horses had almost no energy left, or so it had seemed to him.

'Sir. Battle, get a splash o' water from everyone and two mess tins on for a brew, shall yer? Screen yerself from the village, mind.' Kelly knew that hot tea would restore the men and, tired as they were, the lads quickly set about the precious concoction.

Morgan was always amazed by this performance. Even in normal times, the troops would be lacklustre about so many things – it would take them an age to stack coal or to sweep a floor – but just mention the words 'brew', 'char' or 'mash' and the boys would set to with rare energy. First, he watched Battle select a point where his fire would be invisible to searching eyes in the village. Then each man produced a handful of twigs and dry grass from his haversack – carefully hoarded against such an occasion. Predictably, Battle had a few Snider rounds in a pocket: he poured the powder on to the kindling and drew a lucifer along one of the rough stones that had been placed around the pyre. The smudge of smoke and the flare of yellow flame was enough to set the wood alight, but it took endless puffs from Battle's pursed lips to get the blaze going properly. Two D-shaped mess tins full of scummy stream water were placed on top of the stones. A little more cartridge powder speeded the process along before Battle commanded, 'Let's be having the makings, then.'

Two men conjured up twists of brown paper that contained tea leaves and some sugar. Battle sprinkled the tea into the now bubbling water, then dropped in a piece of matchwood, around which any floating leaves might cluster. As the sugar was spooned in, the char master demanded, 'Give us your mugs, boys, one between two.' Then the sweet dark-brown nectar was poured out and shared.

''Ere you are, sir, 'ave a swat o' that.' Sergeant Kelly had taken a few sips from his own tin mug before passing it to his officer. In the light of the flames, Morgan could see how Kelly – probably when he was still a young private soldier – had carefully whipped the handle in thin cord to protect his fingers from the heat of the liquid.

No sooner had he taken his first pull of the elixir than he heard the clatter of hoofs and the nasal Scouse of Private Wardle, the sentry, demanding, 'Halt! Who comes there?'

'Lieutenant Maclaine and two.'

'Advance one and be recognised.' Wardle, despite his fatigue, continued the ritual – probably more scared of Sergeant Kelly's

266

displeasure than anything that the Afghans might throw at him, Morgan guessed.

'All right, Wardle, well done. Let them through, please. I know who the officer is.' Morgan took a quick sip, handed the cup back to Sergeant Kelly and wearily pulled himself to his feet to find out what Hector Maclaine, scourge of the Afghans – and his father's nemesis – wanted.

But as he approached a voice he knew too well rasped from one of the horsemen: 'Morgan, that is you, ain't it? Why have you got a bloody fire burning when the enemy's still about?'

'The fire's well shielded from view, Keenan. You would see that if you took a moment to look – and it's a judgement I've made for the good of my men, not that it's any business of yours.' Morgan was tired and had had enough of his brother's haughtiness; he didn't bother to conceal this from the troops. He saw that Sergeant Kelly shifted uncomfortably while he crouched near the fire and he thought he heard Private Battle mumble, 'Jaysus, they're at it again like bloody kids,' but it stopped any more interference from Keenan.

'We're desperate for water, Morgan.' Maclaine thrust himself into the confrontation before things got any worse. 'Our nags are on their last legs. Thomas, show Mr Morgan your horse's tongue.'

The two officers' escort, a stocky lad whose breeches were stiff with dried mud almost up to his waist, dropped from the saddle. 'Shush, Lily, shush.' Gently he opened the mare's mouth. Even in the dark, the young officer could see that the horse's tongue was grossly swollen, while Gunner Thomas went on to inform him, 'She's got 'orrible blisters all over 'er gums, she 'as, and the rest of the troop's no better, sir.'

'What have you done for water, Morgan?' asked Keenan, in a more emollient tone.

'We found a trickle of pure stuff mid-afternoon and have had what we could find from the dead along the way. We dealt with some Herati cavalry a while back and they had a saddle

267

bladder. We can offer you a little, but nothing like enough for your mounts, I fear,' answered Morgan, soothingly, responding to his brother's brutishness the day before with sweet generosity.

'That's good of you, Morgan,' replied Maclaine before Keenan spoilt the *rapprochement*, 'but you're right. We need more than you can provide and gallons more for both the gun teams and the cavalry.'

'Are those buildings I can see over there?' Keenan asked no one in particular, staring towards the houses from which the shots had come.

'They are, your honour,' sparked up Battle. 'It's a wee village that'll be bound to have a well.'

'Yes, indeed,' Keenan answered, apparently not recognising Battle's voice. 'Have you had any men in there, Morgan?'

'Not yet.' Morgan added nothing more.

'Right, Gunner Thomas, you stay here and nurse that horse of yours. Come on, Keenan, let's you and me go and find some water.' Morgan could hear the impetuosity in Maclaine's voice, despite the obvious tiredness.

'But, sirs—' Sergeant Kelly started to object, even as Morgan caught his arm to silence him as the pair of subalterns trotted away into the blackness.

Kelly looked at Morgan but said not a thing. Officer and sergeant crouched by the fire, sipping the last drops of the now cool tea while Gunner Thomas fussed over his stricken horse. Their silence continued for they were listening to the night. As the noise of hoofs disappeared, some camp-followers appeared, with a pair of wounded Sappers shuffling along the track behind them. A dog started to bark in the distance.

'That sounds as though they've arrived at the village, Sar'nt Kelly,' muttered Morgan, still listening intently.

'It does, sir,' replied Kelly, unhappily, just as angry cries and a ripple of shots came from the huts and shanties they could almost make out in the dark. There was the sharp crack of a pistol, a long pause, more shouts and then silence.

'That's the officers in trouble, that is, sir.' Gunner Thomas left off tinkering with Lily and went to pull his carbine from its leather bucket by his saddle. 'Shall we go and help?'

'No, lad,' Sergeant Kelly replied quietly. 'Our job's here on the road. They'll either be back in a minute or there'll be promotion for another couple of young gentlemen.' He looked at Morgan reproachfully.

'An' that'll be more promotion than Jim Sutton or Josh Cooper will ever get.' Battle's voice came bitterly from the darkness.

TEN

The Siege

I'd been back in Kandahar a couple of days and was pretty
well recovered. As I stood in Primrose's headquarters I'd
nothing worse to show for my trials than a handful of scrapes
and bruises and the need for a complete new suit of khaki
drill. Some solid sleep had set me to rights, but I knew that
the ghastliness of the last few days would stay chiselled into
my memory for ever.

Now I'd been called for by my chief. He'd made it clear
that he wanted to speak to me alone and I'd been treated
with great courtesy, gentleness almost, by the staff officer who
had shown me up to the low-ceilinged, poky little room, with
its narrow Asiatic window, that was my commander's inner
sanctum.

'So, Morgan, you're feeling more yourself now, are you?'
said General bloody Primrose. I suppose he was doing his
best to be kind, but I just couldn't take to him. But, then,
that was probably more guilt and weariness than anything
else – and it wasn't the most pleasant of tasks explaining to
your divisional commander why you had lost your command,
had your arse whipped by a bunch of savages and your son
butchered to boot. But the general wouldn't let me indulge
in self-pity. 'We've not managed to talk in any detail before,

but I'm clear about the major events and where the enemy have got to now. Others have filled me in while you were getting some sleep and, I imagine, slaking your thirst.' He really was trying to let me down gently – the peppery runt was even attempting to smile sympathetically. 'But what do you think went wrong?'

'It was entirely my fault, General. I've lost over a thousand men, two guns, countless vital animals and ruined two regiments of cavalry and three battalions of infantry. What went wrong was my judgement and I've only got away with a bit of my force intact by virtue of some very brave men – officers and soldiers, Bombay and British.' I'd been watching from the wings during the recriminations after the Light Cavalry Brigade's débâcle at Balaclava back in '54. The one thing that I'd learnt from that was that superiors of all sorts might forgive failure, but they would never tolerate the sort of blame-spreading that milord Cardigan tried – and that was before the gentlemen of the press had properly got their teeth into things. My disaster was already headlines back in England. There could be only one thing for it. 'So, General, I would like to resign my commission immediately.'

'Don't be a damn fool, man.' Primrose gave me no opportunity to continue. 'Why, there's argy-bargy about who did what and when, about whether I should have let such a small force go into the field when we didn't really know what the enemy's strength was – oh, and all sorts of other things. But the one name that stands out for sheer dogged bravery is yours. Now we need to think about how we make the best of this. They made a virtue out of a skirmish at that drift on the Buffalo river last year in Zululand – d'you remember how practically everyone got the VC? That was to distract folk from Chelmsford's little nonsense at Isandlwana . . .' He prosed on about what the viceroy would make of it all, how the papers would follow it up, even what effect it would have on that arch clown Gladstone. In other words, how he could come out of the whole wretched affair as undented as possible.

I tried to listen, but all I could think of was the men who lay in the desert behind me. I'd seen some things in the Crimea and the Mutiny, but for utter bloody horror, nothing compared with an angry Ghazi topped up with *bhang* and *jihad*. They'd overwhelmed the young jawans of the Rifles and the Grenadiers – just as I had feared they would. The 66th had stood firm and died in droves but it was really down to the first-class and numerous guns that Ayoob Khan had deployed. Our Horse Gunners – except for the idiot who had triggered the whole damn thing prematurely – and Slade's battery had fought magnificently. But then there was the cavalry . . .

'And to whom do you attribute the blame for all this, Morgan?' Primrose had to have his scapegoat and I suppose that I was too senior, too much part of the group who had agreed to the general's overall plan, to be an easy target. Blame me and some of that would stick to Primrose. 'Seems damned odd to me that Malcolmson of the Scinde Horse should be almost the first person to arrive back at Kandahar. And what of Nuttall, your cavalry commander? That retreat across the desert must have been hell on earth, yet he looked pretty dapper when he got here. How useful to you was he when the Afghans closed in? You had two horses – it was two, wasn't it? – shot from under you and your staff cut to ribbons. Why was he so spruce?'

Why indeed? The cavalry, my so-called eyes and ears, had never really done their job. First, apart from Sam's patrol, there had never been any reliable intelligence from their reconnaissances. Then there had been a lot of loafing around on the battlefield getting shelled and not much aggressive action. Even when they had charged, everything had been half-hearted, which only gave our gracious foes even more to go for. And to think of all the tosh I had had to endure from bloody Malcolmson: how he'd fought over that same bit of ground more than a year before, how he knew it and the Afghans like the back of his horse-sweaty hand, yet when he came to it, who had he left commanding the 'post of honour'? Who had he left in charge of the rearguard? My son – and him just a subaltern. Mark you, Tom Nuttall was never strong enough or knowledgeable enough to control the likes of Malcolmson – Nuttall was an infantryman by trade and knew as much about horse-soldiering as I did about the Vicar of Rome's underwear.

'General, there's no one to be blamed except myself.' I wasn't trying to sound like a boy in the headmaster's study: I just understood that if things went wrong the *burra-sahib* had to take responsibility – there was too much swerving by half, these days. Besides, I was sick at heart over what had happened.

It was the retreat as much as the battle. I'd seen men behave worse under fire than any of my regiments did that day, but when the bloody drag back to Kandahar started, all discipline just dissolved. The 66th and the Horse Gunners were splendid – what was left of them – but the others and all those wretched camp-followers just invited the enemy to do their worst. The 3rd Light Cavalry jumped at every shadow and interpreted musket shots as enemy artillery; the Sappers and Miners got at the drink; the Grenadiers immediately supped every drop of water they could get their hands on and were constantly pleading thirst; and the Rifles – well, they had no officers left and became a rabble. By the time Harry Brooke's brigade had thrown out a protective screen to receive us seven or eight miles west of Kandahar, my precious regiments were nothing more than a mob. What the Afghans had failed to do, panic, exhaustion, the sun and dehydration achieved for them. Thirty miles seemed like three hundred and I don't mind admitting that when Brooke came up to me and clapped a manly arm around my shoulders, I blubbed like a baby. It was the shame and the waste of it all.

'Anyway, Morgan, we can deal with all these recriminations once we've survived whatever Ayoob Khan has in store for us next. His leading troops were spotted about four hours ago up on the Baba Saheb Ghar.' He loved his *bat* did our man Primrose. I guarantee he'd never been near the rocky outcrop that dominated the western approach to the town, but he'd learnt its name off the map and trotted it out like a bloody local. 'As you've seen, we've pulled everybody within the walls and I'll ask you to take your share of its defence − I kept very few troops behind to garrison the place once you deployed, as you'll recall.' I did. He'd kept a full Bombay battalion and the excellent Second Battalion of the 7th Fusiliers. If I'd had that lot with me four days ago, it would have been a very different story. But, oh, no: James Primrose wasn't going to leave himself short. Still less was he going to command troops in the field.

'Now, I suggest you get Brooke to show you round the defences. He'll explain how we've cleared the shanties and lean-tos in order to get some decent fields of fire . . .' He was a bugger was Primrose. Brooke and I had been urging him to do that for months. 'By the way, how did my political officer serve you, Morgan?'

Serve me? Jock McGucken? More like bloody save me. 'General, he was a tower of strength. When we have a minute to discuss decorations, I'd like to put his name forward. He stopped the Bombay Grenadiers collapsing almost single-handed when their commandant was struck.'

'Is that a fact? I'm delighted to hear it. Oh, and one more thing, Morgan. I'm very sorry to hear about your step-son, young Keenan. I'm told he did great things throughout the day, but nothing more has been heard of him since he and that Horse Gunner went off to find water, has it?'

The words caused me a physical ache. Ever since I'd come to after twelve hours' exhausted sleep and been told that Sam was missing, the truth had lingered at the back of my consciousness like some hideous spectre. I was busy and still deeply tired, but my mind kept going back to the fact that my boy, Mary's and my boy – the lad I'd never treated as properly as I should – was probably now cut to strips and nothing more than carrion. It didn't help that he'd been with that showy eejit Maclaine – what a bloody mess.

God knows why Primrose put me in charge of the garrison. Sometimes I despaired of the Army and its hidebound thinking, for I don't mind admitting that I was still in a pother after the events of the last few days. But I was the most senior brigadier general, I needed something to stop me falling into a decline and – while I hated to say it – it was good of the general to continue to demonstrate his confidence in me.

Harry Brooke had practically carried me to my room in our shared mess after I'd finished weeping all over the poor man. McGucken and I had stayed with him until the last scarecrow of what had once been my brigade dragged himself under the guns of Brooke's people and then we'd all walked our nags back inside the walls of the town. As soon as the news of my little embarrassment had reached Divisional Headquarters, Primrose had ordered everyone from the cantonments to come inside the walls and prepare the place for defence. Now Brooke was showing me the measures he'd taken before handing responsibility over to me.

'It took me so long to convince the Bloom that we had to unblock every single well inside the town if we were going to survive a siege.' Brooke and I were trotting past the tomb of Ahmed Shah, right next to the Citadel where Headquarters had at last been established. 'I'm sure you've heard that Roberts and Phayre are leading relief columns? Phayre's got a hell of a job on his hands. He has to concentrate his people all along the lines of communication while Roberts can make a much quicker start from Kabul.'

I had heard. I knew nothing about Bob Phayre, but Roberts,

in my opinion, was a bloody showman. He'd practically admitted that he'd deliberately set out to win a Victoria Cross in the Mutiny to boost his career — I'd never seen such a frank and immodest account of what he had done when it was published a few years back. Now he was setting off to march three hundred miles from Kabul in double-quick time to come to our aid amid press hullabaloo and all sorts of fanfares. What really smarted, though, was that, whatever the circumstances, it was my defeat that had caused the public's favourite soldier — 'Bobs Bahadur', if you please — to come to our rescue.

'How long does the Bloom reckon it will take the columns to get here, Brooke?' I was finding it difficult to concentrate. All I wanted to do was to sit in a darkened room, nurse my shame and mourn the loss of my fine young lad. But that wasn't what the likes of me and my kind were supposed to do. The music halls and the *Graphic* told us how we were to behave and think:

> *As we fell on them fiercely, rank after rank,*
> *Invincible seemed those brave children of Mars . . .*

We weren't supposed to have thoughts for anything beyond the business of war and death. We weren't supposed to have any finer feelings at all. More to the point, how was I going to tell Mary about Sam? She would . . .

'Are you with me, Morgan?' Brooke had to pull me out of my miserable reverie. 'They reckon Roberts won't be ready to march for a week or so yet. Then he'll be about four weeks on the hoof — and that would be quick. So, we've got to be able to last for a month and a half before the Strong Deliverer might reasonably be expected here.'

Brooke had done a good job in a remarkably short time. The heavy forty-pounders were well sited with the lighter guns on the walls and in the Citadel. He'd formed a picked body of sharpshooters and made the best possible use of the new barbed wire. I suggested to him that we might link the crucial parts of the defences to Headquarters with telegraph wire and he told me that it was already being attended to, but it was the troop disposition that made me realise just how many of my men had been rubbed off the ration roll. The remains of my Bombay battalions were clubbed together and put to defend the Citadel while the Light Cavalry and the Scinde Horse − both of whom had lost more than half of their horses − were given sectors of the walls to defend, acting as infantrymen. The rump of the 66th were told off to hold the Idgah Gate just beyond the Citadel at the north end of our defences and it was here that I asked James Brooke to leave me at the end of our tour of inspection.

I just wanted to be among ordinary lads for a moment, to hear the accents of London, Reading, Birmingham, and the brogue of Ireland − and I wanted to hear those voices saying day-to-day things, not bellowing their last while staring at death. I wanted to feel the pulse of an English battalion and travel back a few years to McGucken's and my time in the old 95th when responsibilities had been lighter and failure was a rusty rifle barrel, not a slaughtered brigade. I wanted to clap those lads on the back and thank them for holding the line and dying like the warriors they were, but most of all I needed to break all the protocols, all the etiquette, and make sure for myself that Ensign Billy Morgan was in one piece.

I breezed through Battalion Headquarters, pretending I was just nosing about, and blundered through lines of boys filling sandbags in their shirt sleeves and digging pitfalls.

'Stand up!' Sergeant Kelly − I wasn't going to forget *his* name, was I? − had one of the Ordnance Board's larger filled sandbags slung across his shoulders when he called the work party to attention. It must have weighed forty pounds if it was an ounce and behind him staggered a line of other men similarly laden.

'Well, now, Sar'nt Kelly, I hope I'm not disturbing you. I thought I'd just come and see you all and thank you for everything you've done over the last few days. I saw you last when the rearguard was forming up. How did it all go?'

'A bit naughty, sir, but those that's 'ere are all rarin' to go now we've 'ad a bit of rest and summat to drink.' Kelly was running with sweat but appeared none the worse for an experience that would probably have laid Lysander low.

'And how are you, my man?' There was another fellow behind Kelly, dripping just as hard but doing his best to keep his burden between me and his face.

'Fine, sorr,' the man mumbled: he was awfully familiar.

'Ah, Private Battle from Sligo, if I remember rightly.' I know my memory is not the best, but I wasn't able to forget this tough and his crimes.

'Sir, I can explain. Sir, Colonel Galbraith—' Sergeant Kelly started.

'There's nothing to explain, Sar'nt Kelly. I think you'll find that all the brigade paperwork was left somewhere between here and Khusk-i-Nakud and I've a terrible memory for names and details sometimes.' I've never seen a man grin so hard in all my life. I knew that if Battle was slaving willingly away next to a man like Kelly, his sins had probably been atoned for. Queen's Regulations could go hang while Private Battle would not.

'You ain't seen Mister Morgan have you, Sar'nt Kelly?' I tried to sound as casual as possible.

'Aye, sir, he's yonder.' Kelly turned and pointed as best he could with the bag on his shoulders to a pit where I could see picks working methodically above well-muscled torsos. 'Digging spoil to fill these bags, he is.' I thanked Kelly, but just as I was about to walk off he added, 'Sir, I 'ope it's all right to say this, sir, but no one could 'ave done better than you did the other day. You only need to say the word an' we'll go again so long as it's you that's leading.'

278

'Thank you, Kelly. That means a very great deal to me.' Off I stalked so that he couldn't see my face — though I suspect he heard the catch in my voice. I didn't trust myself to say more to Kelly but with those words a great blanket of misery and self-reproach began to slip from my shoulders.

'Officer present!' I was never quite sure how useful all the saluting and standing to attention was, but that was the Army and it didn't do to challenge such shibboleths. Now half a dozen lads ceased wielding their picks and braced stiffly in the textbook position, all work suspended while they showed their respect. And there was something so reassuringly familiar about the whole thing that it was almost too much for me. A hatful of lads all stripped to the waist, tanned on their forearms, necks and heads but otherwise milky white, all of them tattooed, all of them moustachioed — I could guess what their attitudes, aspirations and hopes were, for I'd been serving and living with such men since I was a boy, and that was why it was all so comforting and homely, in a sweaty way.

'Ah, Mister Morgan.' Billy looked just like one of his men, except for the tattoos. He'd been working alongside them — good fellow that he was — setting just the right example. 'May I have a moment or two of your time?'

'Of course, sir,' my younger son replied, pulling himself from the hole and reaching for his shirt and jacket. 'I'm glad to see you about, sir. You were covered in muck and riding two to a horse last time I saw you.'

'Aye, and you looked as if you were having the time of your life.' He had. Even in the moment that the battle was clearly lost, when it was obvious to me and to any other right-thinking person that we were going to be damned lucky to see another dawn, there had been a gleam in Billy's eyes, a keenness about his manner that reminded me of a foxhound in full cry. 'Tell me about the rearguard and what happened.'

'Well, Father, we took up our first delaying position—'

'No, lad. I can fill in the details for myself — I know what rearguards are meant to do, and the appearance of Beresford-Peirse and the lot of you when we reached Kandahar told me all that I needed to know. Except one thing. What exactly happened to your brother?'

'Well, Father . . .' Billy told me about Maclaine and Sam heading off to find water and about the ambush '. . . and there was no question of our sending troops after them. There were few enough of us left and we working under Cap'n Slade's orders.'

'Yes, I understand that, son. But had you cleared the village at all?' There was something odd in the way that Billy was answering me. I knew him better than anyone else on earth – except, perhaps, his step-mother. I'd spent as much time as I could with him after I'd come back from India until the lad went away to school and I'd seen him in all sorts of scrapes and dramas. But now he wouldn't meet my eye.

''No, Father. There wasn't time or need and when Hector Maclaine and Sam came along in a tearing hurry looking for water, we told them that the enemy was about but they wouldn't listen. The rest you know.'

Billy wasn't being straight with me, I knew he wasn't.

'Do you think there's any hope for your brother, Billy?' I watched very carefully as my son answered.

'No, Father, I don't. There was a lot of shooting from the Afghans and we heard only one pistol round in return. I very much regret that he's dead.' But Billy answered just a little too quickly, slightly too keen to bring the subject to a close.

'Hmm. Thank you, Billy. Please don't write home to Herself until I have. I shall make it very clear that we don't know for sure that he is dead and that the tribesmen will do their utmost to keep men of rank as hostages. I'd be obliged if you'd do the same.'

'Of course, Father,' Billy replied. I was desperate to take the boy away somewhere private, to throw my arms around him and seek some sort of solace for Sam's death of which

280

– and there was no escaping it – I had been the ultimate architect. But I couldn't, not just because I was a general speaking to a subaltern in full daylight in the centre of Kandahar, but because the boy was all stiff and formal. He sounded more like an official despatch than a son talking to his father. I hadn't heard a scrap of sympathy or regret in what he had said.

'So, General, I can see no reason at all why we don't turn these people out of the city. They're a drain on our food and water and impossible to control. You have seen how they come and go as they please.' Harry Brooke had really got the wind in his sails and Primrose didn't like it. Initially, the general had taken over a light and spacious room in the Citadel as his headquarters from which he could look down on the city walls. But when one of Ayoob Khan's gunners had put a shell just above the main lintel, the Bloom had decided to retire into the depths of the place for safety. Now we were all crushed into a stuffy little room, jabbering worse than bookies at Fairyhouse.

'I understand the logic of what you're saying, Brooke, but if we expel fifteen thousand native men just as the siege is beginning to get into its pace, there'll be the devil to pay in the press. Why, the Afghans are bound to slaughter those whom they don't regard as their people, and we shall be blamed for that, and then it'll be "Kandahar Atrocities, read all about it", just like it was last year in Kabul.' I felt sorry for the little trimmer, I did. What Brooke was saying made perfect tactical sense, now that we were properly besieged with shells landing regularly within our defences and Johnny Af creeping nearer to the walls, using all the houses that we hadn't levelled as cover. But he was right. The Liberals and their newspaper lapdogs would make mincemeat out of the Bloom if there were needless civilian casualties. Then where would his field marshal's baton and seat in the Lords be?

'Well, Morgan, you're in command of the garrison, what's your view?' I could see both sides and, if I was honest, I recoiled at the thought of innocent folk being thrown out and then at the mercy of the same devils who had butchered almost half of my brigade. And then I remembered the child Ghazi whom Billy had put to the sword. What price our survival if crazies like that came to life *inside* the city while their pals were malleting us from outside? There was no shortage of stories of intrigue and duplicity in Afghanistan – you had only to think of Louis Cavagnari last year.

'No, General, these lads must be sent out into the cold to fend for themselves. The greatest disadvantage I can think of is that some of them, inevitably, will end up staring down the sights of one of Ayoob Khan's rifles, shooting at us, but I'd prefer not to be feeding and watering them at our expense in the meantime.' My lord and master was treating me differently since the battle. I could see him nodding slightly, almost deferentially, when I spoke; he would never have done that before. I guessed he must have been feeling guilty for not sending me into the field with enough troops or guns.

'And what's your view on this move, McGucken?' asked Primrose. I'd been watching the major since he had arrived at the meeting – 'meeting', mark you, was the Bloom's word: I would have called it GOC's Orders, but then I'm old-fashioned. We'd seen each other only briefly since the battle and he looked none the worse for those terrifying few days: just as whipcord tough, just as full of energy. But there were creases across his forehead that did not bode well.

'General, it'll be a bloody disaster afterwards. We'll disaffect both those who are for us and those who are merely indifferent, an' we'll have trouble around here for years to come. The wali will not thank us, for many of his people will be at the mercy of Ayoob Khan's men. Yet I see no other solution. We canna have a knife in our backs and that's exactly what we'll get if some of these folk remain. So, let's sling 'em oot, General, and worry about our own skins now and the finer points later.' Good old Jock: typically uncompromising. The whole room gaped at his assessment for none of us 'proper' officers, none of us 'gentlemen', had given so much as a thought to what lay beyond the siege we were now enduring.

Primrose, though, broke the silence: 'Well, that's decided, but please make a record of the way *we all* talked this through . . .' I saw the chief of staff taking notes furiously '. . . so that when General Roberts's or General Phayre's column arrives and kicks our enemies where they deserve to be kicked, Simla will know what factors affected our judgement.' There were a few too many 'our's and not enough 'my's there for my liking. What he was really saying was that he would do anything except take the blame for another false move.

'So, gentlemen, is there anything else before we—' Primrose was interrupted by the crash of one of our howitzers replying to the foe.

'Yes, General.' I'd known when he'd started blethering on about moving the natives out of Kandahar that he would try to duck the real issue. 'Our enemies are getting a damn sight too close to the city walls for comfort. You know how worried I am about them up here at De Khoja.' I pointed it out on the map for him because I doubted that he'd even bothered to put his binoculars over the place. And I had reason to be worried: the battered village was only about four hundred paces from our defences and the Afghans had been creeping up there night after night, loop-holing the buildings and sniping with increasing accuracy at our men on the walls. 'If we're going to have to last out for at least six weeks, we should try to drive these gentlemen back, for if we do not, they'll have artillery or mortars there before we know it and that would not be good for the health.'

'Yes, you've mentioned this before and I know that the

Seventh Fusiliers have been taking regular casualties from there. What do you want to do about it?'

He must have read reports about the place and heard the Fusiliers' worries, but had he been to see it for himself? Had he buggery. 'We need to teach Ayoob Khan to keep his distance, General. If we mount an assault, probably by night, clear the place, destroy his earthworks and knock down any masonry cover, things will be easier for us.' I'd spent as much time up at the north-east sector as I could, talking to the 7th and anyone else who knew the ground, and I'd got a pretty good notion of what was required. 'But before I present my plans to you, General, I'd like to send a couple of patrols out, if you'll allow me to.'

'Certainly, please do so.' Primrose delegated the sordid business of fighting as quickly as he could. 'If there's nothing else, gentlemen, I thought I'd close by telling you that we've received a message from our chivalrous opponent telling us that he has five sepoys and two officers as prisoners. He claims that he is treating them well and suggests we might like to exchange them for a couple of hundred of his brigands that we're holding. So, young Hector Maclaine and Samuel Keenan are still drawing breath. I am delighted to hear it – now all we have do is get 'em back, eh, Morgan?' The little runt positively beamed at me.

'Get 'em back'. Dear God, I'd expended far too much blood and sweat getting Sam back from captivity once already – not that he remembered much about it, for he was only a young 'un when he and his mother had fallen into the hands of the Rhani of Jhansi back in the Mutiny in '58. Nearly cost all three of us our lives and led to the nastiest thing I'd ever had to do – the killing of a man I'd once admired and called a friend. My spine crept at the thought of what might be happening to Sam even now and I don't mind confessing that I didn't fancy crawling about Ayoob Khan's back yard looking for him. Falling into the wrong hands was turning into a bit of a bad habit of his.

Mark you, lucky old Primrose hadn't been on the receiving end of an angry Ghazi yet; neither was he ever likely to be unless things went badly wrong. I wondered why he was so pleased with the news he'd just imparted. My first instinct was to jump for joy – my heart had skipped when he told me. Then an icy feeling gripped my vitals. Ayoob Khan was said to be a civilised fellow – some of McGucken's spies had reported that he'd said quite openly he hoped that the British would be friendly towards him rather than seek battle. But I'd seen how civilised his troops' behaviour was during the fight. I'd watched men being pulled from the ranks and literally torn to pieces as hounds might break up a fox. Worse than that, on occasions when we'd driven the Afghans back, I'd seen lads who'd been wounded and overrun, then literally butchered – slashed at with knives, ears, fingers, any extremity cut off, balls and pizzles stuffed into mouths. I wondered if Sam might not be better off dead – and I also wondered why Billy had been so certain that he was.

'Only a few days now, sahib.' Naik Shyamsingh kept his voice as low as possible. His English was good – almost as good as his Pashto, thought Keenan. Shyamsingh claimed some sort of blood link to the scruffy warrior who stood guard over the seven prisoners. '*Gora-log* all sick, water in Kandahar bad and many wounded from the great battle. Ayoob Khan *bahadur* will attack soon and the town will be his. So he says, sahib.' Naik Shyamsingh had already proved himself invaluable, bringing food and water for Hector Maclaine when his wounds had made him immobile and getting extra titbits of information from the gaolers.

Even before they were captured, Keenan and Maclaine had seen more than they wanted to of the Afghans. Keenan knew how stupid he had been to go off into that wretched village with no proper escort, but he had been exhausted, water had become a vital necessity and, of course, he'd had

Hector – reckless – Maclaine driving him on. Odd, though, he thought, that his brother and the 66th hadn't thought to put a patrol into that little hamlet – it was an ideal point from which to ambush the retreating column. Still, there was no point in worrying about that now.

He'd been sensible enough not to resist once he'd realised how badly outnumbered the pair of them were – but not Maclaine, oh, no. He'd had to fire his pistol and holler and, he believed, it was only because the tribesmen were canny enough to realise they were officers and might be worth a ransom that they were still alive. That said, the five sepoys had been brought in still breathing – though in various states of disrepair – and they had all been treated reasonably well.

Then, Keenan had wondered if Ayoob Khan's advance from Maiwand to lay siege to Kandahar would ever stop. The prisoners had been forced to march, carrying their own injured, through the hottest part of each day, although periodic stops for prayers had come as a profound relief. Finally, after five excruciating days on the march, passing the bloated corpses of his father's brigade and the stinking bodies of oxen, camels and horses, they had been told to halt. A canvas tent looted from one of the sepoy regiments, Keenan guessed, judging by the quartermaster's markings, had become their cell. They had been made to erect it themselves as a sea of felt, animal skin and cloth shelters sprang up nearby, looking more like a circus, he thought, than the lines of a besieging army.

But the smell inside was so misleading. There was little to do except doze and, with the sun beating down on the panels of the tent, the whole edifice took on the musty scent that he associated with the annual village fête at home. As Keenan drifted in and out of sleep, he was delighted with memories of summers in Cork, seduced by the nostalgia of warm canvas and damp ground. The dreams were grand, but the reality was sordid.

'What's that he says, Keenan?' Maclaine asked. His shoulder

had been grazed by a bullet when he and Keenan had been seized eleven days ago. The wound had become infected, despite Keenan's using his own piss to clean it, and Maclaine had wandered in and out of consciousness for forty-eight hours or so, with Naik Shyamsingh doing all that he could to beg dressings and clean water from their conquerors. 'What is he talking about?'

'The sentry is mouthing some rot about our garrison being on its knees and Ayoob Khan being about to attack. It's balls, obviously.' Even as Keenan answered, a fearsome salvo roared out from the Afghan battery of Armstrong breech-loaders.

'Aye, I hope you're right, though I reckon our chances of survival would be better if Monsieur Khan won the day. A hostage has no value to a defeated general,' retorted Maclaine, morosely.

'Don't think about that, Maclaine. *Lalkurti* here *ek dum*.' Keenan did his bathetic best to talk to the gang of sepoys, cursing himself, yet again, for having no real grasp of their language. They all smiled politely at his attempts to cheer them, but it struck him that the little group of war-stained jawans was just going through the motions. Naik Shyamsingh talked fluently to them, explaining, no doubt, the content of what the guards said in much greater detail than he could to the British officers and, behind the grins, despondency was written on the soldiers' faces.

Billy Morgan beckoned in the darkness. He waved his hand for Sergeant Kelly to bring Privates Battle and Hughes 06 to join him as the patrol moved as silently as they could across the sandy track that marked the start of the village of De Khoja.

'Over there, Sar'nt Kelly. Take the lads to that junction and watch me forward. I'm going to have a shufti round the next corner.' Two hours before last light, Ensign Morgan and his sergeant had reported to Captain McMath — the new brigade major – to have their tasks and routes pointed out to them for that night's patrol. The 66th had been told to provide an officer and three men for the dangerous little job of scouting the Afghans' forward positions and gaining enough information to allow the brigade commander and his staff to prepare plans for a sortie to drive the enemy back from the remains of the village. Casualties had mounted on the dilapidated stonework opposite De Khoja and Brigadier General Anthony Morgan had become convinced that Ayoob Khan's men would assault from there.

Billy Morgan had learnt much from Sergeant Kelly's quiet instructions to the two private soldiers who were to provide covering fire and muscle in the event of trouble before they left the safety of the city walls.

'Right, you two. No belts and pouches tonight. You'll need forty rounds in yer pockets but don't unwrap 'em 'cos the brass cases will bash about something rotten when you run. Put one round in the chamber and stick another five in the top fold of your puttees – but make sure you wind 'em good and tight. Get rid of your sun-helmets an' wear yer woollen comforters. I'll ask Mister Morgan to make sure that our sentries are ready to recognise us outlines. Next, gerran extra rifle sling, take yours off yer bundooks and put the two on 'em round your waist like belts. Fix yer spikes now and wrap a bit of lint from a field dressing round the rifle muzzle so you get no rattles – oh, and take an extra couple of dressings apiece an' stick 'em in your hip pockets. One water-bottle each, topped up – use the slings to stop it banging about. You'll both have your rifles. Mister Morgan and I will carry pistols. Grab a Khyber knife, both of yer: if you ain't got one, borrow one off of the others – there's enough around after the big fight. An' one last thing, each get two pairs of extra socks. I'll tell you when to slip them over boots; they'll deaden your footsteps until the heels wear through the wool – then change 'em. Any questions, you two? No, well, I'll inspect

288

you in twenny minutes and Mister Morgan will tell you what we're on fifteen minutes after that.' Then they had crept out to see what they could see.

Kelly stood by with an illuminating rocket in his hand, while the two men crouched, pointing their rifles up alternate alleyways. As Morgan shuffled forwards, he caught a lungful of the foetid smell to which he had grown more than accustomed in the Afghan towns and villages, a combination of stagnant puddle water and animal dung.

'Have a care, sir − I can hear 'em purging about something. Listen.'

Sure enough, as Morgan fought to control his breathing and rising excitement, he could make out a whispered conversation in an almost familiar language just a few feet away from the patrol around the next scarred wall. He braced himself to go forward, silently thanking Kelly for the muffling socks and luck for enough stars to see but no moon. Then he crawled along on all fours, his Enfield pistol held firmly in his mouth. Edging round the wall, he slid his head forward at ground level. No more than eight feet from him lolled five Afghans, all armed with rifles, but only one alert, his head just poking over the top of the broken masonry, looking carefully towards Kandahar's bastions. Slowly, Morgan withdrew, wriggling backwards like a khaki snake, before pressing his mouth to Kelly's ear. 'Five of them, dozy as hell. Only one on stag.'

Kelly simply nodded in reply, put a thumb up and then described a route round their enemies with his hand.

'No, Sar'nt Kelly.' Morgan's hand fell to the bone hilt of his knife; he drew it silently from its red-dyed leather scabbard, the starlight dancing on the polished blade. 'We'll have this lot.'

Kelly held up his palms enquiringly, but Morgan ignored him, signing to the two men that there were five targets and to be ready to move. Before Kelly could reason any further with him, Morgan launched himself, abandoning caution and skittering in the grit around the corner of the alley, his knife blade flashing.

The first Afghan was propped against the wall, almost asleep. Morgan watched his beard nodding gently with the rhythm of his breath as he reached low and pulled his arm far back to strike. But he'd never used such a weapon before. Fourteen inches of beautifully balanced, razor-sharp steel did not need all twelve stone of an athletic subaltern behind it. The knife was designed for short slashes and quick, lethal pokes, not a deep thrust fuelled by fear and revenge. While the victim died with a gurgle almost instantly, his spleen and stomach fatally stabbed, the knife lodged its point between two vertebrae that held it like a pair of pliers. Morgan tried to wrench it free but, try as he might, two hands now tugging hard at the handle, all that happened was that the dead man rose and fell in time with his exertions, the pair of them blocking the rest of the patrol's attempts to close with the remaining sentries.

What had started as a silent assault quickly degenerated into a match of shouts and ugly yells of terror. Kelly stumbled over Morgan's feet, jabbed his man through the buttocks as he rose to resist. His victim screamed as though death had sprung from nowhere – which it had. With a frenzy of blows, Kelly eventually subdued him, blood flicking widely over wall and ground. Battle leapt clean over his superiors, kicked the third Afghan in the chest as he landed, but only managed to get his bayonet into a meaty shoulder joint. Suddenly the alley was full of noise and pain, anger and fear, followed by a booming shot as Hughes missed the fourth, running, man and another bang as the fifth sentry fired his Snider into the air – the signal, Morgan assumed – for a general alert.

'Come on, sir, run like fuck!' Kelly grabbed his officer, caught a handful of Battle's jacket and pulled him away from the Afghan whom he was now bludgeoning with the butt of his rifle and summoned Hughes: 'Eh, Oh Six, you come 'ere an' all. Now get bloody going, all on yer.' There were many Hughes's in the Battalion, so Kelly always addressed him using last two digits of his army number; now he manhandled the other three back into the open and away over a couple of hundred yards towards the now friendly outline of the town.

Morgan's lungs were sucking and his legs pumping so hard that he sensed more than heard the musket, matchlock and rifle bullets that spurred them on their way. He saw stabs of flame coming from the rifles of the 7th Fusiliers, replying over their heads, and then he identified the two bits of white tape with which the gap in the wire obstacle was marked to allow them back into safety. His chest ached and his thighs seemed to be tipped with molten lead when a judas gate in the great wooden portal swung open, just as Private Hughes fell with a heavy thump and a rattle of metal just behind him.

'Bastard Afghans.' Kelly swore without malice, more as an observation. 'Give us an 'and, sir.' Morgan threw himself into the safety of the gateway, hard behind Private Battle. The young officer's every instinct was to stay put, to shelter from the fast-moving metal that was kicking up the dirt and humming off the decaying stone walls, perhaps to shout encouragement at his sergeant, who had immediately grabbed at Hughes's belt of slings, but not to expose himself to danger yet again. But he knew that would never do, that he owed Sergeant Kelly the same support and loyalty that the NCO gave to him, so he spun round, jumped over the gate-step and went back out into the lethal storm.

'Grab 'is leg, sir. No, leave that fucker, it don't matter — we'll get it in daylight,' shouted Kelly, who had made little impression by himself on Hughes's inert form. Morgan had instantly gone to grab the man's rifle but soon realised that if both he and Kelly were to stand any chance of getting the casualty and themselves back into cover there was no room for finesse.

'Get on, yer honour, that's it, Sar'nt.' Private Battle had

sheltered behind some solid cover, encouraging both of them loudly but without exposing too much of himself. But even Irish shouts didn't make Private Hughes any easier to drag. Morgan and Kelly were skidding in the dirt as Hughes's arms flopped back like anchors leaving two long furrows behind him in the dust. As subaltern and sergeant at last reached the gate, strong, capable hands reached for the injured man, pulling him to safety. But as Morgan glanced back towards the ruin of De Khoja, he saw a small grey scruffy blur bounding over the ruts and tussocks towards them.

'Well, I'm buggered!' Sergeant Kelly crouched with Morgan just outside the vastness of the Berdurani Gate. 'That's Bobby, ain't it, sir?' Not even bullets splintering the wood or the sting of stone chips that lashed both men's cheeks and necks could stop them gaping. ''Ere, pup, come 'ere,' yelled Kelly, as Morgan watched the rough-haired terrier-cross launch himself bodily through the air into his master's arms. Even as the judas gate slammed shut behind the pair, more bullets thumping into it, all Kelly could say was 'Give over, yer daft little sod! Stop bein' so soft, won't yer?' as Bobby licked his chin and throat with a darting pink tongue.

'Why, I never thought I'd see you again, you rogue.' Morgan bent to ruffle the dog's coat, but as he did so, the animal cringed and whined in pain. 'I'm sorry, pup. Have I hurt you?'

'Aye, sir, look 'ere.' It was hard to see anything in the dark shadows within the walls of the town. ''E's 'ad a nasty gash on 'is shoulder, 'e 'as. Just scabbed over.' Kelly was parting the coarse strands of hair, holding the little dog firmly but gently. 'Should be all right. So, you deserted to the enemy, did you, you little bugger?'

'I bet he's got a story or two to tell, Sar'nt Kelly. Last time I saw him was with the colour party in that garden just as the Ghazis closed in.' Morgan shuddered at the memory.

'Aye, sir. I never expected to see 'im again, I didn't.' Kelly stroked the dog's head.

'An' that would have been a devil of a waste of the ten bob you paid for him, Sar'nt, would it not?' Now Battle had joined in the petting and the patting, Bobby responding with obvious pleasure to the familiar scent and sound of the big Irishman.

'Sorry to spoil the dog-show, sir.' A sarcastic London accent brought the trio back to reality. 'There's nothing I can do for your lad, sir. Dead before 'e 'it the ground, I'd say. Look 'ere.' By the dim light of the stars, a medical orderly from the 7th Fusiliers pointed to a hole the size of a child's fist at the base of Private Hughes's throat. Blood, black in the darkness, had spread far down the front of the soldier's jacket.

'Yes, I see. Thank you, Corporal,' Morgan replied, forgetting the dog worship and looking with sad fascination at Hughes's open, unseeing eyes.

Sergeant Kelly knelt down next to Private Hughes. 'Sorry to lose 'im, sir. Good lad 'e was, bloody excellent with a shovel. Remember 'im joining us in Karachi with that big new draft in '76. 'E got stick-man on 'is first barrack guard – d'you recall that, Eddie Battle?' Morgan had never heard Kelly speak like this before. His sergeant was normally unemotional, matter-of-fact, almost laconic, and while he never doubted his gruff kindness towards both himself and the men, he'd never heard him being reflective like this. And he'd certainly never heard him use one of the men's Christian names.

'I do, Sar'nt. And d'you remember him in the fight with the Field Gunners when he leathered that big Scottie?' replied Battle. All of this had happened a long time before Morgan had joined the regiment; he'd heard of it, for it was H Company lore, but he wondered if the two men were deliberately excluding him.

'It's a fucking waste it is.' Kelly straightened up. 'Tek 'is effects, Battle. Mek sure you go through 'is kit so nowt dodgy gets sent back to 'is next of kin.' Morgan knew how worried

293

the men were that some bit of carved erotica or evidence of contact with native women might find its way to a mother or a sweetheart in England. 'An' will you pen a line to 'is mam in Oxford?' The task of writing to the nearest and dearest of the dead man fell not just upon the officer but also upon the soldier's closest 'mucker'. Again, Morgan had seen how important such rites were to the troops.

'I will, Sar'nt. I knew Oh Six well enough and liked the lad, so.' Battle's voice was hushed with respect.

'Stay with 'im, then, Battle, until I send a couple of the boys back to get you both. Come on, sir, you'll need to get a report in as soon as possible.' As Kelly turned back towards the company's lines, Morgan thought he had detected a troubled note in the man's voice.

They walked silently for a minute or two, Bobby in his master's arms as the crackle of musketry they had stirred up began to settle down. Then Sergeant Kelly asked, 'Did we need to take that lot on, sir? What 'ave we got to show for it except three of theirs and one of our'n gone west? What are we going to tell Cap'n McMath at Brigade that he don't know already? Weren't we supposed to find out where Johnny Af was in greatest strength, not just knife the buggers an' get Oh Six killed?'

'What are you suggesting, Sar'nt Kelly?' Morgan asked stiffly. 'You don't want me to shy away from a fight, do you? The Sixty-Sixth's got a reputation to maintain, you know, and we'll get endless misery from the other regiments when the word gets round that we lost our colours the other day.'

'Sir, with respect, ye're a cheeky young fucker, you are! I don't need lessons from a griff like you about this regiment – I've sixteen years' service an' given more to the Old Berkshires than you ever will, just like Hughes Oh Six an' Battle.' The two men had stopped in their tracks, staring at each other. 'So don't give me all that "born to lead" bollocks. I'm bloody worried about you, I am. Killing has got to be done, sir, but ye're not supposed to enjoy it – I've said that to you before. Sometimes it's right to avoid a fight. That's not being scared, that's good soldiering. We've got fuck-all from tonight except one less bloke an' more bloodstains to wash out of our kit. Thing is, sir, the lads are beginning to think ye're a bit too rash – I don't want them sayin' they won't go out on patrol with you. You've seen how most of 'em shake like fuck now when they're warned for duty. That punch-up the other day's left its mark on 'em an' I don't want you gettin' a bad name.'

Morgan stared at his sergeant. Kelly had made similar remarks before but never as blunt as this. It had rattled him. 'I see, Sar'nt Kelly. What do you suggest?'

Kelly paused for a moment's thought. 'Be more like your dad, sir. He's a gentleman, he is, who'd never risk one of his own men's lives needlessly. He's been in more scraps than any of us, 'e 'as, yet you don't see 'im thirstin' for more, do yer? Finest officer an' bravest man I've ever seen, sir – an' decent as well. Look how he dealt with Battle.'

'Yes, I see,' Billy Morgan answered quietly.

'And another thing, sir, now I've started. That was wrong what you did during the retreat when Mr Maclaine and Mr Keenan came up to us. You knew that village was dangerous, sir. Now both young gentlemen is missing. Why didn't you warn them?'

Morgan could see that Kelly was deeply aggrieved. 'Mr Keenan was perfectly happy to abandon Sutton and Cooper to the enemy, wasn't he, Sar'nt Kelly?' Morgan replied quickly. 'Am I my brother's keeper?'

I'd lost count of the number of towns I'd besieged. From Sebastopol to Kotah and Gwalior, I'd seen 'em all, some hard on the defenders and some hard on the attackers, but I'd never been under siege myself before. Well, it was mid-August now and we'd had more than two weeks of Ayoob Khan's clowns sitting outside our walls and sniping, throwing the odd Armstrong round into our defences and creeping gradually forward. It was just so damned frustrating, squatting impotently and waiting for someone else to deliver us from the wolves who circled our camp fires. But now, as I stood in front of Primrose, ready to give him my plan for a sortie against the enemy, I had no confidence that I would be allowed to deliver the punch that Brooke and I wanted.

'No, I'm sorry, Morgan, but I simply cannot risk your using all those troops. We've little enough left to hold the city if anything goes wrong with your plan, so you'll just have to make do with fewer infantry and use our heavy guns to rake De Khoja before the assault.' I should have expected this from the Bloom. It was exactly the same when we'd been sent to the Helmand – I simply wasn't given enough troops to do the job while Primrose kept more than he needed to ensure that he was nice and safe. Look what had happened as a result of that.

Now I wanted to sweep round the enemy from the north to the east with two squadrons of cavalry, isolate the dangerous little village of De Khoja and then launch three battalions at it to kill the garrison, spike whatever guns we could, then let the Sappers demolish the strongpoints. I'd spent bloody days studying the place from the city walls; McGucken's touts and spies had brought us all sorts of useful information about Ayoob Khan's intentions to attack from there very soon and I had personally debriefed three patrol commanders, including my own son – not that he'd found out anything of much use. Now Primrose, the daft little bugger, failed to grasp the lesson that I and my brigade had learnt the hard way. Clausewitz and his ilk would have called it 'concentration of force', I've no doubt, but in plain Paddy it would have been simply 'If you're going to have a crack at Johnny Af, go mob-handed.'

'I'm sensible to all the effort and risk that has gone into these plans of yours, Morgan, but the guns will do the job

296

of two battalions. You can have two companies of the Seventh Fusiliers — they're still quite well up to snuff and damn good — and two companies of the Twenty-eighth Bombay, who are as fresh as daisies. The cavalry part of the plan can stand, but I must insist on fewer infantry. Now, who's going to lead this adventure?'

'Well, I am, General.' Who else did the silly sod think would do it? I shouldn't have been surprised, of course — after all, he'd stood even this bit of my planning on its head.

'Oh, no, no, no. I know how anxious you are to get back at these people, my dear Morgan, and I can only guess how much the business with Keenan must be playing on your mind, but you are my *garrison commander*, my *senior* brigadier. No, your duty is to direct operations. Brooke can command this — he's been burning to prove himself.'

I could see that Primrose was not for turning.

Burning to prove himself — why, Harry Brooke damn nearly burst into flames when I told him the news. It took me a while to find the man, so busy was he about his own part of the defences, but when we eventually got together he'd already absorbed my written warning order and was in a positive lather of excitement.

'Well, Morgan, I'm most grateful to you, I really am,' he bubbled away, supposing — though he was too good a man and too good a friend even to hint at it — that a successful conclusion to his sortie might help to expunge the black mark I had run up a couple of weeks ago. 'I would like to put the assault time back just a little as I've been observing the precise moment of dawn for the last week and . . .' He battered on about a whole series of other details — all practical enough — but ignoring the main point.

'But, Harry, I just don't think you've got enough infantry to do the job. De Khoja's been filling up with Ayoob Khan's people ever since the siege started and you can see the loop-holes as plain as pikestaffs. They've got some light artillery in there now and the heavier pieces can enfilade the approaches from the high ground further east. Now, I've no doubt that one battalion would be enough to plod through the place systematically, supposing that the enemy couldn't bring reinforcements up, but I asked for three battalions so that everything could be done simultaneously . . .' I tried to point out the obvious bloody faults with the plan – I even offered to tell Primrose that it couldn't be done – but Brooke trumped me.

'Well, Tony, if you think the whole thing's hare-brained, why didn't *you* refuse to do it when you still thought you were to lead?'

And, of course, he had me there. It's all very well for a superior to forbid a plan on behalf of a junior, but no officer could say he wouldn't lead such an assault and hope to keep his reputation intact. Besides, if I was honest with myself, I was still so done up with the consequences of my last failure that I would have tried almost anything to get back into the field in order to clear my name, or be killed in the process. But I could hardly admit that to Brooke, could I? He had already seen me at my weakest.

ELEVEN

The Sortie

Even with your eyes closed there are smells that conjure up a whole scene and a litany of images − wet sandbags, Army disinfectant, that ghastly grey foot liniment, overcooked *burgoo* − but the most powerful of the lot, for me at least, is Irregular Cavalry. I got it in full measure when I went to see Tom Nuttall's force, which was assembling just inside the Idgah Gate. His two-hundred sabres − a squadron of the Poona Horse and another of the 3rd Scinde Horse − were dismounted by the sides of their animals in the dark just before dawn, waiting the order to mount and sweep out of the gate in order to stop reinforcements coming to the help of the enemy in De Khoja − this was the only bit of my plan that Primrose hadn't scrapped.

Now the breath of man and beast hung heavy in the air, lit by a half-moon. Weapons and equipment clinked and rattled, horses snorted and whickered while the men talked quietly, nervously. But above all there was the smell. An Indian cavalry mount got a different mix of oats and bran and it was cut with herbs when the men could find them. So, the horses' sweat and piss smelt distinctive − even their dung was a slightly different colour from that of British chargers. Then there are the men. British troops, especially when they were fresh out of their blankets, smelt of booze and tobacco mixed with a bit of onion; Indians smelt of *dal* and leather. That sounds like a bloody cliché, but they just did. Mix the scent of horse and man and you had an aroma that couldn't be mistaken.

There was another smell that was the same the world over − the stink of fear. I'd smelt it on the Russians, the Pandies, my own men but never on myself, of course − unless you counted the sudden wetness in the armpits or the sheen of moisture either side of the nose that was instantly cold and had an animal scent so different from the smell of ordinary exertion that it shocked you and left you thinking that everyone could sense your fear a mile off. Now, in the stark moonlight, the men sweated and farted their terror. The dawn was cold, yet they mopped foreheads and cheeks while bowels erupted, suddenly loose and foetid. At the same time, every mouth chewed betel; every bearded jaw was set a little too firmly; gauntlets were incessantly, compulsively removed and put back on. As I walked Tommy − I'd renamed the whaler that had been found for me at Maiwand − through the mass of waiting troopers, I noticed a familiar face among the Scinde Horse.

Daffadar Sayed Miran was tightening his girth for the twentieth time when we saw each other. 'Sahib, will you not be riding with us this morning?' he asked, with no side to what he said, just a simple question − at least, that was what I thought he meant − but I prickled back, 'No, Daffadar, *huzoor*, you ride behind your own colonel, Malcolmson sahib, this morning, as you did at Maiwand.' I doubt he detected any trace of irony. 'And with no Keenan sahib to lead you astray.' I tried to sound light and unconcerned.

'No, indeed, General *bahadur*. But he's a man I will miss. He may be too bold sometimes, but it's a boldness that the men need,' replied Miran.

'And how are your jawans, Daffadar sahib?' They looked

pretty seedy to me. All the sparkle had gone from them. They moved mechanically, almost as if they were in a trance, with none of the chatter or any of the interest that a visit by their general would have occasioned a few weeks ago. They didn't ignore me – not quite – they just seemed sunk in their own thoughts.

'They are scared, sahib.' There, he'd said it. Such phrases weren't meant to be in the lexicon of such bold irregular cavalry; braves such as Miran were never meant to utter such things. 'They will do their job, sahib, of course they will, though almost too much has been asked of them. But, sahib . . .' Miran held my eye with a suddenly raised chin and beard '. . . we will pay them back for Keenan sahib, of that you need have no doubt.'

I was just on the verge of thanking my son's troop daffadar and turning my horse away from the troopers, when the commanding officer, Malcolmson, and his wordi major walked their chargers up to me. 'Ah, Malcolmson, Wordi Major sahib.'

Both men saluted me, the Indian smiling through his beard as his hand quivered at the folds of his turban. But the colonel of the Scinde Horse seemed rather more reserved. There was no smile, no warmth from him.

'General, thank you for coming to see my men.'

Was that resentment from the stuck-up, windy sod? This was the man who'd pressed me not to seek battle at Maiwand despite my orders telling me to do just that. He'd urged me to run on back to Kandahar – perhaps he'd been right. What wasn't right, though, was that he'd been one of the first back to the safety of the city, his cavalrymen outstripping the retreating infantry and guns, leaving the rearguard in the hands of junior officers, like Lieutenant Sam Keenan. He knew that he had been in the wrong: no wonder he was being so damned stiff.

'You'll be with us, will you, General?'

That was just bare-faced cheek. He knew bloody well that

his own brigadier, Tom Nuttall, would lead the cavalry and that I was in overall command from back here in Kandahar.

'Not directly, Colonel Malcolmson.' I wasn't going to let him get away with such gall. 'But I shall be taking a very close interest in your command and I trust that, today, you will remember your duty.' He'd pushed me too far. Whatever I'd got right or wrong at Maiwand, whether we should have fought there or not, Malcolmson had behaved badly and he knew it. Now he said not a thing – what could he have said? He just saluted drill-ground style as I turned my nag away.

It should have been a full moon, so oddly were people behaving. Malcolmson had just been outrageously rude, but as Lynch – my trumpeter – and I turned down one of the alleyways leading towards the Charsoo, I soon forgot about it for a full-scale row was going on between two mounted figures. In the dark just before dawn, I could only see their outlines, but I recognised the voices.

'But what in the name of God, General, d'ye suppose bloody artillery is going to achieve against a place like De Khoja?' I could see Jock McGucken leaning out of his saddle, tearing a strip off Primrose, even though the general outranked him many times over. 'My people have told me time and again that the village has a rabbit warren of cellars and tunnels below it where Johnny Af has learnt to shelter – and all my reports have repeated that. There'll be a damn sight more of the buggers in there than we know, General, and our guns will do nothing except give 'em a headache and mek 'em even more irritated with our men when they show up.'

'Goddamnit, McGucken, will you people never stop arguing with me? You know what the decision is and it's final. I have no more infantry to add to this assault.' There was a sneer in Primrose's voice. Normally he was courtesy itself – idle, half-thought-through courtesy, mark you. 'Ah, Morgan.' The relief in his tone was palpable – he must have been bloody irritated with Jock McGucken to be glad to see me. 'Now, I hope I've made myself clear, McGucken. Please be so kind as to attend to your duties while I speak to General Morgan.'

I'd seen a few furious salutes from McGucken in my time, but never one where his palm quivered at his forehead with such mute contempt. But all he said was 'Sir!' before hauling his horse around and trotting off with his escort.

'Wretched people,' Primrose muttered in the dark to me. 'I cannot see why we commission such types. He may have a DCM and a strange affinity with the Indians and Afghans, but that doesn't make him really suitable to be an officer, does it? You've known him a while, ain't you, Morgan?'

Now, I'm a pretty affable type and − I'm prepared to confess it − I'm chary of going against the Army's mores and contradicting my superiors, but this was the limit.

'General, we've been together off and on since '53 and I cannot hear a word said against the fellow. You're right, a DCM don't mean a thing except that a man's uncommon brave, but McGucken's had promotion after promotion without ever buying a step, and been mentioned in despatches until he's lost count. I know he's still rougher than most rough diamonds, sir, but the men worship him and I reckon Queen Victoria got a bargain and a half when she lifted him out of a Glasgow orphanage.' That made the Bloom sit back a bit. It would have been the easiest thing in the world just to listen to what the bitter little chap had to say, neither agree nor disagree, just play the dumb, loyal type. But I couldn't give a fig any more. I'd hoped that Afghanistan might see me through at a gallop in the last furlong, that I might just squeeze a major-generalship on the back of a little good fortune − stranger things have happened: look at that bucko Wolseley. But, no, Maiwand had put paid not just to my ambitions, but also − and I knew the odds were slight of my ever seeing Sam again − to one of my sons' careers, while the other seemed to be well on the way to becoming a professional killer. So,

303

I wasn't going to hear anything disobliging about a man whose boots Primrose wasn't fit to black.

'I see. I knew you'd served together before, but I had no idea you were so close. I cannot apologise for my sentiments, Morgan, but I can for my clumsiness. I didn't realise how comfortable you are with men of McGucken's stamp.'

'General, you're talking tripe. If you give a damn about what school a man comes from or which London club he belongs to, then you're more of a fool than I took you to be. If you'd seen McGucken win that DCM or watched him take the bayonet to a gang of Ghazis while men half his age were swooning like sixpenny whores, then you would realise just how ridiculous your comments are. May I have your leave to carry on, sir, please?' I used the old Army formula, utter contempt hidden behind ritualistic phrases, while Primrose just gaped. It was turning into a morning where salutes expressed more than words: I threw the Bloom a most articulate one.

My mood needed improvement and Trumpeter Lynch could normally be relied upon to achieve that. 'Fookin' 'ell, sir, you told 'im, din't you?'

'Thank you, Lynch.' The lad had done well at Maiwand, but sometimes he failed to grasp that informality on a day-to-day basis should not translate into familiarity; he was the Yorkshire equivalent of Private Battle to whom Billy had grown so attached. 'That's no way to talk about the divisional commander.'

'That's a bit bloody rich coming from you, sir. You ripped the poor little sod a second arsehole just then, I heard you.'

'But that's the point, Lynch. You were not meant to be listening, and as you were, you ought to have more sense than to refer to it, lad.' Sometimes I wondered about the boys they were sending us these days. When I'd joined, the men were good types – they knew when to turn a deaf ear – but this lot? No respect, no understanding of the proper order of things. Why, show someone like Lynch a little kindness and he'd assume you were offering him your daughter and putting him up for White's — now I was sounding just like Primrose! 'Anyway, that's enough of that. Who's in command of this gun, Lynch?'

I'd watched the infantry and Sappers build the gun platform right next to the Berdurani Gate looking out towards De Khoja and I could see how the Afghan guns had tried to neutralise the nine-pounder that now poked its muzzle through a thick embrasure of grit-filled sandbags.

'Sar'nt Mullane, sir. D'you remember him? His was the patrol what your lad shot up outside that camp we had near Khusk-i-Nakud before the big battle.' Lynch replied, expecting me to be as intimate with his own circle of comrades as he was. But, funnily enough, I did remember the name, not because of the horse-shooting incident, but because of Slade's having mentioned how well he'd done at Maiwand.

'Actually, I do know the name, Lynch. Didn't he do rather well when the guns were overrun?' I replied in all innocence, not thinking what I was implying to a Horse Gunner.

'Dunno about losing guns, sir. Best ask 'im yersen — he's just there — but 'ave a care, sir. 'E won't want to 'ear nowt about givin' pieces away to savages, 'e won't,' replied Lynch, worried, no doubt, that the redoubtable Mullane would invite his brigade commander to settle any difference of opinion behind the stables as he might do to any errant Gunner who belittled him or his men.

'Thank you, Lynch, I'll bear your advice in mind.' But Lynch missed my sarcasm: he nodded sagely as the first light of dawn began to show. 'Now, Sar'nt Mullane.' The sergeant's silhouette stiffened as he recognised an officer's voice, even a strange one. 'I've been hearing great things about you: first serving your gun even while the Ghazis were swarming all

305

over it and then saving a hatful of wounded during the retreat. Grand stuff.'

'Thank you, your honour.' I guessed it was a Belfast brogue that replied. 'But who am I a-speaking to?'

'Brigade commander, General Morgan, Sar'nt,' Lynch answered for me, in surprised tones, as dismayed by his sergeant's inability to recognise me as he had been by my ignorance over the identity of Sergeant Mullane.

'Oh, sorry, sir. Aye, we had a bit of mischief from Johnny *bahadur* but nothin' we couldn't handle. An' what of yerself, sir? Word is that you was on the back of a Scindi's charger at one stage all covered in blood an' shit.' Sergeant Mullane was just like the rest of the long-serving NCOs, respectful but not the slightest bit shy of senior officers.

'Well, I'm good enough now, thank you, Sar'nt Mullane, and I shall be even better when you put a few rounds into Ayoob Khan's men shortly. Are you all ready?' I peered over the steel barrel of the gun, which was aimed directly at the chipped and knocked-about walls of the troublesome village.

'Oh, aye, sir, we're ready. But there's one thing me and the rest of the lads ought to say first, sir, and that's 'ow sorry we are to 'ear about that boy of yours. We had a bit of nonsense with his troop a few weeks back, so we did.' Mullane, God bless him, was doing his best to be discreet in front of Lieutenant Sam Keenan's father and brigade commander. 'But 'e came over as a real gennelman, 'e did, an' a fine officer. 'Ope 'e comes through it all, sir.'

'Thank you, Sar'nt Mullane.' All this emotion from the men was getting too much for me. Odd – it harked back to that nonsense Primrose had blethered about McGucken not being officer material. But the men were much more open about their emotions than the officers, and for someone like me, who'd been brought up always to keep such thoughts to myself, it was uncomfortable. Not that I wasn't glad to hear it, but it didn't stop me changing the subject as fast as I

306

decently could. 'It's in the lap of the gods and the speed at which General Roberts gets here.' I tried to sound offhand. 'Now, do you not think we should have breech-loading guns rather than sticking with these muzzle-loaders?'

'Why, no, sir. We did tests on some Yankee guns couple of years back and they were all right as far as they went, but you can't beat the old and tried methods, can you, sir, especially now they've rifled these beauties?' Mullane patted the barrel of his lethal pet fondly. 'You've seen the Armstrongs that the Afghans used on us and they was no great shakes, was they? Bit faster rate of fire − until the breech mechanism gets fouled, and then where are ye? No, sir, stick to what you know is what I say.'

'Well, we'll see what *our* Armstrongs can do in a minute or two, won't we, Sar'nt Mullane?' I pulled my watch from my pocket and checked the time. I reckoned that there were eight minutes before the cavalry left the northern gate and eighteen before the guns opened fire.

'We will, sir. And just you watch. My first round is high explosive and I'll pop it through that loop-hole, yonder, nice as ninepence.' Mullane was squinting through the sights, gently feeling the elevation wheel and checking, yet again, that the copper initiating tube was firmly in the gun's touch-hole.

'What − that must be six hundred paces at least.' I thought I could see the target that Mullane was pointing out. 'I'll risk twenty rupees that your first high-explosive round won't touch the target.' The new guns were still a bit of a mystery to me. I'd served smooth-bore pieces myself and knew full well that there was an awful lot of luck in whether they hit or missed. But the rifling had, to all intents and purposes, given the artillery a new generation of weapons. There was no need to warm the barrels with a shot or two as there used to be and they even had sights now − no need to rely on a wrinkled old bombardier and his 'lay of metal'. Anyway, even if I was

307

breaking every rule in the book by wagering with one of the men, it was worth every *anna* to get a good shot off first.

'Twenty rupees it is, your honour, that you'll see Afghans reaching for the Prophet as soon as we get the word to fire, so you will.' Mullane was positively rubbing his hands with glee at the idea of taking money from his brigade commander – and that he was a Protestant brigade commander made the idea even sweeter, I guessed.

But even as I played out this bit of nonsense with the Gunners, the Idgah Gate was swung wide open, its hinges pre-greased to aid some element of surprise, and the two squadrons of cavalry walked calmly out on to the *maidan*, jingling ominously in the cool dawn before they broke into a quick trot that almost amounted to a canter.

'There's the donkey wallopers, sir. Reckon they'll draw any fire?' Lynch voiced my own thoughts as I watched, stomach tight and breathing shallow, as the files kicked up a low cloud of dust.

'Well, the Ghazi sentries need to be broken all the way down from madman to idiots if they fail to spot that lot. I'm more bothered about the enemy guns, though. If they're sharp about things they could make a mess of General Nuttall's boys before they get very much further.' I really was worried about the Afghan metal. They'd made mincemeat of us at Maiwand, bolstering the rumour that there were Russian advisers in their gun-lines.

'Don't fret, your honour,' Mullane came back, cool as you like. 'In this sort of light you need to have measured ranges and registered the guns right well to stand any chance of hitting fast-moving horse, and I've seen more signs of them smoking *bhang* than I have of them doing their job properly. No, sir, my guess is that boldness will pay off.'

And Mullane was right, for I could see Nuttall's figure at the front of the column and I even reckoned that I could see Malcolmson and his wordi major leading the Scinde Horse before the whole lot merged into the half-light, riding hard in a threatening sickle curve to get round the back of De Khoja and cut off any reinforcements. There was a sputter of shots, one or two shouts, but within minutes, as the thump of massed hoofs melted away, I knew that that part of the plan, at least, had started well.

'You ready, Sar'nt Mullane?' The luminosity on my watch hands was pretty well gone now, but I could just make out the time as the start of the bombardment approached. 'Forty seconds to go.'

'Aye, sir, I'll wait for the bugle.' He took the slack out of his firing lanyard and had another quick check at his sights and elevation. 'Twenty rupees, weren't it?'

But either my watch had, like its owner, seen too many knocks to be reliable, or the Gunners' timepiece was fast, for there suddenly came a flat bugle note, the rest of the call being drowned in the guns that fired simultaneously from right around the east side of Kandahar. Forty-pounders, three howitzers, and another three RHA steel rifled guns all spat and flashed into the dawn. It was pathetic. Not that I could say that, of course, to my hosts, but if you were brought up on literally hundreds of guns battering each other from inside and outside Sebastopol, this looked like nothing more than a Brock's Benefit.

'Garn, there! You see, your honour? Right on the button!' Even before the bugle's first note had sounded, Mullane had fired and we all watched for where the shot would fall. Now, with a smooth-bore gun or with the old-fashioned spluttering fuses that the shells used, you could positively see the rounds in flight, but with the much faster HE rounds from rifled barrels, it was impossible. None the less, that didn't stop Mullane − the great soft Mick − from going through the pantomime of pretending to see the flying projectile. Sadly, despite his confidence, it was a little too high and burst about two feet above the intended loop-hole with a great dirty splash of dark smoke, powdered mud and brick splinters all riven by an orange flash.

'I don't think so, Sar'nt Mullane – two foot high, I'd say, and twenty rupees in my pocket.' I saw his face fall while the rest of the gun numbers threw themselves at barrel and rammers, pushing home another charge and round without needing orders. 'Double or quits?'

'Forty rupees is a wee bit rich for my blood, your honour . . . Ye're on!' Mullane immediately crouched beside the barrel, twitching his hand to and fro for the trail to be adjusted by a lance bombardier who stood behind him, his own hand caressing the elevation wheel as he peered through the pendulum sight. Satisfied, Mullane then pushed an initiator home, looped the lanyard tight and, with a cry of 'Firing!' the gun leapt back on its wheels, the recoil dampened by the heavy return ropes attached to the front of the carriage.

'There! The luck o' the fuckin' fightin' Irish, yer honour! Right up the Afghans' hoop, straight in among the bastards.' Mullane was delighted – and I had to admit it was one of the sweetest shots I'd seen in all my campaigns. Even more pleasing was the flash that reflected off the inner walls of the village, exaggerated by the light and, no doubt, by all our hopes and the pall of dust and smoke that rose from within the Afghans' defences. 'There, your honour, we're evens now!'

'No, Sar'nt Mullane, that shot was worth every penny.' I didn't normally carry cash around with me – the troops could think of a million good reasons to relieve an officer of any rank of his wealth. Besides, as Mary would say, it only encouraged me to gamble. 'Here's your forty rupees. Buy the boys a swally or two when you next get the chance.' I have to admit that, while it gave me a great deal of pleasure to reward such skill, I knew that whatever Primrose, Malcolmson and even those arses in Simla thought of me, the boys loved such gestures.

But this was all nonsense, of course. I still couldn't help

but think that our gunfire was wholly inadequate for the task, just as I had warned the Bloom it would be. Certainly, the guns made good practice and De Khoja was soon wreathed in smoke and flying grit, but instead of the constant roll of explosions that might keep our enemies in their cellars or even nail them when they came out to defend the place, the fire was intermittent and weak, by no means enough to dominate the place. That was why I had such a dry, sour taste in my mouth when, after only thirty minutes' firing, I watched Harry Brooke through my binoculars lead his four companies out from the Kabul Gate down to my right into a very storm of small-arms fire.

'Come on, Sar'nt Mullane, let's have more shots like those first couple you let go.' Christ, I was worried – and so were the Gunners. I could tell by the way that Mullane's voice had dropped, how he started to urge the men on to get an even faster rate of fire, how the banter disappeared to be replaced by low, urgent cursing when one of his precious rounds flew anything less than true or when dust obscured his next target.

'Yes, your honour, we're doing our best – there, like that fucker!' Mullane crowed a little as his next round – a shrapnel one – burst squarely over a host of Afghans who were forming up behind the cover of a wall ready to throw themselves on a platoon of Fusiliers who were doing their damnedest to clear the houses either side of an alleyway. 'But that's not going to hold the rogues for long, sir. Look at that lot swarming in from the other village to the south.'

Mullane was right. The cavalry could hold off reinforcements from further afield – and, from firing I could now hear in the distance, that was exactly what was happening – but one battalion of four companies was simply not enough to stem the swarm of Ghazis and regular infantry who were now crowding from their hiding places.

'Yes, Sar'nt Mullane, I can see them.' I was trying not to show my fear, but I knew that my voice must have trembled.

This was going to be another bloody disaster unless Primrose ordered forward more troops to help Brooke or told him to pull out. I was doing no more good perched on the battlements admiring E Battery: I had to find Primrose and get him to use the very considerable numbers of reserves while he still could.

Luckily, Lynch had read my thoughts correctly and had my horse waiting for me as I skittered down from the gun platform and threw myself into the saddle. The Bloom, I knew, was due to be watching things from the north-east corner of the walls and I spurred poor Tommy mercilessly along the streets in what was now almost full light.

But even as I approached that point, I could see that Primrose and his staff had already ridden off five hundred paces to the west towards the Idgah Gate. As I got closer, I could see some sort of ramasammy going on with Primrose leaning down from his saddle talking urgently to others who had already dismounted. For the second time that morning, I seemed to be intruding on a full-scale row between my divisional commander and his political officer, though this time there was no darkness to screen them and every staff officer who legitimately could, as well as some who had no business there at all, was listening avidly to every word.

'Morgan.' Yet again, I seemed to be coming just in time to save Primrose from another of Jock McGucken's tongue lashings. 'Sharratt here has just come in to report. Tell the general what you've been telling us, please, Captain Sharratt.'

Captain Peter Sharratt was Brooke's brigade major – he'd managed to get back to the safety of the city walls on a nag that had been shot through the lungs, judging by the amount of bloody foam the wretched creature was hawking up.

'General, we're almost out of ammunition already. The house fighting has used up all the gun-cotton charges that both the infantry and the Sappers had and it's all that we can do to keep the Afghans at bay with constant volley fire – and

312

you know how that eats the lead up. We've cleared all but the top end of the village and demolished a fair amount and we can hold on so long as we get more shot and another four companies of whatever infantry is to hand. General Brooke has sent me back to get orders.'

Sharratt, a young 7th Fusilier, had obviously been badly shaken by his first close encounter with the Afghans – and I didn't blame him. The trouble was, Primrose was playing for time and trying to spread the blame for any decision he had to make.

'General, you know my view.' I wasn't going to indulge the man by weighing the pros and cons. 'We should never have committed to this attack without more bayonets. Now, I suggest that as there are no further reserves warned off, I take a scratch couple of companies from my brigade out there to cover Brooke's withdrawal.'

'No, General, ye canna pull General Brooke's force out.' McGucken gave me the same treatment that he'd obviously been giving Primrose, the little man looking thoroughly relieved that someone else was to be the target. 'We've lost enough men getting this far. Listen to Sharratt. With more troops and ball cartridge we can keep Johnny Af oot of De Khoja and stop the bastards assaulting the town from there. We can't throw this advantage away.'

'But, Jock, it was never the intention to hold the place – there weren't ever going to be enough men to form some sort of forward redoubt. The plan was to knock out the strongpoints, kill as many of the enemy as possible and then conserve our manpower.' I loathed gainsaying the very man who had stood by me physically and morally so many times. But there had never been any intention of garrisoning De Khoja, no matter how successful the assault might have been. Now, of course, Primrose had succeeded in separating the inseparable.

'Sounds like we might be reinforcing failure. Morgan, do

313

you have men ready to cover any withdrawal that I might order?' I had to hand one thing to Primrose: once he'd fanny about until other people had made up his mind for him but then he would stick to his decision.

'General, I have my brigade reserve of two weak companies of the Sixty-Sixth at five minutes' notice to move. If you'll give me ten minutes, I'll have them out of the Kabul Gate and doubling down to help Harry Brooke.' Luckily, I'd expected something like this and had given orders to Beresford-Peirse to carry an extra forty rounds per man, double the amount of water and to be poised and ready. 'Will you have the artillery fire a diversionary bombardment to the north?'

'You may have just that, Morgan. But no more than ten minutes, mark you. Every second is vital now − every minute will cost lives. In exactly twelve minutes from now, I shall semaphore Nuttall and sound the "retire" simultaneously.'

I almost hit the little fool, all cocky and hard-pounding now that he'd been told what to do.

'Well, it may be the last thing I ever do, General, but I shall be at your side.' Thank God, the damn-your-eyes awkward note had gone from Jock McGucken's voice: he'd accepted what was going to be done and, like the wonderful soldier he was, he would follow loyally.

'Don't expect 'e ever thought 'e'd end up like this, sir, do you?' Sergeant Kelly was looking down at the Reverend George Gordon, one of the chaplains, who now lay on his back in the early-morning sunshine, his dusty khaki rumpled and stained, blood soaking down from a corner of his mouth through his coarse beard and on to his clerical collar. Billy Morgan watched with distaste as the flies feasted at the rims of the dead man's open eyes.

'No, a very long way from some country parish, poor fellow. And that's Colonel Newport, ain't it, the Twenty-eighth Bombay's commanding officer?' Morgan, sword in one hand, pistol in the other, pointed across to another corpse, one of a dozen or so that had been collected behind a low mud wall just south of the centre of the village. That wall now provided cover for the double company − in reality only seventy or so strong − of the 66th Foot as bullets and musket balls sang through the air.

'What next, sir?' Sergeant Kelly crouched beside his officer. The dash from the Kabul Gate over the open ground with Brigadier General Morgan and Major McGucken, both dismounted, at their head appeared to have taken the enemy by surprise. The Afghans, Billy Morgan thought, had seemed to be concentrating all their efforts on driving back General Brooke's force − until a few moments ago. Now shots thumped into the tiles and masonry all around them in a positive torrent of lead and iron.

'I expect we'll try to give the Seventh Fusiliers and the Twenty-Eighth some covering fire − but here's Cap'n Beresford-Peirse, he'll tell us,' answered Morgan, as their company commander and his bugler crouched and dodged around the broken walls before throwing themselves down among the sheltering troops.

'Ah, Morgan, Sar'nt Kelly.' Beresford-Peirse's chest heaved, Morgan noticed, yet he'd returned to his old suave ways. 'The brigade commander has linked up with General Brooke and his people a couple of streets further on.' He pointed in the direction from which he had come, while taking in the dead bodies that surrounded them. 'He wants us to get forward and help to extricate a company of the Fusiliers who are acting as rearguard, but who are now all but out of ammunition. We'll move by platoons up to the guides that the Fusiliers have put in place for us and then concentrate our fire on all identified enemy positions. Once we've won the firefight, the Fusiliers will withdraw and we will become the effective rearguard. Be prepared to break clear by platoons on my orders and make your way back to the Kabul Gate. Be ready

315

to counter-attack should the enemy rally or try to cut us off. Any questions?'

It was more or less what both Billy Morgan and Kelly had anticipated – they had warned the men already – but it didn't make the prospect of hurling oneself into intense fire any more welcome. Both officer and sergeant shook their heads.

'Right, on my bugle call, then . . .' A salvo of their own artillery temporarily drowned Beresford-Peirse's instructions. 'I'll give you six minutes to sort the lads out.' He snapped the cover of his half-hunter shut. 'I'll bet that poor reverend gentleman didn't expect to end up here.' He nodded towards George Gordon. 'Don't let the boys bunch up. Good luck – away with you now.' He sent the pair darting among the men to pass his orders on.

Morgan could feel the tension among the troops. As they had paraded inside the town for the job they had been warned to expect, but hoped not to have to perform, there had been none of the normal banter, none of the good-natured name-calling, the older hands trying to demonstrate their experience with cool understatement or well-tried jokes. No, Morgan thought, Maiwand had knocked any of that out of them. They were still pliant, willing, cheerful even, but those hours facing the Ghazis' blades and the Heratis' rifles had taken their toll of their stock of courage. Now they were quiet, mechanical about what they had to do and, when they had surged like a khaki wave out of the gates and down across the open ground towards De Khoja, there had been no cheering, no shout of 'Come on, Sixty-Sixth!' just silent determination as the men sprinted hard in the hope of avoiding death.

'All right, Battle? Know what you're doing?' Morgan rested his hand on the Irishman's shoulder. If there was anyone who could be trusted to come back with a witticism, it was him.

But all he got was a lugubrious 'I am, your honour, better than that poor priest there.'

316

'Indeed.' Battle was clearly as appalled by the red of the blood so stark against the white collar as he was. 'And what of you, Williams?'

'On sparkling form, thank you, sir,' answered Posh Williams.

'Sparklin' form . . . I'll give ye sparklin' fuckin' form, Poshie, you creature. Why don't ye shag off back to yer precious fuckin' Horse Gunners? He's as shit-scared as the rest of us, your honour, don't listen to the fuckin' eejit,' jeered Battle.

'That's the trouble with this lot, sir. A very rough sort of man enlists in the Sixty-Sixth, hardly the sort of fellow you'd want to share a—' But Williams's riposte was cut short by the bugle and then it was all 'Come on, lads,' and 'Move yourselves,' from the NCOs as Beresford-Peirse led them out of the cover of the low wall and into danger's path.

The young officer had hoped for a minute or two's grace while the Afghans grasped what was going on − and he got it. His throat tight with fear, his heart pumping hard and an unnatural sweat trickling down his face, Morgan ran forward at the head of his men, crouched low and waiting for the enemy to respond. And, of course, that was precisely what they did. The initial calm was split with one or two twanging shots that flew high overhead, then a more reasoned fire was brought to bear with musket balls and Snider bullets cracking and whirring off the brickwork, throwing up great clouds of dust when they struck home and ricocheted almost musically.

Morgan felt the sting of a hundred slivers of grit as a round hit a wall just inches above his head, pricking his face and chin, but this only made him run the faster. As the men curved and dodged through the alleyways behind him, he was suddenly aware of Major McGucken and his father crouched below a windowsill, talking earnestly to an officer huddled down in front of them.

'That's a Fusilier officer, ain't it, Sar'nt?' Battle had noticed the white flash of the 7th sewn to the subaltern's helmet cover. 'Why can't they sort their own mess out? Why do we get to do the dirty work all the time?'

'Cos we're better at it than they are, Battle. You know what they say, "If you're in a fix, call for the old Sixty-Sixth,"' replied Kelly, trotting out one of the best-worn phrases in the regiment's lexicon.

'Aye, well, me an' the lads are gettin' a mite bored with bein' called to get other buggers out of the shite that they've got themselves into all the fuckin' time.' The moaning continued while Morgan, Kelly and the other NCOs shook the men out into fire positions from which they could support the embattled Second Battalion of the 7th Royal Fusiliers.

As Billy Morgan returned to the centre of the company's firing line, he heard Beresford-Peirse shout, 'General Morgan, sir, Major McGucken, I'd be obliged if you'd fall back behind my lads.' The two senior officers and Lynch, their trumpeter, were still in front of H Company's muzzles, peering at the enemy. 'We'd like to open fire, by your leave.'

As the trio scuttled back through the waiting 66th, they passed within feet of Ensign Billy Morgan and his sergeant. 'How are you, my boy? Hope he's not proving too much of a nuisance, Sar'nt Kelly?' Billy Morgan looked at his father and wondered. He'd aged visibly over the past few months: his hair was greyer and he was thinner than he'd ever seen him, even at the end of the fox-hunting season − yet he'd lost none of his touch.

'Aye, sir, bloody pest he is. But not as much of a pest as Major McGucken's had to put up with in his time − if the stories are true!'

Both men laughed and the general turned his attention to the next sweaty mass of khaki. 'Private Battle, as I live and breathe. Look after Sar'nt Kelly and Mr Morgan for me, will you?'

'I will, your hon−' He was cut short.

Beresford-Peirse roared, 'H Company, targets front, rapid . . . fire!' Seventy or so rifles kicked and bucked, spewing white smoke, thrashing lead over the heads of the Fusiliers, who were now beginning to fall back.

'Mark your targets, men.' Morgan found himself uttering one of the least understandable musketry instructor's aphorisms, saying anything to make himself feel useful. Meanwhile, the rifles banged at windows and loop-holes behind which the Afghans might be sheltering.

'Them Fusiliers have fair got the wind up 'em, your honour – ain't they just?' Battle, of course, was only too happy to see another unit discomforted, but Morgan couldn't agree. He watched the 7th fall back by sections, one covering another in a well-disciplined way, despite their lack of ammunition. He knew that it would have been only too easy for the whole company to dash back pell-mell once H Company's fire began to tell. But, no, the men were kept well in hand and Morgan saw the company's colour sergeant counting off every surviving man before they trotted back as a body towards the protection of the town's walls.

'Well, it's the least I could do, Brooke.' Poor Harry Brooke had been in a right old flurry when McGucken and I had found him trying not to catch a piece of Afghan lead. He was doing his job, right enough, very much in charge, very much the boss, but all the belief in his own success that I'd seen in him before the attack, all the vim, had gone. There was a great deal of lip-licking going on now and many a harrowed glance; his horse had been shot from under him – the shock of that was enough to unsettle anyone. But he'd been pathetically grateful when my little gang had arrived, not just for the firepower we provided but for the moral support that Jock and I would give him – at least, that was how it seemed to me.

'No, really, Morgan, we wouldn't have been able to do

anything without you – why didn't Primrose send us the men I asked for?' But Brooke knew the answer: he'd been sold a stillborn pup of a job and now he was paying the price in blood and misery.

'You did the same for my people after Maiwand, Brooke, but don't bother to ask why you were sent forward without enough troops. Don't you think we ought to make a move while my men have still got enough shot to keep the enemy's heads down?' Typical of Brooke, the keen, decent, brave bugger had been right at the centre of the fight, lost his horse and had even had to use his own revolver at one stage. Now, like the captain of a sinking ship, he was insisting on being the last man out and he'd paused to help some Sappers and their wounded officer, young Cruickshank.

'Aye, there's no point in staying here.' He couldn't have been more right – even as he said it, three or four rounds hammered into the wall next to us that had me, and everyone else, ducking even lower for solid cover. 'But what of the dead? We can't leave them – you know better than anyone else how the Afghans will abuse them.'

'You're right, Brooke, but that's their lookout. I've no desire to join their ranks, and carrying back dead weights like your man here...' Poor Cruickshank had been bleeding like nobody's business when his boys brought him up to us. I thought his femoral artery had been severed because no amount of dressings could staunch the flow. I wasn't in the least surprised when he succumbed just as the 66th were getting into position. 'No, leave him and the others and let's get cracking while we still have shot to spare and before it gets any damn hotter.' Brooke nodded, waving to Sharratt, his brigade major, to leave Cruickshank in the gory puddle where he lay.

I told Captain Beresford-Peirse that Brooke, McGucken, our escorts and I would move out of the village and wait for him and his men before we all hared across the few hundred yards towards the Kabul Gate together; not really what the *Field Training Manual* would have suggested, but I reckoned it would have to do. It was a shambles, right enough, but I'd been in worse – and at least this one wasn't of my own making. So off we set, myself heartily cheered by the sight of the big wooden gates and the chipped walls lined with crackling riflemen that soon came into view.

But I wasn't so cheered by what we saw next: in fact, I can rarely remember being so fucking terrified. Just as the half-dozen of us came to a dusty junction where the paths of the village gave way to drainage ditches and some scabrous excuses for orchards, two dozen or so Ghazis came up on our left, moving fast, trying, no doubt, to get behind Beresford-Peirse and my lad just as they withdrew. That same *Field Training Manual* would have described what happened next as a 'meeting engagement' or something equally fanciful. If it hadn't been so dangerous it would have been quite funny, for the Ghazis were all wrapped up in *shamags* and so filled with lethal fervour that they didn't see us moving on an almost parallel course.

It was Jock McGucken – predictably, the first to find his wits – who yelled, 'Come on, let's get among the scunners!' as he ran at them, firing his pistol, waving his sword and looking every inch the loon he was.

Well, the first Ghazis to start the journey to Paradise must have done so with precious little understanding of what or who had sent them there, for we ploughed into them with pistols and carbines and then our swords. I can remember firing my Enfield until all I got from it was empty, metallic clicks, then hacking about me with the bit of cutlery I'd bought in Fermoy in '52. I know it's been said before, but a mêlée like this is a little like life: if you're well armed, fit and determined, your enemies will give you a wide berth; if you're wounded or show signs of weakness, Heaven help you. I kept my blade going like a blinking windmill, catching one warrior

321

a good 'un right across the bridge of his nose that sent him yowling and bleating back among his mates, both hands clasped to his phizog, blood pouring from between his fingers. The others soon formed a defensive circle alongside me, Lynch jabbing away with the butt of his carbine, McGucken, Brooke and I doing our best to remember what the master-at-arms had taught us, while Sharratt poked hard with his steel, despite a nasty stab he'd taken in the foot.

'Where's yon Beresford-Peirse when you need the lad?' said Jock McGucken, while parrying an uncommonly well-handled spear. 'This is grand exercise, General.' He grunted as he got the better of his assailant and sank his blade deep into his stomach before pushing him away quite dead. 'But we can't keep it up for much longer.'

And he was right. Sharratt was weakening, Lynch had got a cut across his wrist that was bleeding badly and I'd over-reached my last cut at some damn savage and pulled a muscle at the back of my sword arm; it was bloody agony and I knew I'd never play the violin again.

The bastards could see this, of course, and once they'd recovered their balance and realised how heavily they outnumbered us, they came on in earnest. I tried to gain a breathing space to reload my pistol by stabbing one fellow in the throat, bundling him back into the crowd of his mates who were pressing hard behind and then sending his long knife cartwheeling into the throng – and that did my twanging arm muscle no good at all and bought me not a second. The Ghazis could scent blood and were storming in from all sides, surrounding us, mobbing us, trying to break the screen of slashing steel with which we held our ground. I don't mind telling you what a desperate situation it was. Now, at forty-nine, I was no longer in the same condition that had seen me racing around Kotah and scarcely notice it, but I was still in good shape. I could still scythe an acre of barley without a pause or saw a dozen oak logs without breaking into a sweat, but all this stroke and counter-stroke had me wheezing like a grampus, my right hand wet on the hilt of my sabre.

Then poor Sharratt went down like a sack of spuds; three swordsmen were instantly upon him, hacking and stabbing while Jock and I tried not just to defend ourselves, but also to beat those shrieking devils off Sharratt before they turned him to something fit only for the hounds. In the chaos, I got a nasty slice across my left elbow and was just turning to stop anything worse happening to me when I found myself pushed bodily to the ground. As God is my witness, one second I was trying to keep the howling lunatics at bay, the next a wall of sweaty warriors was sprawling all over me. I was grovelling in the dust, conscious only of the fact that the screaming was worse than ever and that my arms were pinioned to my sides by the sheer weight of bodies – dear Lord, how they stank!

I'd seen it before in the Mutiny. Men become so obsessed by a close-quarter fight that they fail to notice anything else. The Ghazis were so intent upon wiping out our little gang that, in the midst of the noise and general bedlam, they did not see their intended quarry bearing down upon them. Beresford-Peirse and half of H Company had thrown them-selves upon our assailants with such force that the struggling, stabbing mob had collapsed like a bunch of Dublin drunks. As sandals and bare legs scrabbled above me, I was suddenly conscious of shouted English – nothing intelligible, mind, just the feral grunts and curses of khaki gladiators about their brutal trade. I was aware of bayonets rising and falling, of the bang of rifles and the crunching impact of issued boots bruising flesh and breaking bone with vicious ease.

Two beefy lads dragged at McGucken and myself (God, I'd have given half my inheritance to remember their names) only to be greeted by Jock's 'An' where the fuck have yous been? What took you so bloody long? Can't the general rely upon anyone these days?' and similar ingratitudes as he swiped furiously at the dust and grime that now beset his normally faultless uniform.

'You can rely upon H, Major McGucken, you know you fucking can.' This came from Sergeant Kelly, panting in the sunlight, his face obscured by the deep shadow thrown by the peak of his helmet, the long, curvy blade of his senior NCOs' pattern bayonet red with blood and matter.

'And I'm obliged to you, Sar'nt Kelly. Ignore the political officer – there's no pleasing the man.' This produced a bit of a laugh from the pair of them as we all looked at each other and thanked the Lord that we still had something to laugh about.

But I didn't like what I saw next. Most of the Ghazis had beaten a pretty rapid retreat when Beresford-Peirse's group had fallen upon them, but scattered around the place were a number of dead bodies – I saw two of our lads among them – and a handful of wounded who were either writhing about, bleeding heavily, or lying quite still and waiting for death. Now, in so-called civilised wars (and there's a contradiction in terms if ever I heard one) you learnt to look after the enemy's casualties (I saw the Russians being treated with great tenderness on many occasions), but in this form of savage warfare, mercy ran in short measure. It wasn't much good the papers and liberal twats like our esteemed prime minister blethering about the dignity of man if Johnny Af cut the tongues out of our men's heads and stuck their severed balls there instead. No, our fellows fought fire with fire, and while I never saw deliberate cruelty, I rarely saw a wounded tribesman reach a dressing station.

Now a couple of the lads had been detailed off by Kelly to deal with things. They had either taken their bayonets off their muzzles or grabbed one of their fallen enemies' knives and were moving among their foes slipping the blades under armpits or down into the lungs past the collarbone: nasty work, but someone had to do it. Except one man who had no need to be there at all: my son Billy, his face an expression-less mask, was helping them. This was no job for an officer, yet he was jabbing home a Khyber knife without, apparently, any remorse. My very instinct was to yell and tell him to stop; to ask him if he could not see that there were certain necessary brutalities from which an officer – a leader – should stand apart. But I couldn't do this in front of his men: that would utterly have undermined the lad.

I looked away with a shudder and listened to Brooke eulo-gising Beresford-Peirse: 'Grand stuff, Sixty-Sixth, well done, Beresford-Peirse.' I could hear the relief in his voice. 'Now be so kind as to lead us back to the Kabul Gate.' Poor fellow: he must have experienced exactly what I'd felt at Maiwand – a plan going badly awry and his command being cut to pieces under the eyes of his superiors. Added to that, the last bout of swordplay must have left him just as shaken as I was – probably worse, for he'd been among the Afghans since before dawn while I'd been watching from the comfort of the battlements. Now, with safety just a few hundred yards away across a litter of ditches and bushes, he seemed almost euphoric.

Beresford-Peirse gave a brisk reply, croaked – for we were all dry as dust and hoarse from shouting – a few simple orders and off we set, a khaki mass trotting across the open ground covered by a handful of riflemen to the rear.

The unconventional idea of the whole lot of us just belting across the *maidan* in a mob had worked – for a while. True, the lads manning the defences in Kandahar did their best with rifles and artillery to keep Johnny Af's head down, and all we got at first was a few wild shots that flew high overhead. But with about two hundred yards to go, a volley hit the rear of the column pretty fair, knocking down two of the 66th lads.

Then Brooke, the big, brave clown, shouted, 'Go on, Morgan, you get the rest back into the town. I'll stay with the casualties and see that they're not left for the enemy to cut up.'

Well, fifty-odd infantrymen who've just had yet another close encounter with their own mortality ain't keen to stop, particularly when safety is in sight. A couple of the lads paused to help the wounded but the rest swept on and it was all I could do to make myself stop. One half of me wanted to plough on to the sanctuary of the walls, the other told me that if Brooke paused then so should I. It was all very well Primrose telling me that my name was a 'byword for courage' or some such rot, but that would last no longer than a heart-beat if I gave folk the excuse to question it. The fact was, though, that the Afghans had other ideas.

As the dun-coloured scrum pressed past us, Brooke and I were very soon alone with the casualties and their mates. Brooke had just turned to lend a hand when some sharp lad put a Snider round clean through his neck. I saw the wretched thing hit him. Blood sprayed out just below his left ear. The big man staggered, clapped his right hand to the entry wound on the other side of his head and his face took on a look of utter puzzlement as his knees gave and he fell into the dust.

I was with him in seconds, reaching to staunch the flow of blood from what looked like a severed carotid artery, but I might as well have been that little Dutch boy with his finger in the dike. He was leaking so heavily I could see that most of his blood would have pumped out of his body in minutes: the soft lead round had, I guessed, clipped the spine, flattened on impact and torn a hole through the neck that was big enough to stick my thumb in. The poor fellow made a half-attempt to raise himself, but this was probably his nervous system reacting to the unusual, rather than anything else. By the time I managed to prise an eyelid open, he was already dead.

I felt sick. Twice, now, I had failed to stand up to bloody Primrose, losing my brigade the first time and condemning a fine man and his troops to certain disaster the second. Brooke had been keen enough to give the ill-starred plan a try and perhaps green enough to underestimate the Afghans, but that didn't excuse me from saying – in terms that could not fail to be understood – that to try to take De Khoja in daylight with less than three battalions was suicidal. Now Harry Brooke of County Tyrone lay dead in the dirt. I might as well have shot him myself.

'Come on, General! For fuck's sake, don't hang around now.' Sergeant Kelly and two men were suddenly by my side – they must have turned back when they saw Brooke fall.

'Battle, Williams, catch a grip of General Brooke and get a move on yourselves.' I watched, dumbstruck as the two men lifted my broken friend under the knees and armpits and began to stagger towards the sprinting rear of H Company.

'Jaysus, these Prods don't come light, do they, Posh?' Battle had lost whatever slight respect he might have had for an officer now that the man was dead.

'Just save your breath and run, Eddie,' replied Williams.

Now, I don't know if you've ever tried to carry thirteen stone of dead body while being shot at but, I can tell you, it ain't easy. That pair of lads made light of it, though – it might have had something to do with the bullets kicking up the dirt around their ankles but by the time we go to the Kabul Gate, it was all I could do to keep up with them, even though I was encumbered by nothing more than Brooke's sword, which I supposed his family would want, and a heart that weighed heavier than lead.

'So, you've brought General Brooke back, have you, gentlemen?'

As I might have guessed, the first person I met standing just inside the gate was Harry's and my divisional commander, Primrose. And just beside him, as I might also have guessed, was Jock McGucken, who'd been at the head of H Company and who, judging by the atmosphere, which could have been cut with a rusty knife, had already told Primrose what he thought of him and his plan.

'We have, General. He fought like a lion,' I replied – and thought I heard Private Battle remark, 'An' the weight of an elephant, so he is.'

'He stopped a Snider round just as we cleared the edge of the village, General.' I looked down at Harry's torn throat and the great bloodstain that now spread right across the shoulders and breast of his tunic, soaking the Crimea and China ribbons.

'Well, I regret it, but it's a soldier's death and the end that he would have wanted,' said Primrose, without a shred of remorse that I could detect. I gasped at his coldness. I could think of nothing to say that would express my contempt adequately.

Luckily, Jock McGucken did it for me. 'No soldier that I've ever met wants death, General . . .' he paused to let his words sink in '. . . an' if you'd given him the troops he needed, instead of hedging your bets, this fine man that now lies here would still be drawing breath.'

Sam Keenan felt fear clutch at his belly. He'd recognised the disciplined fire of the British artillery – it had woken them as they lay in the prison tent before dawn. The wind had been from the east so they had all been able to hear the pulsating rifle fire, the volleys of the British being quite distinct. At first, they had thought that the noise marked the arrival of a relief force of some sort, but as the hours crawled by and the firing lessened, it became obvious that their hopes were false.

'What are they saying, Naik Shyamsingh?' he demanded of the sepoy, but he was hushed with the flap of a hand as the non-commissioned officer tried to follow the excited babble of the two guards.

'What's all this about?' Hector Maclaine's condition had worsened over the past couple of days. His wounds had swollen badly and he was spending most of the day asleep on a rough charpoy that had been provided for him by his captors. The noise of gunfire had been enough to penetrate his unconsciousness in the early morning, but since then he had drowsed fitfully, only waking now at the hubbub the guards were making.

'I don't know, Maclaine, but it seems that our masters are mighty pleased about something and, judging by the fact that no one's decamping here, I can only presume that things have not gone well for our people.' Keenan watched the other sepoys who were doing their best to pick up whatever scraps they could from the sentries' obvious bragging. Eventually, with a laugh, the two Afghans withdrew from the tent, which was stifling in the mid-afternoon sun.

'Well, sahib . . . there is some good news.' Naik Shyamsingh made the most of what little he had heard, thought Keenan. 'We are to be given a special meal tonight at the orders of Ayoob Khan *bahadur*.' Keenan hated the way that Shyamsingh used the honorific title for their captor, almost as if the naik's loyalty had passed automatically to whoever was feeding and watering him. 'It is to celebrate their great victory.'

'The city can't have fallen, can it?' Keenan asked, appalled at the prospect.

'No, sahib, but a grand attack was made by our men from the garrison to try to raise the siege. It was beaten back with hundreds killed. The Afghans have taken many mounts, which pleases them greatly, including the horse of a general, who fell during the *gora-log*'s retreat.'

A general killed? Keenan tried to digest such news. Why and how could the Afghans know such a thing? It would just be wishful thinking, surely. Perhaps an officer's charger had been taken and the rank of its owner exaggerated – that must be the explanation.

But, on the other hand, the natives passed fairly freely from the lines of one army to another; letters were exchanged between the commanders, and if a general had fallen, the British would be desperate to recover his body before it was abused. Could it be his father? He knew how badly the loss at Maiwand had affected him and he could imagine his wanting to avenge that defeat at almost any cost to himself.

Keenan listened to the Babel of the guards and the sepoys. Maclaine had joined in now and was demanding, with what little strength he had, that Naik Shyamsingh go out to the guards and glean whatever further information he could. Then, through his hunger and despair, Keenan saw a chance. Might it be possible, he wondered, to inch his way up to the pile of rugs and bedding that lay at the far end of the tent without any of the others noticing him? If he could, he might be able to pull up the canvas skirt of the tent from the ground and worm his way under it. But what then? Was the camp in such a state of excitement that he might pass unnoticed? He was filthy and unshaven, tanned and ragged – he might pass for a native, but wouldn't an unarmed, bareheaded creature be just as noticeable as if he'd been in full uniform? One thing was for certain: he must not risk the lives of the others; if he went at all, he would go by himself.

As the din continued, Keenan crept away from the rest of the group – it took no more than a couple of minutes and no one seemed to notice. He ensconced himself among blankets and mats, hunkered down, facing his comrades, his back to the sun-hot wall of the tent, his fingers groping blindly under the lip of coarse cloth next to the soil. As his hands found a loop of rope that he knew must be secured on the outside by a wooden peg, he caught the musty aroma of crushed grass and warm canvas that took him straight back to a dozen gymkhanas at home in Cork, or to school cricket matches under a summer sky. With eyes half shut, the others became a gaggle of matrons sipping tea around his mother, or teenage boys grabbing for sandwiches at close of play. He snorted silently at the absurdity of the image while his hands tugged and probed, trying to get at the peg. At last his fingers closed around the wood, but it was all he could do to get any purchase. Long minutes passed while he waggled and grappled with the picket as unobtrusively as he could, but eventually he was rewarded: it began to move in the ground. Keenan paused for a moment and considered waiting for dark, but he was desperate to be free, to find out exactly what had become of his father and to end the torment of captivity.

Desperation clouded his judgement: he pulled too hard, whisking the peg from the ground with such force that he dragged the cloth skirt of the tent clear of the ground, half tumbling as it came free and letting a great flash of sunlight pierce the gloom of the tent.

'No, Keenan, please don't think of that.' The light had caused the hubbub to stop at the other end of the tent and every face to turn towards him. Maclaine had realised at once what his intentions were. 'You'll be dead within seconds looking like that and running around out there in broad daylight. I know how damnable this is, but we need you to see us through all this. I'm no use now and someone's got to give these lads . . .' Maclaine pointed a feeble hand at the gang of tattered sepoys '. . . some leadership. Be a good fellow and push that flap back down before our gaolers discover it.'

'You're right, Maclaine. Now's not the time.' Keenan wondered at himself: had boredom caused him to lose his senses? Maclaine was, indeed, right – there was no point in trying to escape by himself while the Afghans' dander was up: it would be suicidal. The moment would come when the garrison or reinforcements would fall upon Ayoob Khan, wouldn't it? Then they might try something together.

Until now, Keenan had thought of his father sitting in Kandahar and fretting about him in enemy hands – he could see him conjuring up all sorts of pictures of horrible tortures and privations and swearing bloody revenge. But now the

331

boot was on the other foot. Now he imagined his father stabbed, riven, covered with blood and flies, while he sat on his arse in a bloody marquee. If he ever got home, how on earth would he explain that to his mother?

In the early light it was hard to make out, but I reckoned I could just see the naked feet and legs of half a dozen of our lads sticking above a fold in the ground right next to a building on the edge of De Khoja. I'd gone back to Sergeant Mullane's gun position on the walls of the city and he'd drawn my attention to it; he reckoned he'd seen the Afghans stripping the corpses at one stage and heaved a shell at them for good measure. The light was beginning to fade now, but even if I twisted the focus wheel of my binoculars, I still couldn't be certain. A pie-dog was pulling at something, for sure, and the shite hawks were circling overhead, but it still wasn't clear.

Things were quiet now. After the latest confrontation with Primrose I'd not even tried to tell him what had happened. I'd just gone to my room in the miniature mess I'd shared with Harry Brooke, shed my filthy clothes, bathed, had my wound dressed, eaten as much as I could stomach – precious little – gathered up my friend's things and written to his wife. I'd hoped that that would be enough to propel me into a sleep born of physical exhaustion, sadness and fear, but it didn't happen. I'd lain and turned below my mosquito net, sweated, reproached myself time and again, and thought of the house and stables in Tyrone that were going to be awfully quiet now that there was no master to bring life to them. It could so easily have happened to Glassdrumman, my own house in Cork. Perhaps it should have.

With such cheerful thoughts swirling round my head, I dressed and returned to the walls to study no less cheerful sights. I'd seen some battlefields and bodies in my time: the battery at Inkerman where our boys and Russians lay in great piles; the Chumbal river after Kotah where you could almost walk to the other side on the bobbing dead; or the fortress at Gwalior, which had looked more like a charnel house once we'd finished with the mutineers.

But there was something special about the lads who littered the ground around De Khoja. They were no different from any other corpses I'd seen, just bundles of rags, shrunken in death, lying anyhow – I think it was just the sheer futility of it all. We'd told Primrose that the plan wouldn't work. I'd told Brooke the same yet I'd failed to get the enterprise cancelled; and there was something about that look on his face when the bullet had ripped his neck. It was surprise mixed with the disappointment of failure. Now he was dead and a trunkful of sun-bleached khaki would be all of him that returned to rain-drenched Ulster.

We'd lost a hundred good men during this little nonsense, a hundred good men that we could ill afford, especially as there was no news whatsoever of when one or another relief column might arrive. And all this time, of course, my lad Sam was a guest of Ayoob Khan. Word had come back that he was unhurt and in company with Maclaine and others, and I suspected he would be cared for decently enough so long as things went well for our enemies. But if they didn't, if we attacked again or Roberts or Phayre arrived, what then? Hostages would be of no use to a routed host. I guessed that when that happened, Sam's life might become, as someone once said, nasty, brutish and short.

TWELVE

The Battle of Kandahar

'Mother of God, these fellas stink, so they do,' exclaimed Private Battle, through the rag that was knotted around his nose and mouth.

It was late August and the men killed during the sortie to De Khoja had lain where they fell for almost a week and a half. Their comrades watched them from the battlements of Kandahar as they swelled, blackened and burst. Billy Morgan knew there was nothing that could be done – well, nothing that didn't risk a bullet from the besieging Afghans. Then, twenty-four hours ago, as dawn broke, there was no muezzin's call, no smoky cooking fires and no sniping. The rumours that Ayoob Khan's men would lift the siege and move to block Roberts's column were obviously true so the garrison was free to recover its dead.

'Well, so would you if you'd lain in the sun in these temperatures for the last few days, Eddie,' replied Posh Williams, through a similar piece of cloth.

'Right, lads, get 'im over 'ere an' on that cart. Can you lift 'im or will 'e fall to bits?' Sergeant Kelly was supervising the work detail that had been sent out to collect the dead from the sortie against De Khoja. The bodies not only smelt foul, but after eight days in the open, they had started to deteriorate badly, many shedding limbs or heads when the men tried to lift the bloated, blistered remains on to the horse-drawn carts.

'No, Sar'nt, this 'un's in one piece.' Battle had the Fusilier by his shoulder straps while Williams held the dead man below the knees, just where his still neatly folded puttees ended. 'On three, Posh.' As Battle counted down, the two men swung the corpse rhythmically before letting it go, dumping it on a pile of others in the bed of the wagon.

'Have you got 'is papers, Williams?' Sergeant Kelly had a little pile of documents that had been recovered from the top left pocket where each man was required to carry his pay and personal details. Some were clean and dry while others were either crusty with old blood or wet with the fluids that come from decomposing flesh.

'No, Sar'nt, sorry, I'll get them,' said Williams, as he levered himself into the back of the vehicle, trying hard not to stand on the dusty, oozing, repulsive corpses. The young, stiff soldier that he and Battle had just thrown on to the pile lay on his back, arms raised rigidly, both hands scratching at the air, the desiccated flesh pulling the fingers into sickle claws. Williams looked down at the khaki tunic. The cloth was still quite clean and the collar still hooked smartly straight and tight at the neck. But there the normality ended, for a hideous, blackened face lay above it, the eyes pecked out by the birds, the flesh pockmarked by the sun, the lips drawn back over the teeth in a dreadful rictus. Williams gagged as he unbuttoned the top pocket, reached inside and retrieved a fold of papers before he leapt down to the ground with relief.

'Hello, sir.' As Sergeant Kelly took the documents, Billy Morgan, in full battle order, had approached, leading a horse with a handkerchief pressed to his face. Kelly and the men all stiffened to attention.

'Hello, Sar'nt Kelly. Lads, carry on, please,' Morgan mumbled, as he flicked a salute in reply. 'What an awful pong.'

'Aye, sir, but these poor sods 'ave got to be brought in and given a proper burial, ain't they, sir? Someone's got to show 'em some respect. You don't need to get involved in this, sir. Come over 'ere an' tell me what you found out on the recce.' Sergeant Kelly led his officer away from the men's malodorous labour.

'Well, Ayoob Khan's buggered off over the hills and no mistake. Cap'n Beresford-Peirse and I went right up to the Pir Paymal . . .' Morgan pointed to the great hilly outcrop five miles to the west, on the other side of Kandahar from where they now stood. 'Most of the brigade officers were there, and the general led us almost up to the Afghan sentry positions – can you imagine?'

'I can, sir, I can. He's a bloke, that dad of yours, ain't he?' replied Kelly, admiringly.

'Well, that's one way of describing the old sod, Sar'nt Kelly. Anyway, it seems that once the Afghans got word of the relief column's approach, they could hardly wait to decamp and, as far as we could make out, Ayoob Khan's got most of his people bunched on this side of the Argandab, expecting, I've no doubt, General Roberts to try to storm his positions from across the river.'

Three days before, heliographs had warned the garrison of Kandahar that Roberts and his troops were approaching from the west. Almost as quickly, messengers had passed the word among the Afghans and so, on 23 August, Ayoob Khan had moved out of his positions south and east of the city. The next day, he had abandoned the siege altogether. Now he had shifted his flag to oppose the crossings of the Argandab some four or five miles north-west of the town with the high range of the Baba Wali Kotal to his rear and the river in front of him. As soon as the enemy had been seen to withdraw, reconnaissance and burial parties had been despatched.

'Did they say when General Roberts is likely to be here, sir?' Kelly had produced a pouch of tobacco and a small clay pipe from his pocket. Now he fiddled with a lucifer before offering the flame to Morgan, who had ferreted around in his pockets for a cheroot. Both men wanted to lessen the ghastly stench that engulfed the place.

'Not with any certainty, but the staff reckon it'll be at least another four or five days before the leading elements reach us and that we're to expect Roberts to waste no time. It's thought he'll attack straight off the line of march and that our brigade – or what's left of it – will be used to flank him from the south and west. Anyway, no point in worrying too much about that now. How long will you be with these stiffs, Sar'nt Kelly?'

'Almost finished, sir.' Kelly had got his pipe going now and sucked at it with obvious enjoyment. 'Don't you worry about it – it ain't officer's work. You get back into camp an' get your head down. You'll be busy with plans an' orders an' suchlike over the next few days. The boys will be fine – nothing that a good wash won't put right, anyway. Just leave 'em to me, sir.'

Morgan realised how much he had come to depend on Sergeant Kelly. He knew how the man fathered him, how he protected him from the men who would take advantage of a young subaltern and, indeed, from himself. Now he understood how far the stability, order and enterprise of the regiment depended upon the sergeants, kind, hardened, versatile working-class fathers mostly. It was they who lent the backbone to patrols, who steered the men like children around chaotic, terrifying battlefields, standing by and supporting their sub-alterns who flourished brand-new swords and revolvers. Yet the intensity, the sense of injustice in Kelly's next statement brought Morgan up short.

'Had any word of your brother now that Ayoob Khan's moved hisself, sir?' asked Kelly.

'No, not a thing, Sar'nt Kelly,' answered Morgan, knowing what was coming next.

'Hope you don't mind me saying, sir, but there's been a bit

of grumbling among the men about what happened. It's none o' my business to want to know what's gone on in the past between you and Mr Keenan, sir, and – the good God knows – this company's got reason enough not to like either that officer or the Scinde Horse, but word gets around, you know, sir, and the lads are worried – if you're prepared to let your own brother get hisself captured by those cruel bastards, would you stand by them? Don't get me wrong, sir, they more than appreciated what you did for Sutton and Cooper when Mr Keenan wanted to leave them to the enemy during the retreat, but they can't get over what you did to your own flesh and blood.'

This worried Morgan. The whole incident weighed heavily on his conscience, but he had had no idea that the men understood what had really happened. Then he realised he should have known better: the company was a tight, self-contained bubble in which not much happened without everybody getting to hear about it. When it suited the men, they could be slow – lumpen, even – but the same family-like understanding that made Kelly a father to them all ensured that little escaped their simple but shrewd judgement.

'Might be a good idea to put the lads' minds at rest, if you get a chance, sir. There's a deal more fighting to be done yet, sir and – I know I've said this before – I don't want them having any doubts about you,' Kelly answered.

'Thank you, Sar'nt Kelly. I appreciate your telling me that.' And he did appreciate it: he prized above all else his relationship with the men he commanded. 'But what should I do?' Morgan asked, genuinely perplexed.

'Do you know, sir? I ain't got the least idea.'

I didn't know which of them I disliked more. Roberts, being four months senior to Primrose, assumed command of the whole damn shooting-match once he came through the gates of Kandahar and, I suppose, I should have been pleased to see the Bloom's nose put out of joint so royally. But there was something instantly detestable about Roberts as well. It wasn't just the rumours about his VC and his obvious insatiable ambition: he looked and acted tricky. There was bugger-all of him, and what there was was covered with medal ribbons – not that I was jealous, certainly not. His moustaches were too long and too well groomed but, much worse than that, wherever he went he had a newspaper wallah at his elbow. I'll own that Howard Hensman of the *Daily News* scribbled well, except for his gushing admiration of Roberts who, it seemed, could not put a foot wrong with him and his paper.

Now, if you look at the map, it was a hundred miles for Phayre to get to Kandahar from Quetta in the south while Roberts had had to tramp almost three times that distance from Kabul in the north-east. But I always knew that Bobs would do his damnedest to get to us first because – well, just because he would. True, Phayre had more difficult ground, serious opposition, and started later, but the fanfare in the press that the Kabul force made of their dash to help us showed how desperate Roberts was to succeed. But what I wasn't ready for, though, was the state of his troops when they arrived. We knew he was on the way – we had been picking up heliograph signals for some days before we saw his scouts – and I was guilty of expecting a neat, trim, powerful set of braves to appear on the horizon once Ayoob Khan's boys had gone.

Well, I couldn't have been more wrong. Now, I'm not saying that my brigade had made much of a showing when we'd got back to Kandahar after Maiwand, but at least we'd had the excuse of having just been massacred. Bobs's Bengal people looked threadbare without having fired more than a shot or two on the way down. The first mob I saw was a mixed bag of Punjab and Bengal cavalry whose mounts were so thin and saddle-sore that they looked more like Afghans than our own people. Then there had been files of Gurkhas, some reasonable-looking Sikhs, and the 72nd and 92nd Highlanders, whose ghastly pipes we could hear squealing from miles away. They all looked pretty travel-worn – but nothing prepared me for the great column of sick, who were either stumbling forward under their own steam or being carried in an endless stream of dhoolies. I counted more than five hundred as they crowded through the city gates and swamped our meagre medical establishment.

'So, Morgan, it's good to meet you at last – I've heard much about you. How's your wound?'

Was Roberts, the little git, being tricky? I'd been called forward to a council of war in the Citadel almost as soon as the column had arrived. The general had not even shaken the dust off his boots, let alone paused for a meal and a drink – none of this being lost on the newsboys who were jotting admiring things like crazy, though why such creatures should be allowed in to listen to the GOC's plan for battle was beyond me.

'Fine, General, thank you.' I'd almost forgotten about the scratch I'd sustained at De Khoja. 'It's good to meet you, too.' I'd tried to answer as levelly as I could, very conscious that I was the main reason that the khaki-clad pygmy had had to come haring down from Kabul to our rescue. 'I hope your march hasn't been too trying.' I thought I'd get my sally in first and allow Roberts to remind the room and the press of just how damned good he was.

'Well, ten thousand troops and followers marching three hundred miles over this terrain in just three weeks ain't too bad, is it? Daresay Hannibal and his elephants might have done it faster but he didn't have endless bloody oxen and camels to deal with, did he?'

So, there it was, just as I'd expected: Bobs had put himself on a platform with the heroes of antiquity, had he? Why was I not surprised?

In any event, I really didn't care if Roberts despised me or

340

not. My career had run its course and perished with those lads whose bones were bleaching even now between here and the Helmand. All I wanted to do was to find out if Sam was still drawing his pay or not and, if he was, to get the young bugger to safety. God's teeth, the whole situation was so like the last time he had been in enemy hands – mark you, that was more than twenty years ago at Gwalior when he was just a nipper – and he'd had his mother to look after him. Still didn't stop me from having to shed more claret than I cared to, though, did it?

'But have you got any advice for me, Morgan? I've got the better of all manner of different tribes and so-called regular troops over the past few months . . .' He would use 'I' rather than 'we', wouldn't he? '. . . but I've scarce met any Ghazis. I've seen a handful or two, but you've had more swarms of 'em about your ears than anyone else and you're still here to talk about it. What's their Achilles heel? How do you deal with 'em?'

Well, I nearly fell over with surprise. Here was Mars asking me how to fight and I didn't get the impression that it was all flattery. There had been a pretty robust defence of my handling of the brigade at Maiwand in most of the papers and universal praise for me after poor old Harry Brooke's death at De Khoja; perhaps Roberts didn't see me as a complete booby.

'All I can say is, General, keep them at arm's length with plenty of musketry and gunfire. Once they get close enough to use their knives, our men's advantage has gone entirely. And I don't like to have to say it, but use your British troops as the linchpin for your native regiments – both my Bombay battalions were completely overawed by those madmen. It was only the Sixty-Sixth and E Battery that stopped Maiwand being worse than it was, while the Seventh Fusiliers were like a rock at De Khoja.' I thought that would twist Roberts's tail, his being a Bengal Gunner and all. But he just nodded and stroked his moustache sagely. 'I suspect that things might have changed already in Ayoob Khan's lines. He lifted the siege of Kandahar sooner than shit goes through a goose when word reached him your column was on the way.' He liked that: I could see him preening. 'And he'll be terrified that he could be caught from behind while he's on that river position he's occupied. But I'm sure you've thought of all this.'

'No, Morgan, that's very helpful. I can adapt things to use all that you've said. Would you do me the kindness of listening to what I intend to do?'

Well, a little humility goes a long way with me. I studied Roberts's plan and it seemed sound enough. The cavalry had already reconnoitred the enemy's position and that information, combined with all the detail we'd been able to give him, led to a design for battle that would put overwhelming force against Ayoob Khan, involving more than eleven thousand troops and thirty-two guns. Then, with a nod to my experience, he told how Gough's cavalry, with what remained of my E/B Horse Gunner battery and four companies of the 7th Fusiliers, were going to be pushed hard in an encircling movement over the Argandab to threaten the enemy's line of retreat. For the hard pounding in the centre, the position of honour, Roberts proposed to use his three Bengal infantry brigades.

That was the bit I didn't like: he was relegating Primrose's and my troops to supporting roles holding the flanks and suchlike. I could quite see why a commander would want to use his own people – he would know their strengths and weaknesses after all – but this use of new, inexperienced troops almost rubbed the nose of the Kandahar garrison in the shit. *We* were the folk who had a score to equal with Ayoob Khan and a reputation to restore; *we* had had to endure a battering from the bloody man, a siege and countless indignities; *we* should be given the chance to close with the wily bugger, not Roberts's rag-arses, who looked more like bloody scarecrows after their 'epic' march. And that wasn't all. The prisoners were *our* people: *we* should be allowed to rescue them for that was what they would expect – my own precious son included.

But I'd said my piece, had at least part of my advice listened to and, frankly, didn't have the energy to argue any further with the man. Anyway, I had no career to save, so I got my head together with McGucken, hatched a plan and, once Roberts's orders were over, put it to Primrose.

'It sounds suicidal to me, Morgan. The hostages will be well guarded and our sources tell us that they've been kept at the very centre of Ayoob Khan's camp. Now, I quite see you're worried that they'll all be put to the knife if our assault looks like it might succeed, but if that doesn't happen – and I pray it doesn't – they'll be spirited off and you'll end up with nothing to show for your enterprise except heavy casualties. Remind me, how many men do you want to take for this task?' Primrose asked.

'I must lead it, General, for it was my fault that these men fell into enemy hands at all. With your permission, I shall take Major McGucken with me as the potential for intelligence gathering will be enormous.' That was a complete lie: I just wanted Jock by my side in what was likely to be the swansong of my time as a soldier. 'Thirty or so experienced lads will be all I need.'

'And you have no need to tell me that they'll be from the Sixty-sixth – not that they've got any score to settle with the Ghazis,' Primrose snapped.

'General, a platoon of handy lads from the Sixty-Sixth is a grand idea.' I forbore to mention that I would need a particular young subaltern to lead them. If any bugger was going to risk his neck getting Sam Keenan back in one piece, it was going to be Billy Bloodthirsty Morgan whose part in Sam's capture I still hadn't fully fathomed.

'Certainly I have no objection. Your brigade's hardly been given a task that one of the commanding officers couldn't manage so, if you want to try to persuade Our Saviour Bobs of the feasibility of your plan, I have no objections.' Typical Primrose – he'd neither endorse nor forbid my idea, nor support me with the chief: he'd leave me to do all that myself.

Well, I did, and Roberts rolled over nice as ninepence. Actually, I think he understood my position. He might have confused my desperation with a last chance for glory, but I couldn't have given a hang.

'Very well, Morgan. I'll attach you and your little gang to Baker's brigade. If things unfold as I trust they will, you should have the opportunity to be first into Ayoob Khan's camp and to get your hands on those prisoners before anything ghastly befalls them. The people at home have had far too much horror already without having to put up with any more. You have my full authority to do what you need to do to save those two brave young officers' lives – oh, and the native soldiers' as well, of course.'

Damn me for a fool! Without realising it, I'd suggested a scheme to Roberts that had all the ingredients of a real scoop for the press hangers-on. The 'hero' of Maiwand might be given one last chance to salvage his name by rescuing not just one young lion but another who happened to be his son. What romance, what glory, what poetic justice! And if he were to grab a handful of loyal sepoys as well, then so much the better – surely that would rub any stain off Bobs's record after the unfortunate accusations of atrocities last year?

I knew Roberts wouldn't dither around. It made sense, mind you, not to let his men get too settled after the march or, for that matter, to let Ayoob Khan have any more breathing space. No, within a few hours of my outlining my plan to him, he'd issued his orders, extra ammunition had been dealt out to the men, battalions had been assigned to new brigades and fresh tasks, and I'd been given a couple of dozen toughs from the 66th and a certain ensign to command them. We'd moved at

344

dawn behind a battalion of Sikhs, marching fast out of the town, clearing one or two hamlets with hardly a shot and making grand progress up until the late morning.

But why did Johnny Af always fight his hardest at the hottest part of the day? Did he know how bloody awful it was for us, or was it just the nature of things? Whatever the answer, our speed was too good to last and as the brigade approached a bigger place called Gundigan, with one battalion leading and the other two in echelon behind it, Ayoob Khan's men really began to pepper us. The village lay on the plains leading down to the river, overlooked by the hills in the distance and with a few stands of trees and scrub surrounding it. How Johnny Af loved to fight from these places. I'd always assumed that tribesmen would prefer to avoid built-up areas, but that didn't seem to be the case. They'd been rather better than I thought they would be outside Kandahar and now a right wall of lead was coming to meet the leading troops. It did feel odd, though, for my little mob was keeping out of it. Instead of all that dry-mouth and tight-hoop stuff, we were able to sit back and watch and, listening to the men, they were as unaccustomed to it as I was.

'Well, I'll be damned. It makes a fuckin' change to see some other bastard bein' made to do the dirty work, so it does.' Private Battle watched from the shelter of a sturdy wall as a trickle of wounded from the 72nd Highlanders and the 2nd Sikhs came limping and shambling back from the fighting ahead of them.

'You're right, Eddie, but these lot are a right bunch of red-arses. They attacked that last position without any real fire and manoeuvre – no wonder they've taken casualties. You and I know that Johnny Af's no fool – he'll punish the least mistake. You watch; this'll be just some delaying game – his main position will be up ahead somewhere that we don't expect it.' Posh Williams had added his veteran's pennyworth.

The two men were standing easy with the rest of the 66th detachment, sheltering from the Afghan slugs and bullets that whistled irregularly overhead or thumped off the wall behind them. Like me, they'd had little sleep the night before and a start well before daylight, but their lot had, so far, been an easy one. Now they shared pipes and water-bottles and passed expert comments on the efforts of their less-experienced comrades as Baker's brigade tried to clear the village and its dense tangle of brush and gardens, ditches and low enclosures.

'Look there, General. Who's that they've got in a blanket?' Major Jock McGucken was crouching next to me at the far end of the column of 66th lads.

'I don't know, but they're making very heavy weather of it − looks like one of the officers.' Four kilted Scotsmen, rifles slung across their backs, their spats and hose dappled with mud, were struggling at the corners of a grey issue blanket that was pregnant with its burden. Alongside them, in a half-crouch, came a regimental doctor, peering worriedly into the shroud. There seemed to be a sergeant at the head of the party; the rest were non-commissioned officers too.

'What news from up ahead, Sawbones?' I tried to sound light-hearted as the bearers approached. The pattern of the firing told me all I needed to know about the progress of the fight, but I was curious about the casualty.

'We were doing right well, er . . . General' − the doctor was obviously confused to find a brigadier general scuttling about with a clutch of unfamiliar infantrymen in the rear of his own battalion − 'until the last buildings had to be rushed. The colonel was just coming up to give orders to the leading companies when he took a bloody great musket ball in the neck. He'd bled to death by the time I'd got to him, the poor man.'

What a bloody awful place to die. This village was no different from any of the others, mud-walled houses, funny,

346

higgeldy-piggeldy courtyards, the odd bush and fruit tree and as many varieties of turds as there were animals in the Ark. Now the four NCOs had found as clean a bit of ground as they could and laid the blanket down in the cover of the wall, grateful for a rest from their sad burden. As McGucken and I stared down at the dead man, they massaged their hands, trying to get the circulation to flow where the rough blanket had cut it off.

'Freddy Brownlow, McGucken. Did you know him?' I asked, as we gazed at the corpse. Brownlow wore no whiskers except a great walrus moustache that made him look more like sixty than his actual thirty-eight; now it was soaked with congealing blood and black with flies.

'Aye, General, a wee bit. Got himself a CB last year up by Kabul, did he not?' said McGucken, while he studied the long furrow that had been chopped in the side of the dead man's neck.

'He did, and much good did it do him. Looks like a *jezail* round caught an artery,' I answered, gazing at the blood that had pumped out not just over the colonel's khaki tunic but right down to his tartan breeches and the curious Mackenzie tartan puttees he wore.

'A brave man by all accounts.' I knew that the body held little further interest for McGucken: he'd seen too many such sights. 'Has the battalion cleared the village yet, Doctor?'

'Almost, General. You'll be wanting to be up with the action, I've no doubt,' the medico said quizzically, obviously curious about an unfamiliar general-officer's presence with such a small command that was taking no part in the fighting.

'Not just yet, thank you, Doctor. We've our own wee task to attend to when the moment comes. You'd better get back to where you're needed, there's nothing more that can be done for your commanding officer.' I didn't like the way that the 72nd's doctor was being quite so nosy – and I liked his suggestion that we were battle-shy even less – so I was blunt with him. Besides, there really was nothing that could be done for poor Brownlow, while Highlanders were falling to Afghan bullets by the score. With a stiff little salute, the doctor scuttled back towards the noise of firing, leaving the sergeant and the other three NCOs with their load. The group of kilted soldiers seemed perplexed, lost without an aim, faces creased in sadness, almost on the point of bursting into tears, or so it looked to me. But I'd seen Highland regiments like this before. Perhaps it was to do with the clan chief, the laird, having been struck down or just their emotional nature that made them so good in the attack yet so instantly despondent when the pendulum swung the other way.

Whatever the answer, Jock McGucken had noticed the same thing and berated them in grinding Lowland Glasgow: 'Sar'nt, will ye get a grip of yerself and those others? Ye look like a bunch o' greetin' bairns, not soldiers. Put your man down by those buildings yonder. Pull the blanket tight around him and mark the spot like you've been taught – he can come to no more harm. Then get back to the fighting – that's where ye're needed.'

The sergeant seemed startled at first by the harshness of the words and the accent, but the authority of the tone jerked him back to reality and in no time the Scotsmen were hurrying back to the fray, checking their rifles and ammunition as they scurried away.

'They can be just like weans sometimes, those big lads from the hills. Too much Papist nonsense pushed into them when they're young – makes 'em sentimental. Ye'd never see a Lowland regiment behave like that, would ye, General? Ye ken the Seventy-First or the Twenty-Sixth taking on like that? Why, the sergeants would skelp the bums o' the lot of 'em if they behaved so!'

I hadn't, really, the least idea of what Jock McGucken was talking about, except that from time to time he would unfetter his total scorn for all things Roman and Highland. And, indeed, this little incident seemed to set the mood for the next

348

couple of hours. As we followed the 72nd I got a litany of comments: 'Have the big, daft loons no idea? O' course they'll take casualties if they go rushing at Johnny Af hell for bloody leather like that! Have they no' heard o' skirmishing forward?' A steady stream of dead and hurt trickled past us.

But McGucken's cup of contempt spilt over when the main line of Ayoob Khan's defence was encountered about a mile and a half south of his camp. I was familiar with the long, deep, dry watercourse that bisected the plain from my recces up to the Argandab river in the weeks before Maiwand, but I hadn't expected the Heratis to have loop-holed the western lip quite so ingeniously. As usual, the Afghans had shown what bloody good tacticians they could be, for there was no cover to speak of surrounding their position, allowing every rifle and musket the best possible fields of fire. Not only that, but the guns were well sighted to rake any attacking force, and when all three infantry brigades were thrown at it with little preparation by our own artillery, McGucken became apoplectic.

'Christ on a crutch, General! It's just like the fucking Alma all over again . . .' I remembered, as he did, the utter dismay of dashing myself and hundreds of good men against pre-prepared defences. 'I thought Roberts had a reputation for a bit of skill in these matters.' I had to admit that, as Gurkhas, Sikhs and two regiments of Highlanders – the 92nd Gordons had come into our sight for the first time – went pell-mell for the enemy, McGucken had a point. Make no error, there was no lack of gallantry, but our men just charged the Afghans bald-headed with bugger-all plan that I could see, other than a determination to absorb as much lead and iron as the enemy could throw at them.

'Jesus, General, the bayonet's a fine thing, but don't those soft teuchters know the value of volley fire?'

McGucken was right: the Gordons had gone in straight against the enemy's defences without a shot fired. 'They might as well be armed with bloody assegais for all the fucking use they're making of their rifles!'

'I agree with you, but it looks as though our people are getting the better of things, even if they're suffering more than they should.' The whole Afghan line – the entrenched nullah right down to their infantry in the open – was now being engaged by our people. I had to admit it, once the leading brigades had got over the shock of finding the enemy so well entrenched, they'd gone at them with a real purpose, ignoring the casualties that they were taking. Even Ayoob Khan's guns, which had done such execution initially, were beginning to fall silent while their flags and banners, so many of which had floated above their troops at first, now seemed to be far less numerous.

'Aye, the heart's being kicked oot of them, General. I guessed as much when the whole bloody lot scampered back from outside Kandahar to the river line when they heard that Roberts was coming. These people will soldier well enough when it's all going their way, but they hate to be caught between two encircling forces,' replied McGucken.

Hadn't I had much the same thoughts myself and expressed them to Roberts? Not that he was interested in the views of a mere brigade commander, mark you. 'You're right, McGucken . . . but I thought this crew were hardier than that. You and I've never seen better fighters than those buggers at Maiwand and De Khoja.'

'True enough, General, but the really hard pounding was done by yon loons the Ghazis, was it not? How many of them can you see now?' Again, McGucken was right, for I could see precious few white-robed crazies here. 'I reckon that if Roberts keeps up the pressure this bunch'll take to their heels, leave their kit and just melt away. Some of the Heratis may stand and fight it out, but our lads – even this lot o' bairns – will get the better of 'em.'

And that was what worried me most. A victorious army

tended to treat its prisoners well, but troops, especially native ones who were in full retreat, would hardly be bothered to protect, feed and transport anyone but themselves. No, these circumstances were a recipe for a quick exit from the stage of life for Sam and the others. So, the sight of Ayoob Khan's bunch of cutthroats getting a taste of the stuff they'd doled out to us – while satisfying – was a dangerous distraction, yet it took Sergeant Kelly to recall us to our duty. I'd been so taken up with the spectacle of the Afghans being thrashed that I'd not noticed my son and his sergeant working forward of the men and finding some high ground from which to survey things.

'Don't like to intrude, gennelmen, but Mr Morgan's just sent me down to say that he thinks there's a bit of a nullah up ahead that might provide a covered approach right into the enemy's camp. Looks like everyone's so keen on this barney that it's been left undefended. Just a suggestion, sirs, but you might like to come an' 'ave a look for yourselves.'

McGucken and I tore ourselves away from the gory circus act that was unfolding in front of us and scrambled up to where Billy was lying prone on a dusty little knoll, gazing down towards the gaggle of multicoloured tents less than two thousand paces to the north-east.

'Look there, General, you can see the full extent of Ayoob Khan's camp. Looks like we might have taken him by surprise judging by the cooking fires that are still burning.' Among the stretches of animal skin, felt and even some captured British canvas tents, there rose columns of white and wispy grey smoke. By twisting the focus wheel on my binoculars, I fancied I could even see the pall from a mobile artillery forge – but perhaps I was imagining it.

Indeed, a bending, shallow nullah seemed to lead directly towards Ayoob Khan's camp. I can think of any number of examples of prime bits of ground that sometimes go un-appreciated in the heat of battle (hadn't I neglected a very similar stream bed at Maiwand and paid dearly for the mistake?) and now Afghans and British were at it hammer and tongs everywhere except along it.

'That looks very promising indeed, Mr Morgan. Good work.' Billy beamed at me, genuinely pleased by my praise. 'What do you think, McGucken?'

'It might be all right, General, but Johnny would have to be a fool not to leave some form of guard up there.' He was exercising the caution that had saved both his and my hide countless times before. 'Trouble is, we'll have to move in one long column, and we won't have much firepower up front if we do bump into something nasty round one of those bends.' He was studying what we could see of the nullah as the battle raged round about, while the drifting smoke from the musketry made things no easier to fathom. 'What I do know, General, is that we'd best get a move on. Young Mister Morgan's right. The Afs are still in the camp there and, I guess, they won't have moved the prisoners yet. If we're sharp, we might just bounce 'em.'

That was the pleasure of experienced troops. While this bunch of 66th had more reason than most to be war-weary, their officer (sparing his blushes) and NCOs were good and the men trusted them. So, with no more than a few quick orders, the lads were shaken out into column, weapons checked and bayonets fixed, and off up the nullah, as if it were Derby Day.

I was all for leading, but Jock McGucken held me back, slotting us in behind an advance guard of four boys who'd been told to be ready for trouble.

'Well, your honour, it's the pick o' the bunch up here to look after yerselves, so it is.' I might have expected to see Private Battle and the rather superior Private Williams among the crew of ruffians Billy had picked to deal with any enemy interference as we moved forward in the narrow, stifling confines of the stream bed.

'Yes, General, it's the Four Musketeers at your service.' Private Williams bowed theatrically and patted the hilt of a Khyber knife that he, like the others, had stuck among his buff equipment.

'Stop buggerin' about, Posh bleedin' Williams, and just lead off, can't you? The general would do better to trust in Bobby here than in you lot. Just move your idle bodies,' Sergeant Kelly chaffed, as the men shuffled into position. God knows how that wretched dog survived all the scrapes that he and his master got themselves into but it was good to see the little whelp again.

'Thank the Lord we've got that pup with us. At least I'll have someone to ask for advice.' That got a bit of a laugh out of the troops and served to distract them from the task that lay ahead, for generals were not supposed to have a sense of humour, still less to expose it to the soldiery.

That was the last shred of fun we were to have that day, though. Billy and Sergeant Kelly set a spanking pace up the dry stream bed trying to get past the slaughter that we could hear but no longer see on either side of us. We hadn't been going long, however, before we started to come across the first corpses. Regular Heratis, Ghazis and tribesmen who had flocked to Ayoob Khan's standard had crawled into the cover of the earthy banks either to die or to lick their wounds.

But whatever hopes they might have had of being able to cling to life disappeared as fast as Messrs Battle, Williams *et al* clapped eyes upon them. As McGucken and I passed the dead, it was obvious from the fresh blood that justice – if that was what it could be called – had been swift and rough. I knew it was pointless to tell Billy to urge his men to act with a little more restraint and, besides, I was in no mood for mercy as I thought of the fate that awaited Sam and the other captives. But one of the corpses stood out from the rest.

We'd been going for twenty minutes or so when there was a delay. The column came to a stop and, in truth, I was glad

353

of a breather, a chance to take a pull at my water-bottle and to mop the sweat out of my eyes. Then I became aware of a bit of a rumpus going on at the front of the snake of men, of raised voices and Sergeant Kelly serving out a regimental bollocking to someone. I didn't give it much thought because we got under way again, the line of troops stuttering forward between the sandy, crumbling banks.

Then McGucken, who was just in front of me, pulled up short. 'Dear God above, they've made a job of that poor sod!' At first the tangle of clothes next to a scrubby little thorn bush seemed like any other dead Afghan's until I looked more closely. This lad had much the same beard and mat of hair, loose pants and sandals that I'd seen far too many times already. However, he'd made some serious errors, had this young fellow. Pulled over the top of his shirt was a khaki tunic and a buff leather belt, the buttons and brasswork of which bore the number '66' and the title 'Berkshire'. He'd obviously looted a British body at Maiwand and probably thought himself no end of a bucko for wearing the kit of his vanquished foe.

'They've kicked the poor bastard to death – look at his face,' said McGucken – not normally shocked by what one angry human being could do to another. That said, it was something to behold, for the wounded man had been stamped and kicked by four pairs of stout, nailed, iron-shod boots until his face was just a mask of cut, blue jelly set about with stumpy, broken teeth. Now, I regret to say that I've seen far too many people meet a violent end in my time and I'm living proof that the human body is actually much more resilient and difficult to rob of life than most folk would warrant. Granted, this fellow was already wounded, but his very certain state of death, the scrapes and bruises on every bit of exposed flesh and the blood that was splashed around suggested a wild, feral attack that told me more about the set of the men's minds than anything else could.

'Mother of God, Jock, remind me not to get on the wrong side of this crew – and if I do, not to make off with any of their kit.' I tried to sound light-hearted about it, but brutality like this was at odds with the men's normal behaviour. Usually, they would mete out violence with a detached distaste – but this suggested enjoyment.

'We're going to have to watch these lads, Jock. I suspect they've seen almost too much of this sort of thing and they're beginning to get a liking for it.'

'Aye, General, I was thinking much the same myself – but they'll take their lead from their officer, won't they?' replied McGucken, darkly. I was just pondering this answer when shouts and a spatter of firing suggested that the front of the column had met its first serious resistance.

We were no more than a hundred paces from the outer line of Afghan tents and at a point where the nullah petered out to level ground when the firing started. There were the characteristic, sharp cracks of the Martini-Henrys, which had McGucken quivering, alive with excitement, like a hunting dog, desperate to get to the front of the column to find out what was going on. I could hear some popping replies that sounded like carbines or muskets, and then we were all scrambling towards level ground, with the rest of the platoon bunching up behind us in the defile, forcing us towards the sound of the shots.

'Take your time lads, control your breathing and aim low. Go for the prads – we can sort the riders out later.' By the time Jock and I had a clear sight of things, my son Billy was already in control, giving clear orders to the men as they rushed out of the low ground and either threw themselves flat on their bellies or knelt and cuddled the butts of their rifles into steady firing positions.

'We've caught these buggers napping and no mistake.' Jock McGucken rested his pistol on his left forearm and snapped off a shot that I heard thump home into a horse's rump more than thirty paces away. The animal squealed and reared, hurling its master to the floor of the plain before it cantered away from the skirmish. I tried my hand at a tribesman who was in a fearful hurry to be away from the carnage and missed, the man being brought down by Sergeant Kelly's rifle, a ball from which flung the Afghan from the saddle. He landed in a spray of grit and lay quite still.

'You'll 'ave to do better than that, sir. Just wasting lead with them damn things . . .' Sergeant Kelly had smoothly ejected an empty case and slipped another round into the breech of his Martini while expressing his contempt for the under-powered Enfield revolvers with a jerk of his chin. 'Young Mister Morgan's got the right idea, he has, sir.' I saw that Billy had picked up a Snider from one of the Afghan stiffs and was banging away at the horsemen with the rest of his men, who were still rushing up from the nullah to form a firing line.

'I'm sure you're right, Sar'nt Kelly, but it's a pretty thing that I'm having to get involved in this sort of affair at my age, at all.' I stopped firing, leaving it to my son and his troop.

'Give over, sir. You're bloody loving it. And we've caught these sods on the hop — ain't we just!' Kelly paused in his commentary long enough to bowl another fleeing horse and horseman over, his bullet very obviously breaking the animal's off-rear leg and sending it, shrieking with pain, into a tangle of thrashing hoofs, reins and uncured leather saddlery.

'We have, Sar'nt Kelly. Looks like Ayoob Khan's transport wallahs or some such.' The men, who were doing their best to get away, were older than most of the tribesmen I'd seen so far, a few with greying beards. And judging by the number of horses and mules that were now dashing about wildly, some with loads, the animals had been infected by the same terror that was gripping their handlers.

'Let's get through this lot, Sar'nt Kelly. They can't do us much harm and it's not them we're after.' But I could see I was

356

fighting a losing battle for now all the platoon were blazing away at the Afghans and their mounts in an ecstasy of easy killing, which was only delaying us in finding the prisoners.

'Mister Morgan, cease fire . . . cease fire – d'you hear me, damn you?' But Billy seemed deaf to my voice, only giving up his frantic marksmanship when I physically grabbed hold of him. 'Stop all this horse-slaughtering, Mister Morgan, and get your ruffians moving as fast as you like. We've work to do!' But there was a look on his face that worried me. In the orgy of violence, Billy seemed to have forgotten that he was an officer whose job it was to lead – to 'show front', as they would have had it in my young day – and not just another rifleman.

Well, eventually my soldier son came to his senses – helped by burning his hand on the barrel of his stolen Snider (they were the devil for overheating, those old Snider-Enfield conversions: people said that the cartridge was far more powerful than it really needed to be). He shook himself back into reality, issued a few crisp orders and, with Kelly and his mutt at the rear of that gang of avenging angels, we set off in two columns about thirty paces apart from each other, doubling forward at a fast trot through the Afghan camp.

I never really knew what happened next. The left column under Billy's command was slightly in front of ours. We were weaving among the ranks of tents, potting at running Afghans and trying not to shoot women, or the children who came tearing out from under our feet like driven grouse. Billy's lot started shooting at something or someone invisible to us, and I was about to ask McGucken whether he agreed with me that a group of gaudy tents hung about with flags and whatnot was probably the head man's quarters, when the big Scot clapped his hand to his belly, staggered for a pace or two, doubled over and crumpled to the earth. I couldn't believe it. I'd seen McGucken positively laugh at bullets, shrapnel and splinters; I'd seen his binoculars smashed in his hand, his haversack torn from his side, his trousers shot through and through, yet nothing had ever touched him. True, he'd been wounded at Inkerman years ago, but since then nothing and no one had been able to harm him – beyond the contents of the odd bottle of Scotch, which, he said, had made his head smart a wee bit. But not now. Whatever had hit him had done so by chance rather than by design, and from the blood that was spreading fast around the waist of his khaki pants, I guessed that my old friend was in serious trouble.

'Get on, General, don't waste your time with me – this is nothin' but a scratch.' But despite his claims, McGucken was incapable of getting back to his feet. He made a couple of feeble attempts to stand, then dropped back to the ground as the blood seeped through his breeches and began to soak into the dry soil.

'Scratch be damned, McGucken. Let's get these jodhpurs off you and find out what's amiss.' As I dragged at the khaki cloth and ripped his blood-soaked cotton drawers away with my clasp-knife, I lost twenty-odd years. Suddenly Jock and I were back in the Crimea or the Mutiny, sergeant and subaltern depending upon each other just like Billy and Sergeant Kelly. And Jock needed attention. Just below and to one side of his belly button there was a ragged hole the size of a pea; it pumped blood rhythmically, a fount of dark red liquid adding to the lake of gore, with each heartbeat. I placed myself between the wound and his face so that McGucken couldn't see what was going on and tried to reassure him.

'You're right, McGucken, it's only a scratch – nothing that'll hold you up for long.' But even as I pressed my palm to the tear, the blood continued to well, as Jock's eyelids fluttered and his great, leathery face turned an ashen white.

'Come on, General. Potter here will do his best for the major.' Sergeant Kelly was standing over us, shoving one of his medical orderlies forward.

'I'll not leave Major McGucken in the hands of a boy. Why, Sar'nt Kelly, have you any idea how much this man and I have been through together?' I knew I was being unreasonable, and even as I said it, Kelly was gently pulling me away from the casualty and beckoning for Private Potter to set to.

'Father, please, will you not leave Major McGucken? If we don't push on we'll lose the initiative and the birds will fly.'

Now even Billy was trying to recall me to my duty, as my best friend and constant companion from the old 95th days bled to death. I couldn't leave him – but I had to. As I dragged myself away, with a dull feeling in the pit of my stomach, Private Potter was pressing a great pad of snowy gauze on to the wound. Then he caught my eye and shook his head without a word. I paused for a moment and looked at the finest soldier I had ever known. He'd been struck down by a ha'penny slug and now he lay on some worthless bit of desert leaking his very life away. His eyes opened momentarily and I'm sure there was a slight smile on his face as he raised one bloodied hand to me in gory benediction before letting it slump back on his chest.

'Look there, sirs!' Sergeant Kelly's excited shout served to remind me why we were in that hell-hole at all. 'Look – just there in the entrance to that tent.' The NCO raised his rifle and fired at a group of Afghans about fifty paces in front of us, just visible through the confused mass of canvas, guy ropes, fleeing pack animals and the smoke that drifted from the cooking fires. I caught sight of three or four of the enemy, who were bundling out a number of swarthy, scruffy men: their hair swished long and loose and their arms were bound behind their backs at the elbows, Afghan style. Unusually, Kelly's bullet missed, but I shouted, 'Don't fire, any of you: you might hit the prisoners.' For that is what they undoubtedly were: the captive sepoys in loose *dhotis* and with their hair undressed. But there was no sign of two British officers and, as the guards ducked back into the tent and out of sight of any more danger from Kelly and the rest of the men, I wondered if we might not have stumbled across another set of captives, rather than those for whom we were looking.

'Follow me, lads. No shooting now but let's get at 'em.' Billy sprinted to the front of his scattered men, dropping his Snider and pulling out his sword, looking every inch like a plate from the *Illustrated London News*, the thirst for battle lighting his face.

Well, I don't know if it was what I had just seen happen to Jock McGucken, my desperate worry about Sam, or a combination of the two, but my feet and lungs were suddenly those of a much younger man. I flew hard after Billy, Kelly's wretched mongrel yapping madly alongside me, and as my son wrenched the flap of the looted British ridge tent to one side, I was right behind him. Despite the brightness of the sun, the inside was gloomy and stank. I recognised the smell: it was the smell of dirt and fear, the cocktail of sweat and shit that was the same on every battlefield the world over. And as if this weren't enough, there was the heavy stench of the butcher's block, the scent of fresh-spilt blood. Several struggling bodies thrashed around within the canvas walls, but my eye travelled first to a bundle that lay in a corner – it was still twitching. Young Hector Maclaine lay on his back, his throat opened in a great, purple gash, blood still pouring out. His mistakes had been the first that led to the massacre at Maiwand five weeks ago and I had cursed the little bugger at the time, but he hadn't deserved to meet an end like this. And neither did Sam – for he was one of those who was wrestling with one of the guards. Despite his dirty clothes and wild beard I recognised him at once and realised that, in his evidently enfeebled state, he was about to be overpowered by the same man, I guessed, who had done for Maclaine.

The guard had seized Sam from behind, had his left arm in a stranglehold around his neck and was trying to slice at him with one of those nasty little tribesman's axes that you saw all the time in those wild parts. Sam had hold of the man's right wrist and was just managing to fend him off, but he was growing weaker by the second. The trouble was that the tent was full of yelling, panic-filled sepoys who, due to their bonds, were stumbling about like village drunks while the Afghans were using the confusion to shield themselves from the bayonets of the 66th lads who were now crowding into the place as well.

I tried to get a cut at Sam's attacker, but stumbled over someone else and cannoned into the tent pole – that was the last thing we needed, the bloody canopy falling around us. But then I saw one of the prettiest sword strokes I've ever seen in my life. Any doubts I'd had about Billy's regard for Sam were dispelled as my younger son first feinted left, then pricked the tribesman's shoulder with the point of his sword. The Afghan shrieked, swore and loosened his grip on Sam's neck. That gave Billy the chance he needed. The lad didn't hesitate. Almost too quickly for the brain to keep up, he had pulled his blade back, then jabbed it forward, catching Johnny Af under the jaw and driving the steel up through the roof of his mouth and into his brain. The man was dead even before he fell off the bloodstained steel while Sam coughed, spluttered and, I imagine, wondered how he was still alive.

'I owed that to you, Samuel Keenan,' I heard Billy say, as the brothers looked down at the corpse.

'Did you, Billy Morgan?' Sam was now massaging his half-crushed windpipe, but I heard a quizzical, slightly resentful note in his voice. 'Over the past few weeks I've had plenty of time to ask why you let me go into that damned village when you knew it hadn't been cleared.'

'Stop bickering, you two – it's as if you're back in the nursery again.' But it wasn't. It was as if the death of a single Afghan thug had wiped the stain of envy and hatred from the boys' minds. It seemed as if, in those few vital seconds, the years of rivalry and imagined unfairness had ceased to be important. My lads suddenly grinned at each other.

'Now come here, the pair of you.' The three of us, smelly and bloody as we were, threw our arms around each other, the intensity of our feelings causing the yelping sepoys to fall quiet as they watched in utter wonderment. 'And you, Sam Keenan, don't ever put me to all the bother of coming to your rescue again – you're making a damned bad habit of it!'

'Sorry, sirs.' Sergeant Kelly cleared his throat, as a hotel's head waiter might do when he's presenting the bill. 'Don't like to spoil the family frolics or owt, but there's a whole gang of tribesmen a-runnin' as hard as they can away from the Scotties and Sikhs, they are. Looks like Johnny Af's chucked in the towel, sirs, an' I thought a bit more lead from us might just help 'em on their way.'

My two sons shook themselves free, grabbed for rifles and ammunition and followed Kelly and the yapping Bobby towards the sound of firing. Sergeant Kelly was right – but, then, he always was. Ayoob Khan had broken and his ragged troops were being harried from the field by the rifles and guns of Roberts's men. I stood among the 66th and marvelled as round after round scythed into the same folk who had tumbled my brigade to ruin. Ordinary English and Irish boys from the factory and the plough, who had endured the worst campaign that I'd ever been through, had turned the proud Heratis and crazed Ghazis into a rabble. Now those lads loaded and fired as they'd been taught, galling the Afghans with lead just as we had been slashed by their steel. It had been a close-run thing, but finally we'd smashed them.

Then I looked at my two boys and marvelled again. Sam and Billy stood shoulder to shoulder, firing hard at the enemy. I'd seen them like this before, but that had been years ago, over Cork's wet grass and woods where snipe was the quarry, not the Queen's enemies. Then there had been jealousy; now there was comradeship. A few moments ago the two lads looked as though they were ready to fight each other rather than the Afghans. Now they looked like . . . well, like brothers. It was the damndest thing.

Glossary

Aliwal: British victory in the First Sikh War, 1846
anna: low-value Indian coin
Armstrong: breech-loading artillery

badmash: low, rough man
bahadar: term of respect – 'brave one'
bat, sling the: British term for the ability to speak the native
  language
Bengal and Bombay Armies: there were three separate locally
  raised armies in India – Bengal, Bombay and Madras
bat-pony: horse used for carriage of supplies
bhang: hashish
bhisti-wallahs: water carriers
bint: abusive term for a woman
Black Bastards: abusive term for the Royal Irish Constabulary
  due to the colour of their uniforms
Brock's Benefit: firework show
Brummagem: Birmingham
Brydon, Dr: the most celebrated survivor of the retreat from
  Kabul, 1842
bandook: rifle
burgoo: porridge

burkha: all-enveloping robe worn by Muslim woman
burra-sahib: the chief – literally the 'big man'
bus: finished, dead

cantonments: military living quarters
chaggle: large, leather water-bottle carried by native
    bhisti-wallahs
chaplis: leather sandals with a nailed sole
char: tea
cornet: most junior British cavalry officer; later, second
    lieutenant
craic: fun, banter – Irish slang

dal: curry
dhoti: long shirt
dhoolie: Indian cart
Dizzy: Disraeli, British prime minister
Dum-Dum: Indian arsenal

eejit: Irish corruption of the word 'idiot'
ensign: most junior officer in the British infantry; later, second
    lieutenant
ek dum: now, at once

Fairyhouse: Dublin racecourse
Famtoosh: slang for fussy or affected
Feringhee: foreigner
friction tube: small copper tube inserted in an artillery piece's
    touch-hole. Its fulminate content would fire when a rough-
    ened piece of wire was dragged from its centre by a lanyard,
    thus causing the gun's main charge to explode
feu de joie: a ripple of gunfire used to mark anniversaries, etc.
'Fore and Afts': nickname for the 59th (2nd Nottinghamshire)
    Regiment
fyrd: Saxon militia under the control of a local lord

gallus: over-confident – Scots slang

gammon: nonsense or, as a verb, to fool

Gs: refers to musical notes, a Gee being particularly distinctive
   and useful for signalling

gora-log: white people

greeting: Scots slang for crying

griff: a beginner or new arrival

gouger: Irish slang, meaning a ne'er-do-well

hoop: anus

huzoor: respectful term of address

jawans: affectionate term for Indian troops; literally, 'the boys'

jezail: long native musket

jildi: hurry up

*jihad*ist: violent religious extremist

kurta: long tunic

lalkurti: come

lines: military quarters, initially tented

MacNaughton: British governor general in Afghanistan in 1842

maidan: a plain or open piece of ground

mokes: donkeys or mules

mullah: native priest

mufti: plain clothes

nullah: dry water-course

Pandies: British term for the Indian mutineers of 1857

phizog: face

pitfalls: narrow, deep holes designed to break a horse's leg

poshteen: native sheepskin jerkin

prad: slang term for a horse

puggaree: turban

punkah: hinged grass or reed screen hung from the ceiling and used to fan a room

ramasammy: meeting or discussion

Ram-ram: a greeting

ranks:

Indian infantry	*Irregular cavalry*
sepoy – private	sowar – private
naik – corporal	lance daffadar – corporal
havildar – sergeant	daffadar – sergeant
jemadar – assistant troop or company officer	
subadar – company officer	rissaldar – troop commander
subadar/rissaldar – major (most senior Indian officer)	

red-arse: a beginner or new arrival

rooti-gong: the long service and good conduct medal awarded to other ranks

sabretache: leather wallet suspended from mounted officers' belts in which messages etc. were carried

salaah: Muslim ritual cleansing

shabash: well done

shamag: light scarf worn across the face and mouth against dust

shufti: a look or a reconnaissance

shikari: hunter

shukria: thank you

sillidar: the system used in irregular native cavalry where each man owned his own horse

stag, to go on: guard or sentry – from 'staggered duty'

stick man: the man considered to be the smartest when a guard is inspected

skelp the bums: smack bottoms – Scottish slang
swat: midlands slang for a mouthful of drink
syce: groom

tape: slang for a chevron denoting NCO rank or long service
tatt: a pony
teuchter: Scottish slang for Highlanders
tik-hai: 'I understand and will obey'
tulwar: native sword

vedette: cavalry outpost

wadi: dry water-course
wallah: slang for a person carrying out a function – thus, 'char-wallah', tea boy
wet canteen: canteen where alcohol is served as opposed to the 'dry canteen'
whaler: British horses from New South Wales

Historical Note

The Victorians saw the fighting in Afghanistan between 1878 and 1880 as two distinctly different wars and often referred to it as such. Certainly, the events in the north of the country concluded with a natural pause until that was broken by Ayoob Khan's march to Kandahar that started in May 1880. For the sake of this story, it matters little whether we refer to this period as the 'second' or the 'third' Afghan War. What is important is its relevance to today's campaign in exactly the same area.

In 2006 I wondered long and hard about the wisdom of sending a tiny force to the Helmand valley, suspecting that the British government of the day had not opened its history books, still less heard of the battle of Maiwand. It has been with a deep degree of pessimism that I've watched the same tribesmen being fought on the same ground by many of the same regiments against a political backdrop that is all too similar to that of the 1880s. Anthony Morgan clearly disapproves of Gladstone's approach but at least the Grand Old Man (later, of course, dubbed the Murderer of Gordon) understood the need to get British troops out of Afghanistan as soon as he possibly could. I suspect that his grounding in history was more thorough than that of many of his political descendants.

The relationship between British and Indian units has been fascinating to uncover. The intense rivalry and suspicion that existed between Bombay and Bengal regiments in Afghanistan has stuck out from the pages of diaries and manuscripts almost as obviously as the scorn of the British troops for their Indian comrades in arms. Bearing in mind that this war was the first serious test for the reformed Indian armies since the Mutiny of 1857–9, this is hardly surprising – but it's unfair.

The fact that the Bombay Grenadiers and Jacob's Rifles were all but overwhelmed in July 1880 was as much to do with the flawed British policy of deliberately arming them with outmoded weapons as any lack of fighting prowess. The theory that if native units were less well equipped than Queen's units they would be less inclined to mutiny can hardly have added to their self-confidence.

However, the conduct of the cavalry is rather less easy to understand or justify. Certainly, regiments like the 3rd Scinde Horse fought valiantly until Maiwand, and at the battle itself they did well when they came into action. But they appear to have been badly led. Morgan complains of their commanding officer being among the first to reach Kandahar during the retreat from Maiwand when he should have been one of the last. In fact, the débâcle of the cavalry's action led to the arrest and subsequent court-martial of Malcolmson and Nuttall, who were charged with dereliction of duty. Both were found not guilty, which strongly suggests that theirs was a show trial based more on a desire to spread blame rather than a burning wish for justice.

I find it hard, however, to recount the conduct of the 66th (Berkshire) Regiment of Foot with anything other than breathless admiration. In the 1980s when I was stationed in Omagh as a company commander, I paid several visits to the church in which Colonel James Galbraith's monument rests. There he kneels, petrified in marble, holding a Colour in one hand

and surrounded by his officers and men, ready to fight to the last. I marvelled at it then, but it was only my research for this novel that revealed to me the depth of this fine old regiment's steadiness and gallantry.

Over the forty-eight hours or so that the battle of Maiwand and the retreat to Kandahar lasted, the 66th lost eleven officers and 317 men, the vast majority stabbed or bludgeoned to death. They endured not only the fighting, but also the burning thirst and hollowing hunger of the long trek back to Kandahar apparently without flinching. There is no doubt that they were a splendid battalion and thoroughly deserved the decorations they received – although it has to be asked why no Victoria Crosses came their way.

E/B Battery of the RHA won two VCs. Again, I cannot detect anything but cool dedication from this handful of Horse Gunners, for without their steel guns and the faithful service of the crews, the story would have been an even bloodier one. I've taken some liberties with the doings of Sergeant Mullane VC, of which I hope his descendants will approve.

One of the most interesting characters to emerge from my research is 1397 Private Frederick Williams – or 'Posh', as I've dubbed him. In reality, he was the son of Lieutenant Colonel Caulfield of County Dublin. He was educated at Heidelberg College, but some unknown misfortune overtook him, forcing him to enlist in the 66th under an assumed name, one of Kipling's original 'gentleman rankers'. Queen Victoria insisted that he should revert to his real name of Algernon Montgomerie Caulfield when she decorated him with the Distinguished Conduct Medal on the regiment's return from India. From there, his career became even more remarkable. Commissioned into the 66th, he fought in Burma and in the Boer War, where he was again decorated, this time with the Distinguished Service Order, before he retired in 1902. He volunteered for the First World War, and was killed at Gallipoli, 'as if walking down Piccadilly', as second in command of 6th Battalion the

Border Regiment, aged fifty-five, and with the extraordinary combination of DSO and DCM after his name.

All the other characters in the 66th are real, including Sergeant Kelly, Private Battle and Bobby the terrier. In the best traditions of the time, Bobby was presented to Queen Victoria in August 1881, when she hung a special medal around his neck. Today Bobby's stuffed and bemedalled form has pride of place in the 66th's regimental museum in Salisbury.

There was no Sam Keenan in the Scinde Horse, but there was a Lieutenant Edward Monteith. Similarly, there was no Billy Morgan in the 66th, but an Ensign Harry Barr of H Company did carry the Queen's Colour, although he was cut down alongside Galbraith.

There was no Anthony Morgan at Maiwand, either. The brigade commander was one George Burrows. Here, the comparison between 1880 and today is uncanny, for Burrows's brigade was sent into the field badly equipped, under-manned and with little intelligence. He did well at Gereshk (the site of a current British headquarters) but was simply outgunned and mobbed at Maiwand when his tactical advantage was spoilt by a junior officer. Nonetheless, it is said about him in the official history, '. . . wherever the fighting had been most desperate, there was Burrows to be found'. I hope that Brigadier General Morgan does justice to his memory.

In this novel, Alan 'Jock' McGucken is modelled on the divisional political officer, Major Oliver St John. McGucken has been like a rock to Anthony Morgan throughout all three novels: killing him was not easy!